MW00471189

GOATS IN THE TIME OF LOVE

A Martha's Vineyard love story
with goats, a dog, and some recipes

Pabodie Press books may be purchased for educational, sales, or business promotional use.

Pabodie Press
Washington, DC

First Pabodie Press paperback printed 2019

ISBN: 9780692910382

Library of Congress Cataloguing-in-Publication data not available at this time.

Book design by Tilden Bissell and Felicia Wang

10 9 8 7 6 5 4 3 2 1

For Chris

Starry-eyed and strongly-thigh'd

Melanie hops from side to side

Over branches, rocks, and sties

Leaving untouched, her furry hide.

DBM

ONE

You can do this, Schuyler Harrington. Sky took up her knife, pressed her lips together and set the blade along the thin line that separated the shells.

"Place your thumb on the flat edge of the blade, pushing into the gap in a smooth motion until it glides into the clam," she recited. "Bullshit," Sky muttered as the edge of the littleneck broke off into flakes. Sure, she could have had the woman at Larsen's shuck them, but when the crusty guy in line in front of her ordered a dozen unopened, she'd followed suit. She was an Islander now. (Well, sort of.) And Islanders opened their own clams.

Sky banged the clam on the counter. The shuckers made it look so easy: push the knife in, twist off the shell, a swish of the blade to loosen the clam. Then, the delicious, ocean-y reward. She threw the failed clam into the pile of busted-lip rejects. Sky had a fantasy of impressing her city friends with her newfound skill. She wasn't giving up.

She was sure (well, pretty sure) she'd had the clam and knife in the correct position. She picked up a new victim, set it in her potholder, and took a few deep breaths to clear her mind. Be the clam. No, she didn't want to be the clam. It was about to be spritzed with lemon, dabbed with cocktail sauce, and eaten. Be the knife. No. Be the force. That sounded like Yoda. Not helping. Sky snorted a laugh. Then, carefully setting the knife in the groove between the shells, she visualized the blade sliding in and gave a gentle push.

There was the knife, halfway through the clam. Her eyes widened in surprise. She torqued the blade to separate the shells and twisted. The lemon and cocktail sauce sat waiting. At last. Sweet, briny success.

🐐 🐐 🐐

"Well, finally, I've got you on the phone," said Sky's mother in her tight, cultured voice. "Didn't you get my messages?" Sky could see Lucretia at her desk, hair in a perfect French twist, tapping her pencil.

Just seeing her number pop up on the cell gave Sky a stomachache. "Sorry. I've was going to call you later today," she lied.

"What have you been doing up there? Mimi told me she invited you to dinner and you said you were busy. What could you possibly be busy with?" Sky had moved the phone from her ear, letting her mother's voice fade to a tinny whine. "Are you listening?" She wished her mother would learn to text.

"Yes, I'm here."

"...It's rude to turn people down. Mimi went to a lot of effort to find fun young people for you to meet. She was quite put out."

A thought occurred to Sky. "Mother, did you ask Mimi to set up a dinner party for me?" Manipulative Lucretia. No wonder Mimi was so surprised when Sky had declined.

"I might have mentioned something, but that's beside the point."

"I'm sorry I made trouble for her, but I told you, please, do not do things like that. I'll make friends here when I'm ready. I like my quiet life."

"Never mind. That wasn't the reason I was calling. Your father and I were talking about you." This translated to Lucretia talking while Sky's father was in the room. "We've decided you're coming with us to the Galapagos." Sky couldn't think of anything worse than being stuck on a ten-day cruise with her parents and a bunch of wealthy retirees. The temptation to push her mother overboard would be too strong. "I've reserved your stateroom and your flights. We were extremely lucky; the yacht has only twelve cabins and had been fully booked, but one of the passengers passed away."

"No, Mother. I told you before I wasn't interested in your cruise." Sky was finally able to say no to her mother, but to her own ears, she sounded like a petulant child. "You know my plans. I'm spending the summer here." She held the phone out at arm's length. She picked up "being ridiculous," "wonderful opportunity, do you realize," and "wallowing in self-pity over that Gil."

Sky put the phone back to her ear, determined to end the conversation on a civil note, but her mother filled the gap. "Well, I must say, Schuyler, I only want what's best for you. I just don't know what I'm going to do."

The old dog whistle. Blood rose to her temples. "Yes, I know, Mother. Someone's at the door. I need to go," she lied again.

Sky hung up and put her head in her hands. How was it that hearing her mother's voice could still affect her like this? Always a lecture, delivered in that tone. Decisions made without consideration for her wishes. But worst of all, the constant criticisms: stiletto jabs that slid past Sky's defenses and—even now—left her wounded and bewildered.

Sky vowed not to answer when her mother called back. A beach walk. That's what she needed. And the phone would stay at home.

🐐 🐐 🐐

Her New York plates and new Jeep pegged Sky as a summer person, but she tried not to drive like one. It was always the cars with New York plates that failed to yield to oncoming vehicles on the Island's one-lane dirt roads. ("Don't scratch the Lexus, dear.") Nor did it occur to the drivers to smile and wave thank you to the car in the pull-out as they drove past. Sky always did both.

Two miles of bumpy dirt road led to the Quansoo beach gate. Sky unlocked the chain, swung the big metal gate open and drove through. Then, reversing the process, she secured the gate behind her. Quansoo, on the south shore, was one of the Island's many private beaches, inaccessible to all but its owners by lock and key. Those less fortunate battled for parking at one of the Vineyard's few public beaches.

Sky paused on the footbridge to check for crabs (none today), then climbed the path over the dunes separating the pond from the ocean. The threat of rain in the gray marble sky had kept the beachgoers away and made the beach all the more wild and beautiful.

Waves crashed, spewing foam. Sky walked along the edge of the surf where she'd spent so many hours fishing with her grandmother. Childhood summers on the Island with Grams were the highlight of Sky's year, weeks of pure joy. Breakfasts of wild blueberry pancakes with real maple syrup would be followed by lazy days at the beach, fishing rods at the ready. Family friends would come for dinner and stay for games of Dictionary and pocket change poker. Cloudy weather called for a ferocious round of miniature golf, the loser buying the ice cream cones: black raspberry for Sky and peppermint stick for Grams (Mad Martha's, of course). But best of all was the quiet evenings on the porch, just the two of them, talking about anything and everything as the moon rose and the stars spangled the dark.

The damp breeze caught the hood of Sky's windbreaker as she sat down to watch two fishermen cast for striped bass. Maybe tomorrow she'd bring her rod, throw in a line. The idea of fishing made Sky feel better, closer to Grams. With a short rod and live minnows, her grandmother had, early on, knocked out any squeamishness about hooks and wriggling fish. When Sky was big enough to handle the seven-foot surf rod, her grandmother moved her lessons from Dutcher Dock to the beach. "It's feeling fishy," Grams would say as she nudged Sky awake in the cold, gray predawn. "Get up, sleepyhead. We'll miss the sunrise." Sky would grumble and moan, but she never regretted seeing the sun slide up over Chappy with her tummy full of hot chocolate and a rod in her hand.

But the most fun was when Grams would splurge for a fishing charter to go in the Sound after the albies and bonita and the fierce, fighting bluefish. Although Grams claimed she had the power to call the fish to her, Sky knew it was the skill of their favorite charter guy. But Grams did have one special power. She loved Sky unconditionally.

As Sky grew older, her visits to the Island got shorter as her mother insisted that Sky go to the 'right' sleepaway camp in the Adirondacks and then build her résumé through fancy summer internships. Trips and friends and parties kept Sky away too. Grams was changing too. Her quick long stride slowed to an old lady shuffle, and her balance was none too good, but her mind stayed sharp.

Then, just like that, Grams was gone. Sky was supposed to be grateful that it was fast, a massive stroke. She'd ignored her grandmother in the chaos of wedding planning, canceling lunch after Friday lunch at the club. It broke Sky's heart that she'd had no chance to say goodbye, to tell Grams one more time that she loved her. Or to thank her for the unexpected inheritance that allowed her to buy Pennywise cottage on the shore of beautiful Tisbury Great Pond.

The wind whipped Sky's hair around her wet face. She took a deep breath and wiped her tears. Lucretia was right about one thing; self-pity did her no good. Then Sky heard her grandmother's voice: be true, Sky, and be kind. That's how you find happiness.

She picked up a clamshell and turned it over in her hand. She'd made Grams's favorite dinner tonight, linguini with clam sauce, smoked bluefish to start, and a bottle of Sancerre. A real meal, for a change. Grams had taught her the recipe, simple enough to boil pasta and chop garlic and parsley. Besides, she already had all those stubborn littlenecks; heat would succeed where her knife had failed. Sky's stomach rumbled its approval. Then a gust of wind brought the first raindrops. Sky headed for home.

TWO

Nate rested his head on the steering wheel. "Not again," he muttered, tossing his phone onto the seat. "C'mon, Nan. Let's go get the goats." A black and white dog leaped panting into the truck.

Nate shook his head. He couldn't figure how they'd gotten out this time; he'd double-checked that enclosure. At least the lady who phoned had sounded amused at finding goats in her yard. But no one had ever called the cops before. Nate didn't think he'd broken any laws; nothing on the books about reckless endangerment of hydrangeas. But he'd be paying for whatever damage the beasts had caused. Every time the goats got loose on a job, it was as if he'd tossed them his wallet to eat. Twenties, fifties, down the gullet.

Nate pulled up to find the goats, all five, scattered across a large pasture bounded by old stone walls. The farm was lovely, with distant water views beyond the fields and a thicket of beetlebung trees. A dozen shaggy, horned cattle turned unfriendly eyes on him, and the ruff on Nan's neck stood up. Nate hadn't anticipated horns.

"Hi. You must be Nate with the goats. I'm Adrienne."

Nate turned to shake the hand of a smiling woman in a paint-splattered shirt. "Thanks for rounding them up," Nate said.

"Oh, it was fun. I was working in my studio and looked out, and there they were. I didn't know what to do or whose goats they were, so I called the police. They suggested I get the neighbors to help. I think I got my ten thousand steps in today!"

"Yeah, chasing them is a lot of work."

"They are such silly things, the way they jump on everything." Silly wasn't the word Nate would have used, but he smiled and nodded. "Oh, and a photographer from the *Gazette* saw us and took some pictures. I hope you don't mind. Maybe you'll make the paper!"

Nate held his smile as he stifled a groan. That was not the kind of publicity his business needed. "Sure, I'll have to look for it."

Adrienne bent to pat Nan's head. "This your helper? She looks like she's got some border collie in her."

"A bit, I think."

"Such a sweet doggie," she said, giving Nan a good scratch behind her ears. "I'll leave you two to your work. Just bang on the door if you need me."

Nate paused. No escaping this part. "After I get the goats into the trailer, I'll check out the damage to your garden. I can either have the plants replaced or get an estimate and write you a check."

"Oh, don't worry about that. A bit of early pruning. I really don't think they did anything serious, but I'll let you know."

"I'll check anyway. Goats eat pretty fast." He shifted on his feet. "Um. One more thing. Are your cows going to mind me going into their field? The horns?" Man Gored While Capturing Goats, the headline would read.

Adrienne laughed. "Oh, don't worry about them. They'll keep out of your way. They look fierce but are as sweet as cupcakes. Good luck!"

Good luck indeed. Nate checked that he had a rope in his satchel and headed to the field. Well, hell. Another effing goat rodeo.

🐐 🐐 🐐

Nate's eyes drifted back to the newspaper. Centered under the masthead of the *Vineyard Gazette* was a big picture of a goat— his goat, Bugs, standing on a shaggy Highland cow. The headline read "Gallivanting Goats Greet Summer Guests." Nate read the caption again and groaned. *Goats happen! Ms. Adrienne Copeland of Chilmark was surprised Wednesday morning to find a flock of goats in the garden at her Middle Road farm. They were retrieved later by their owner, Mr. Nathaniel Batchelor (aka Nate the Goat Guy) of West Tisbury. Keep a closer eye on those goats, Nate!*

He'd had a sleepless night. The photo was bad enough, but the goat damage was worse, an entire bed of dahlias gone and two hydrangeas. Suzanne at Island Gardens would send the estimate for replanting by the end of the week. He rubbed tired eyes, imagining that bill going on the wrong side of the ledger.

The screen door banged open. "Hi, Zeke," Nate called without turning around.

"Hey, man, you're up early."

"Getting a head start on the paperwork. Coffee's made."

Zeke poured himself a glass of water from the sink, then headed for the bathroom. "First things first. Stink warning, sorry." Zeke lived in a surplus army tent on his ex-girlfriend's farm. Nate didn't begrudge Zeke the free rent but wished he'd invest in a composting toilet.

"Open a window, please," Nate said.

"Yeah, sure. What time is it?" Zeke asked. "I'm supposed to be on at 9:00, I think."

"Not even 8:00. You mowing today?" Zeke's wake-and-bake approach to life made him unsuitable for most occupations. Landscaping was an exception.

"Yup."

Nate turned back to his yellow pad: Finish the Calhoun and Watson estimates. 4:00 p.m. pitch at Hidden Creek Farm off Indian Hill Road. Send email re Mackissac overdue bill. Call Chris re setting up backhoe for cut opening. Move fences in Aquinnah, Windy Gates. He added, Write apology letter to the bottom and got out his laptop. Nate hated the paperwork part of the business but set to working up the estimates. No new jobs, no new money.

Zeke came out grinning. "Fine doody this morning, if I say so myself." Nate shot him a look. "Hey! I opened the window, like you said."

"Whatever," said Nate. "Just spare me the details."

Zeke rummaged in the kitchen cabinets and refrigerator for breakfast. "Yo, dude, don't you have any milk that isn't sour?" Zeke called. "If you have ten bucks, I could run up to Alley's. You need cereal too."

"Yeah. Wallet's on the counter. There should be a ten in there."

"I'm taking the twenty."

"Sure. Get me some peanut butter too."

"No problemo. But first, caffeine, my morning friend," Zeke said, sprawling with his mug in the chair across from Nate. He blew over the top and took a careful sip. "Mmm…."

"Fresh bag of beans," said Nate.

Zeke sat up and pulled the newspaper over. "Whoa! No way. This your goat?"

"Yeah," Nate sighed. "It's Bugs."

"How'd he get up there?" Zeke asked.

"I don't know. He's a goat. He jumped."

"Man, it's like a free front-page ad," said Zeke, holding up the paper. "Look how cute he is on that cow. Everyone's going to want their own goat."

"Or like the worst review ever," groaned Nate. "They escaped, remember. The *Gazette* must've gotten my name from the police report."

"Naw. People won't notice that. Cheer up, dude. No such thing as bad press, right?"

Like most Islanders, Nate could do almost anything and everything. Fisherman, carpenter, line cook, landscaper, roofer, scalloper, musician (never going to make a living at that), organic farmer, bike mechanic, part-time cop, caretaker, and probably a few others he'd forgotten.

He had the idea to start his goatscaping business after hearing a piece on NPR about using goats to clear brush on golf courses. If they'll pay thirty bucks for artisanal local cheese, he figured, the Vineyard summer folk would probably pay anything to rid their fancy properties of poison ivy and bittersweet. It seemed like a no-brainer. What he hadn't fully appreciated was the actual goat aspect of the business.

Nate had grown up with farm animals. Placid, well-behaved, cooperative farm animals. His parents had bred Belted Galloway cattle—the ones that look like Oreos—along with the usual assortment of pigs and chickens on their Tiasquam River farm. But goats were different. Different in evil, tricky, unpredictable ways. Sure, they'd happily run up wagging their cute little tails like a pack of puppies. But behind the yellow eyes with those weird horizontal pupils lurked a cunning goat brain. Every time Nate would think he was about to turn a profit in his business, the goats would escape their enclosure on some big job in Aquinnah or Chilmark or West Chop and eat hundreds of dollars' worth of landscaping. Sure, goats liked to eat poison ivy, but, as Nate soon found out, they liked azaleas and hydrangeas and David Austin heirloom roses better. A lot better. Plus, the wicked little things' ability to leap meant that the rolls and rolls of forty-two-inch fencing he'd invested in served as little more than a suggestion.

And they reproduced. Like rabbits. Ha. The expression should be like goats. Before Nate knew it, his seven goats had become fifteen goats and then twenty-eight goats, with no sign of stopping. Sure, selling the goats for meat was an option. But after he'd bottle fed the babies, he just couldn't sentence them to the stake, even though that would be sensible for his bottom line.

And now the latest escapade over in Chilmark that landed his goats on the front page of the *Gazette* and made him the butt of more than a few jokes. At least he got some free publicity out of it. And a new client, he hoped.

THREE

"Hi," Sky said to Nate the Goat Guy. "Sky Harrington. Come in."

"Nate Batchelor. Nice to meet you," he said, surprised to be shaking a woman's hand. With a name like Schuyler and the bucks to buy Pennywise, Nate assumed that he was meeting another smugly wealthy, balding executive type. But Sky, dressed in some sort of floaty top, yoga pants, and bare feet—besides not being old or a guy—gave off a different vibe. Definitely not your typical WASP-on-a-stick-in-heels.

"I liked the picture of your goat in the newspaper," Sky said.

"Oh, that." Nate glanced at the copy of the *Gazette* sitting on the kitchen counter. His sales pitch didn't include the risk of runaway goats.

"Can I get you something to drink? I was about to make myself some iced tea."

"Sure. Thanks," he said, walking over to the big picture window. Beyond the yard, a thick tangle of bittersweet and underbrush nearly blocked Tisbury Great Pond from view.

"See my problem?" Sky said.

"Thanks," he said, taking the glass from Sky. "It's pretty overgrown. But if we take all that brush out, over there by that big oak, you'd see across the pond. Maybe even down to the beach."

"That would be great." Sky gave Nate a warm smile and waved at a pair of antique captain's chairs. "Please sit down."

Nate sat and looked around the room. "Nice place," he said.

"I just moved in a month ago," Sky said.

"Yeah, I heard this place was for sale. You know, if you go way back, this was part of my family's original land grant." He shot Sky a wry grin. "Too bad we ever sold any of it."

She tilted her head to give Nate an appraising look, taking in his faded tee and stained work shorts. She sat down and tucked a strand of pale hair behind her ear. "You're from one of the really old Island families."

"Yup. There's still a bunch of us around, and my uncle runs a farm across the cove. But that—and my house—is about all that's left of our land." Nate shifted in his chair, not sure if he should launch into his pitch or keep making small talk. He always hated this part of the job, meeting a client for the first time, explaining his services, quoting a ballpark price. Today, he was feeling more nervous than usual.

"So tell me how this works. You drop off a bunch of goats and they walk around and eat everything?" Sky found Nate almost disconcertingly good looking. He was tall and rangy—she guessed six-one—tan, lean, and muscular. No surprise there. He worked outdoors. Wavy brownish-blond hair streaked by the sun and in need of a haircut, hazel eyes creased at the corners. Clean-shaven, which she liked. And, unexpectedly, he didn't smell of goats.

"…so they aren't wandering loose. The other thing about goatscaping is that it's environmentally friendly…" Sky tried to concentrate on the environmental benefits of goatscaping over machine clearing, but again, her attention faltered. If he lived out West, he'd have a big ranch with a herd of cattle, not goats. New England laconic and a bit of awkwardness that Sky found attractive. She'd spent too many hours in the company of charming, egotistical, and arrogant men. He smiled broadly in response to her question about goat poop, and Sky felt a warm glow. Nice-guy-next-door with a subtly sexy charisma wrapped in a very attractive package, she concluded. Too bad he was a goatscaper.

FOUR

That night, Sky dreamed of Gil. It was the same dream, nightmare really, that she'd had almost every night since the breakup months earlier. Sometimes, the woman changed, sometimes the place, but the story stayed the same. This time, they were in the apartment that she and Gil had shared in the city. As always, it began with Sky picking up a bottle of Gil's favorite Barolo. She'd been working extra hard to get her projects wrapped up before the wedding and wanted to surprise Gil by coming home early for a change. They'd go to the little Italian place where they'd had their first date and then become regulars because the food was good and cheap, and their favorite waitress called them her little lovebirds. Sky turned the key in the door to the studio apartment and opened the door. There she found Gil and his assistant in bed. Time and time again. Night after night. Nightmare after nightmare. Except it was no dream. It really happened.

Untwisting herself from the sheets, Sky felt her heart pound and that familiar, sick feeling tightened her chest. She put on her robe and wandered into the dark living room to pull herself together, flopping on the sofa. She leaned her head back against the cushion and stared up at the hand-hewn beams barely visible in the dim moonlight.

Especially at night, it was so hard to push all the ugliness of splitting with Gil—and leaving her friends and her job and her life, really—back into the box where she had hoped to keep it locked until the pain faded. Sky had met Gil during freshman orientation at Brown. A scholarship kid, which you wouldn't know to look at him, with his preppy Izod shirts, khakis, and broken-in docksiders (all from the thrift store, it turned out). Tall and athletic, sandy blond hair, clear blue eyes. Even his name sounded patrician—Gilfillan Smith. They ran in overlapping circles at college. Sky registered him as good-looking, but not much more.

Years later, they met again at a Cinco de Mayo party. At that point, the mutual attraction—personal, intellectual, sexual—exploded, the last, helped along by the bottle of Reposado they'd polished off in the wee hours of the night. Gil had grown up. He'd used his charm and network to build his client base as a stockbroker, as well as a great group of friends ranging from artists to investment bankers. By all accounts, they were a perfect couple. (Sometimes, harshly, Sky would think that they were like a matched pair of purebred yellow Labradors—only smarter and not quite so drooly.) They followed the usual pattern of attractive, successful young adults in the city: they dated, fell in love, moved in together, got engaged.

But with no warning, the happy story Sky had been living came crashing to a painful end. The breakup, combined with the final push to close the financing for the San Juan airport project, pushed Sky to the edge. Then her grandmother died, and Sky found herself in a very dark place.

Sky walked out onto the deck to clear her head. The half-moon shimmered silver across the pond, and restless horses nickered in the stables across the cove. The Island had been a salve over the past weeks. Sky had arrived scraped raw and in pieces. But the clear air and silence had begun to knit the edges and heal the hurt.

She yawned, took a long last look at the moon, and went inside. Milk would help her sleep. She poured a glass and sat down on the white-linen sofa. Such incredible luck that Pennywise cottage had been for sale and that Grams had left her enough money to buy it. Sky loved her house. The former owners had added a light-filled wing that echoed the antique cape's plain but graceful proportions. But it was the sloping floors and narrow stairs of the original cottage, like Grams's old summer place, that sealed the deal. Fortunately, the sellers' money woes meant they'd mothballed their plans to gut the old house. But for the paint colors, it was perfect just as it was. Sky sipped her milk. Oh. Mothballs. Better double-check the drawers in the old house didn't still stink of mothballs. Ugh. She propped her feet on the coffee table, an old sea chest. Quiet, simple furniture accented with a scattering of nautical antiques, nicer than anything she would have bought, had come with the cottage. So different from the city, where her studio apartment's small windows opened onto a dirty brick airshaft, and Gil's icky black-leather sofa sucked what little light there was out of the room.

But that was all behind her. For good.

The next morning, Sky rose with the sun, pink fog softening the trees outside her bedroom window. She yawned and stretched, putting the night's bad dream behind her. First coffee, then the early-bird yoga class. The rest of the day, well, she'd decide that later.

The Yoga Barn opened its massive arched doors to a bliss-inducing view of a pond and rolling fields. Sky took a deep breath of clean air as she sat cross-legged on her mat.

"Good morning, class. And it is a lovely morning. Thank you for coming. Please stand for Tadasana, mountain pose." Sky unwound her legs and stood. Even the yoga instructors seemed happier and more relaxed than in the city. Duh. Why wouldn't they be?

"Start by pressing all four corners of your feet evenly into the mat. Feel stable and strong." Sky focused on her feet. "Now that you've connected to the earth, steady your breathing. Breath in and breath out as you shift your focus inward. Lift your arches and ankles as you begin to engage the muscles of your legs." This class, too, had helped Sky reconnect. So different from the ghastly mat-against-mat experience in her city classes, where she felt lucky if she didn't have a tush in her face. "Straighten the spine as you tuck your tailbone down and lift the crown of your head…."

Back home, fully relaxed and energized from yoga, Sky wandered to the one place on the deck where she got good cell service. Six new texts. First, her mother: *Schuyler, dear, you should really come back for the gala, Francisco will be there….* She'd take a pass on that. Next, Hadley: *Hey, girlfriend, am I still invited for Labor Day? What's up? We all miss you! And big news, Rolin and Avery are pregnant!!* Sky texted back, *Absolutely invited! Will call you later to catch up.* Then Alexandra: *I miss you, Sky. Can we come over for Labor Day? Russ wants to fish, and I want to see you!* It would be a full house for the holiday weekend. Time to move the painting project up the list. Then a voicemail from a 508 number she didn't recognize. "Hi, this is Nate. Uh, Nate the Goat Guy. I have that estimate worked up for you and can drop it off later." Sky surprised herself by hoping she'd be home when he came by.

Sky stretched and sniffed, then went inside to pick up a fluffy white towel before heading to the outdoor shower. The best shower in the world. Sunshine and the spray of water warmed her shoulders as clouds drifted overhead. She washed her hair, then scrubbed with French-milled soap (the only kind that didn't dissolve into a gooey mess in the rain), checking for deer ticks as usual. Lyme disease was epidemic on the Island, and tick checks were a daily necessity. She gave an appreciative glance to her body—generous breasts, narrow waist, and full hips—glad that curves were back in fashion. Sky had taken advantage of West Tisbury's three-acre zoning to sunbathe topless on her deck, tanning her pale skin to the shade of a lightly toasted marshmallow. She wrapped a towel around her waist and, tucking some wet strands of hair behind her ears, opened the shower to find Nate bending to slip a piece of paper under her screen door. The black and white dog standing next to him gave a friendly yip, vigorously wagging her tail.

"Uh, nothing like an outdoor shower," Nate stammered as Sky adjusted her towel upward.

Red-faced with embarrassment, Sky was surprised to also feel another warm flush under Nate's gaze. "Yeah. It's one of my favorite things."

"Mine too." Nate nearly smacked himself for that remark. "Anyway. Sorry to bother you, I was just dropping off the estimate."

"Right," she said.

Nate made sure to look at her face. Potential client, albeit a half-naked one. "I gave you a couple of different options," he said.

"Thanks."

"Here it is." Nate stepped forward to give her the estimate then froze, hand out, as Sky grabbed at her slipping towel.

Beet red, she set a firm hand on the terrycloth and her teetering composure. "Why don't you wait inside. Since you're here, we'll go over it together. I'll put some clothes on and be with you in a minute."

🐐 🐐 🐐

Sky leaned over and gave the dog a good scratch behind the ears. "What's his name?"

"Her. This is Nan." Nan had been a skinny, skittish stray who had been found last fall near the Registry of Motor Vehicles office in Oak Bluffs, likely left behind by thoughtless vacationers. The animal rescue people had named her Reggie, but she seemed more of a Nan to Nate.

"Does she help herd your goats?"

"Yup. She's really good. Supersmart. I'm not sure I could do it by myself," said Nate.

"I'd love to have a dog someday. Oh, look, here come my turkeys," Sky said, pointing through the window to the flock of feral turkeys pecking across the yard. Nan's ears perked up. "You can chase them. Go, Nan!" she said, opening the door. The dog bolted across the deck and leaped over the rail, setting the ungainly birds to reluctant flight.

"Turkeys are about Nan's favorite thing to chase. After seagulls. And rabbits," Nate said with a grin.

Such a cute smile. "OK. So how would this work?" Sky asked.

"I set up a forty-by-forty-foot enclosure. With three or four goats, the brush should be completely cleared in about a week," Nate explained. "Then we move the pen over to another spot...." Nate continued to describe his plan. Yup. Just as good-looking as she'd remembered.

"OK. To open up the area almost to the pond's edge will take a couple of weeks. Faster if we set up two enclosures." Sky noticed Nate's hands, so different from Gil's manicured fingers, as he pushed the estimate across the table. She wondered how Nate's calluses would feel. Rough, like sandpaper or just firm?

"The options are one enclosure or two. It just depends on how quickly you want the clearing done."

Sky picked up the paper. "One, I think." Might as well stretch out visits from Nate the Goat Guy.

"Great," Nate grinned. "I could start as early as next Wednesday. I'm just finishing up a job over at Cedar Tree Neck, and I have an open schedule until after August.

"I hope you don't mind that I'll be around every couple of days to check on the goats. If they get through all the underbrush they can reach, then they'll start to try to get out to eat what they can see outside the fencing," he explained.

"And sometimes they succeed," Sky said with a half-smile.

"Uh, yeah. Half the time, I can't figure out how they've done it. Then it's a pain to get them all back in the pen." Nate paused. "By the way, I really am sorry about earlier. Nan and I were going for a walk along one of the ancient ways. You know, the old footpaths? So I thought I'd just swing by to drop off the estimate," he explained with a sheepish look. "I'll call ahead of time in the future."

"Really, don't worry. Not a big deal," Sky said. In truth, she hadn't minded. Not at all. "I get cell service in only a couple of spots, so calling doesn't always work. Just give a loud hello or something. So I'll know you're around. But I'm curious about the path. Will you show it to me?"

FIVE

To market, to market.

Sky pulled a straw hat out of the closet, slipped on a pair of old Birkenstocks, and added a plaid cotton shirt against the sun. A couple of canvas bags, her camera, and wallet, and she was ready to go. She loved wearing her shabbiest, best-loved clothes out in public and not getting a second look. It was impossible on the Vineyard to tell the local organic farmer from the billionaire hedge fund manager—if you didn't look at the nails, that is. At least that was true of what Sky thought of as "her" part of the Island. Edgartown was a different world, Nantucket-like, where Lily Pulitzer sundresses were common and men unironically wore pants with whales.

Sky walked down her driveway, noting where Nate had pointed out the ancient way across her property. She loved that her house was connected to the web of the Colonial-era cart tracks that crisscrossed the Island. Her Grams's house had been off one, the King's Highway. Something to explore another time. Today was market day.

It was a lovely morning for a walk. The dirt roads and narrow lanes that led to town and the farmers' market took Sky past grazing sheep and fields of wildflowers. Sky slowed her pace. Queen Anne's lace waved for attention, but Sky loved the bachelor's buttons best, lacy cobalt petals around a purplish center. Taking out her camera, she snapped a couple of close-ups of the blossoms, then some wide-angle shots of the field, blurring the focus like an impressionist painting. It reminded Sky of the summer she was twelve and decided she would be a photojournalist (or maybe an art photographer, she couldn't decide which), shooting picture after picture with Grams's old 35mm camera.

Sunshine and quiet open spaces had not only been healing her hurt but had also been gradually peeling back the shell that had protected her against the assault of urban life. In New York, she'd escape her cubicle for lunch and head onto noisy, crowded sidewalks to look for the patch of blue between the towering buildings. Here, the sky was everywhere. Sky looked up and slowly turned in a circle. So blue. So much blue.

It took her but three minutes to walk through blink-and-you'll-miss-it West Tisbury: Alley's General Store, the library, town hall, the Grange, a handful of houses, and the old Congregational Church. Sky paused to look at the tiny white clapboard structure with its modest steeple. Sprays of pale pink and white flowers hung on the church doors: perfect for a wedding. Bizarrely, her mind flashed a vision of white goats wearing, then eating, garlands of pink roses in the churchyard. Shaking her head to clear her apparently goat-addled brain, Sky arrived at the busy outdoor market.

The stalls of Island-grown produce looked as if they had been painted with a child's art set: piles of red and yellow heirloom tomatoes; heaps of lettuce, zucchini, and beans in shades of green; bright orange carrots; pinky-maroon radishes. flowers, in coffee can vases. Should she buy the bold, cheeky zinnias or the English garden-style mixed bunch with the cosmos and dahlias? Or maybe a big bunch of sunflowers that reminded her of a Monet? She'd shoot some photos first—it would be fun to try supersaturating the colors later—then shop.

Sky moved from stand to stand with her camera, sometimes just trying to capture the flowers and vegetables, other times widening the focus to include the reactions of the pleased shoppers. The mushroom vendor's wares caught her eye, especially the giant Dr. Seuss-like tubes with their tiny caps. "What would be good in an omelet?" Sky asked the scruffy vendor in a Gone 'Shrooming tee shirt.

"Ah," he said, running his eyes over his offerings. "For a delicate flavor, I would suggest the oyster mushrooms. Healthy too. Wonderful at breaking down toxins." He picked up a pale floppy clump, took a deep sniff, then held them out to Sky. "Or, if you want a meatier flavor, try the shiitakes or the trumpets," he said, pointing them out. "The maitakes are lovely too in an omelet. They crisp up almost like bacon."

Sky pursed her lips. So hard to decide. "I'm not sure."

"Or, special for you, I could make up a bag of my magic mushroom mix. Chop up a bit of each, sauté in butter, dash of salt, then slip that into your omelet. Mouth magic, I promise."

Sky smiled. This was so much more fun than the supermarket. "Yes, please, and a bag of sprouts."

"Excellent choice."

Now, for the rest of her shopping. Having grown up in the city with a live-in housekeeper-cook and being surrounded by restaurants and takeout options, the cooking-challenged Sky found the farmers' market a bonanza: bakers offered meat pies and cookies; smoked fish made an excellent quick lunch; and anyone could make a salad. She ticked off items as she filled her bags: cheese, tomatoes, and basil—caprese salad was within her skill set. Honey, bread, eggs, peaches, granola.

Next, Sky loaded up with prepared food from the Asian stand: sesame noodles, cold rolls, tofu with chives. A fresh bag of locally roasted coffee beans and a bunch of zinnias finished her list. She took another slow loop around the market, just in case. Oh, wild blueberries. Her favorite. She'd almost forgotten them. They'd be great with yogurt and granola in the morning.

Nearing the exit, Sky spotted a familiar face that she couldn't place. Clearly, the woman was having the same problem as they smiled at each other with that awkwardness that comes with almost—but not quite—recognizing someone. The brunette's smile broadened. "Oh my gosh, are you Schuyler? Sky? I'm Elly. Elly Cooper. You probably don't remember me, but our grandmothers were friends. We used to go to Quansoo together as children." Sky did remember Elly; they had been best summer buddies for years. The small, slightly chubby girl had grown into a lithe, tanned, athletic-looking woman, but she still had the same winsome smile and big green eyes.

"Of course I remember! We were Elly and Sky-Sky, the Wonder Girls! It's so great to see you," Sky said with genuine pleasure. "I'm up for the summer. I bought a house just down the road. How are you? It's been so long."

"Really well. I live close by. Where to start? I'm married and a teacher," Elly replied. "Gosh, that sounds so boring. How about you?"

"I'm…" Sky paused, not sure how to answer the question. Not a lawyer, at least not at the moment. "I'm sort of between things; it's a bit of a long story. But would you like to come by for a cup of coffee sometime? We could catch up." Sky had been kind of lonely, she realized, in her hermit existence.

"I'm not doing anything now, if that that works for you," Elly replied with a big smile.

"Let's stop at Bolla's first. I've got a craving for that bacon-cheese bread thing."

There was a line, as always. Sky studied the big framed photo of the owner with her husband and their daughter happily holding up a straight flush of blue ribbons in front of a table of baked goods. "Remember when you got so mad at me when my brownies beat yours?" Elly asked.

"Are you sure?" Sky retorted, amused. "I remember it the other way around."

"Uh-uh," Elly said, shaking her head. "I still have the ribbon to prove it. Only time I ever won a blue." They reached the head of the line. "One breakfast bread, please," she said to the counter girl, then turned back to Sky. "Will you stay through the fair?"

"I think so." Sky paused and looked down. "I really don't know."

"I hope you do," Elly said, touching Sky's arm. "Maybe we can even go together. Like the old days."

They compared life notes as they walked back to Sky's house. Elly: married to her high school boyfriend, college off-Island at the University of Massachusetts-Lowell, now teaching middle school English. Sky: unemployed junior attorney, taking the summer to figure things out.

"I missed you so much when you stopped coming up for the whole summer," Elly said, stirring sugar into her iced tea.

"I know. When I got old enough, I thought I'd get a job at Morning Glory Farm, like you did. But my mother had other ideas." Sky made a face.

"We had so much fun though. Such good memories." Elly tapped her chin, thinking. "OK. I've got one. Do you remember the stinky whale?"

"Oh, jeez. Ew, I'd forgotten about that. Not a good memory, Elly!" Sky laughed, a real belly laugh, her first in months. "You'd be floating through the cut and there'd be a glob of dead whale floating next to you. So gross!"

Elly joined in laughing. "Then they brought the bulldozer to bury it, but that oily film stayed on the pond all summer." She wrinkled her nose.

"Bleah," Sky said. She broke off another piece of the breakfast bread. "How about that time our grandmothers let us camp on the beach? Then it poured rain in the middle of the night, and we had to drag our wet sleeping bags like two miles back to Grams's."

"Was that the time we ran into the skunk in the dunes? And the poison ivy?"

🐐 🐐 🐐

In the excitement of her reunion with Elly, Sky had forgotten to buy milk. With nowhere she needed to be and nothing she needed to do, she picked up her canvas bag and started back to town. She felt lighter. Elly's visit had opened a door, a wonderful door, to her childhood memories of the Vineyard.

As she walked along the path in the bright July sun, Sky recalled the utter contentment of those long, simple days. They'd spend hours playing in the ocean and sunbathing on the beach, Elly bemoaning the way her pale Irish skin did nothing but freckle and turn red as Sky toasted a golden brown. She flipped through scene after scene as if they were a stack of old photos: She and Elly taking beach walks and giggling when they ran across the nudies down by Black Point

Beach. Convincing one grandmother or the other to take them to Menemsha, please, for a hamburger and root beer float. Rainy days curled up in the big wicker chairs on the porch at Grams's farmhouse, watching the rain move in sheets across the ocean and falling over with laughter at the torrid love scenes in the bodice-rippers they'd sneak from Grams's secret shelf. They'd bike to Alley's for Necco Wafers and Fun Dip, and Pop Rocks to hide inside a dog treat for Elly's old black mutt, Hendy, just to watch the surprised expression on his dog face.

Sky's eye was caught by a round white pebble in the dirt road. She stooped to pick it up. Her beach stones—she'd almost forgotten about them. Elly had collected shells and wampum, but Sky loved best the smooth pebbles brought up by the surf. Lucky stones with their unbroken ring of quartz earned spots on her childhood windowsill, and the others— pink granite silvered with mica flecks, translucent quartz, the rare violet and green stones—sat in a glass bowl on her dresser.

There was so much time, day after day. She'd wake and realize that the hours that stretched empty were hers to fill, or not. Elly and Sky would disappear for hours. Sky's grandmother fondly called them her feral girls, which, for the longest time, Sky thought meant happy. She'd felt safe, free, and joyful. No wonder this is where I ran after the split with Gil. Sky felt a wave of gratitude to her Grams, who'd known how hard it was to be Lucretia's daughter and allowed Sky's summers, for a time, to be a place where she could simply be.

SIX

After a long day of meeting with an irritating prospective client and building three goat pens, Nate wanted nothing more than a beer and a shower. He grabbed a cold 'Gansett from the refrigerator, went out onto the deck, and flopped down into a peeling Adirondack chair.

"Ah," Nate sighed. A few minutes of peace and quiet with a cold beer. Until he heard the sound of Zeke's rattletrap car, followed by its owner's banging through the door.

"Yo, dude," Zeke said.

"Hey, Zeke. Help yourself to a beer."

"Already did." Zeke came out and lowered himself carefully into the other chair. "Payday. Replenished your supply. Cereal too. Good deal at the Stop & Shop."

Nate took a satisfying gulp from the sweating can. "Thanks. I was almost out."

"Happy to be of service." Zeke shifted in his chair and pulled out a joint. "Man, riding that mower all day does a job on my tailbone. You want a puff?"

"Naw. I'm good." The fields across the cove glowed gold and bronze in the late afternoon sun.

"Nice," said Zeke, blowing out smoke.

"Yeah." A flock of geese landed with a chorus of honks. "Batty left a message. She's having people over tonight and wanted me to tell you. You doing anything?"

"Nope. You going?"

"Uh huh. Laurel'll be there and the rest of the gang. Good food. You should go." Nate had been distracted all day by visions of his new client wrapped half-naked in a towel. "The lady that bought Pennywise hired me today."

Zeke gave a thumbs-up as he took another hit and slowly released the smoke. "Laurel pointed her out to me the other day in Alley's." Zeke's voice went up an octave. "I'd like to open an account, please, like my grandmother had." Zeke's voice dropped back down. "Like some Princess Barbie, dude."

"Alley's doesn't do that anymore."

"That's what they told her." Zeke shifted gingerly in the chair and leaned back. "Laurel was updating the listings for West Tisbury and saw the sales contract. Princess Barbie paid cash."

Nate whistled. He couldn't fathom having enough money to buy waterfront in Martha's Vineyard these days, let alone pay cash. "She seems really nice."

"That she may be, but she's out of your league, dude, if that's what you're thinking. In more ways than one." He took a big slug of beer and belched. "Unless she wants to go slumming."

"Way to make me feel good, Zeke."

"Just sayin'. Hey, I'm going to shower. I've got grass clippings where they are not meant to be."

"Save me some hot water."

Nate stretched his legs in their muddy boots and leaned his head back against the chair. Yeah. Zeke was right. It wasn't like she meant to flash him. But it reminded him how long it had been since he'd had a girlfriend. The breakup with Linda had put him off dating for a while. A long while, it turned out. He still didn't like thinking about how much that one had hurt.

Nate's mind drifted to his other exes. His first true love had been Marianne, his college sweetheart. He'd been attracted to her curves, dark curls, and bubbly personality, so unlike his, and had fallen in love with her goodness and pure heart. That split, he blamed on fate. He'd moved back to the Island when his dad had gotten sick; she'd stayed in school. Marianne had married a classmate and now had a kid, he'd heard. They'd probably be at the Labor Day weekend wedding of his college roommate, which would be great, awkward, or both.

Then Caroline. Sweet, outdoorsy Caroline, who was the photographer for the *Gazette*. They'd dated pretty seriously for a year but somehow never completely clicked. He wasn't entirely surprised when she told him she wanted to take a break. Still, it hurt when Caroline and her German shepherds moved in with the assistant harbormaster in Edgartown.

His last serious girlfriend before Linda had been Tory, the hard-partying waitress at the Black Dog. She'd broken his heart too. Tory was an off-Islander, and while she'd managed to make it through one winter with her sanity more or less intact, when the sun started setting earlier and earlier the next fall…. Well, better she leave him and the Vineyard than end up a drunk or crazy.

I guess there's a pattern here: I find a great woman, and then I get dumped. Nate sighed. Zeke was still singing in the shower, so Nate opened a second beer.

Zeke poked a wet head through the door. "Hey, I think I used the last clean towel, dude. Sorry about that."

"Whatever, Zeke. See you at Batty's. At 8:00?"

🐐 🐐 🐐

Nate piled what he'd need into the back of his truck: wire fencing, tall metal stakes, sledgehammer, waders, and his tool kit. No response to his text that he was coming by; she must be out of cell range. He whistled for his dog. Streaking across the field, a panting Nan launched herself into the truck. "You like Sky, right, Nan?" Nan did not like all Nate's clients, especially the poodle people in Chappy.

His truck tires crunched loudly on the gravel driveway. "Hello? Anyone home? OK to set up the pens today?"

Nate heard a reply from somewhere inside the house, and the screen door opened. "Sure, Nate, no problem. Come on in." He followed Sky into the kitchen. "Please sit down. Can I get you something to drink?"

"Just some water, thanks."

Nate went over the options for the project. "First, you have to decide where you want the clearing done and whether you want one main sightline or multiple views," he explained.

"OK."

"Then decide how much you want cleared. You can take it close to the pond, but you have to leave a buffer of low bushes," he continued.

Sky nodded. "That's fine." She liked his eyes: grayish-greenish blue, shading to a dark-blue outer band with flecks of warm brown near the iris. The type of eyes that probably turned blue by the water and green in the fields.

"And how do you want the clearing to look when you're done? Even fifty years ago, there were almost no trees here because there were so many sheep on the Island. It was all overgrazed. Like Iceland."

"Oh, that's interesting," Sky replied, now distracted by Nate's muscles. "I didn't know that."

"You can make it a meadow, then have it bush-hogged a couple of times a year, or make it a yard, throw down some grass seed and keep it mowed."

"OK," said Sky. Nice voice too.

"But you really shouldn't use lawn chemicals or fertilizers if you do grass. They poison the pond."

"Right. That would be bad."

"I'll sketch some ideas, then we can go outside and look around." Nate took out paper and a pencil and started to draw.

"You can decide to keep bushes—the more attractive ones—and we take out the straggly guys. Really up to you, but if you decide not to take it all down to meadow or grass, then I need to pull the goats out early before they start stripping the bark off." Nate stood up. "Ready to go outside? We can either look from the deck or go into the brush, but you'd need pants and boots."

"I'll go put some on. Meet you outside?"

They pushed their way through the tangle of wild cherries and bittersweet toward the water. "I think a big meadow for wildflowers; not a lawn," said Sky.

"That's what I'd do." Nate lopped off a couple of branches to make a path. "You've got some nice bushes hidden in here. This is a wild blueberry," he said, pulling off a few berries and handing them to her. "And you've got a big clump of beach plums over there," he said, pointing left. "They get ripe in late August."

"Can you keep the goats from eating those?"

"Yup. I'll fence them off. It's pretty thick. Do you want to keep going?"

"Please. I'd like to get to the pond."

"Watch out for the poison ivy." Nate worked for a few minutes with his loppers to clear a tangle of bittersweet. Sky tripped over a vine and Nate reached out to steady her. She liked how his hand felt: hard, warm, and secure. "Careful," he said, "we're almost there."

"Wow," Sky said when they'd reached the water's edge. The cove widened to reveal nearly all of the two-mile-long Tisbury Great Pond. "Is that the ocean?" Sky asked, pointing to the dip in the line of dunes barely visible in the far distance.

"Yup. That's the cut."

"I had no idea this would be my view." Horses grazed in a paddock across the cove, and a pair of black-crowned night herons stood in the reeds.

"Pretty great."

Sky agreed. This was better than great. "Let's make this area nice and big so I can put some chairs here."

"Can do. Ready to head back?"

They turned around and crashed back through the brush to the house. "I can get started now on building a pen if you want," Nate said. "I brought my tools."

"Sure. Do you need a deposit check?"

"No. I can bill you later." Yup, just business. "Don't forget to scrub well in the shower." Nate winced, what made him bring that up. He took a breath. "There was a lot of poison ivy in there. And ticks."

Sky beamed. "I'll take one right now."

After her shower, Sky ran her fingers through her drying hair. Things would work out in the end, even if she couldn't quite see how to get there yet. But never again would she live in a claustrophobic apartment with a cheating fiancé. Long run, Sky wanted what most people did: a rewarding career, husband, family, good friends. But now, she wanted a summer off. Like she had as a kid. To wake up with nothing she had to do and do only what she wanted to. Selfish? Perhaps. Self-indulgent? Definitely. With time and space to think, the right next step would come to her. Or so she hoped.

Nate strode toward her with the sledgehammer in his hand. Sweat had made his shirt stick to his chest, his arms were covered in bleeding scratches, and twigs stuck out of his hair.

"Done here with the pens. I'll bring the goats by tomorrow or the day after."

"Great. You look like you could use some water?"

"Thanks. Hot work."

Hot Nate. "Be right back."

Sky had changed into a short swingy sundress after her shower and her wet hair had dried into blond waves. Zeke was wrong; Sky wasn't Princess Barbie. She was just a princess.

"Here you go," Sky said handing him a glass of ice water.

"Thanks."

"I was thinking that maybe next summer I'd put a dock in so I could get to the beach by boat. But I'd have to learn how to run an outboard."

"Happy to show you," Nate said. "I keep a boat over by my place."

"When?" Sky asked, delighted.

"Uh," Nate said. "I'm going down to the cut in a couple of days to take a look around. We're going to need to open the pond soon."

"Just tell me when. I'll be ready."

🐐 🐐 🐐

Nate usually just grabbed whichever of the unfortunate little beasts came into reach when stocking a client's property. Today, however, he found himself examining the goats to select the most appealing, attractive, and good-natured of the beasties, as Sky was going to be living with them for a while. It was a bit weird that he wanted to impress Sky with nice goats, but he did.

Doc Holliday was a handsome, even-tempered creature, but he bleated pretty much all the time. Too noisy. Pretty Boy Floyd had a glossy black goat and a nasty streak. Billy and The Kid had brown and white antelope-like markings and rambunctious but sweet dispositions. They could go. So could Pearl Hart, a solid white goat, and her nursing baby, Lizzie Borden. The Sundance Kid had been the perpetrator of the past two goat escapes; he and Butch Cassidy would stay behind. Jesse James was a soft blondish goat, one of his friendliest. Yup. Baby Face Nelson was very pregnant, and that was making her cranky: she had even bitten him the other day. Definitely not. Let's see, one more. He decided on Patty Hearst, a bit temperamental, but cute, with her long floppy ears and black and white cow-spotted coat. Belle Starr and Dillinger would also stay behind; Al Capone, Wyatt Earp, Bugs Moran, and the others were out on jobs.

Nate attached the makeshift goat trailer to his truck. He'd taken an old farm wagon and built a semiopen structure out of spare wood to hold the goats. Then he'd had his artist buddy Liza paint a sign for the back gate: Nate-the-Goat-Guy Goatscaping. His logo: a white goat reaching on its hind legs to eat a giant poison ivy leaf. The goats hated the trailer. Even though he always hid it around the side of the barn whenever he was getting ready to load them into it, their goat ESP told them something was up. They'd go from happy creatures munching hay to four-legged demons in an instant. He decided to start with Billy. Billy gave him the slip before Nate could get the rope around his neck, leaving Nate flat on his face. He heard a muffled chortle from behind him. Nate sat up to see a grinning Sky leaning against the fence. Nan stood next to her, looking up and wagging her tail.

"Uh, hi," he said, blushing red under his tan.

"Sorry, sorry," she replied, laughing. "I didn't know I was coming here. That ancient way you showed me? I wanted to see where it went. Then Nan ran up."

"Yeah. It's a nice hike."

"This is a great old barn," Sky said.

"My uncle's. But I grew up playing in it."

"Can I look inside?" she asked.

"Sure, go ahead."

Sky walked around to the side, pushed open the door and stepped into the dim interior. The massive posts and beams looked ancient. Sky took a deep breath of the familiar scent of hay and manure and watched dust motes floating in strips of light. She peered into a few stalls and said hello to the black and white cows inside, then opened the side door to the view. The barn, like Sky's house, was situated on one of Tisbury Great Pond's many coves. An open mowed field ran down to the water.

"Neat barn," she said, coming back outside. "How old is it?"

Nate was securing Billy in the trailer. "I'm not sure. Late 1700s maybe." He walked back to the pen. "It's falling down. Big sag in the roof, probably structural problems too."

Sky looked up. "You can fix all that, though?"

"With enough money." Nate gave a wry smile. "Which my aunt and uncle don't have."

"This would be a great place to build a house."

"Yeah, the cows got the best views. There used to be a farmhouse here, but it burnt down in the '30s, I think."

She walked over and leaned on the gate. "Can I help? I'm pretty good with animals."

"Uh." Nate looked down at his filthy work boots. "There's a lot of goat poop around. I'm not sure you want to. You can watch though; it's pretty entertaining."

"I'm quite familiar with poop. I used to ride horses. Besides, I have my Blunnies on." She lifted one boot-clad foot.

Sky raised the rope securing the gate to the pen and walked in, the goats eyeing her with spooky, sidewise pupils and obvious distrust. She gave Nate's arm a squeeze. "Time to get to work!"

She was pretty darn good with the goats, Nate had to admit. Sky knew to ignore her target until she was able to sidle up beside it. She'd then turn and quickly throw an arm around its neck, and, as the creature bleated with indignation, Nate would secure it with a rope. With a few nips from Nan, the grumpy goats were escorted one-by-one up the ramp and into the trailer.

"My truck's kind of a mess, but you're welcome to ride back with me," Nate said.

"I'll take a ride. Hey, is this a Willys?" Sky asked as she climbed up into the bench seat next to Nan.

"Yup, it was my grandpa's. How'd you know that?" Nate was used to being teased about the truck, its chassis more or less held together by body filler and the bumper by WMVY and off-road vehicle stickers.

"My grandparents had a country estate in Connecticut. They had a Willys there," she explained. "My dad taught me how to drive when I was fourteen. I even got a farm use license. It was so much fun to bounce around the back fields. How did that song go? It's something about a Willys in four-wheel drive?" Sky hummed a tune.

Man, she is full of surprises. "Grateful Dead, 'Sugar Magnolia.'" He shook his head, laughed, and started the motor. "Yeah, this beater's a great old truck. The engine is indestructible. Mid-Island keeps it running. But the rest is mostly Bondo and duct tape."

Sky settled back onto the seat and petted Nan's head, which was resting on her knee. "Tell me about my goats. And what are they—a herd or a flock or what?" He'd never had a client ask about their goats; it was like quizzing the landscaper about his mower.

"Usually people say flock or a herd, but officially it is a tribe or trip of goats."

"Oh, my friend Trip will love that. He and his wife are coming from Vermont for a visit. OK. I've got a trip of goats. Do they have names?"

"The brown ones are Billy and the Kid…."

"Your goats are named after outlaws?" Sky interrupted with a giggle.

"Yeah. Uh, that seemed to fit." Nate described the personalities and foibles of her trip as they headed down South Road towards Pennywise, hauling the trailer of bleating goats. They pulled into Sky's driveway and parked in the field next to the new goat pen. The diabolical little beasts had hatched an escape plan, and Billy, as usual, was the ringleader. Nate freed the latch and stepped back to pull out the ramp. As he did so, Billy shoved open the door. The goats cascaded off the back of the trailer, quickly scattering out of sight. Only Pearl and Lizzie remained, fixing Nate and Sky with baleful stares.

"Meh. Meh-eh," Pearl bleated, disapproving of the breakout. Sky started laughing.

"Oh, shit," Nate said.

"Come on, Sheriff Nate. Let's catch those desperados."

SEVEN

Why had she picked up Lucretia's call? She'd answered without looking, assuming it was Nate, calling to confirm the details of their date. Well, their outing on his boat. And now here was her mother chiding her about skipping the gala, refusing the Galapagos trip and, once again, telling her she'd wasted all that money buying a house she'd barely ever have time to use. Taking a deep breath, Sky pushed the phone away from her ear in a graceful motion and, holding it steady, turned her head in the opposite direction. *Outward mother*, she could call it, a new yoga pose. Lucretia was just background noise and Sky could think about Nate and his sweet offer to teach her to run an outboard motor.

She was waiting for him on the dock with a cooler of goodies: gooey brie, smoked bluefish from Larsen's, a screw top bottle of rosé, and a couple of cans of beer in case Nate didn't like wine. Her towel and a fleece jacket (in case it got cold) were stuffed in a canvas beach bag.

"What did you do today?" she asked, handing Nate the cooler.

"Goats. And grocery shopping." He held the little boat steady as Sky stepped in and took her place in the middle seat. He whistled and Nan flew down the path at top speed. She leaped into the boat, claws skittering on the metal seat, and settled in, panting, at Sky's feet.

"I feel like a little kid," Sky said. "It's been years since I've gone to the beach in a boat!" Nate smiled at her enthusiasm. "Now show me what to do." Nate took her through the steps: lower the motor, throttle in neutral, kill switch connected, choke out full, then half-way, squeeze what Nate called the Clinton to get the gas to flow. Then hard, fast pulls on the starter rope. She leaned over him to watch.

"Do you want to try?" Nate asked, discomfited by Sky's closeness. She smelled of lavender.

"Nope. That was enough lesson for today." Sky moved back to the middle seat and turned to face the bow. Nate steered the boat slowly into the deeper waters of the cove and opened the throttle to full. The boat began to plane smoothly, the wake cutting widening ribbons across the surface of the pond. Farms, meadows, and discreetly landscaped vacation homes slipped past.

Sky's face wore a ridiculously large grin. "This is great!" she shouted to Nate over the motor.

"Smooth ride today," he yelled back.

As they neared the beach, Nate slowed the motor to navigate around the sandbars, jumping out into the warm knee-deep water to pull the boat the last few feet to shore. "You have to be careful around sandbars," Nate said. "If you run into one, you'll break the cotter pin."

"I'll remember that," Sky said. "Looks like almost everyone's gone for the day."

Nate pulled the anchor from the bow and set it in the sand as Nan ran off in search of cheeky gulls. "Best time to come down, I think."

"Me too. The ride was absolutely gorgeous," Sky said, taking off her flip flops. "Did you see how the sun lit up the sheep over at Flat Point Farm? Golden fleece."

Nate hadn't noticed the sheep, but it was impossible to miss Sky's glowing incandescence in the late afternoon light. "It's a nice afternoon."

A pebble caught her eye as she climbed over the side. "Oh look, Nate. A lucky stone!"

"That's a good one," Nate said, studying the smooth oval pebble with its continuous quartz ring. Sky dropped it into her pocket. She'd put it on her bedroom windowsill, just like she used to do at her grandmother's house.

They lugged the chairs, stakes, and bags along the edge of the dunes that separate the pond's south shore from the sea. Nate stopped where the beach opened wide and flat to the ocean. "Let's dump our stuff here."

"What are the stakes for?" Sky asked.

"I need to figure where to dig the next cut and mark it. The idea is to reach deep water so it doesn't close too soon," he explained. "We need a good exchange of salt and fresh water when it gets tidal. That's what makes the shellfish happy. Want to go check it out?" Nate asked, picking up the stakes and the mallet.

The simple pleasure of a beach walk with this sweet, good-looking guy. Sky was grateful that he didn't feel the need to talk; Nate's easy, quiet company was a balm. A few more taut strands relaxed in her body as she breathed in the clear air carrying the brine of the sea and the sun's fading warmth. The sand scrubbed between her toes as the ocean crashed and withdrew, the receding waves chased by sandpipers and the happiest of dogs.

Nate surveyed the pond as they strolled. "See that sandbar? Look there and there," he said pointing to areas of lighter water. "The channel should dig itself between them. I also want to get closer to Long Point so we don't cut into the dune on the Quansoo side."

"Oh, I see."

Nate hammered a stake into the sand. Walking toward the ocean, he set additional stakes about thirty feet apart.

Task complete, Nate went over to where Sky stood watching an osprey hunt for fish in the shallows. "Ready to head back?" he asked. "We're going to get a good sunset tonight over Black Point. That is, if you want to stay that long."

"Are you kidding me? Of course, I want to stay."

Returning to their picnic spot, Sky poured herself some rosé into a plastic cup and sat back in her chair. She watched Nate's face, noble in the bronze light. He is of and a part of this island, this pond. I'd bet that if he were transplanted anywhere else he'd be absolutely miserable. She felt a deep connection to the Vineyard but had always had her city life to return to. What would it be like to be so deeply rooted in a place, all those generations in this one spot?

Nate unwrapped the bluefish and handed Sky a chunk on a cracker. "Mmmm," she said. "I forgot how good this is. My grandmother had a smoker. It was this metal box called Little Chief. She'd pull it out when we got into a mess of bluefish."

"Do you fish?" Nate asked. He still threw a line in from time to time when he could. But not as much as he'd like.

"I used to. A lot, actually. I've been meaning to start again," Sky said, sipping her wine. "My Grams was crazy about fishing. She'd enter the Derby every year. Never won anything other than a daily pin, but she'd be out all day, every day."

"Yeah. I like to fish—for eating." He stabbed the brie with a knife. "I've got an extra rod. I'll bring it down next time and, we can throw some lines in." Next time. Shit. Way to be cool, Nate.

"I have my own rods—they were Grams's—but I'd like that." OK. This was a date. And he'd just asked her on a second one.

The sun grew larger, turning a reddish orange as it slid toward the horizon and set in a spectacular display of shooting magenta rays before dropping down behind the rise of low hills beyond Black Point Pond.

"That was just beautiful," Sky said, putting on her fuzzy gray-green fleece against the chill. "My Totoro jacket," she told Nate.

"Totoro?"

"You don't know Totoro?" He shook his head. "From the Miyazaki anime film?" Nate still looked blank. "The other big one was *Spirited Away,* I think. Anyway, Totoro is this magical woodland spirit who's huge and superfuzzy." She stroked her jacket. "My ratty old stuffed Totoro even went to college with me."

"Me, I was a Pooh man," said Nate.

"'You are braver than you believe, stronger than you seem and smarter than you think.'"

"I hope so."

"Silly old bear," she said, patting his arm.

"The moon's coming up."

Sky smiled. "I want to see that."

They walked across the beach to the ocean. A half-moon hung over the sea, casting a wide, bright path onto the dark waves. With a tingle of excitement, Sky slipped her hand into his.

🐐 🐐 🐐

"We'd better pack up. Fog's coming in."

Sky stood and peered at the white, faintly glowing shape sliding over Squibnocket Point. "Look at that," Sky said. "It's like someone took a big eraser to the Island down there."

"Yeah. It's moving in pretty fast." They repacked the bags and cooler and carried the chairs to the boat. By the time they were done, the beach by Black Point Pond had disappeared. A few moist white wisps floated by in the light breeze.

Once Sky was in the boat, Nate walked it out to deeper water and clambered in, quickly starting the motor. He opened the throttle to full. The dune where they had had their picnic faded and disappeared into the fog bank. Nate looked over his shoulder. "We won't outrun it," he shouted over the motor.

Now worried, Sky watched the wall of white move across the pond toward the boat, a ghostly apparition chasing them down. "What happens? Will we get lost?"

"Naw," Nate replied. "I've been out on the pond in the fog a bunch of times. At worst, we head up the wrong cove and have to bump around for a while until I figure out where we are," he reassured her. "One time, Zeke and I were a hundred percent sure we were in Tiah's Cove, but it was Deep Bottom. Then we ran out of gas and had to row home. That took forever." He lifted the red plastic gas tank and sloshed it. "Full tank, no worries."

Soon the small boat was enveloped in a cocoon of white. Nate throttled down and angled toward what had been visible as the west side of the pond a few minutes earlier. "When you get your own boat, don't forget to keep an eye out for fog. Best thing is to go slow and stick to the shoreline, but you've got to be careful around Big Sandy," Nate said. "There's a big concrete thing in the water you don't want to hit."

The moon gave the fog an eerie luminescence. Sky, disoriented, looked for something on the shore to ground herself, but all was water and white. The fog had not only blocked her sight but had also muffled the sounds of the pond. She felt as if they'd been loosely wrapped in a roll of damp cotton wool. She was scared, scared of the idea of being out in a boat alone and having to find her way back.

Nate broke the silence. "The native people—the Wampanoags—had settlements all around this pond. Good place. Lots of fish, shellfish. Even a spring eel run up Mill Creek. Flat, fertile land for beans and corn. Then the English came, and it was the usual story: epidemics, land grabs—the English got the great ponds in the treaty of the Middle Line—Christian conversions, the works." He peered through the fog for a recognizable landmark. "But the Island's Wampanoags sat out King Phillip's War. That was one bright side to the Christianity thing. Still, the 1600s were not good for the native people."

"No surprise," Sky said, reassured by Nate's voice.

He went silent again. Ghostly shapes—a tree, a patch of shoreline—came and went as the fog lifted and thinned and then thickened again. "The old timers," Nate continued after a while, "swore that you could sometimes hear and see old Wampanoag camps here on the pond in the fog." The hairs on the back of Sky's neck prickled.

"Could that be true?" Sky asked.

"I would have said that was all an old wives' tale, but my dad would tell me a story of when he was a kid out on the pond with his dad, my grandpa." Sky gave a little shiver and snuggled closer to Nan. "And my dad never made up a single thing in his life. So, the story goes that they were out fishing late and got caught in the fog on their way home. When they got to Tiah's Cove, the fog lifted and they could see a campfire surrounded by people. My grandpa thought that they were having a bonfire or something, which seemed weird. So he called out, but they didn't seem to hear him. Dad could see clearly enough that they were dressed like the Indians you see in your history books. You know, the ones hanging out with the pilgrims at the first Thanksgiving." Sky patted Nan's ears, trying not to be spooked by Nate's story.

"So, what happened?"

"The fog dropped back down as they went past. Still, my dad knew exactly where he'd seen them: by that big oak tree where the cove begins. So the next morning he canoes down. No signs of a fire, or footprints, or trash, or anything. He does find an arrowhead, though. A nice one." Nate fell silent again. "He wasn't scared or anything by what he saw, though. He always looked for them, the Indians, in the fog, but he never saw them again."

They continued their slow progress up the pond. After a while, Nan perked up her ears and gave a sharp bark. Off in the distance, muffled by the fog, came a bleat in reply. "Good dog, you smell the goats," Nate said.

EIGHT

The first drops of rain beat against the windows. Sky loved that sound. She looked at the clock. Time to get ready. Showering in the light rain, the cool drops mixed delightfully with the warm water as Sky scrubbed away the day's grime with her lavender soap. She dressed in a loose gauze tunic and white pants, only half-drying her hair so it would dry the rest of the way in waves. Sky liked Nate. He was like the Island. Gorgeous and uncomplicated. Poor guy, she'd kind of talked him into inviting her to his house for dinner. But truly, she was curious to see the inside of one of the oldest houses on the Island—even if Nate did describe it as a dump. And to get to know him better.

Her contribution to dinner would be wine and cheese. Sky picked a nice white from the refrigerator and a round of local goat cheese. Goat cheese for a goat guy. Grabbing a yellow slicker, Sky slipped her feet into her Birkenstocks and set out for Nate's. The directions were a bit tricky: start on South Road, heading toward Chilmark, then take the first left past the orchard. After about half a mile bear right at the wooden whale sign, go another quarter mile past a field with horses, and take another left.

Unfortunately, Sky was one of those people afflicted with no sense of direction. She'd heard stories of people who ended up spending hours bumping around and going down what might be a road but was just another really, really long driveway, never finding the house they were looking for. Please don't let that happen tonight.

Nate surveyed his beloved Blacksmith's Cottage. He'd tried to tidy up the many stacks of books and had shoved as much clutter as he could into drawers and his one closet, but he was stuck with the threadbare brownish sofa and mismatched chairs. The rain and damp had refreshed the familiar smell of mildew that he was almost fond of but that put most people off. Nothing he can do about that.

And fish for dinner. What was he thinking? The fishy smell will just make it worse. Too late now. He had started preparing Betsy's Bluefish with an extra fillet from his cousin's last charter. This was one of the recipes he knew by heart: breadcrumbs, butter, and lemon, broiled with a cup of white wine at the end to cut the oiliness of the fish. Nan knew this was going to be a good night to clean plates. Fish—any kind of fish—made for a very happy dog. She stared at Nate drizzling lemon over the fillet, her drool making a small puddle on the scarred wooden floor.

The rain had become a steady downpour, and he was wondering what was taking Sky so long when, finally, he heard the sound of a car pulling up. She was at the door in a moment looking mad as a wet cat as she stood dripping water. "I couldn't find the whale sign. Then I got all turned around, and it started raining really hard. I must have gotten out of the car a half-dozen times looking for the damn sign." Her white pants had glued themselves, not unflatteringly, like a wet paper towel to her legs, and her feet and sandals were covered with mud. Strings of wet hair were stuck to her face. She looked lovely.

Soon Sky was curled up in his favorite armchair in a pair of Nate's flannel pajama pants. He had started a fire in the woodstove next to her and hung up her sodden trousers to dry. Candles were lit on the table, and the old oil lamp on the wall put off a warm glow.

"This place," she said sipping her wine, "I feel like a time-traveler to a different century."

"It's over two hundred years old. It wasn't always a house. It used to be a blacksmith's shop."

"How cool. Has it always been in your family?" Nate nodded. "How long have they been here on the Island?"

"Oh. Um. 1600s."

Sky laughed. "Come on Nate, this is really interesting. Tell me more."

Nate drank his wine and wished he was better at storytelling. "The legend goes that my earliest ancestor landed here in the 1630s with three other soldiers. They met a tribe of Wampanoags and he gave the sachem—that's the chief—his red coat as a gift."

"Of course, he'd be a red coat!" Sky exclaimed. "Go on."

"Supposedly, the sachem was so pleased with the coat, he gave him a big chunk of land. They spent the first winters in dugouts. But the official record shows 1652 for the land grant."

"Wow. That's incredible." Sky had had no idea that Nate's roots went back that far. Her family was a bunch of carpetbaggers in comparison.

"We haven't been able to hold onto much, like I told you. There's this house with a couple of acres, and you saw the barn. My uncle has about twenty acres there." Nate stood up. "I should check on the fish."

"Can I help?"

"Nope. I got it."

The fish was delicious, moist and not fishy at all. "I love smoked, but I didn't think I liked cooked bluefish. This is really good," Sky exclaimed. He'd heard that before; the dish had never failed to convert a bluefish hater into a bluefish lover. "Is it an old Island recipe?"

"Not really. My Aunt Betsy came up with it."

"Did she grow up here, too?"

"Nope. New York City. She'll tell you stories about roller skating to school on Riverside Drive." The wine had finally loosened Nate's tongue. "She's an old hippy. Bunch of them came here in the '70s. They tried to set up a commune on Tea

Lane," he explained. "You want some dessert? I got some key lime gelato squares from Alley's." A splurge, at six bucks a box, but she seemed the gelato type.

"Sure, yum. I love those. Tell me more about Aunt Betsy," Sky said.

Nate tried not to be distracted by Sky licking the edges of her ice cream. "All the hippies had were tents and a lean-to. So most gave up after the first winter. But Aunt Betsy had met my uncle—apparently, she was quite a looker in her day—and ended up staying and becoming a teacher. Great lady. She knows everybody on the Island."

"I'd like to meet her," Sky said, wondering if she could ever be accepted too.

After dinner, Sky and Nate sat on his sofa. "Do you mind if I stretch out? I'm as full as a tick," she said.

Nate didn't mind. She propped up some pillows and lay back, putting her feet in his lap. Unsure where to put his hand, Nate shifted in his seat and rested his fingers on her shin, resisting the temptation to pull the flannel up.

"Tell me about yourself," Sky said.

Like many New Englanders (and Islanders in particular), Nate was taciturn by nature and especially disinclined to talk about himself. Still, Sky gently prodded and managed to extract a few facts. An unexpected late-in-life baby, he was an only child. He'd gone to college at UMass Amherst on a partial scholarship but left after three semesters when his dad was diagnosed with cancer.

"It was really hard. We had to sell the farm after my father died. It broke my mom's heart. She had a stroke a couple of years later and died, too."

"I'm sorry, Nate," Sky said, sitting up to reach for his hand.

"It's OK. It was a long time ago," Nate replied.

"Some more wine?"

"Sure," he replied,

Sky stood up and got the bottle from the refrigerator. After filling his glass, she went over to the bookcase. A second precariously balanced stack of books stood in the corner. "Wow. You've read all these?"

"Yeah. I don't watch much TV."

She skimmed the titles, mostly history (the McCullough books and the Banks *History of Martha's Vineyard*), natural ecology, and nautical yarns (*In the Heart of the Sea, Moby Dick*—the unabridged version, with all that business about rigging and rendering pots), *Two Years Before the Mast*, and several of Patrick O'Brian's novels). That was something they had in common: a college semester at sea on a tall ship had made Sky a fan of the genre.

"You've got some great books. Have you read *Blue Latitudes*?" she asked.

"No. I've meant to take that out of the library."

"I'll lend you my copy. Can I borrow this one?" she asked holding up *The Perfect Storm*." Nate nodded. "Thanks. I've wanted to reread it. But I should go; it's late. It was a wonderful evening," she said. Sky meant what she said. All of it—Nate's house, the food, his company—were exactly what she wanted. "I hope I don't get lost again."

"It's easier going back. Take a right out of the drive, stay to the left, then a right onto South Road. Or I can take you." Nate stood up.

"I'll find my way. Do you mind if I wear these home?" Sky asked gesturing towards her legs. "My pants are still wet."

"Sure." Nate paused, wondering what came next.

No need for him to decide. Sky walked over and put her hands behind his neck, then pulled him into a kiss that rocked his boat on a tempestuous sea.

NINE

Nate wakened early to the muffled honks of the pond geese. His washed-thin sheets were damp from the morning mist drifting through the window. He'd had a restless night. Sky's lingering goodnight kiss had left him rattled, feeling horny, and wondering what the hell he was getting himself into. Still, not seeing her would be like passing up ripe wild blueberries because they last only a few weeks. He'd just play it by ear, keep it light. He could do that, right?

Sky was stretched out on a cushioned chaise on her deck with the *Times* and a cup of coffee. "Hi, girl," she said, patting Nan's head. The dog's tail spun in happy circles. "Where's Nate?"

"Morning," Nate called as he walked around the side of the house.

"Hey, you," Sky said, greeting him with a high-wattage smile. Nate handed her a bowl and flopped into a chair. "What's this? Oh wow! Blueberries. I love these. Thanks." Sky popped a few in her mouth. "Yum. Where'd you get them?"

"Uh, from my blueberry bushes."

"Oh, right," Sky laughed at his expression. "I'm a city girl. Remember?"

"I remember." Nate grinned. God, she was sexy, lying there eating his berries.

"Thanks again for dinner. That fish was terrific."

"You're welcome." Nate searched for something to say. "Uh, have the goats been making much noise?"

"Just a couple bleats now and then. I think maybe Lizzie lost her mother in the bushes at some point, but she's quieted down. You know, they come up to the fence and let me pet them if I walk down there?"

"They probably think you're bringing them food. I forgot to tell you that you can feed them vegetable scraps and stuff. Nature's garbage disposal."

"Good to know."

Nate stood. "I'll be right back. Going to check on them."

Sky watched Nate stride across the field with Nan at his heels, then she wiggled the itchy spot on her back. Better not be a deer tick. She'd ask Nate to check. "How are they?" she asked.

"Goats look good." No reason for him to stay. "Um, guess I'll take off now."

"Nate, could you do me a huge favor and look to see if the bump I felt in the shower might be a tick?" Sky stood up and lifted the back of her tee shirt. "There, right between the shoulder blades. I tried to check it with a mirror but it's in a hard place to see."

"No problem. My buddy Zeke had a bad case of Lyme last summer and felt like shit for weeks." Nate moved closer to peer at the tiny black dot on Sky's back. "Hold still, it's so small I'm not sure what it is yet."

Sky felt Nate's hands touch her back and his breath brush her skin. "No, no legs. Just a tiny mole." Nate's voice had a husky edge to it as he tried to keep his attraction in check. Sky, on the other hand, let her thinking brain turn off. "And could you check one other place?" She slid down the waistband of her shorts. "Here."

"No, that's just a red spot, probably a spider bite," he said with a catch in his voice. "I can keep checking. Just tell me when to stop."

"No reason to stop." Sky turned around and put her hands around Nate's neck, pulling him into a deep kiss. She tugged his shirt up and over his head, running her fingers across the muscles of his back. Smiling, with a naughty look in her eye, Sky stood back and took off her tee and bralette. For the second time, Nate stared at her, transfixed. She next slid off her shorts, enjoying his ardent appraisal of her assets. Reaching for Nate's hand, Sky pulled him to the chaise.

"Here?" he asked.

"Here."

He'd never look at deck furniture in quite the same way again.

Zeke sat happily munching his second muffin. "Whoa, man, muffins? Spill, dude, who is she?" Zeke asked. Blueberry muffins were Nate's tell.

Nate grinned. "Heaven fell from the sky," he replied.

Zeke looked puzzled as he chewed the still-warm muffin. "Man, these are awesome." A sudden look of disbelief crossed Zeke's face. "No way," he said.

Nate's grin broadened. "She asked me for a tick check the other day. Then things just sort of, uh, went from there."

Zeke's eyebrows shot up. "Sure. A 'tick check.' She knew what she was doing."

"Oh yeah. She did." Nate's eyes went wide and soft. He looked like a lovesick cow.

"Oh no, buddy. I know that look. Please be careful. Like I told you before, she's way, way out of your league."

"She's really nice," Nate said. "You'll like her."

Zeke rested his cheek in his hand and sighed. One roll in the hay and Nate loses all sense. "I hope she's nice. But come on, Nate. Plus, she's a summer person. Don't forget that," he warned as he reached for another muffin.

"Last one, Zeke. I'm taking the rest over to Sky."

"Will you at least think about what I'm trying to tell you, dude?"

"Yeah, yeah. I hear you. She's an out-of-my-league summer person." That dopey smile again. "Summer Sky," he mooned.

Zeke sighed and gave up. "But hey, I didn't think I was ever gonna eat these again! Maybe she's not the right chick, but good on you. It's been too long, bro."

"Tell me about it." Nate put the remaining muffins on a paper plate. "Oh. I almost forgot. Katya wanted me to ask if you could help out at the Livingston Taylor concert," Nate said. "You know, tickets, selling CDs."

"Sure. She's singing with him, right? When?" Zeke asked.

"This Saturday night, at the Old Whaling Church."

"Ah shit. I've got a shucking job that night. Some hoity-toity party in Chilmark." Nate moved the plate as Zeke tried to grab another muffin. "Bet they won't let me put out a tip jar."

"Too bad. We're going to the Tank for beers afterward. Batty'll be there," Nate teased.

Zeke's eyes widened in mock terror as he put his hands over his zipper. "Lord almighty, protect me from that woman."

🐐 🐐 🐐

"I have to go meet my cousin Jak at the landing to help him trailer a boat," Nate said, tracing a gentle finger along the curve of Sky's cheekbone and planting a kiss on her lips. "I'd tell him I'm going to be late, but he and his phone took a swim in the Lagoon a couple of days ago," Nate explained.

"How'd that happen?" Sky asked.

"Who knows with Jak. He was trying to get into a rowboat or something and fell in."

"I should get over to Vineyard Haven anyway," Sky replied with a contented smile on her face. "Are there any muffins left?"

"One, I think." Nate reluctantly left the softest female and bed he'd ever been in. Man, I was totally right. Heaven did fall from the sky and somehow *I* caught it.

The sun lit Nate's bare backside as he walked outside to retrieve his clothes from the deck. "OK to move the pen tomorrow morning?" Nate asked as he pulled on his khaki shorts. "We'll have to tie up the goats while I do that."

Sky sat up in bed and stretched, sunlight warming her naked torso as the sheets fell to her waist. "Baaa," she replied, grinning at Nate.

"You sound like a sheep, not a goat," he laughed.

"Teach me, then."

"Later. I promise. Gotta go." Nate leaned down for another kiss, resisted the urge to blow off his cousin, and stood up. With a shy smile and a wave, he let himself out.

Sky listened to his truck rumble down the drive. Like an eraser, Nate was rubbing out the pain of Sky's breakup with Gil. She stretched again. That was unexpectedly wonderful. Call it what you will, hormones, chemistry. It's there. She looked out the window at the clouds floating by. Mmm, that delicious body. A cuddler too. So nice to snuggle against warm skin and inhale clean Nate-smell. Well, maybe just a touch of goat.

Sky flopped back onto the pillows, blissfully relaxed. What had gotten into her the other day? While her first request had been legit—she really couldn't check that spot between her shoulder blades—the second was not. Still, no regrets. She felt great. Really great. Besides, a guy that good-looking surely got plenty of offers from women. And her friends had been nagging her to stop thinking about Gil and get back in the game. Though they probably didn't mean making a stealth attack on Nate the Sexy Goat Guy. Sky giggled.

This summer was exactly what Sky needed. Her life had been a pressure cooker of scripted expectations. Get into the right schools, run in the right circles, choose the right career, marry the right man. She'd followed the rules. And until the breakup with Gil, Sky had been happy (or so she thought). Jumping into bed with a goatscaper was most decidedly not in the script.

She double-checked Grams's advice. *Be true.* Being with Nate made her feel truly horny. And she truly liked him. *Be kind.* Yup, that worked. *That's how you find happiness.* Well, there'd been happy endings for them both.

Sky shrugged her shoulders. Why not?

TEN

The two women resumed their friendship as if no time at all had passed. Elly struck Sky as someone who could be relied on for advice that would be both sensible and sensitive. And this was a topic that she couldn't (at least not yet) bring up with her old friends.

"Elly, do you know Nate Batchelor?" Sky started after they'd ordered their salads: a Niçoise for Sky and a Cobb for Elly.

"Of course," Elly replied. "Nate was a couple of years ahead of me in school. He dated my friend Caroline seriously for a while. He's goatscaping over at your place, isn't he?" Elly's curiosity was piqued. Nate was a good-looking guy, but hardly Schuyler Harrington's type, if that was where this was going. "Why do you ask?" Sky's hesitation in answering—and the look on her face—gave Elly her answer.

Sky jumped in. "Well, we probably seem like chalk and cheese to you, but he's a nice guy and we – um…." She wasn't sure what category their daily check-on-the-goats-then-have-sex sessions fell into. "Not really dating-dating. But I like him, and we have a good time together." An understatement, for sure.

"Nate's a good guy. And cute."

"He even made me homemade muffins with wild blueberries he'd picked himself. How amazing is that!"

"Wow," Elly said. Oh dear.

Sky took a deep breath. "My problem is that I have friends coming from the city later today, and, well, they're probably not going to, uh," she stumbled for what to say and decided on a different tack. "Well, it's just that I want to keep this out of the gossip circles back home. And Nate's been coming by every day."

Elly tilted her head, still trying to wrap her brain around the idea of Nate and Sky as a couple. "Just tell him that you want to keep things private for now. He'll understand you not wanting to say anything to your friends."

"You don't think that would hurt his feelings?" Sky asked. "I don't want him to think I'm embarrassed by him or anything like that."

"Then tell him that too." Elly was firmly in the just-say-what-you-mean-camp of advice-dispensing. "I suspect he really won't care. Likely he wants to keep his private life private too." Elly took a sip of iced tea and thought about whether she should say more. "But, Sky," she said kindly, looking her childhood friend in the eye, "relationships are different here. We Islanders have to live with each other no matter the outcome. Nate is a good guy, and you don't seem to have changed at all since we were kids." Elly glanced at Sky's décolletage and smiled. "Maybe a little." She became serious again. "But when you leave in a few weeks, you go off to a world full of other people, new people. And Nate's world—my world too—contracts."

"Sure." Sky didn't like where this was going.

"I'm always ready for things to quiet down, but not everyone does so well with it. We have a lot of issues here: alcohol, opioids, depression. So do other places. Nate doesn't have problems like that, so far as I know. But winters are hard. Especially if you have a broken heart."

Sky thought about what her new-old friend had said. It wasn't what she had expected to hear. "So I should break it off now?" she asked Elly, feeling like she'd just been kicked in the gut.

Elly shook her head. "I'm totally not advising one thing or another. Really not my business. Just promise me you'll be honest with him—and with yourself," Elly said.

Sky's bright expression had dimmed. "I will."

"I probably shouldn't have said anything,"

"No, I'm glad you did. I needed to know that. It's just that I've been feeling good about life for the first time in months."

Elly's empathy antenna went up. "Do you want to tell me about it?" she asked, reaching over to rest her fingers on Sky's arm.

Sky looked into Elly's kind eyes. Maybe it was time to talk about what had happened between her and Gil, at least the part of the story she was willing to share.

"Oh, Elly. I was engaged. But we broke up."

"I think there's more to the story than that," Elly said with an encouraging smile. "Spill, girlfriend. I'm a good listener."

Sky took a deep breath. "Gil and I had been together for a year. I met him in college, but we only started dating later. We hadn't even talked about marriage, but Gil had a business trip in Hong Kong and I'd come along. We were on the ferry boat to Lamma Island when he pulled out a ring and a bottle of Dom he'd hidden in his backpack." Sky gave her friend a sad smile. "Gil had had the ring in his sock drawer for months, trying to figure out how to ask me. I was so surprised but so happy. Then the wedding plans. Well, I don't know if you remember my mother at all, but it was just way easier to let her have her way. She's really good at organizing galas, and I was superbusy at work anyway. But then...." Sky paused and bit her lip. "I caught Gil cheating. In our bed." She looked down at her plate as tears threatened. "Two weeks before the wedding. It was horrible."

"Oh my, Sky. I am so sorry." Elly patted Sky's hand. "So, you had to cancel the whole wedding? That must have been awful." The waiter came by with the dessert menus. Elly didn't even look at hers.

"Two of whatever is chocolate," Elly told the waiter.

Sky choked back a sob. "You remember," Sky said, smiling as she wiped her eyes. "The chocolate cures." She blew her nose into her paper napkin. "You'd think I'd have stopped crying by now."

"Don't be silly. You literally caught your fiancé with his pants down."

It was much worse than that, but Sky had vowed not to tell anyone, ever. After the breakup, she'd guessed Gil's password and read his emails. It was wrong, but she'd had an irresistible, irrational urge to cut deeper into the wound. But what she'd found was even more painful than she could have imagined. Gil had been cheating on her the whole time they'd been together. That was why he'd always wanted to know exactly when she'd be done with work. It wasn't sweet as she had thought. It was so he wouldn't keep her waiting. Gil was setting up his trysts around Sky's schedule. Even in Hong Kong.

Sky had searched "meet me at" and there were the names. Such terrible, tacky names that at first she thought Gil had been hiring hookers. She felt betrayed, furious. And so, so stupid. The clues came to her later, piecemeal: Gil showering at the gym when he couldn't have had time to work out. All those last-minute emergencies at work that kept him out until midnight. His eyes lingering on the trashy, tight outfit worn by that cheap-looking blond.

"Your mother must have been upset," Elly said.

"Mortified. She had to tell all her friends the wedding was off. She lied, of course. Said it was 'postponed while Gil and I worked a few things out.' Everyone found out the real reason eventually." Sky stabbed her brownie sundae. "She couldn't have cared less about how I felt. It was all about her." Anger welled up, and she took a deep breath. "She canceled the wedding part and threw a huge charity benefit instead. Same ballroom, caterer, band, florist. Even the cake. Gil and I had picked chocolate with ganache. None of the guests knew that they were eating my wedding cake." Lucretia's adroit repurposing of Sky's wedding was deemed by society to be a generous and elegant move on her part. She avoided creating a gap in the social calendar, got her picture in the society pages, and netted a tidy sum for the new neonatal wing at the Children's Hospital to boot. But Sky was devastated.

"That is so weird," Elly said. "Maybe not weird. I don't know what to call it."

"All Lucretia had to do was reissue the invitations. She wasn't going to waste a guest list like that." Sky looked down at her dessert. "But she raised a lot of money for a hospital, so I guess that was one good thing that came out of it."

"You didn't have to go, did you, to the event?"

"Geez, no. I was an embarrassment. She packed me, sobbing, off to a spa in Arizona with my bridesmaids. But tell me about your wedding. Did you get married in West Tisbury?"

"Where else? Did you see the church was decorated for a wedding the other day? Pink roses and daisies? It looked so cute!" Elly said.

"It's such a pretty little building. Did you have a big wedding?"

"Not really. We wanted to keep it simple, so we just had a clambake on the beach for the reception."

"That sounds wonderful. Nothing like what mine would've been like!" Sky said, with barely a twinge of the old pain. "I bet you were beautiful."

"I hope so," Elly said. "I wore my grandmother's lace dress. I'll show you pictures next time you're over."

"I'll remind you." Sky motioned to the waiter for the check. "Thanks, Elly. Talking to you has really helped. I should go soon, though. I've got a ton of things to do before Winky and Prescott get here."

ELEVEN

Sky wandered around putting the final touches in place before her friends arrived (flowers in the bedroom, soaps and towels in the bathroom, an extra bottle of wine in the refrigerator) as she mulled over Elly's comments about her and Nate. Sky was well aware of having been born with a silver spoon—Tiffany, to be precise, with a matching silver porringer. She had no intention of leading him on a merry chase. Sky didn't play games.

But Elly was right: it was important to be honest with herself and with Nate. Sky was still thinking about what to say to him about her friends' visit when gravel crunched in the drive.

Sky expected to see Nate, but instead it was Winky, Louis Vuitton duffel in hand, running to greet her with a huge hug and kiss.

"Sky! I hope you don't mind that we're early. One of Prescott's clients was coming over in his jet, and we were able to catch a lift."

Sky was delighted to see her oldest and dearest friend. "Of course not. It's so great to see you." She and Winky had been friends forever. They'd met in Mrs. Bloch's class at the *right* preschool, the one their mothers had chosen to maximize their chances of getting into the *right* private school—one that would lead them to the Ivy League. The tiny, thumb-sucking

Winifred had turned into Winky, a willowy, auburn-haired woman with an easy smile.

Winky had the rare ability to make everyone feel comfortable. Seat her next to Uncle Dick at a dinner party, and their conversation about his beloved bird carvings would be the liveliest at the table. She was the kind soul who'd spot the pimply teenage nephew sitting alone at a wedding and get him to chat with her about lacrosse or football. At last year's Opera Ball, she'd been seated next to Merrilleon Finch, as intimidating a dowager as their social class could produce. Sky came back from dancing to find them in an animated tête-à-tête about the best breeds for dressage. Winky, who didn't even like horses, had the old bat smiling. Sky loved her.

Prescott followed behind Winky with his Burberry hold-all and a big white shopping bag, clearly unimpressed with Sky's modest house.

"Come in. Let me get you something to drink," Sky said.

"Here, Sky. We brought you a house gift." Winky said pulling out a square box tied with a bow from its bag. "Prescott and I saw the Chihuly exhibition at the Botanical Gardens. I just love his stuff."

"Thank you." Sky undid the bow and took out a slumped glass bowl—chartreuse stripes, purple and red spots, a yellow lip, and a bright raspberry interior. It sat like on her table like a shiny alien sea creature: smashing in an all-white penthouse, hideous here.

"Isn't it amazing," Winky said.

"Amazing," Sky repeated, horrified. She pulled herself together. "Thank you so much." She gave her friend a hug. "I love it."

"I knew you would. I remembered that was your favorite shade of green. We got one too, in turquoise and orange!"

"I'll have to find the right place for it." In a cabinet, after they leave, hidden from view.

"Prescott," Sky said. "Here, let me show you your room." Sky had created a main guest suite in the original part of the cottage. The previous owners had more or less gutted the first floor, leaving the original steep staircase, fireplaces, and other architectural details. The guest suite ran across the back of the house facing the pond, offering lovely views through all the windows. Sky had furnished the room with an antique four-poster bed she had snagged at a yard sale at one of the big estates on Edgartown Great Pond, adding a new mattress, luxurious linens, and a fluffy down comforter. A bunch of dahlias from the farmers' market sat in a silvery former-tomato-can vase. The suite's private deck, with French doors and a second outdoor shower, faced one of the sightlines that Nate's goats were clearing. Prescott gazed at the shower with something close to horror.

"You do have indoor plumbing, I hope?" he remarked, as he set their bags on the bed.

"Of course she does," said Winky.

"Why don't you freshen up. Then we'll decide what we want to do today," Sky said.

"Excellent plan," said Prescott. "Do you mind getting my briefcase? I think left it outside."

Sky was heading out to the drive when Nate pulled up. "Hey, Sky. I've got news. Baby Face gave birth to triplets!" He strode over to give her a big hug. A flash of pain moved quickly but unmistakably across Nate's face as she drew away, with a glance toward the house. "I saw the car. Do you have guests?"

At that moment, Sky changed her mind about keeping their relationship under wraps. Damn the consequences. She moved close and gave him a gentle kiss, reaching up to run her fingers over the stubble on his cheek. Putting her hand on his arm, she said, "Yes. Some very old friends! Let me introduce you."

Winky's baffled eyes moved from her dear friend to the admittedly good-looking but grubby Nate at Sky's side. Prescott looked appalled. Both had seen Sky kiss him.

"Winky, Prescott, this is Nate Batchelor. He runs a goatscaping business. Those are his goats you see out in the field. They're, uh, clearing the brush. So you can see the view."

Winky recovered her poise, generations of good breeding kicking in. "Very glad to meet you, Nate." She shook Nate's dirty hand and shot a look at Prescott.

"Prescott Hale," he said, stepping forward to grip Nate's hand. Prescott was now privy to perhaps the juiciest piece of gossip all summer.

"Winky and Prescott are visiting this weekend," Sky said.

Prescott's client-dinner-fed belly pooched over his belt as he sat down, gesturing to Nate to do the same. "Interesting business. Goats?"

"Um," said Nate. "Well…"

Oh boy. "Goats are much better for the environment than, say, gas-powered tools," Sky volunteered.

"Yeah,. There's that," Nate said.

"And high profit margins, once you cover your fixed costs? That is, the investment in the goats?" asked Prescott, amusement clear in his eyes behind his horn-rimmed glasses.

Nate shifted in his seat, painfully aware of his grimy clothes. "I'm making a profit this year, yeah."

"And the competition?" Prescott leaned back and crossed his legs. "Goatscaping a big business here on the Island?"

"There's one other guy. Bigger outfit. More goats." Prescott's eyebrows went up. Sky's new boyfriend was only the second-most-successful goatscaper on the Island. "But the competition is mostly from the landscaping companies."

"Har. This business of yours just reminded me of one of my favorite jokes," Prescott began.

Winky rolled her eyes. "Oh, Pressy."

Prescott cleared his throat. "So. A gentleman taking a long ramble through the countryside comes across a field full of goats. He spies a man having sex with one of them. 'That's not right,' he says to himself and knocks on the door of the nearest hut. A young man answers and asks if he can help. The gentleman says, 'I hate to bother you, but there's a fellow out in the field having sex with a goat.' The young man replies, 'Thaaats okaaay. Thaats my faaaather!'"

Nate managed a weak smile. Winky stepped in to rescue him. "So sorry to interrupt, Pressy. But don't you have a conference call in a few minutes? We still need to get you connected to Sky's Wi-Fi."

"I'd better be off. Nice to meet you," said Nate.

"Bye. We'll talk later. OK?" Sky said with a worried look.

Poor, sweet Nate.

TWELVE

It didn't take long for the fallout to begin. Returning from a drive down to Menemsha for a lobster roll lunch, Sky found her phone stuffed with texts. *Sky, are you OK? A goatherd????"* one friend asked. Another had sent a photoshopped picture of Sky with a herd of goats and the caption, *Anything you want to tell me?* Even her mother had left a voice message. "Schuyler, dearest. I have just heard the most alarming news. I am quite sure it isn't true, so please call me ASAP."

Sky and Winky took glasses of lemonade out onto the deck. "I'm really glad to see you looking so rested and healthy," Winky began. "Almost glowing. You were so drawn and pale when you left the city. You looked shell-shocked, to tell the truth. We were really worried about you."

Sky nodded. "The Vineyard's been really good for me. It has—I know this sounds sort of crystals and new agey—healing power."

With a twinkle in her green eyes, Winky asked, "And maybe a little manly medicine has helped too?"

"He's a good guy," Sky said. "I expect you're surprised."

"I'm not one to judge. You're single and attractive. Why shouldn't you have a fling? Sow your wild oats, as the men used to be told." Winky sipped her lemonade. "Nate isn't exactly my type, but I grant he'd turn a few eyes at the club if you cleaned him up a bit."

"I like him. A lot, I think." Her cell buzzed. "Oh no. Look at this." She handed her phone to Winky.

Winky tried to hold back her laughter as she handed it back. "Colin is nothing if not creative," Winky said. "Do goats really do that?"

Sky looked again at the photo of a goat and the caption: *Roses are red, violets are blue, I peed on my face 'cause I love you.*

"This isn't going to end. Is it?" Sky asked.

"It won't take long for people to get tired of the goat jokes. I'll do what I can to make the gossip fest short-lived. You'll be old news before you know it."

"Thanks, Wink." Sky smiled in relief. "I'll show this one to Nate. It is pretty funny."

"How about we head over to Davis House Gallery while Prescott finishes up his calls? I'm redoing our bedroom and might commission a beachscape for over the mantle," Winky said.

Sky stood up. "I love that gallery. Let's go."

🐐 🐐 🐐

Winky's visit coincided with the sort of social events that she'd been trying to avoid. Sky had zero interest in Winky and Prescott's party, but unbeknownst to her they'd asked the hosts to invite her; it would be terribly rude for her not to attend. A totally A-list crowd, Prescott said, as if that would be an inducement.

The evening's weather was perfect—just a touch of cool in the air—and the property spectacular. The multimillion-dollar farm was set at the top of a hill with views stretching from Aquinnah along most of the Island's south shore toward Katama. Fat, black-faced sheep grazed in fields bounded by ancient stone walls, adding a charming note to the bucolic scene. Sky hoped the Cupertons appreciated what they had.

She hesitated after handing her keys to the valet. This type of event was well within her social wheelhouse, and the food would be fantastic, but Sky wasn't in the mood to make small talk with a bunch of strangers.

"Schuyler," Prescott called, "the party isn't going to come to you."

"On my way. I was fixing my sandal."

The party was A-list, as advertised. A-plus, Sky corrected herself, studying the guest names listed on the chalkboard outside the lavishly renovated barn. The money-and-power crowd, most of the guests closer in age to her parents' generation than hers. Sky recognized CEOs, some high-ranking political appointees, and many who were merely enormously rich. Clever to have the guest names on display: both so guests don't fumble and forget names they should know—here's your crib sheet—and also so they have a road map to those they should be sure to talk to. Or avoid, as was the case for her when she spotted Francisco's name near the end of the list.

Sky rested a hand on the barn door and looked around. Caterers had set up fresh hay bales, covered by Hudson Bay blankets, as seating. Extravagant, colorful arrangements of dahlias, cosmos, and roses filled zinc buckets, and Pinterest-worthy hors d'oeuvres spilled out cornucopia-style from baskets on antique tables. She wandered over to nibble on a mound of fresh lobster served in a grain scoop. The party flaunted its lavish expense against the barn's rough-hewn walls.

"How do we look?" Winky giggled as she posed for a selfie. Prescott had plunked green John Deere caps on their heads from a stack thoughtfully provided for guests seeking their inner farmer.

"Not your color, I think," Sky replied, disliking the caps worn as a joke.

"Come on. You should try one on," urged Winky.

"No thanks," Sky replied. "Look, they have an alpaca." She wandered over to the horse stall to stroke the animal's oh-so-soft coat.

"Time for a drink," announced Prescott, putting the hats back on the stack. They moved deeper into the barn where a bartender, dressed like a farmhand in overalls and tatty straw hat, stood behind a horse trough.

"Our signature cocktail tonight is a sheep dip," he explained, unscrewing the top from one of the mason jars resting on ice in the trough. "It's my variation on the classic Aviation cocktail: a mixture of Hendrick's gin, St-Germain, Crème de Violette, a splash of maraschino liqueur, and lemon juice, muddled with fresh basil." Sky, Winky, and Prescott eyed the grayish drink and its bits of greenish leaves with some suspicion. "Trust me. It's delicious," the bartender coaxed.

"He's right," Sky said to Winky with some relief after taking a sip from her mason jar. "This is good. But strong." The three made their way over to greet their hostess and then headed outside to the field where a raw bar had been set up in an old wooden dinghy.

"Oh, look, littlenecks. Let's get some before the hordes descend," Sky enthused. Her appetite for the tiny, briny bites was only whetted by her ineptitude at opening them.

"Prescott. Good to see you," called an overstuffed man in a purple striped shirt. "I've got an idea I want to discuss."

"Sorry, Winky, Sky. Business," Prescott said over his shoulder, a sucking-up-to-the-client smile already plastered on his face. "Get me a few oysters."

"Good evening. I'm Zeke and I'll be your shucker this evening. What can I do for you, ladies?" asked the scruffy young man dressed as a fisherman in waders and a yellow Sou'wester rain hat. Sky was too busy looking at the clams to notice that the shucker was staring at her.

"Littlenecks, please," she replied, mouth already watering. "Did I tell you I tried to teach myself how to do this? It's much harder than it looks," she said to Winky. Zeke deftly slid the knife through a clam and popped off the shell. "I got only two open out of a dozen."

"I can't believe you even tried. You could have sliced your hand open! I always leave things like that to the experts." Winky smiled at the shucker, who grinned back.

He handed them six juicy bivalves on a tin plate. "Lemon and cocktail sauce?"

"Yes, please."

"And three oysters," Winky said.

They carried their plate over to an antique tractor and set it down on the hood. "Poor Pressy," Winky said. "He never really is off work." A brilliant investment advisor and one of the top performers in his field, Prescott had always been fascinated by money. He'd started as a stockbroker, relying on his father's contacts, and eventually opened his own private wealth management business. This party was exactly his kind of scene.

Sky had just raised another shell to her lips when a masculine arm slipped around her bare waist; she almost spat out her clam in surprise. It was Francisco. Handsome, charming, egotistical Francisco. He moved in close to give her a European style two-kiss greeting, pressing himself against her.

"Schuyler, I am so happy to see you! We've all missed you. Your mother said you have become some sort of recluse up here. You're looking fabulous. Obviously, this charming island lifestyle agrees with you." Francisco stepped back to give Sky a head-to-toe appraisal. A wolf sizing up his prey. Neatly, Sky sidestepped Francisco's attempt to return his arm to her waist, positioning her drink defensively.

Winky had been dragged away by a tight-looking woman in a silk tunic. Sky was trapped. "Yes, it's lovely here," she replied, resigned to the conversation.

"Everyone has been asking for you at the Hamptons. How have you been keeping yourself busy?" Francisco asked, leaning in closer. Too close. She hated men's cologne, the smell bringing back the unwanted memory of a major-mistake night she'd spent with him.

"Nothing really. Just putting the new house in order. But what have you been up to?" Sky asked politely, automatically. She should be nicer to Francisco. In truth, Sky liked him when he wasn't in pursuit mode. Anyway, it wasn't entirely his fault that he thought he had a chance, considering the night she'd seduced him and that Sky's mother had been working to convince him that patience and persistence would win her over.

Sky feigned interest in his reply—Francisco could talk about Francisco for hours—as she scanned the crowd, searching for an escape route. Prescott was still deep in conversation with his client. Winky was now over by the farm tables laden with food, buttonholed by a balding man and the hard blonde in the tunic. Sky felt unmoored: here she was on the Island, her refuge, engaged in a conversation that seemed to be coming from her "other life." The disconnect made her dizzy, and she was relieved when Francisco knocked her hand by accident, splashing her with sheep dip. "This is silk, I need to wash it out," she explained, moving toward the farmhouse.

Sky located the bathroom with its floating sandstone sink and dabbed at her top. When as much of the stain as possible was out, she caught a glance at herself in the mirror. She looked like she belonged with these people. She was exactly the type of intelligent, highly-educated, attractive, and socially adept female who'd be the perfect arm accessory for Francisco. But was that really her, and why was she feeling the need to flee this party?

Still feeling shaky, she found Winky. "I'll see you back at the house. I'm not feeling well. Bad clam, I think."

With her excuse in place, Sky called a cab and escaped.

Picking up her book and settling onto the sofa with a cup of peppermint tea, Sky tucked an alpaca throw blanket around her legs. She was rereading *Caleb's Crossing,* the story (imagined, but based in fact) of a Vineyard Wampanoag boy who went to Harvard in the 1660s and the daughter of a Puritan minister. The book was a good distraction, and Sky was feeling settled and sleepy. She was about to head off to bed when she heard a car pull around the drive. Winky and Prescott were back.

A red-faced, slightly unstable Prescott reeled through the door, followed by Winky. Winky had never been much of a drinker, but clearly, Prescott had gotten into the sheep dip. "Great party, dear Schuyler, such fun. You should have stayed." His voice filled the room.

Winky walked over to check on Sky. "How are you feeling? I've been worried."

"Much better, thanks. I think I'll be fine tomorrow. Tell me what I missed," Sky said patting the spot next to her on the sofa.

"Got any decent scotch around here?" Prescott bellowed. "Anyone join me for a little nightcap? That Francisco friend of yours was looking for you everywhere. I told him you had gone home to feed your goats!" Prescott laughed at his own joke.

Winky sat down, eyes bright, to recap the party for Sky. "Guess who came after you left. Obama. He didn't stay long; someone said Michelle was waiting for him at another party, but we were chatting with the Cupertons when he walked right up and introduced himself." Winky melted back into her cushion. "He has such a wonderful smile. I can't believe you missed meeting him."

"That must have so been exciting," Sky said feigning enthusiasm. A lifetime of watching her mother finagle introductions to celebrities had left Sky immune to the appeal.

"After dinner, there was contra dancing in the barn. They had a caller and professional dancers to teach us the steps," Winky said. "It was so much fun. And you should have seen Prescott. At one point he tried to dance with the alpaca!"

"I got confused. I thought I was dancing with Meg Ryan," Prescott chuckled as he flopped down in the armchair with his drink.

"Oh, Pressy," Winky said.

"I can see why you like it here," he said, slurring slightly. "Private beaches—no hoi polloi. Even Nantucket can't say that. No shortage of social or business opportunities. I bet I could pick up a dozen new big-ticket clients up here if I put my mind to it. Maybe we should call a realtor after tomorrow's brunch, eh Winkster? You'd like being up here with your old friend Schuyler here, wouldn't you? And I've been saying we need to diversify into some more real estate."

Winky turned from husband to friend. She bit her lip as she tried to read Sky's reaction. "What do you think? Should we do that?"

Sky's stomach had dropped. She adored Winky. It wasn't that. And Prescott, beneath the supercilious exterior, was funny and generous. But if they bought a house it would be impossible to resist the orbit of the Vineyard's summer elite: the tennis matches, rounds of golf at Farm Neck, and the endless, endless cocktail parties.

"Great idea," she replied with a weak smile.

THIRTEEN

Even Nate wasn't immune to the classic beauty of the Old Whaling Church. He ran his hand across one of the mast-like pillars of the Greek Revival building as he waited for Katya to arrive with the amps and gear and wandered over to look at the event poster. There was Katya's name (as special guest) under Livingston Taylor's, right next to the red sold-out-show banner. No wonder she was so excited. If seasonal work as a goatscaper was hard, try being a musician.

A horn beeped and he turned around. "Hi, Nate! I'll pull around the corner," Katya said.

"Is there a lot of stuff?"

"No, we're using Liv's speakers."

Nate carried in the guitar cases and gear as Katya parked. "Omigod, Nate," she said as she came bounding into the church. "I can't believe it's tonight. Thanks heaps for helping."

"No problem. I don't often get to be a roadie. Did you want to check out the stage?"

Katya took her guitar out of its case, climbed onto the platform, and strummed a few chords. "How does it sound in the back?"

He walked to the rear of the church and flopped into a pew. The room's acoustics, designed for a minister's sermon, naturally amplified Katya's warm, husky voice. The night's concert couldn't be any better than this.

"You sound great, Katya. You barely need the amps."

"I figure Liv knows what to do. He plays here a lot." Nate set to work hauling speakers that Livingston's crew had brought in earlier and taping down cords. Wound up with pre-performance jitters, Katya went to the bathroom to put on her stage outfit and makeup as the ticketholders lined up outside.

Livingston Taylor's familiar, folksy tunes drew mostly families and older couples. Nate watched the show, leaning against the rear doors, having also been designated usher for the latecomers and CD salesman. Liv was in fine form, interspersing songs with humorous anecdotes. Katya relaxed under his gentle ribbing as Liv played off the difference in their ages, claiming her songs got louder applause than his own. Their encore, a duet version of his "I Will Be In Love With You," gave Nate goosebumps.

Katya came out after the performance even higher than before. "Omigod! That was so great," she said, spotting her husband, John, and throwing herself into his arms. Katya's daughters jumped up and down with excitement.

"My mom'll take the kids," John said. "You're coming to the Tank with us, right, Nate?" The Earl of Tankerville, the closest thing to a locals' bar in tony Edgartown, would be packed with weekend tourists and summer people on a Saturday night, but a beer sounded good.

"You bet. Let's get the stuff packed up."

Nate spotted Batty waving from the rear of the pub. "I got us a table," she shouted, her bullhorn voice cutting through the din.

"Katya," Nate called through the press of people at the bar. "Tell John we'll be in the back."

Nate made his way over with his beer. "Hi, Felicia. Hey, Batty," he said.

Batty slid over on the bench to make room. "Nate, this is Mary and Lauri. They're two of my kayak guides this summer."

"Hi," said Nate, sitting down next to Lauri.

"Is Zeke here?" Batty asked, searching the crowd. Batty (short for Bathsheba, an old Island name, justifiably despised) and Zeke had been an item in high school and she had, for years, indicated in no uncertain terms that she would welcome a rekindling of their relationship. Nearly six feet tall with a figure like a sturdy oak and short sun-bleached hair, Batty was a formidable woman. No wonder Zeke protected his crotch whenever Nate mentioned her name.

"Naw. He's got a shucking gig up-Island somewhere."

Batty's smile dimmed. "That's too bad. Who's he working for?"

"Jodi, I think."

"Ah. Fancy party, then."

Nate took a deep, satisfying slug of beer. "Yeah, I guess so. Long day, I think he started mowing early today."

"Poor Zeke. He'll be exhausted," Batty said, sun-creased eyes softening.

Nate raised his eyebrows. "Yeah, but it's not like he can afford to turn down the work." He drank another inch and wiped his mouth with the back of his hand. "Any of us."

"You got that right," Mary chimed in. "Batty's been working me like a dog," she teased, mock-punching Batty in her man-sized biceps.

"Busy is good," Batty said. "Nate, you want to order some food?"

"I'm OK. I'll eat some of your fries though," he said, reaching over.

"They're delicious," said Lauri. Nate pushed a lock of hair out of his face with his nongreasy hand and caught her flirtatious look. Nobody knew about Sky, except of course Zeke. Nate sighed. Sky was probably having a great time with her hoity-toity friends right now. Maybe meeting some rich guy who'd ask her out on his yacht and make her wonder why she'd ever hooked up with a goatscaper.

He realized Batty was talking to him. "So I was tinkering with my Nonna's lasagna recipe again the other night. I meant to bring some over for you and Zeke to try." There were always leftovers from Nonna's Italian family-size recipes. "Did Zeke like the stracotto I left? The pot roast thing?"

Nate suspected Batty was trying to fatten Zeke up for the kill. "Loved it. Me too. I'll swap you the lasagna for some wild blueberries."

"Ooo. I love blueberries," said Lauri, still ogling Nate. She slid a little closer.

"Me too," said Felicia. "I still miss Eileen Blake's blueberry pies. They were the best."

"Pie Chicks makes a good one," said Mary.

"Did I tell you I tried your coffee cake recipe?" Felicia asked. "Only I used frozen wild blueberries, and it came out purple. I think I let the berries defrost."

Batty slid the basket of fries over to Nate. "Hey, I saw the picture of the goat escape in the paper," she said.

"Oh man. Yeah. But it got me a new client, Nate said. Lauri pressed her thigh against his. Yikes. He moved his leg away. Maybe he'd picked up some pheromone off the goats that was working for women too.

"Free publicity. I could use that." Batty thought for a moment. "Nope. 'Escaped kayaks' isn't going to land me on the front page."

"Unless the goats used the kayaks to escape," Lauri said, giggling.

Katya and John wove their way through the crowd with their pints, followed by Nate's cousin Jak. "Big night," John told the table. "Katya totally stole the show."

"I did not," Katya protested, beaming.

"I respectfully disagree." John raised his glass in a toast. "To my talented wife and a sold-out show. As they say, making hay while the sun shines."

"Congrats, Katch," Jak said, planting a kiss on her cheek. "Always knew you were a star." He said hi to the rest of the table then turned to Nate. "Sorry for the short notice, but any chance you can cover for Bobby tomorrow morning? I just found out he's not coming." At a thousand bucks for an all-day charter fishing trip, Jak couldn't risk white-knuckling it solo, or, even worse, canceling. "I can get Colton, but he just tangles the lines."

A day on the water (and some extra cash) sounded fine to Nate. Besides, he hadn't done any fishing all summer. "No problem," Nate replied. "What time you need me at the dock?"

FOURTEEN

Sky and Winky walked in silence down the damp path. The lifting fog painted a pink and gray-green palette, softening trees and bushes into vague shapes and amplifying sounds: the faint gabbling of the geese, Lizzie's bleat as she sought her morning breakfast from Pearl.

"This is pretty magical," Winky said. "I wasn't sure it was such a good idea, your leaving everything behind to run up here." She raised an eyebrow. "But you've found at least one thing to keep you busy. I didn't know you had a weakness for the rugged workman type."

"Me neither," Sky laughed. "How are things going with Prescott? She asked, deflecting the conversation from Nate. "Still wedded bliss?" Winky and Prescott's extravagant Saint Kitts wedding had been *the* event of the season a few years back.

"Pretty much." Winky smiled. Prescott adored his wife. "Though I get tired of his bad jokes sometimes—sorry about that goat one. But he really is sweet. Especially now."

"Why now?"

"You know we're trying to get pregnant, but it isn't going so well," Winky confided. "The doctors started me on that thing where I have to get a shot of hormones in my tush every day." She shuddered. "And unless I want to go to the doctor's office to have the nurse do it, it has to be Prescott." That, Sky could not see. The man once turned green and nearly fainted when Winky got a splinter from a wooden dock in Palm Beach. "At least for me, it's just a couple of shots. Not like what you'll have to go through."

Sky shook her head. "Nothing I'm worrying about right now," she said with a smile. Surgery at seventeen for ovarian cysts had left her infertile but delighted not to have to ever worry about birth control. "When will you find out if it worked?"

"This next cycle, we hope. We're keeping our fingers crossed."

"I'll cross mine too," Sky said, reaching over to squeeze her best friend's hand. Wisps of fog danced across the pond. "I've been terrible about staying in touch with people. What's everybody up to this summer?" Sky asked.

Winky filled her in with details of the latest gossip and parties and glancing at her watch, asked, "Ready to head back? I'm supposed to get my shot the same time every day."

Prescott sat on the deck in his old-fashioned black-watch plaid nightshirt and bee-embossed slippers. "Morning ladies. Where have you been?" He asked, stretching his arms overhead. "I slept like a log. Wonderful bed, by the way."

"Yes, and you sawed logs all night again," retorted Winky, engaging in their standard morning repartee.

"Oh, pshaw. You just make that up. I am as quiet as a mouse. What's our schedule? Over to the Hand's in Edgartown at for brunch at 11:00? I think I have enough time to get in a few practice swings at Farm Neck first." Prescott yawned broadly. "I didn't expect to get up this early, but I was having the damnedest dream about a dinner party where the other guests were two sheep, a giant goose, and some goats, and a talking alpaca was the host. It was terribly difficult to come up with a topic of dinner conservation," he added.

Sky laughed. "That works. Winky and I can drop you off and then head to Oak Bluffs to see the Campground. You'll love it, Winky. The houses are adorable."

"Perfect," said Winky, looking forward to seeing the tiny Victorian gingerbread cottages, painted like dollhouses in pastel shades.

"I'll go get dressed."

Sky felt both relief and a twinge of guilt as she kicked one of Nate's dirty tees to the back of her closet. Just as well that they'll be out when he comes by to check the goats.

Nate chipped away at a block of frozen squid bait as Jak welcomed the charter boat's passengers onboard.

"Scott, Jim. Great to see you guys again," said Jak with a hearty handshake. "John, Greg. Ready to catch some fish?" All middle-aged guys, lots of Orvis. Jak stepped off the dock and onto the deck of *Island Girl*, his thirty-five-foot Duffy. He extended a hand to steady the men as they climbed on. "My cousin Nate's my mate today."

"Hiya, mate Nate," said Greg. Nate grinned and waved his pick, then moved to the bow of the boat to release the lines.

"What do you guys want to go for today?" Jak asked.

"Whatever's biting. We're just out to have a good time," said Greg.

"Nate, I know these guys. Double supply of beers in the cooler, right?"

Nate switched on his friendly-to-the-paying-customer persona, wondering how Jak did it day after day. "Triple, I thought you said."

The guys laughed. "Good thinking. We'll drink 'em," said Jim.

"Wind's coming in from the south, so it's a bit rough over at Noman's. I thought we'd head over toward Cuttyhunk. I've been having good luck there—if you don't mind catching blues. Then we can go try our luck finding some stripers."

The clients settled in for the ride while Nate checked over the rods. One guy, Scott, had just returned from fishing the Atlantic salmon run on the Whale River in Quebec at a fishing camp so remote that the only way to get there was to charter a plane.

"Best fly-fishing there is," he said. "You know, I was flipping through the guest book. They even got Ted Williams in there."

"What did you land?"

Nate listened with half an ear to Scott's day-by-day list of fish caught, numbers, lengths, and weights.

"Maybe it's not fly-fishing, but nothing tops the Kenai," Greg said. "I'm out there one morning last summer—they tell you where the grizzlies are so you know where you shouldn't go—and damn if a big bear doesn't come out of the woods directly across from me. I've got a big old king salmon on my line, and he's looking at me like breakfast is served. I thought I'd shit my pants," Greg laughed, opening his second beer of the morning.

"What did you do?" asked Jak, looking over his shoulder from the wheel.

"Cut my line and walked very slowly backward. Then I ran like hell."

"Ah, salmon fishing is for bears and wusses," Jim declared.

"Yeah, we know, Jim: the only real fishing is bonefishing," Greg shot back.

"Hey, Redpath. I heard a rumor you landed a permit," Jim said.

"Come on. Tell us the story. You know you want to." The men listened to the tale of catching a fifty-three-pound permit in the Marquesas Keys on a ten-weight fly rod. They'd laid theirs out on the table and, considering everything—length, girth, and difficulty of the conquest—had lost.

"Yeah, permit. That's one hell of an elusive fish," said Jim.

Lines began zinging as they hit a school of blues. Nate rushed around netting and rebaiting hooks as flopping bluefish thumped in the fish cooler. How much money did these guys spend flying around the world to catch fish? Nate liked fishing as much as the next guy, better than most, but jeez, you can't even eat a bonefish.

"Yo, squidboy," called Jim. Nate sliced a squid up into smelly, slimy white strips and brought it over. His hands would stink for days.

Goats and bait. What a prize. Nate couldn't figure out why Sky was interested in him. And that other day, what was that about? First Sky looks at him like he was the hired help, then she's kissing him and introducing him to Winky and her stuffed shirt of a husband, Prescott.

Then the lightbulb came on. It hurt. Bad. Zeke was right: Sky was slumming. Nate would be an amusing story she'd tell at cocktail parties: that time she had a summer fling with the goat guy. He'd save Sky the trouble. And a bit of his pride. Before he got in too deep.

FIFTEEN

"Thanks for dropping us off," Winky said as Sky pulled up to the graceful clapboard captain's house overlooking Edgartown Harbor. "I'm sorry to be deserting you for the morning, but you know how it goes. Prescott always has these client things, and I'm expected to go too…" she said with a wave of her hand.

"Don't worry about me. A couple of hours on the deck with my book suits me fine." Winky was so good, the way she endured those endless rounds of business-related socializing.

"See you later, alligator," said Prescott.

Prescott offered his arm to his wife and they walked inside. It was a lovely house, quintessentially Edgartown. The classical façade featured two columned porches, a triangular pediment, a bullseye window, and a widow's walk perched on top. Rose gardens bounded by immaculate picket fencing stretched from the street to the water. But Sky was happy to be dropping off, not going in.

A Doris Day parking spot right in front of Murdick's Fudge changed Sky's plan from reading to shopping. She wandered around the boutiques and galleries for a while, then splurged on a sexy-casual pale-blue sundress she thought Nate might like if they went out to dinner. A new floppy sunhat caught her eye, perfect for the beach, and she'd pick up some addictively delicious penuche-pecan fudge on her way back to the car. Tired of shopping, Sky had just sat down at a dockside cafe for an iced coffee when her cell buzzed. Francisco. Sky stared at her phone and considered ignoring the call. "Hello," she said instead.

"Schuyler, it's me." She would be expected to know who "me" was. "I meant to call you earlier but got roped into a killer set of doubles. What happened to you last night? I looked all over, and Prescott made the oddest comment about you needing to go back to feed your goats?"

"I wasn't feeling well, so I left early. Bad clam, too much sun, I'm not sure," she explained. "I'm fine now. And I've got goats on the property clearing brush. That must have been Prescott's idea of a joke or something," she added.

"Can I see you? Have you eaten? I'm staying at the Charlotte Inn. How about you meet me here for lunch in, say, half an hour, then you can show me your place, and we'll change and go to the beach." The idea of an entire afternoon of macho Francisco, preening in his swim trunks, held small appeal. She was about to say sorry, she was tied up with houseguests, when she spotted Francisco walking down Main Street, still in his tennis whites. And he saw her. Crikey.

Francisco was at her table in a minute, his double-kiss and full chest-to-groin body press lingering even longer than last night's. His sweat-dampened tennis clothes didn't help, nor did the rank combination of cologne and perspiration.

"Schuyler, what luck. Here you are, looking even more lovely in the daylight." He sat down and leaned in close then reached over and took her hand, wetly kissing her palm and pressing it against the club logo of his snug white tennis shirt. "So beautiful. Here, feel my heart beating for you."

Where does he get these lines? She extricated her hand and surreptitiously wiped her palm on a napkin. "I'm sorry, but I am really tied up today. I've got to pick up Winky and Prescott in a bit, and I've promised to show them around before their flight."

"Ah, a perfect plan. I will quickly shower and be back in ten minutes. You order for me—a salad, no bread—and we can have a bite together. Then I'll join your little tour. I'm quite sure that Winky and Prescott won't mind." He clasped her hand in both of his and made another attempt to look deeply and soulfully into her eyes.

"No running off to your goats this time, mi cielo."

🐐 🐐 🐐

The afternoon seemed endless. And not in a good way. Winky and Prescott's brunch went on longer than expected, leaving Sky to sit in Edgartown and chat with Francisco about, as usual, Francisco. Francisco's vacations (Barcelona, Rio, Miami), Francisco's new apartment (park view, spa bathroom), Francisco's new diet (a soy-, gluten-, and sugar-free regimen). After resisting his attempts to stroke her bare thigh, she'd finally placed his hand on the table and secured it under hers, preventing further unwelcome forays. He was the most clueless man she'd ever met. Maybe it's a macho-culture thing, she speculated, and the man expects the woman to reject him before she says yes. Nah. Probably just Francisco.

Finally, she heard from Winky that things were winding down and they were ready to be picked up.

"How was your brunch?" Sky asked as Prescott climbed into the front seat.

"Very nice. Met some good prospects. Fertile fields here," Prescott said.

Winky leaned forward to pat her husband's shoulder. "Always working, aren't you, dear?"

"Well, you keep planning all those trips to Aspen and Saint Lucia," he teased. "Somebody's got to pay for them."

"Because that's where you want to go too," Winky said with an affectionate swat. Then, turning to Sky, she said, "Addy Hand took me on a tour of the house after brunch. Up to the widow's walk. You would have loved the view. I could see all the way across to Chappaquiddick." She smiled at Francisco. "It's so lucky you two ran into each other. I felt bad leaving Sky by herself."

"Lucky indeed," Francisco said. "Schuyler and I had a wonderful time catching up."

Sky's eye twitched. "Small island, you never know who you'll run into."

"Milt made me a list of places to check out," Prescott said. "Of course, he thinks Edgartown is the only place to buy, but I told him we wanted to look around." He turned to face the back seat. "What do you think, Wink? Up-Island, down-Island, waterfront, water view, or maybe a big swanky farm? Then we could get you some goats, like Sky," he chortled. "But hands off the goatherder." Sky grimaced, hoping the comment would drop unnoticed.

"You're going to buy property here?" Francisco asked.

"Well, we haven't decided, but I think it would be a capital use of our capital," Prescott quipped. "Let's see, where's that list. Oh, here we go." Prescott pulled out a piece of paper. Edgartown, West Chop, Chilmark, and Katama. He said not to bother if the real estate agent tries to show us anything in Oak Bluffs or Aquinnah."

Sky's heart sank down to join a knot forming in her stomach. "I'm happy to drive you around, but you won't be able to see much of anything. It's not like Nantucket, with that low scrub. Here, you can see the big houses only from the water." Still, there would be splendid views around each turn: ocean, pond, pasture, forest, farm. And sometimes, breathtakingly, all at the same time.

"That's OK," Winky said.

Sky had an idea. "Have you thought about buying on Nantucket? A lot of people say it's even lovelier, more exclusive." Nantucket would be close enough to see Winky and Prescott without their being able to draw her into their social orbit. "And they've got a fast ferry that runs all the time between the islands, so we could visit each other."

"Oh, I like it here," said Winky. "And Prescott says the values are on the Vineyard. He can't help but think like an investor."

"Why wouldn't anyone, dear? And the golf course at Farm Neck is excellent"

"Schuyler, did I tell you about our villa on Lake Como?" Francisco asked.

"Oh, I love Lake Como. Prescott, we need to go back; it's been years and years. Tell me about your place, Francisco," said Winky.

"It's in Bellagio, you know, where the lake forks. Eighteenth century and tucked into a cliff. It's my parents' actually, but they rarely use it. We just restored the boathouse and dock…"

Dutifully, Sky drove them around the Island, pointing out landmarks—West Chop Light, the big barn where the Martha's Vineyard Agricultural Society Fair would be held in August— as Prescott used his phone to look at listings. The views, at least, made the ride talking real estate bearable. In the back seat, Winky and Francisco chatted about his Tesla.

Prescott quizzed Sky about the famous people who summered on the Island: Where did the Obamas stay? Didn't David Letterman have a house on the Island? And Meg Ryan? And where was Jackie O's spread? Prescott was well-meaning and just being Prescott, but it was one of the least interesting conversations she'd had in ages.

"Should we stop in Menemsha, pick up some a lobster rolls?" Sky asked. The quaint fishing village never failed to delight visitors.

"Yes, please. That would be wonderful," Winky said. "It's been such a long time since I've been there. Is it still the same, with all those little fishing shacks?"

"Not changed a bit," Sky replied. "Looks just like it did in *Jaws*."

"Now Schuyler, looking at this as an investment, where do you think the best values are?" Prescott asked. "Appreciation-wise."

"I don't know, Prescott. I honestly didn't look at it that way when I bought Pennywise. I just fell in love and put in an offer."

"Ah, my dear, you should never buy real estate that way," Prescott reprimanded.

"I disagree," Sky said as she parked the car. She was tired of him. "I think it's the only way." She turned to Winky and Francisco. At least Francisco didn't talk down to her. "Let's get our rolls, then I'll take you up to one of my favorite secret spots for a late picnic."

Sky turned up the unmarked road that led to the top of Peaked Hill. Almost the highest point on the island, it had 360-degree views of Aquinnah and Chilmark, the Elizabeth Islands in the distance on one side, and Nomans Land on the other. Sky and the men wandered around, taking in the view and the immense round boulders that rested in the field like a giant's marble set. Winky, anxious about poison ivy and ticks, stayed near the car.

"These huge boulders are called erratics. They were left behind by retreating glaciers," Sky explained what she'd learned from Nate. "We're on the moraine, and the great ponds are all part of the outwash plain." She was not surprised that Prescott didn't care about the Island's geology. Francisco probably didn't care either, but he feigned interest and kept touching her arm and making moony eyes.

"So I think it's between Chilmark—to be near Schuyler—and Edgartown," Prescott announced as they were driving back. "We'd need to buy a beach lot, of course."

"But Prescott, you don't even like the beach," Winky said.

He turned to smile fondly at his wife. "Kiddies love to play in the ocean." Sky's heart went out to her friend. She truly hoped that Winky's daily tush shots would jumpstart her ovaries or whatever they were supposed to do. "Besides, it's a good investment, dear Winkster. They aren't making any more beaches, you know. Back at the office, I'll have my girl look into a few things." Sky flinched. "And Milt had a recommendation for a real estate agent. Unless you want to use Schuyler's."

Sky pasted on a smile. "Sure, I can give you his name." She clung to the thought that this Vineyard real estate idea would be just another of Prescott's fancies, like the Scottish castle he almost bought after a whisky-tasting trip, or that French chateau in Fronsac following their stay with the Ferenburgs. Winky, with her common sense, had talked him out of those.

"Let's interview both of them!" Winky said. Sky's hopes went thud.

They stopped back at Sky's house to pick up Winky's and Prescott's bags before heading to the airport. Francisco insisted on a full tour. Not that it took very long. "So charming, so quaint, so quintessentially New England," he exclaimed. "Like a Yankee version of my little villa. I could see staying here and being very happy."

Fortunately, Francisco also had a flight out that evening, and there was barely enough time for Sky to drop him back in Edgartown to meet the car at the inn. Another lingering embrace and double kiss marked his goodbye, with the added ick of hands sliding low and slow down her back.

"I will call and let you know when I'm coming back; this beautiful place, more beautiful with you, mi cielo, I need to visit more often."

No, nope, uh-uh, no way, nothing doing, not going to happen… Sky repeated to herself as she finally drove home.

SIXTEEN

Sky flopped, exhausted, onto the outdoor chaise and closed her eyes. Her best friend in the whole world comes up for the weekend, and she's relieved that she's gone? The disorientation that had plagued Sky on and off all weekend returned. She felt as if she had one foot on a dock and one in a boat and was about to lose her balance. The world that would be—constant parties, tennis matches, and fancy dinner parties—jostled against the quiet, simple life that she had been building on the Island. Farmers' markets, yoga, beach walks. And Nate. Poor Nate, she'd never had a chance to explain.

Next thing she knew, Nan's soft furry nose was resting on her chest, tail wagging circles. Sky sat up and petted the dog's black and white coat. It was dusk, and Nate was heading back across the yard from the goat pen. Sky got up to greet him with a huge sleepy smile.

"I missed you," she said, leaning against his chest. Nate smelled of sea and salt and—fish?

"You were busy with your friends."

"I was. Did you have a good weekend?" Sky wrapped Nate's arm around her waist as she nestled into his shoulder.

"I worked," he replied.

Leaning against Nate was finding firm land again. "I'm sorry yesterday morning was so awkward. I wanted to talk to you first but Winky and Prescott came early, and I didn't get a chance. Then, when I tried to call later to explain, you didn't answer." Sky tilted her head up. "You're not upset, are you?"

Nate stayed silent.

"You are upset," she said. Nate looked unhappy. Sky felt a sick tilting motion, like getting off an amusement park ride. She put her arms around his neck. "I guess I'm not surprised you didn't like them. I'll be honest, Nate. I was going to tell you not to come by."

"Because you didn't want them to meet me."

This wasn't going the way Sky imagined. They were supposed to be passionately kissing by now. "No, it wasn't that at all." She struggled for how to say the obvious without hurting Nate's feelings.

"Let me guess." Nate pressed his lips together. "I'm a goat guy, and he's a money guy, and you…."

"I'm Sky."

"Schuyler Harrington."

Sky dropped her arms and took a step back. "Yes. I am. But that sounds like you're accusing me of something." If she didn't care that he was a goatscaper, what was his problem?

Nate sighed. "I'm not accusing you of anything." His practiced speech about "different people, different worlds" flew out the window. Nate swept his hand around the room. "This is your vacation house. Your best friend is named Winky and her husband is Prescott, which sounds like some sort of cracker."

Sky, wide-eyed, felt her anger rise. "It's Prescott, not Triscuit."

"Right. Winky and Presss-cott," Nate said, drawing out Prescott's name.

Her mouth set into a firm line. "You don't even know Winky. Or Prescott."

"I don't need to," said Nate. "Give me credit for seeing what's in front of me."

"What are you trying to say?" Sky asked, not wanting to hear the answer.

Nate took a deep breath. "It's not going to work out between us." He closed his eyes. "I don't need you using me."

"I'm using you," Sky said, now fully angry. Another girl would have started yelling, throwing things, hitting and kicking even. But Harrington women pressed their lips together and turned their anger into deadly, icy spikes. Sky was, after all, her mother's daughter. "And on the basis of exactly what did you decide that I was using you?" She was horrified to hear Lucretia's voice come from her mouth.

"It's late, and I need to go." Nate turned to leave.

"You can't go," said Sky. "Not until you explain. I don't use people. That's a horrible thing to say to me." Her anger burned hot behind stone-cold eyes.

Nate searched for signs of the warm, loving Sky he'd grown so fond of, but he found a different woman looking back at him. The hair prickled on the back of his neck. "I just don't see the point of talking anymore."

"You're just going to walk out of here without telling me why you said that."

"It's obvious, Sky."

"Not to me."

Nate shook his head. It was time to go. "I'm sorry." He felt awful, but it had to be done. No way would it work out, and he'd had too much heartbreak. "Goodbye, Sky."

Sky stood shaking with rage as the man and dog walked away. She was just dumped by a goatscaper. Sky gave a sour laugh. The joke was on her.

SEVENTEEN

At least it was clean, simple anger, nothing like the roil of emotions triggered by arguments with Lucretia. Her ire grounded her. No more wobbling: Sky vowed to herself that she would get excited about the idea of Winky and Prescott buying a summer place on the Island. And she would put Nate out of her mind.

Mug in hand and energized by coffee and the fight, Sky wandered around the old house. The previous owners had painted the bedrooms bright colors, so, she supposed, they could say, "You'll be staying in the green bedroom." But the shades they chose were atrocious. Lipstick red, vivid delft blue, kelly green. And the bathrooms were yellow and violet. The house was like a box of Crayola crayons.

The rooms should be painted soft colors, inspired by sand and sea. Muted and pretty. Sky was excited. The new project would keep her busy her mind off Nate. Sky had never painted a room before, but she had watched HGTV and knew the "power of paint to transform a room," as one host had put it. There was a ladder in the back shed, so she figured that with a few cans of paint and some brushes, she'd be ready to go.

Sky had recently discovered the mind-boggling inventory of Cape Hardware. She'd learned to ask for Dick, the handsome older fellow who not only showed her what she needed and where to find it but also carefully explained each step of the process, writing notes and diagrams to make sure she understood. So far at Pennywise, she had managed under Dick's tutelage to install a new towel bar and replace a screen all by herself.

It was work, of a sort, but Sky wondered whether she should miss her old job more. Her decision to quit was sudden, part of the horrible time. She hadn't been particularly happy or unhappy in her junior associate position, drafting documents and reviewing hundreds of legal papers for the complicated international project financings her law firm specialized in. Impossibly long hours, of course, but that was to be expected. Mostly nice people, a few assholes. It was the kind of first job that would look good on her résumé.

This time she was spending on the Island was just a pause, a break to get herself back together and operating at full power before picking up where she'd left off. She was OK painting and puttering and putting her career and ambitions on hold. Just for a little while.

The wall of thousands of paint chips filled Sky with dismay. OK. Not so easy to pick the right pretty color. She pulled strips from the wall and put them back as she fingered the lucky stone in her pocket. Inspiration struck. She held the pebble to the chips and found one that matched its pale beigey-grey color. Make-up Kiss was the color. Such a silly name. Sky walked to the counter. "A gallon of Make-up Kiss, please."

"Sure, but I'll need the formula number for that," replied the young woman behind the cash register. She must have been Dick-the-helpful-hardware-guy's daughter, tall with his deep-set green eyes. Sky handed her the chip. "That's a lovely greige," she said. "I've used it. Latex, I assume? And do you want it in matte, eggshell, satin, semigloss, high gloss?"

"Uh, wall paint?" was Sky's reply.

"First painting job?" the woman asked, lifting her eyebrows.

"Yup, afraid so," Sky admitted.

The woman smiled. "I'm Kris, I'll get you started."

Kris, as helpful as her dad, shared her tips and tricks as she helped Sky select brushes, rollers and pans, blue painter's tape, Spackle, a tarp, and a scraper.

"You want to spend as much time taping as painting," Kris explained. "And use the best paint. If it covers in one coat, you've saved yourself a ton of time and money."

Kris looked familiar, then Sky remembered where she had seen her before: Kris was one of the artists who sold paintings at the weekly Artisans Fair at the Grange. Sky had been admiring one of Kris's beach scenes, a four-foot-long panorama-style painting with a wall of beach stones in the foreground and ocean breakers behind, set in a gorgeous driftwood frame. It would look great in the Make-up Kiss bedroom.

"Don't you show paintings over at the Artisans Festival?" Sky asked.

"Yup," Kris said as she bagged Sky's purchases.

"I absolutely love that big one of the rocks and the ocean in the driftwood frame," Sky gushed.

"Thanks," Kris said, with a big open smile. "I like it too. I did that *en plein air* over at Stonewall Beach earlier this summer, and my dad made the frame." Kris thought a minute. "Listen, I'd really like to sell it before the end of the season. If you're still interested and it hasn't sold by Labor Day, I'd be happy to cut you a deal. No room for it in my studio, and the money never hurts."

🐐 🐐 🐐

Nate was miserable. Zeke had come by to mooch a bowl of cereal, and Nate told him about the breakup. "Good you're out early, dude," he'd consoled. He told Nate about seeing Sky and the rich guy lunching together in Edgartown, looking "all hot and heavy" and that she'd been with the same guy at the party Zeke worked Saturday night too. Nate felt sucker-punched, not better. Sky had been so angry, yet she was the one messing around.

Nate was still sitting on his deck staring out at the pond when Batty stopped by with a container of lasagna.

"Hey, what's wrong?" Batty asked, putting her man-size hand on his shoulder.

"It's nothing. Thanks for the food. I promised you blueberries. I'll pick some later."

Batty sat down across from him. "Come on. What happened? Something with the goats?" Batty's tough exterior belied a marshmallow-soft center. Nate was hurting, and she wasn't about to walk away. "A woman?" Nate's face twisted. "You want to tell me?"

Nate didn't, really. Batty would think him an idiot too. But the telling would make it better. Two sentences later, he was done with his story. The details would only make it worse.

"C'mon Nate. You did the right thing," Batty said. "Don't you remember what happened to your cousin Jess with that guy in West Chop? What was he? The son of some TV newscaster or something? With the sailboat?"

"Gus," Nate said.

"Right. They were going to sail all winter in the Caribbean together. Then he just took off."

"I remember."

"I think too much money messes with your moral compass or something."

"Maybe."

Batty tilted her head. "Lauri likes you. You sat next to her at the Tank the other night. You want me to fix you up?"

"No," said Nate.

"Sue, the architect?"

Nate shook his head. "Really, I'm fine."

Batty sighed. "I'm sorry I missed Zeke. Don't forget to give him the lasagna. I've got to go." Batty stood up and wrapped Nate in a massive hug. Her breasts squashed against him like giant water balloons as she all but squeezed his breath out. "Feel better. OK?"

"Yeah."

The gray sky matched Nate's mood. He didn't feel like it, but the goat pens in Windy Gates needed to be moved. Small favors. But Sky's pens would be OK for a while. He didn't want to see her.

"Let's go, Nan," Nate said, standing up. "We've got work to do."

EIGHTEEN

Sky set her little Bose radio to WMVY, the local station that played everything from the Grateful Dead to the latest alt-indie hits and also reported on the number of cars in the ferry standby lines. First, the tedious job of edging the room with painter's tape. Kris had emphasized that this was *the* critical step. The blue tape was hideously patriotic against the red paint and white trim.

"Soon, this room will be transformed into an oasis of calm," she said to an imaginary TV camera. "The matelassé coverlet can stay; and the white chaise. But those red poppy print throw pillows must go!" She threw the offending pillows into the closet. She'd donate them to the Dumptique later. Once she had started working on her house, Sky quickly discovered the attractions of the Dumptique, West Tisbury's popular freecycle exchange, located in a shack at the town dump. "We'll replace them with raw-silk-covered pillows and find an antique trunk for over there," she said pointing to a spot under the window.

The afternoon passed quickly as Sky laid out precise lines of tape. She still hadn't given Prescott the contact info for her realtor. Not that it mattered. They wouldn't hire Doug. He'd been an old Island friend of her grandmother's. Whip smart, but the most gentle of gentlemen. Prescott would want the sharp-toothed go-getter type.

It would be nice if Winky and Prescott bought a house nearby, Sky told herself. Prescott would spend most of his time in the city working, which would leave Winky free to hang out with her. They could lunch and shop and sit together under an umbrella on the beach reading books. No one could make her go to cocktail parties every night if she didn't feel like it. Her social circle (consisting of Elly) did need to get bigger. She'd meet new men. It would be better than good. It would be wonderful to have them on the Island.

Right?

Sky scrolled through the images on her screen. Nothing wrong with them, but the Island's iconic views had been photographed so many times that half her shots looked like the cheesy postcards they sold at Alley's. Then she saw in her mind Menemsha harbor with a goat face in the foreground, staring at the viewer as if it had photobombed—goat-bombed?— someone's vacation photo. A quaint picket fence in Edgartown with the jaunty tail and hindquarters of a goat walking out of the frame. A goat's eye perspective of Waskosim's Rock. Maybe make a silly calendar. Why not a goat version of the Vineyard Seadogs calendar? She could do video too, even put a GoPro onto a goat and see what she got. It would probably be awful, likely ridiculous, but fun. A tingle of excitement ran through Sky as she went to get a head of lettuce from the refrigerator.

"Now, let's see if this works, Patty," Sky said to the lop-eared goat. "I think you're Patty." She held out a wilted romaine leaf with one hand and a loop of rope in the other. As the goat moved to take the leaf, Sky slipped the rope around Patty's neck. "That was easy," she told the goat. "Good goat."

For fun, Sky used to borrow her friends' pets as subjects, with the best shots printed, framed, and given as gifts. Sky loved the challenge of catching an animal's expression, the fuzziness of an ear or long back-lit whisker. Dogs were easy, cats much less so, but she had no idea about goats.

The summer as a would-be photojournalist with Grams's camera had lit a passion. Growing up, Sky had taken as many photography classes as she could. While Sky's friend, Trip, had followed his dream to New York University film school, Sky had followed her parents' script. Law school was better than she'd expected. It engaged her intellect, and her classmates were bright and interesting. Being a junior lawyer, however, was a different matter altogether.

Sky led Patty out of the pen to her goat photo studio, which was her deck with a chaise on its side as a gate. She had tied a head of sad lettuce to the open deck umbrella so that it dangled from a string: leafy payment for her caprine model. Patty spotted the treat and went right up the steps. Sky slid the chaise into place and slipped the rope off the goat's neck as she stood under the lettuce on her hind legs. Sky grabbed her camera and got to work.

"Nice. You've got lovely long legs," Sky complimented the goat as she stretched to reach the leaves. "I wonder if you'd be any good at yoga." Sky had read about goat yoga and vowed to take her yoga mat out to the pen to give it a try one day.

The late afternoon sun imparted a golden glow to the goat's brown and white coat as she danced under the dangling vegetable. Sky shot a few portrait-style closeups, then shifted her angle to take in the background as well. After a few futile moments, Patty dropped to her feet, stared at Sky, and said "mehhh." Sky zoomed in capturing the grumpy goat's expression. Excellent. "Meh, mehhh," Patty said, advancing on Sky. "Mehhhhh."

"OK, OK," said Sky, laughing. She'd gotten some great shots. "I'll give you some lettuce." Sky pulled off a leaf and handed it to Patty, who closed her eyes in apparent food bliss. Click, click. Sky's imagination was unleashed. A goat in a Black Dog hat. A goat standing on a rock at Lucy Vincent beach, perched on a piling in Vineyard Haven harbor with the tall ships anchored behind. A goat riding the Flying Horses Carousel, a golden ring in its mouth. (That one might take some work.) She could put the goats on Instagram. Or play around with effects on her computer. Sky could create an art gallery of goat portraits: Andy Warhol-style goats. Picasso goats. Cezanne goats. Video, too. Maybe a minidocumentary for kids. Or something funny to post on YouTube: goat tricks or an accelerated-speed clip of Nate chasing runaway goats in a field.

Nate. She missed Nate. Not just the wonderful sex and that delectable body, but his company too. She missed when he'd drop in for a sunset beer on the deck, or just to say hi. Everything was going fine, then somehow Nate got it into his head she was using him. Sky hated that they fought, hated hearing Lucretia's words coming from her mouth. He was wrong about her. It wasn't fair. She'd tell him so when she got the chance.

Sky took off her Black Dog hat and stuck it on Patty's head. Patty paused, looked confused, then dipped her head to drop the hat and chewed on it. "No, Patty, don't eat my hat!" Sky put her camera down and lunged for the cap. The goat scampered off and leaped to the flat board topping the rail, hat still dangling from her mouth. Patty paused to look at Sky as if daring her to come closer. The great beyond beckoned.

Sky yanked the lettuce off its string. "No, no, no goat! Don't jump! Look, lettuce!"

🐐 🐐 🐐

Sky wandered around the gallery, not really looking for anything in particular. "Let me know if there is anything I can help you with," said the woman with salt-and-pepper hair, lifting her eyes from her book. No pushy salespeople here.

"Just browsing, but thanks. You have some wonderful things."

"Thank you. Everything is by local artists, and my husband makes the frames."

The store's art reflected a maritime theme: paintings of sailboats, seascapes, fishing boats, beach scenes. And, naturally, lots featuring Menemsha's quaint-to-decrepit fishing shacks and picturesque docks. Sky recognized a couple of small beachscapes by Kris, but what caught her eye were the few pieces of painted furniture scattered around the gallery. The artist had replicated eighteenth- and nineteenth-century paintings of schooners and other tall ships on the front of dressers and trunks in intricate detail. Intrigued, Sky picked up a shoebox-size chest featuring a pond scene with a small gaff-rigged sailboat.

The screen door banged behind her. "Hi, Joan, I brought that dresser from Uncle John's barn. Where do you want me to put it?" Nate froze when he noticed Sky.

"Take it around back, if you don't mind. I'll keep it in the shed for now," said Joan.

"Hi, Nate," said Sky.

"Hi."

"You two know each other?" asked Joan.

"Nate's been goatscaping over at my place," said Sky.

Joan turned to Nate. "How are those goats, Nate? I saw the photo in the *Gazette*."

"Business is good, thanks," he replied.

"I'll go unlock the shed for you. I'll be back in a minute."

Nate shifted on his feet. "How have you been?" Sky asked.

"OK. Busy," said Nate.

"Isn't this amazing," asked Sky, showing Nate the small chest. "I've never seen anything like it."

"Joan paints the furniture," he explained. "She's pretty famous." Sky was not by nature an acquisitive person, so she was surprised when she'd found herself coveting the piece.

"That's a catboat," he said. "They used them for oystering in the old days." OK. Normal conversation. So far, so good.

"It's so lovely," Sky said. She carefully turned it over to look at the price, and her heart dropped. "This is the one I'd buy."

"Yeah, it's nice. I have to go get the dresser out of my truck. See you."

"Wait, Nate. Have you had lunch?" Turn her down, said his brain.

"Not yet," said his mouth.

They lucked into two open seats at the counter overlooking the harbor in the Galley's back porch. Sky hadn't planned what she'd say to Nate. She just knew that she wanted to set him straight.

Sky glanced at Nate's handsome profile. He didn't look happy to be there. "I've been painting the bedrooms in the old part of the house. I'm almost done with the red one. It's going to be sort of a beigey-gray."

"OK," said Nate, still staring at the fishing boats. "Um, that'll look nice."

"It's fun, but a lot of work. And I'm getting back into my photography," she said. "I've taken some great shots of the goats. I should send them to you, maybe you can use them on your website or something."

"Sure, thanks." C'mon man, just make some normal conversation. He forced himself to look at her. "Uh, my ex-girlfriend Caroline is a photographer. Does a lot of weddings. Good money," said Nate.

"Yeah. Mine was going to charge a fortune. I almost got married. In May. There's a lot you don't know about me."

"Yeah, I guess so."

"I caught my fiancé cheating on me with his assistant."

"Oh."

"That's why I'm here, on the Island." She took a sip of her root beer float. "I needed to get myself together. It was a bad time. My grandmother had died too. I think I told you a little about Grams. I was really close to her." A shadow crossed Sky's face.

"That must have been tough." Nate glanced at her. Shit, Sky was even lovelier than he remembered.

"It was. I've been thinking about what you said. You're wrong about me, Nate."

Nate pressed his palms into the counter. He didn't want to talk about that fight. "I wonder when our food is coming out." Two burgers shouldn't be taking this long.

"I didn't want you to meet Winky and Prescott and think that's who I was. Or have our relationship become gossip back home." Sky sighed. Nate didn't even want to look at her. She pressed on. "I've known Winky forever. We were even in preschool together. She's my oldest, dearest friend. But I knew they'd look like rich snobs to you."

"I get it. Really. It's fine."

"I mean, I guess now I can see why you thought I was using you. But you're wrong. I was with you because I like you; we were good together." She touched his biceps. "You're not just some goat gigolo."

Nate cracked a faint smile. He hadn't thought of himself quite that way. "OK."

"I'll be honest, Nate. I liked the sex and you, but I'm not looking for anything more. Not now," Sky said, keeping her voice low so the other customers wouldn't overhear. She laid her hand over his. "But I understand if that's not what you want." She drew her fingertips back to rest in the tender spot between his fingers. Nate's resolve flapped its wings, ready to take flight. "I've missed you, Nate."

Nate sat silent, heart pounding, staring at their hands. He'd missed her too. He considered what was on offer: a hookup relationship, no-strings sex. "You'd keep seeing other guys."

"What?"

"A friend told me he saw you last weekend a couple of times with some guy. At a big party, then at lunch in Edgartown."

Then it came to her. "Oh. You're kidding me. Francisco? Someone saw me with Francisco, then told you."

"Yeah."

"That's too funny. This is a small island. He's an old friend. I ran into him by accident." She leaned forward to try to catch Nate's eye. "I've got zero interest in dating Francisco—or sleeping with him."

"Oh," Nate said.

Sky remembered her promise to Elly to be honest. "I mean, never again. I did once, but it was a huge mistake. Not my finest moment." The too-vivid memory of her drunk, post-Gil slip-up rose to mind, their blurry, sweaty coupling on his black satin sheets. Definitely a never-again event.

Sky turned Nate's hand over and drew a circle in his palm. The electric current from her fingertips coursed through him.

She took a deep breath. "We'd be free to break it off—no hard feelings—if it doesn't work out. Or if either of us started getting serious with someone else." Sky moved her hand down to his thigh. "Eyes wide open," she said. And maybe something else, soon, if she got her way. "No games."

Nate looked down at her hand and melted like a Mad Martha's ice cream cone on a hot day. He nodded. "OK," he said, thinking with his little head.

She kissed him with root beer lips. "Let's get those burgers to go."

The now-cold burgers sat on the kitchen counter in their greasy paper bag. Mug of tea in hand, Sky made her way back to the bedroom. There her lover slept, sprawled on her sheets, his sun-streaked hair tousled on her pillow. She reached out to smooth a lock from his sleeping face, wondering at her shamelessness in getting him back into her bed. But it had been a stupid fight after all. No reason they shouldn't be together if that's what they both wanted. And he had seemed to want her as much as she wanted him.

"No more napping. Time to get up, sleepyhead," she said. Nate opened his eyes, stretched, and grinned at Sky. Their post-breakup sex had been phenomenal as if the time apart had been supercharging their batteries with extra endurance. Sky leaned over to hand him the tea and let her robe fall open. Nate sat up and took the mug, reaching over to run a hand over his unwrapped present, pausing to gently tweak a pink part. Eyes wide open, and he liked what he saw.

"Mmmm, that's a nicer wake-up than I get from Nan," Nate said. Nan cocked her head, trying to figure out what Nate had said. It didn't appear to involve food or a ride in the truck, so she lay down at Sky's feet.

"I certainly hope so," said Sky.

Nate smiled, glad he had been wrong about her and even more glad to have her back. "How long did I sleep?"

"I don't know, maybe half an hour. Are you hungry? We never ate our lunch."

"Food," Nate said. "Sure." He yawned.

"I can make us something unless you want those cold burgers."

"Nan can have those." Sky sat on the side of the bed. "I should probably go soon, but do you want to meet the triplets tomorrow? Then I'm heading over to Chappy to move some pens, but you're welcome to come along." Nate wasn't sure if their deal included spending time together outside of bed. "The Homets have a really nice place over there."

Sky stroked Nate's chest. "Chappy sounds great. And baby goats. Count me in."

Damn, he felt good. "I can't believe I took a nap. You done tuckered me out, ma'am" Nate said in a bad imitation of a cowboy. Sky let her hand drift where it may.

"A-yup," she replied. Sky leaned over to give him a long deep kiss. "All rested and ready to ride again?"

NINETEEN

The fuzzy newborn goats were beyond adorable. The biggest one, a male, was all black with a white tuft that looked like a toupee on his head. His siblings were white with black inky spots.

"The black one there is stealing the others' milk. See how he keeps butting them away from the mother? I started bottle feeding them yesterday if you want to help," Nate said.

Soon Sky sat with a tiny black and white creature on her lap sucking on its bottle as if there would never be more. Its golden eyes were fixed on Sky's face. She stroked one irresistibly soft cotton puff ear. "Nate, she is just the sweetest thing."

"The babies are cute, aren't they?" Nate agreed, shifting his bottle.

Soon the two fuzzballs were fed and back frolicking with their brother, and Sky and Nate were on their way to Chappy. "Have you named the babies yet?" Sky asked.

"I was thinking Bonnie and Clyde for the spotted ones, but no ideas yet for the black guy. I'm starting to run out of outlaws. Know any bad guys?"

"Hitler?"

Nate shot her a look. "I am not naming a goat Hitler."

"Guess Jeffrey Dahmer is out of the question too?" Sky couldn't keep a straight face any longer, and Nate realized she'd been teasing him. "Sorry, sorry. Let's see. What's the

name of the guy who hijacked a plane and parach
money out over Idaho or someplace and was never ⌐

"D.B. Cooper?"

"Cooper the goat?"

"Cooper it is. You've just named your first goat," Nate said with a grin.

The summer crowds meant long lines for the Chappy ferry. The tiny three-car vessel and its 527-foot trip hadn't changed since Sky had last ridden it as a teenager.

"This is really great," Sky said as the ferry chugged out of Edgartown. "It's exactly like I remember."

"Yup. The ferry never changes. Just the line gets longer," Nate said. "Time to get back into the truck. We're almost there."

Chappaquiddick's single paved road took them to the client's property which, as Nate had said, was an impressive spread overlooking a wind-whipped Cape Poge Bay. Sky and Nate wandered across the field to check the goat enclosures.

"Everything looks good to me. You want to walk over to Wasque Point, or take a look around Mytoi since we're here?"

"What's Mytoi?" Sky asked.

Nate explained how one man's obsession—my toy— became the spectacular, if somewhat contextually challenged, Japanese gardens now open to the public. "Umm, hard to decide. How about the beach walk? I'd like to see the ocean today with all this wind. We'll do the gardens some other time," Sky said.

They walked down the dirt road to Dike Bridge with Nan trotting at their heels. The wind picked up as the pair reached the empty beach. Sky snuggled into Nate's side and he wrapped his arm around her shoulder, wind whipping her hair around her face. The ocean roiled with whitecaps. Huge breakers battered the shoreline.

"Windy day, huh?" shouted Nate. A gust sent a sheet of sand across the beach, scouring their ankles.

"This is so wild and beautiful, but, ow, the sand. And poor Nan. I think I'm ready to head back to the truck," Sky said.

"Fine with me."

"Grams and I used to drive out here to fish. We'd start at Katama and let the air out of tires and drive all the way here across the sand. It was superfun. I'd love to do that again."

"The breach at Norton Point closed, but I'm not sure if they're letting people drive around yet. You can get onto the beach here, though. But the over-sand permit will set you back a couple of hundred bucks."

"It would be worth it," Sky said. Nate widened his eyes. He'd almost forgotten that she was a rich girl. "I'm hungry. Should we stop in Edgartown for lunch?"

Rob was shelving pint glasses behind the bar at the Tank when they arrived. "Hey, Nate. How goes the goat business?"

"Pretty good, right now."

"Just a sec and I'll be over with the menus. Sit anywhere. You're lucky. You beat the crowds."

"I wonder why I've never noticed this place before," said Sky sitting down at a window table.

"Off-season, it's all locals. Really nice in the winter when they get a fire going in the hearth over there." Sky looked around the comfortable pub with its huge, rough-hewn beams, ballast brick walls, and wavy-paned windows overlooking the docks. She imagined herself and Nate curled up with pints by the fireplace watching lamplit snow fall in the darkness outside.

"Do you know how old this place is? Look at the size of those beams," Sky said looking up at the ceiling. "They look like they could have come from ship masts."

"Late 1700s, I'd guess," he said. "Rob'll know."

Rob walked over holding the menus. "Good to see you, man," he said whacking Nate's shoulder.

"You too. Rob, this is Sky," Nate said without further explanation. "She was asking how old this building is."

"1749 is what I've been told," Rob answered, looking at Sky with intelligent, friendly eyes, clearly trying to figure who she was and what she was doing with Nate. "And they say we've got a ghost too, a whaling captain's wife who offed herself when her husband was lost at sea. I've never seen her."

He put the menus down. "The specials today are my secret-ingredient clam chowder and a grilled cheddar and tomato sandwich. Katie's brewed up a new summer IPA, which I highly recommend. You guys need some time?"

The specials were the way to go, according to Nate, so they ordered two chowders and the sandwich to share. Rob soon returned from the kitchen with two steaming crocks and a plate with a huge crunchy-brown sandwich, its melted cheese oozing into the pile of chips.

"What's the secret ingredient in the chowder?" Sky asked.

"Wouldn't be a secret if I told you," Rob said, then leaned close to whisper conspiratorially into Sky's ear. "Don't tell anyone, but I add a glob of sour cream at the end." Sky ate a spoonful of chowder. Smoky bacon, real cream, lots of clams, small cubes of tender potatoes, and not too thick (the way Sky liked it). And she could just detect the faint tang of the sour cream. It was delicious.

"So, how are things with you, Nate?" Rob asked, straddling a chair. Sky ate her chowder and listened with half an ear as they chatted about Nate's business, Rob and his co-owner Richard's progress on restoring Bella, their forty-foot Hinckley sloop, the referendum to allow hard-liquor sales in Tisbury, and the odds of the first traffic light on the Island going in at Five Corners.

I guess this is how Nate spends his days, Sky thought. Outside all day, driving around the Island to clients' gorgeous estates, taking plenty of time to drop in for lunch and a chat with a friend. A world different from my old job. Sky took a bite of the gooey sandwich, and her mind wandered back to the days when she was tied to a computer in a windowless cubical, gobbling a granola bar because she was on deadline, working long and late hours, and canceling weekend plans because of some unexpected crisis.

Rob turned his attention to Sky, still clearly curious about Nate's dining companion. "What brings you to the Island?" he asked.

"Oh," she said, pulled back from her reverie. "I just bought a place last month over on Tisbury Great Pond. Nate's doing some goatscaping there," Sky said, assuming Nate didn't intend for their relationship to be public. "He offered to take me over to Chappy today. I haven't been for ages."

"Nice on Chappy, but the ferry is a real headache in the summer," Rob said, his curiosity far from satisfied and suspecting more than a goatscaper-and-goatscapee relationship. "You've bought in the best part of the Island, in my opinion. Congratulations on the house." A big group of noisy tourists carrying Black Dog and Vineyard Vines shopping bags came through the door, and Rob reluctantly stood up. "Back to work. Catch you later, Nate, and, hey, nice to meet you, Sky. Nate, let's go sailing when crazy season is over."

Next was a stop at the hardware store for paint. The normally grumpy lady behind the counter was delighted to see Nate. "I'm going to get some more stakes next door at the lumberyard. I'll be back in a few minutes," Nate said. Now confident about what she needed, Sky walked to the back of the store where Kris helped her pick out some white paint for the trim.

"I thought maybe something like the inside of a scallop shell for one of the other bedrooms," Sky said.

"You have to be careful with pinks. They come out much brighter and darker than you expect. You'll want to get a couple of test quarts."

The wall of paint strips was still overwhelming. "Maybe these?" Sky asked, pointing to a row of pinky-peachy strips.

"Too bright." Kris moved to the off-whites and picked three in a dull blush." Why don't you take these home and look at them in the light," Kris said. "I can mix half-tints too."

"Hey Kris, how are you doing? You've met Sky, I take it," Nate said, not taking his eyes off Sky.

"Oh hi, Nate," Kris said. Kris's expression froze as Nate slipped his arm around Sky's shoulders—a handful of ice dropped into a warm cup of tea. "Yes. I've been helping her out. She's got what she wants."

TWENTY

Sky looked at up the water-stained ceiling, listening to Nate's gentle snore and the rain beating down on the roof. His house reminded her (in a good way) of the cabins at her sleepaway camp, cozy with a touch of mildew. She swung her legs over the edge of the high four-poster bed and stretched. The downpour provided a lovely excuse to sleep in. But now, Sky was in the mood for tea.

"Mmm, why are you getting up?" Nate mumbled.

"I'll be back in a minute."

A pool of water sat next to the stove. "Nate, your ceiling's leaking," she called from the kitchen.

"That always happens when it rains. I'll put a bowl under it."

"Don't bother. I'll do it."

Sky mopped up the water and put saucepan under the drip; a gentle ping ping joined the sound of the rain. "Where do keep your tea?"

The front door banged open to a dripping wet Zeke. "Yo, man. Flood in the hole! Where's your wet vac? I need it again." Zeke's eyes widened in surprise when he saw Sky. "Oh hi. Uh, I'm Zeke." *Ah shit. She's back in the picture.*

"Nice to meet you, Zeke, I'm Sky," she said, putting out her hand and very conscious of her near-nakedness in Nate's tee. "You have a flood in a hole?"

Nate wandered in wearing boxers and shaking his head. "You didn't get around to sealing the seams?"

"No, man. You were supposed to help."

Nate sighed. "Wet vac is back in the shed. Generator too. Gas can's in the back of my truck." Nate gave Sky a lopsided grin. "Zeke lives in a tent over at the next farm. But it leaks."

Zeke shivered. "Do you want tea?" Sky asked. "I was just making some."

"Yeah, thanks," Zeke said. Sky filled the kettle and reached up to get the tea from the top shelf. It was easy enough to see why Nate was interested, that idiot.

"You live in a tent?" Sky asked, pulling out three mugs.

"Best place. Stays cool in the summer, I get the breezes, hear the birds. All that. I've got a sleeping bag for winter, but when the temp drops too far, I have to find someone to shack up with. Right, buddy?"

"We've got to find you a winter girlfriend, Zeke," said Nate.

"Yeah, maybe," Zeke said to Nate, then turned back to Sky. "You see, there's a positive energy field when you sleep on the ground, womb of Mother Earth and all." He was passionate about the benefits of earth living, as he called it.

"Yeah, but Mother Earth always seems to lose in the battle against the rain gods," Nate added.

"I almost got that figured out. How about you come help instead of giving me shit, dude." Zeke finished his tea and got up to leave. "Nice to meet you, Sky. Thanks for the loaners, I'll bring the stuff back later."

"So, Zeke's an old friend?" Sky asked after the door closed.

"Probably my oldest," Nate replied. "He's almost like a brother. And he saved my life once. So, I figure I sort of owe it to take care of him."

"He saved your life?" Sky asked.

"Yeah, he got me out of a riptide at Quansoo when we were like eleven." Nate made a fresh mug of tea and told Sky the story. It had been off-season, and the boys were alone on the beach. Zeke thought to grab both his boogie board and Nate's before entering the rip to go after Nate. They had been told since they were tots to swim parallel to the beach until you got out of a rip—no matter how quickly you were being pulled out—and never to swim back in toward the beach until you were out of the pull of the current. But Nate had panicked, and a very freaked out Zeke had managed to get them both back safely to shore.

"So we've had this bond since then. Zeke can be a flake and all, but he's a good guy and a really good friend."

🐐 🐐 🐐

"Well, that was relaxing, but I like our morning class better," said Elly, opening the car door and tossing in her yoga mat.

"Me too. I fell asleep. I hope the instructor didn't notice. But it was something new to try. Could you do that square-breathing thing?"

"I think my breaths were trapezoids," Elly smiled.

"Mine wanted to be triangles." She started the Jeep. "How about a glass of wine at my place, or do you have to get home?"

"Love to. John's out tonight anyway."

Back at Pennywise, Sky poured two glasses of white, and they went out onto the deck. "See how much more of the pond you can see now?" Sky pointed toward the water. "A couple more weeks and the goats will have it all cleared out."

"It looks great. Did you know you had this view?"

"Sort of, but not this nice. Do you want some cheese and crackers too?" Sky asked. "I stopped by the Grey Barn the other day and got some Eidolon. That's my favorite."

Sky fixed a plate and brought it back outside. "You know, rumors are starting to get around about you and Nate," Elly started. "Do you know Cassie, the lady behind the front counter at the hardware store? She saw the two of you together at the store yesterday, so she told her scrapbooking club last night, and my mom called me first thing this morning to tell me." Elly sighed. "I know, small-town gossip. Have you met his friend Zeke yet?" asked Elly.

Sky nodded. "This morning, over at Nate's."

"Well, in that case, it might as well be printed on the front of the *MV Times*. Zeke's sweet, but he can't keep a secret to save his life. Unless, of course, he's forgotten it."

"So is it a bad thing?" asked Sky. "People knowing about us?"

"Not bad, it's just that you may start getting some funny vibes off people. Everybody likes Nate, and there is, um, how do I explain it?" Elly paused and stuck her tongue in the corner of her mouth as she thought. "OK. It's sort of like a tribe whose members disapprove of you going outside your tribe to find a mate. Or like how marrying outside your race or religion was decades ago—and I guess still is—for a lot of people. Most people will be fine and friendly. But not everybody."

Sky remembered Kris's face turning cold in the hardware store. The look in her eyes was probably disapproval, not jealousy. "I think I know what you mean. Is there anything I can do?"

"No, not really. Just don't take it personally. You're a summer person in a relationship with an Islander. Islanders don't think that's a good idea. That's all. How's it going with Nate, by the way?" Elly asked.

Sky filled in Elly about the awkward meeting between Nate and Winky and Prescott, the unexpected fight, and the delightful reconciliation. "I think Nate and I are good. We're clear on what this is and isn't. I know that sounds kind of unromantic, but it's working."

"I see," Elly said. Maybe working for Sky.

"I'm really comfortable with him. I don't know. There's this fundamental compatibility despite not really having anything in common," Sky said. "It sounds dopey but being with him makes me feel like a whole person again. And I haven't had that awful Gil dream I told you about since I met Nate. You have no idea what a relief that is."

"Just be careful, Sky."

"I will. I promise."

TWENTY-ONE

Sky had never paid much attention to where she lived or what the place looked like. Not that she had much say in the matter growing up. Every three years, she'd find a folder marked "Schuyler's room" on her bed with the interior designer's plan for a do-over of her bedroom. Arguments that she liked her room the way it was or that she didn't like either toile *or* cabbage roses fell on deaf ears. Lucretia's decorator even designed Sky's half of her freshman dorm room (nautical motif, for Rhode Island). Grams, of course, would have let Sky do whatever she wanted, but Sky loved coming back every summer to her nubby white cotton bedspread and faded rag rug.

Later, she was busy with school and friends, then it was her job and parties and restaurants and travel and shows and weekends out of town. The small apartments she'd shared with roommates, and then Gil, were just places to sleep and shower. But now, she was finding contentment in having a house being made just right. Just for her.

Speckled with paint, Sky rested the roller back in the paint pan and stood back to admire her work. As Kris had promised, the pale-blush paint covered the kelly green in a single coat. She couldn't wait to finish and pull off the blue tape. Sky's pocket buzzed.

"Hi, Winky."

"Oh, Sky, I meant to ring earlier. I really hope you don't mind that we're not staying with you?"

"No, of course not," Sky replied.

"Prescott had already accepted the Hands' invitation before I got a chance to call. I think they want to convince us to buy a house in Edgartown."

"No worries. I've got other houseguests that weekend anyway. You remember my friends Eva and Trip? They're coming over from Vermont."

"Maybe. I'm sure I've met them. But I'll get to see you. Won't I?" asked Winky. "Prescott has picked out nine—nine!—properties he wants to look at and two beach lots, so we're going to be running around like crazy. But maybe we can squeeze in coffee or a drink?"

"How about Sunday before you leave? Then you can give me a full report. I hope you find something you like." Sky was swinging back and forth between loving and dreading the idea of Winky and Prescott buying a place on the Island. The lovely thought of relaxing under a beach umbrella with a book and her dear friend collided with one of Nate, all sweaty and sexy after a long day of pounding stakes. Try as she might, she couldn't get the two to fit in the same picture.

"Perfect. I'll call you when we get there," Winky said. "Gotta go, bye."

Sky finished the last spots around the window with a brush and then pulled the painter's tape off the walls. She'd refused Nate's help on the paint job: this was her project, and she'd do it all by herself. The walls of the room were as smooth and warm as the inside of a scallop shell. It was just as she'd imagined.

She was wadding the sticky tape up into a ball when Nate's work boots clumped up the stairs. "Wow. Hey, it looks great," Nate said.

"Thanks! See, now, without that awful green, you want to look out the windows at the view."

Nate didn't resist the temptation to kiss the paint dab on the end of her nose. "I see you painted more than just the room," he teased.

"Just a little bit." She gave Nate a giant hug. "I'm very proud of myself. Two rooms down."

"You want to do something to celebrate, Michelangelo?" asked Nate.

"Sure. Hmm," Sky considered. "Go to Menemsha? No, let's do a picnic dinner at the beach. I want to practice running the boat again." It felt good to be gaining practical skills for a change.

"Beach it is. It might be a nice night for a fire if you want. But first, let's get you clean."

"Only if you help," Sky said. She gave Nate a sly look. "But I get to paint you first." She'd gotten an idea while painting the room and, well, he was going to be her canvas.

"Uh, OK."

Sky walked over to the cardboard box holding the rest of the painting supplies. Was she going to paint him, like a subject, or really paint him, like a wall? Pulling out a new roller, she slid on a fuzzy white cover, then selected a 1-inch dry brush.

"OK. I'm ready. Off with the clothes."

Nate pulled off his tee shirt and started to take off his shorts. "What do you have in mind to do with those?"

"You'll see."

🐐 🐐 🐐

Nate lay on his beach towel staring up at the clouds turning pink in the late afternoon sun, blissed and relieved that there'd been no actual paint involved in Sky's "painting project." It would never have occurred to him to use a roller and brush *that* way. Sky reached over and patted his arm. "You want to take a walk and look for driftwood for the fire?"

"Sure," he said.

Nate got up and pulled Sky to her feet. They started walking in the soft sand by the dune line toward Long Point. "I've always loved this beach." Sky said. "Did I tell you my grandmother left me the Quansoo key in her will? My mother must not have known or she would have sold it when the prices got so high."

"Lucky that." Nate whistled at Nan and pointed to a piece of driftwood.

Sky was in a talky mood. "Grams was an awesome lady. In the city, she was all martinis and heels and going to the club. But here she totally let her hair down. She called the Island her happy place, which I totally get."

"When did she start coming to the Vineyard?"

"I'm not really sure. I think maybe the first time was in college. She and my grandfather bought the Chilmark farm in the mid-1960s. He died really young—heart attack—but she kept coming up every summer."

A flock of birds circling caught Sky's eye. "Shoot, we forgot the rod. Grams taught me to surf cast. I told you that, right? I think I even have her old leather fingerguard somewhere." She stooped to pick up a beach stone; she still had a couple of paint colors to choose. "I loved going to my other grandparents' place, the one in Connecticut with the horses, the Newfies, and the farm truck. But summers with Grams are my happiest memories, I think."

Nan ran up with the stick and dropped it at Nate's feet. He added it to the bag. "Where was her place?"

"It was an old farmhouse up above Allen Farm, with those incredible views you see from South Road, you know, across the sheep pastures to the ocean. Big stone walls, too, the really old ones with all the lichen." Sky paused as her memories flooded back. "My favorite place was the front porch. It had big old-fashioned wicker chairs with horsehair cushions and ticking-stripe covers. I'd sit there for hours reading and looking at the ocean. Then my mother made me start going to sleepaway camp when I was thirteen. But once I was at Brown, I could come up on weekends with friends. That was fun."

"What happened to the house?" Nate asked.

Sky's face fell. "My mother made Grams sell it after she fell down the stairs the second time and broke her arm. She thought my grandmother would sneak out of the old folks' place and come up here to live by herself." Sky smiled. "Mother was probably right about that. Grams planned for me to inherit it, but my mother lied and told her I didn't want it. She told Grams that I said it was too much hassle to maintain an old house." Sky stopped to pick up a greenish pebble that had caught her eye. "I didn't find out until after it was already under contract. I was really upset, furious with my mother. My grandmother was mad at her too."

Nate reached for her hand. "I'm sorry."

"At least the new owners didn't tear it down. I can show you where it is sometime." Sky turned to Nate. "I'm probably boring you."

"Nope," Nate replied with a smile, planting a kiss on Sky's sun-freckled nose.

"What about you? I mean, you grew up here so what's that like? Is the Island special or do you just sort of take it for granted?" They veered off to pick up a chunk of driftwood too heavy for Nan.

Tough question. Finally, Nate answered. "It's hard to describe. Special is not the right word, but I don't know what is. When I went away to college, it just felt wrong. Not going-to-college-as-a-wrong-choice wrong but being-in-the-wrong-place wrong. I tried to tell myself I was just homesick but…" He stopped, at a loss for how to explain the profound sense of displacement, how wrong it felt to be so far from the ocean, and his keen—almost primal longing—for the Great Pond. "It was more than that. You know when they catch a wild animal and put him in a zoo or an animal park and it doesn't matter how nice they make it, he just pines away? I think that's how I felt. I came back when my dad got so sick, and I knew I wouldn't leave again." They had reached the driftwood chunk and added it to the bag. "That's funny. I guess I'm remembering that now since I'm going over to Amherst on Labor Day weekend for my freshman roommate's wedding."

"That should be fun."

Nate thought he saw a brief flash of relief on Sky's face. Ah hell, her Labor Day houseguests were probably a bunch of Winkys and Dinkys. Just as well to be out of town. "Yeah, well, Geoff's a really good guy. He came out summers to help at the farm until we sold it. Runs a couple of bars in Northampton now." Nate was pretty sure he was not going to have a great time with a bunch of people he didn't know, but he wouldn't miss Geoff's wedding for the world. "I think we probably have enough for a fire. Ready to turn back?"

Nate and Sky walked back hand-in-hand along the hard sand by the ocean's edge. She had almost forgotten about Labor Day. She'd invited four couples for the holiday weekend—mostly old friends from Brown. Alexandra had finished her doctorate in theoretical chemistry at Stanford and was now teaching at Harvard, and Ruslaan—Russ—was an up-and-coming McKinsey associate. And Colin and Keke: Colin started as an actor but found success as a tech entrepreneur; Keke graduated from Yale Law and was a rising star at one of the old white-shoe law firms. Hadley was coming, of course. She was a tech wiz working for a high-speed algorithmic trading company and (if you included her bonuses) earned more than the rest of them combined. Her new boyfriend was Maxim, a psychiatrist. And finally, Cole and Inez: he'd started in his father's commercial real estate business, and after a time, his dad had staked him so that he could open his own company. Inez, also a Brunonian, was an editorial assistant at *The New Yorker.*

But for Nate's trip to Amherst, the weekend would have been a professor, three executives, a lawyer, a doctor, a writer—and a college dropout goatscaper? A pang of relief and guilt washed over Sky. She didn't really think that any of her friends were snobs, but it might have been awfully awkward.

No one knew about Nate yet, except for Winky and Prescott, of course, and they were committed to Prescott's annual family gathering in Maine at Prouts Neck. Winky had successfully squashed the gossip about her and the local goatscaper by telling everyone that Prescott was fooling them with another of his silly jokes. That, combined with Francisco (mis)leading everyone into thinking that he was just one Latin dance move from becoming an item with Sky, put the off-island rumors to rest.

Sky slid under Nate's arm. Just kicking the can down the road, but things would be easier if she could just sidestep questions about her love life. Her friends knew about Gil and wouldn't press if she hinted the topic was off limits. They would, however, insist on knowing when she was coming back to the city, and what she was doing about finding a new job.

City, new apartment, new job. Ugh. She didn't know, hadn't planned, hadn't thought about it, hadn't wanted to think about it.

"Deep thoughts?" Nate asked.

"Nothing important. Just happy to be here."

TWENTY-TWO

They'd fallen into a comfortable routine. Nate would work moving pens or doing paperwork and then stop by Sky's in the late afternoon. If the day was fine, the two would head down to Quansoo, where they'd have the beach to themselves. Dinner (usually cooked by Nate) would be something simple: pasta or grilled something and a salad. Nate kept a clean change of clothes at Sky's place and she at his, and Zeke learned to knock before coming into the Blacksmith's Cottage in the morning to mooch coffee and breakfast.

Sky relaxed into her own schedule. Mornings, she'd go to yoga or hike a Land Bank trail. Afternoons were dedicated to repainting the bedrooms. Pleased with her success at matching the color of the lucky stone, Sky found a round pinkish-tan granite pebble and a piece of pale-gray driftwood as inspirations for her next selections.

Sex fit in anywhere. After a shower together to scrub sweaty grime off Nate and paint flecks off Sky. Twice, hidden in the dunes at sunset. Unhurried, inventive evenings in bed. Even the hayloft of Nate's uncle's barn, a bit prickly but fun. And best of all, morning delight.

No expectations. No strings.

Sky and Nate made it through the usual August backup at the Five Corners intersection and arrived early for the ferry, unexpectedly finding parking for Sky's Jeep in the Stop & Shop lot. "Want to stop by Coffee and Clog?" she suggested.

"Sure, we've got time. That's Zeke's sisters' place," Nate said as they strolled up the busy street holding hands and looking in store windows, Nan trotting at their heels. "They got a great deal on the lease when Bunch of Grapes moved up the street. Sarah wanted to open a vegan coffee shop, and Claire wanted a shoe boutique, so they compromised."

"I wondered about that!" Sky said, laughing. "It seemed like a funny combo."

They arrived at the glass door with its logo of steaming hot coffee served in a clog, which Nate thought (but would never say) looked more like a stinky shoe. The owners were behind the coffee counter, apparently disagreeing over where to put a basket of granola bars. Sarah was tall and Claire small, but they both shared Zeke's dark hair and wide smile. They beamed at Nate when he and Sky walked through the door.

Their smiles turned polite on Sky as they sized her up: attractive face, good figure, no jewelry or makeup. The faded Red Sox cap, tank top, jeans shorts, and Birkenstocks made her look more like an assistant goatscaper than a rich lady. The sisters exchanged a glance that said, could *this* be the new city girlfriend? Nate introduced Sky who, uncomfortable under the sisters' scrutiny, briefly said hi before wandering upstairs to look at the shoes. Nate shrugged and ordered Sky a latte and a regular joe for himself, along with a carrot muffin and lemon scone.

Nate liked the cozy cafe with its comfortable thrift store armchairs, vintage Bally shoe posters, and eclectic library of books about coffee and the history of footwear. He sat down at the small table in the window where Nan had flopped down to wait. No meaty or fishy table scraps here. "When are you going to get my crazy brother out of his muddy hole?" Sarah asked as she made the latte.

"Love him to bits," Claire added. "But he's got no common sense whatsoever." Nate chatted, filling the sisters in on their brother's latest flood relief efforts. He heard Sky clumping down the stairs a few minutes later wearing a pair of bright-yellow fisherman's boots. "What do you think? I don't have any muck boots. You know, for the pond." She stuck out a shapely leg in its big yellow boot.

"I like 'em," Nate said, pulling her down to plant a much-more-than-friendly kiss on her lips. "And you can wear them oystering in the fall." Nate caught Sarah and Claire pass a look between them. Nate groaned. In addition to the coffee-cum-shoe shop, the sisters also ran the Island's equivalent of Gossip Girl. He and Sky would be headlining within minutes. The sisters turned iced-coffee-brown eyes on Sky. If Kris-the-artist's reaction had been an ice cube in a warm teacup, this look was a whole iceberg in her latte. The message was unmistakable: you don't belong here. He's one of ours.

"Are you sure you don't want the Hunters?" Claire said in a polite waiting-on-the-customer voice. "Usually, only the locals buy those," she added, pointing at Sky's yellow boots. "What's your size? I'll bring you some to try. Hunter has some new colors and styles you might like." Sky knew exactly what was being implied: she could afford to pay a hundred and fifty bucks for status symbol rainboots, so what was she doing with the cheap pair? Nan lifted her head from under the table to sniff the rubber with suspicion.

"Thanks, but I like these."

Nate handed Sky the latte and took a bite of muffin. It was moist and dense and carroty-delicious with bits of apple and pineapple. "That's the best one," Sarah said to Nate, still eyeing Sky. "I'm tinkering with the gluten-free recipe for the scone, let me know what you think. What are you guys in town for?"

Sky sat down, trying not to show her discomfort, and took a bite of the scone. It was lemony, bitter, and dry, with a faint hint of garbanzo beans. Crumbs stuck in her throat, and she washed down them down with a sip of coffee.

"Picking up some friends of Sky's at the ferry," Nate said. "But we should go soon. You getting those boots, fishergirl?"

Sky bought her boots and wandered with Nate toward the ferry. She hadn't gotten the stink eye like that since, when, maybe high school? Yeah, it felt exactly like when the cool girls in ninth grade turned on her like a pack of jackals after she'd had the effrontery to date the Carnegie boy.

"Sarah and Claire don't approve of us," Sky said to Nate as they neared the ferry terminal.

"What? Maybe they'll spread a little gossip, but that's all." He put his arm around her and gave her a squeeze. "I like your new boots."

Sky's mood lifted when she spotted Trip and Eva at the top of the ramp. The ferry ride had long been one of Sky's favorite memories. The drive to the Island with her grandmother had always seemed endless until they finally got off the highway and onto the narrow two-lane road to Woods Hole. When she was small, Sky would watch carefully—a quarter to the one who was first to see Martha's Vineyard from the road.

That was the moment when Sky's beloved summer vacation would really begin. She and Grams always sat out on the ferry deck, no matter the weather, sipping cups of clam chowder and chattering about everything they'd do when they got to the Island. Even now, just watching the ferries come in and disgorge their happy passengers brought back an echo of excitement.

The day trippers and weekend visitors poured down the ramp, lugging rollaboards, backpacks, and beach bags and holding leashes of dogs of every size and shape. Finally, Sky's enthusiastic waving caught the eye of tiny Eva, who was bouncing up and down like a four-year-old, and bearded, sandy-haired Trip.

TWENTY-THREE

"You're sure these guys aren't going to be like Winky and Triscuit," Nate said.

Sky whacked Nate's arm. "It's Prescott, not Triscuit. Don't worry. You're going to love them." Like Sky, Trip came from old money and had attended an exclusive prep school and elite summer camps. He was expected to aspire to an Ivy League education and a career in law or on Wall Street. But Milton Blair Hamlin Page III, nicknamed Tripp, lost the second "p" after discovering ecstasy at Vassar and his heart when he met the free-spirited Eva Dawson. Trust-funded and free-thinking, Trip traded life on the Upper East Side for a farm in Vermont.

Eva had been raised poor as a church mouse, the adopted daughter of Baptist missionaries in Taiwan. She was one of those eclectically educated off-the-grid kids who grow up reading the entire encyclopedia out of curiosity and boredom. Now a "lapsed Bap" as she termed it, spirited Eva embraced life (and her dear friend Sky) in a giant cosmic hug.

"Here, Nate, sit in the back with me. Are you really a goat guy?"

"Goat, like in 'greatest of all time'?" Trip asked.

"No. Real goats. Don't tease Nate, Trip. You already know that," Eva said, swatting him. She turned back to Nate. "I can't believe you have goats. That's awesome. I think my spirit animal is a goat since I love overcoming obstacles. And I was born in the Year of the Goat."

"I thought it was Year of the Sheep," Sky said.

"Yeah. You can translate the Chinese symbol, yang, as either, but Chinese people will tell you it's a goat. I want to get goats for the farm, but Trip isn't so sure. I was so excited when Sky told me she had some at her place. I'm sure we'll convince him!" Eva leaned forward to tug on Trip's man bun.

She rattled off goat question after goat question to Nate as Sky and Trip caught up in the front seat. Nate wondered if there was any limit to Eva's curiosity about goats. He had sort of a love-hate relationship with his four-legged brush cutters. Nothing like Eva's apparent passion. They stopped to pick up sandwiches at Humphreys Bakery (a Turkey Gobbler for Sky and Nate, and a Tree Hugger for Eva and Trip) and made plans to go for a hike around the Gay Head cliffs in Aquinnah. The tide would be low around 3:00, which would be perfect. They'd be able to get all the way around from the Land Bank beach on the ocean to Dogfish Bar on the sound side.

As expected, Eva beelined to Bonnie and Clyde as soon as they got to Sky's. Cooper had entirely blocked Bonnie and Clyde, his two siblings, from their mother's milk bar, so the babies, at Sky's insistence, were staying at her place, where she could bottle-feed them. Nate had set up a pen around a boulder in the yard where the tiny Bonnie and Clyde scampered and sproinged about—up, side to side, back and forth—knocking each other off the rock like a baby goat version of king of the hill.

"OMG! I can't believe it!" Eva exclaimed as the tiny balls of goaty fluff trotted to the fence bleating their tiny mehs in expectation of a bottle. "So cute! Oh, look, Trip, I have never seen anything so cute. I think I'm in love. I've got to send a picture to Tiphanie." Trip rolled his eyes, Sky stood laughing and shaking her head, and Nate wondered briefly if there might be any money in running a petting zoo.

Eva sat down and held up her phone to take a selfie with the fuzzy kids poking their heads through the fence behind her. Bonnie made a quizzical bleat, then firmly bit down on Eva's black ponytail and chewed. "Guys? Some help here?"

"Oh, they're always hungry," Sky laughed. "We'll be out all afternoon so we should probably feed them now anyway. Want to help?" Sky asked as Nate convinced Bonnie to nibble on some hay instead of Eva's hair. Soon Eva was sitting, blissfully holding Bonnie on her lap as the kid sucked on a bottle—a kind of Madonna and goat.

With the babies fed, sandwiches demolished, and backpacks and a cooler packed, they set off for Aquinnah. "I'll drop you guys off at Philbin and park on the other side. That way you can walk all the way around the cliffs. I'll meet you halfway," Nate said.

Nate drove to the far end of rutted Oxcart Road on the Vineyard Sound side, where the caretaker at the Orvis fishing camp let him park whenever he fished at Dogfish Bar. He scribbled a note, anchored it under a wiper on the car's windshield, and headed up the sandy path over the dunes to the beach, following Nan who had run ahead fueled with doggish enthusiasm for chasing seabirds.

Pausing at the crest of the dune, Nate could see for miles, from Menemsha on his right and across to the Elizabeth Islands, 180 degrees to Devil's Bridge where the Aquinnah headlands rose up to form towering clay cliffs streaked red, yellow, blue, and white. Unlike the ocean side of the Island, the waters of the Sound were calm and crystal clear, almost a tropical blue in the shallows.

As always, the stretch of rocky sand was almost deserted; today, there was but one fisherman trying his luck on the bar, and a couple of groups were picnicking far down the beach. Nate was grateful for a bit of quiet after Eva's chatter. And even more grateful that Eva and Trip were, as Sky had promised, nothing like Winky and Prescott.

Nate had been walking for about three-quarters of an hour and had reached the point where the Gay Head cliffs rose steeply from the ocean in all their photogenic glory. He was wondering when he'd run into the others when Nan barked a greeting and dashed off, veering around the edge of a brightly streaked cliff.

There in a semi-secluded spot at the base of the cliff were Sky, Eva, and Trip, wearing nothing but streaks of clay. Trip was sprawled out in the sun, arms and legs akimbo, more or less covered from head to toe in blue slip. He sat up and greeted Nate.

"Hey! There you are! Come join the paint party!" He pulled a cold Bud from the cooler and lit the joint that had been tucked behind his ear, handing both to Nate with a wide stoned smile. Eva's boyish body was covered in dots of clay, and she was busy painting what appeared to be clay stripes on the back of Sky's legs. Sky propped herself up on her elbows and gave Nate a huge grin.

"Yay! You're here!" she said.

"What's your Chinese birth sign? Trip's a pig. That's why he looks like he's been wallowing in the mud. I'm a goat, of course, but it's sort of hard to paint so we did spots like Bonnie and Clyde. And Sky's a tiger, so she gets stripes," said Eva.

"Year of the Dog, I think," replied Nate as he took a drag on the joint and sat down on the sand to help Eva paint Sky's stripes. He hadn't smoked for a while, but he could tell this was good stuff.

"Medical-quality sativa," smiled Trip, taking another hit. Sky tugged on Nate's swim trunks.

"No no no no. Off they go! No clothes!" Gay Head was well known for nude sunbathing, but Nate hadn't been naked there since he'd lost his virginity to Marie-Claire Dover in the tenth grade. What the hell. Nate stood and stripped off his tee shirt and shorts under the intent gaze of both women.

"Nice looking guy, Sky," giggled Eva, her eyes pausing over his pale parts. Nate wasn't sure he'd ever felt so naked, both women ogling him like he was a Chippendales dancer. He quickly sat down.

"Thanks, Eva," Sky said, then burst out laughing. "Your expression, Nate!"

"OK. OK. Dog, hmm. Dog is the very best match for a tiger girl, you know. My parents thought it was all heathen nonsense of course, but I'm not so sure. Gil was a snake, so that was doomed to failure." Eva crawled over on her knees to Nate and started dabbing clay on his face. "Here's your nose." Nate started to wonder if Gil was the guy Sky had been engaged to, but he was highly distracted by Sky pushing herself up to sit cross-legged in front of him.

She dipped her fingers into the clay puddle. "And I'll give you patches, just like Nan's."

🐐 🐐 🐐

"Goats were the first animals to be domesticated by humans, some think as long as ten thousand years ago." Eva was chopping vegetables in Sky's kitchen, back on the topic of goats. "And they're just as intelligent as dogs."

"I know goats, and I'll take Nan over a goat any day. They're tricky, though; I'll give you that," Nate said.

"But did you know that they can climb trees?" Eva proved her claim with a YouTube clip of sixteen goats in a tree. Nate wondered if that solved the mystery of a couple of his goat breakouts. "Goat yoga is a great stress-reliever. Hey, Sky. Want to try it tomorrow with Bonnie and Clyde?" A Google search of that had Nate shaking his head. But Eva was only getting warmed up.

"And the goat stuff in mythology is really interesting. You've got goats all over the place—Norse, Celt, Greek, Roman myths. You guys ever heard of Loki, the Norse trickster god? I forget why, but he had to make this pissed-off giantess laugh and nothing was working, so he tied one end of a rope to a goat's beard and the other end to his testicles and started to play tug of war…" Nate and Trip exchanged a glance and squirmed.

"Uh, did that work?" Nate asked.

"Oh yeah. It totally worked. The giantess thought it was really funny and didn't kill anyone." Sky pulled out silverware and Nate helped her set the table. "And then there's the whole satyr business. If you look at the images, those goat-guys ran around with permanent erections, like Priapus." Eva paused to pull up some more images.

"Eva…" Trip said, looking over his shoulder from the stove.

"Naw. It's OK. I'm learning stuff," Nate said, walking over to see.

"Wow. Look at that," Sky said pointing to a particularly graphic Roman mosaic of a satyr and a nymph. "Pompeii porn." Nate raised his eyebrows.

Sky poured ice water into glasses. She opened a fresh beer for Nate and sat next to him on a kitchen stool to watch her friends cook. Eva, for the moment, had run out of goat facts. "What are you making there?" Sky asked, opening a soybean pod and popping the beans in her mouth.

"Three-pepper tofu hot pot with stir-fried veggies and brown rice. We brought a bag of Szechuan peppercorns with us on the ferry—along with Trip's other baggie," Eva said with a poke at Trip. "We're addicted. You're OK with spicy, right?"

Sky took her first bite of tofu. It didn't look hot but soon her tongue tingled, the tingling turning to a mouth-numbing burn. "Fantastic," she said and looked over at Nate, who had started to flush red. Poor Nate had never tasted or experienced anything like it before. There was the Vietnamese couple with the delicious spring rolls at the farmers' market, but their food was nothing like this. Nate tried to cool the fire in his mouth with a big slug of cold beer.

"Really good," he said, taking another bite and feeling his eyes water. "Spicy."

"Glad you like it," Eva said and paused. "There's one more thing I'm trying to remember about goats."

"Eva, enough goats," Trip said, sighing. When Eva got passionate about something, it had to run its course.

"No, you'll like this." She then closed her eyes for a moment, concentrating. "I've got it." Taking Sky's hand in her own, Eva recited, "'Your eyes are doves behind your veil/ your hair is like a flock of goats leaping down the slopes of Gilead/ your teeth are like a flock of shorn ewes that have come up from the washing, all of which bear twins, and not one among them has lost its young.'" She smiled at Sky. "It goes on with something about pomegranate cheeks and a stone tower neck and breasts like fawns, but I forget the rest."

"Eva, you've got some weird stuff lodged in your brain," Trip said, helping himself to more tofu.

"The Song of Solomon, Trip. The most erotic book in the Bible."

"Yeah, well I'd like to pet your fawns there, wife."

"Later. If you're nice to me. Now, who would like some dessert?" Eva asked. "I got us some Fenway Fudge."

"I think I'm starting to feel my tongue again," said Nate, taking another soothing bite of chocolate ice cream. He looked up at the sound of tires on the gravel drive. "Who's that?" he asked.

"No idea," Sky replied as she got up to open the door.

"Sky!" Winky exclaimed, giving her a hug. "Prescott and I were driving by, and I couldn't stand being so close and not stopping to say hello," she said, lovely in a fluttery dress and heels. "We'll only stay a minute."

"Hello, Schuyler, my dear," said Prescott, planting a kiss on her cheek and peering over her shoulder.

"But we're interrupting. You're still having your dinner," said Winky.

"No, please. Come in. We were just finishing up. Have you eaten?

"Yes, a wonderful meal at the Beach Plum Inn," Prescott said, walking inside. "Well, hello again there, Nate." A sardonic grin split Prescott's face.

"Hi, Prescott. Winky. Nice to see you again," Nate lied.

"And these are Eva and Trip, my friends from Vermont," Sky said.

"Please, please, don't get up. Winky and I'll settle here in the living room with a nightcap while you eat your dessert."

Winky tugged on her husband's sleeve. "Prescott, really, we should go. I'll visit Sky later. We should let them finish."

Ignoring his wife, Prescott wandered over and leaned on the counter, leaving Winky standing by the door. "Quite a good meal. Do you eat often at the Beach Plum?" Prescott asked Nate, casting a sidelong glance at Sky. "Lovely place for a romantic date."

"Uh, my cousin waitresses there sometimes. She says the food's good," Nate said, looking up at Prescott.

Winky sighed and followed her husband into the room. "It's nice to be back on the Island. We had such fun with you the other weekend. I can't wait to start looking at real estate tomorrow." She scanned the room. "So where did you decide to put our vase?" Winky asked.

Sky had a moment of panic. "Oh, the cleaning lady was here, and I was afraid she might bump into it dusting," she improvised. "I forgot to put it back out." Sky pulled out the hideous multicolor thing and set it on the sideboard. Nate's eyes widened.

Trip was staring at Winky. "Mrs. Shippen's?" he asked.

Winky's eyes lit up. "No. Trip Page?"

"See? We have to stay. Old friends here." Potential client, you mean, Sky thought ungraciously. "Now, where did you keep that scotch, Schuyler?" asked Prescott. "It was this cabinet, right?"

"I'll get it for you, Prescott. One cube?" Sky asked.

"Good girl, you remembered."

"Who is Mrs. Shippens?" Eva asked.

"What is Mrs. Shippen's, you mean," Trip said. "Our dancing school."

"Weren't you the boy who oiled the dance floor?" Winky asked.

Trip grinned. "You do remember me."

His answer had failed to enlighten Eva. "What kind of dancing? I thought you were into sports."

"Ballroom dancing," called Sky from the bar. "Waltz, foxtrot. That sort of thing. Manners and etiquette too. I did Cotillion instead."

"Terribly important," added Prescott. He took a sip of his drink. "Hmm, fine stuff here," he said examining the Tiffany-blue bottle of Bruichladdich Trip had brought as a house gift.

Eva rolled her eyes at Nate. She stood up to clear the bowls, and Nate joined her in the kitchen.

"Scotch all around," announced Prescott. "And we'll put on some music. A little Frank Sinatra?"

Trip put out his hand. "Care to dance?" he asked Winky. "Music, dear Schuyler, if you please?"

Sky searched for "Sinatra foxtrot" and clicked on "Fly Me to the Moon." Sinatra's baritone voice filled the room, making it feel like a cruise ship lounge.

"Omigod," Eva whispered to Nate. "What are they doing?" Trip, with his man bun and tee, made an incongruous partner for elegant Winky as he began to spin her around the room. Eva burst into giggles.

"Bravo, Winky!" Prescott exclaimed, draining his scotch.

"Didn't they kick you out of Mrs. Shippen's?" Winky asked, trying to keep her balance after a particularly deep dip.

"Indeed, they did. The first Page to so dishonor the family. But they reinstated me when my parents sprang for a live band at the holiday ball." Trip spun Eva under his arm, then brought her in close for a twirl, running both of them into the back of Sky's loveseat.

"That reminds me, Schuyler. I need to polish up my steps before the Opera Ball. Your mother still running things?" Prescott asked Sky as he poured himself another large drink from the bottle. "Wonderful event. Such a good cause."

"She's behind the scenes now, technically only on the board. But, yes, she still runs it."

"I think I'm ready for a scotch," said Eva, wiping her hands on a towel.

"Happy to pour one for you, my dear. Rocks, water?" Prescott asked.

"Straight up, if you please," replied Eva.

"Nate?" Prescott called.

Nate was reluctant to leave the kitchen. "No thanks. I'm drinking beer."

"Your loss. Fine stuff, this," said Prescott, holding up his glass to eye the brown liquor.

The song ended, and Trip and Winky fell laughing onto the sofa together. "That was so much fun," Winky said. "We should put on another song and you and Sky can dance," Winky said to Prescott. "Unless Nate would like to instead."

"Uh, I'll pass," said Nate.

"Me too," said Sky. "I'll take a scotch, though. Rocks and a splash."

Prescott pulled out a glass, held it up to the light and pretended to polish off a spot with a bar towel before adding a cube, then the liquor and a splash of water. "Here you go, my dear."

"So where are you looking, Prescott?" Sky asked.

"Oh, Elisabeth has us going all over the Island tomorrow. A couple of places look promising from an investment perspective. But my lovely bride gets a veto, of course."

"Anybody want to come look for shooting stars?" asked Eva. "It's the Perseid meteor shower."

"Oh, I do," said Sky. "I saw a couple the other night." Nate moved to follow but Prescott caught him by the arm.

"You passed up the Bruichladdich. Fireball man, are you?" Prescott asked.

"I don't drink much hard liquor," Nate replied.

"Good move. Keeps you out of trouble, eh?" He slapped Nate on the back. "But you're missing out on one of the finer pleasures of life," Prescott pronounced. "Single malts. I'm partial to an Islay myself. The Laddie here…" he said, pausing to take a swallow. "… isn't as peaty as, say, the Laphroaig. I might even prefer it to the Lagavulin. Even better paired with a Cuban cigar, of course." Nate stood feeling doltish and drank his beer. Prescott ran his eyes over Nate's faded tee to his work boots. "You're taking good care of Sky's *goats*, eh?" raised eyebrow making his meaning clear.

"Yeah. They're fine." Trip was deep in conversation with Winky. No rescue there.

"Ah, but I've got another joke for you. Tell me if you've heard this one." Prescott leaned up against the bar and loosened his tie. "It's a rainy day in Scotland, and a stranger comes into a bar. After a time, the older man next to him looks up and says in a thick accent." Prescott switched to a Scottish brogue and continued, "'You see this bar? I made this bar with my own two hands. But do they call me MacGregor the bar builder? No.' He polishes off his pint and orders another. 'And did you see that stone wall outside? I found every stone in that wall, set them just so to last forever. But do they call me MacGregor the stone wall maker? No. But you fock one goat..." Prescott guffawed.

Nate managed a laugh.

"What's so funny?" Sky asked, coming inside with Eva. "You guys should come out. We've already seen three shooting stars."

Winky yawned and stood. "Time to go, Prescott. We've crashed Sky's party long enough." She laid a hand on his shoulder. "And we're supposed to meet Elisabeth at the first house at 8:00."

"One more wee dram. Eva? Sky? Join me?"

Winky compressed her lips. "Yes, dear. I see I'm being cut off. Wonderful to see you again, Nate. Fascinating chat. And nice to meet you, Twinkle Toes," he called to Trip.

"Same here. Thanks for lending your wife," said Trip. Sky closed the door to the sound of Prescott's drunken voice singing as he walked to the car with Winky trying to shush him.

Sky found herself a lonely goat-guy
Yodel-ade-dee yodel-ade-dee-oo
Now he's not such a lonely goat-guy
Yodel-ade-dee yodel-ade-dee-oo

Nate put on his boxers and wandered out to his truck to get a clean change of clothes. He could hear Sky and Eva chatting on the deck. Someone (and he could guess who) had traced something in the dust on his Nate-the-Goat-Guy logo that showed a goat standing on its hind legs to eat a three-leafed plant. The goat was now indisputably male and excited by more than the opportunity to eat poison ivy. Nate blew an amused whistle as he swiped a hand across the dusty door.

Sky and Eva could barely contain their giggles as Nate joined them on the deck. "Notice anything on your truck?" asked Eva. Sky snorted some coffee out her nose.

"Yeah, yeah. Very funny."

You want to see something else funny?" Sky stood up. "Eva, you too!" The two turned around and giving Nate mock-seductive smiles over their shoulders, pulled down their pajama bottoms in unison. Nate burst out laughing. Sky's bottom wore the same pattern of stripes as yesterday, now only in white and sunburn red. Eva's was pink with white polka dots.

"Have you looked at yourself yet?" Both made a move for his boxers.

"Wait, I'll do it! What is it with you two always trying to pull my clothes off?" He pulled out the waistband and looked down. Yup, pink with white patches.

"Well, if you're not going to show me, then I'm going to go brush my shorn ewes," giggled Eva, "and I'll get that lazy Trip up. Don't forget that you promised me you'd show me how to milk Pearl this morning after we feed Bonnie and Clyde."

It hadn't once crossed Sky's mind that you could milk Pearl, though she saw Lizzie nursing every day. Nate went into the kitchen to get a couple of bowls and a soapy paper towel, and he fetched a rope from his truck. He'd never bothered with the milking end of the goat business—too much trouble—or wanted to participate in the Island's active raw-milk black market.

Nate wandered to the pen, led Pearl out, little white Lizzie tagging at her heels. and brought them to the deck.

"We don't have a milking stool, but, Eva, you can sit here on the step." Pearl looked suspiciously at Nate and Eva. She stamped her hoof. Nate had never tried to milk Pearl, but he knew how. "OK. First you need to clean her teats with something. A soapy paper towel works. Then you have to discard the first squirt from each teat since it can be contaminated with bacteria," he instructed Eva. Sky stood holding Pearl's rope. Nate had forgotten a key element: food to distract the goat from the human's unwelcome attention to her back half. He reached down to clean a teat, and Pearl neatly sidestepped out of reach. They heard Trip laugh from the deck.

"Need some help down there?" Trip asked. With Sky on the rope, Trip blocking Pearl's sideward motion, and Nan in position at Pearl's heels, they were finally ready to start.

At the first squirt of milk, Lizzie figured out someone was stealing her lunch and dashed full tilt into the back of Trip's legs with her tiny head. Then she sprang furiously to butt him out of the way. "Hey, hey! Ow!"

They finally had some success once Lizzie had been locked in the pen with Bonnie and Clyde, but she pushed her head through an opening in the mesh and bleated piteously for her mama until they were done. Eva took to milking as if she'd grown up with goats. Sky took a try next and found the process not unpleasant. She found the sensation of the teat in her hands rather bizarre. It was like squeezing a warm, fuzzy water balloon. She jumped when the squirt of milk emerged at full force. Trip declined to try. "I'm good getting my milk from a carton, but thanks!" Soon they had filled half a bowl.

"We can leave the rest for poor Lizzie," said Eva, looking at the jailed little goat.

Eva insisted they stop at Nate's uncle's farm to meet the rest of Nate's goats. Little did Trip know that Eva had already hatched a plan with Nate: she wasn't going to leave the Island without a goat of her own. She needed a goat with a psychic connection. The goats at Sky's place were placid and sweet, and babies Lizzie, Bonnie, and Clyde were as cute as can be, but none of them spoke to Eva.

Sky pulled her Jeep up to the swaybacked barn and parked. A young woman with blond braids and wearing cutoffs came outside. "Hey, Nate. What's up?"

"Guys, this is my cousin Jessie. Jess, this is Sky, and Trip and Eva. Eva's into goats." Jessie gave a Sky a calculating look. She'd heard about Nate's rich-girl girlfriend.

"Nice to meet you," said Jessie.

"We're going to go look at the goats," said Sky, uncomfortable under Jessie's blue stare.

"Be with you in a minute," said Nate.

Jessie leaned against the door and picked a piece of hay from one braid. "Has Dad called you about coming to dinner Monday night? He wants to talk to us about the barn."

"No, not yet. What about the barn?"

"I don't know. Whatever it is, he wants to tell us in person." Nate's heart sank. He hoped his uncle wasn't going to take out a second mortgage on the property to pay for repairs.

"That your girlfriend?" Jessie said.

"Not exactly, but we've been spending a lot of time together. You'd like her."

"I doubt that. She's waiting for you. See you Monday, cuz."

One look and Nate knew who was going home with Eva. All the goats had turned to look at Eva when she opened the gate to the pen. But it was Baby Face who walked up, little Cooper trailing alongside. Eva smiled at Baby Face, and Baby Face said "meh." Eva had found her soul goat.

TWENTY-FOUR

"Do we have everything?" Eva asked. An impressive pile of coolers and beach bags sat in the kitchen. "You don't think it's too far us to kayak?"

"About two miles. You should be fine. We can tow you if you get tired," Sky said. "The paddles and life jackets are in the shed, and the second kayak is under the deck."

Sky inventoried their supplies for an evening beach fire: meat and vegetarian hotdogs to roast on sticks, clams wrapped in foil to pop in the fire, and, of course, Hershey bars, marshmallows, and graham crackers for s'mores. Beach chairs, towels, flashlights, sweatshirts for after the sun went down, and a cooler of beer and seltzer. Trip, a serious single-malt aficionado, had filled an empty water bottle with what was left after Prescott's foray into the scotch. Sky added cups, plates, and napkins, as well as a trash bag for cleanup. Still waiting for Nate, Sky stripped the leaves from branches to use as sticks for roasting the marshmallows for s'mores as Eva and Trip paddled out of the cove.

Sky threw the bags into the back of the truck. "Oh good. You remembered your guitar."

"Yup," said Nate.

"Your cousin wasn't very friendly," Sky said, slipping into the passenger seat. "What's her story?"

"Ah, she's OK. She's got a thing about summer people."

Sky huffed her disapproval. "What's wrong with being a summer person?" she asked.

"Nothing at all," Nate replied, kissing grumpy lips.

"Hmph," Sky said, mollified. "That was a surprise. Winky and Prescott dropping by."

"Sure was."

"You didn't mind?"

"They're your friends," said Nate. And never, in a million years, would they be his.

They rode in silence. "Is something wrong, Nate?"

"You didn't tell me they were back. Or that they're going to buy a house on the Island."

"Winky and Prescott? I didn't think you'd see them." Sky cocked her head. "You don't like them. I get it. You do like Eva and Trip, though, right?"

"Yeah, they're great." Nate made the turn into his drive. "Prescott reminds me of some of my clients. That's all."

"Not this one, though," Sky said as she leaned over to kiss his cheek.

"Not this one," he agreed.

It seemed that every possible watercraft was out on the pond and heading home: Sunfish sailboats, kayaks, small aluminum jon boats like Nate's, paddleboards, Zodiac inflatable boats, and even a sail-less catamaran that had been reconfigured with solar panels to run a small electric motor. Nate's boat cut a gentle wake through the smooth surface of the pond as they waved to people in the passing vessels.

He maneuvered the boat among the sandbars, and Sky jumped out into the shallows to pull the boat the last few yards to shore. They set up in their favorite spot, where they could watch both the ocean waves and the pond, staying far enough from the surf that they wouldn't have to move when the tide came in.

Sky spread out two towels and motioned to Nate to join her on the sand. She rolled over and lay across him, resting her head to listen to his heartbeat. "I'm so happy," she murmured into his chest. Nate rolled his tee shirt into a pillow and felt Sky's breath deepen as she slid into sleep. He'd failed, utterly failed, at keeping his pledge to keep it casual and easy and light. He knew he was looking out at a broken heart. But... No regrets, right?

Sky's cell rang in her beach bag. "Can you get that?" she murmured.

"Hello," Nate said into the phone.

"Who is this? Put Schuyler on," said a woman sharply.

Sky opened her eyes and grimaced. "My mother," she silently mouthed to Nate as she took the phone. Way to ruin a perfect day.

"Hello, Mother." Sky rolled over on her back and took a deep breath. Nate propped himself up on his elbow and dug around for a pebble to put into Sky's bellybutton.

"A friend. Sorry, I've been busy. I haven't listened to your message yet. I've got friends visiting this weekend. We're at the beach." Nate put the stone in place and looked for another.

"I'm sorry, I did forget. I hope you have a nice trip. Yes, I know it's a long flight to Ecuador." Nate laid the next pebble three inches lower.

"I'm sorry the cat sitter fell through. I'm sure Queen Catty will be fine with Georgie." The third stone went above her bellybutton.

"No, I can't come to stay at the house. That cat hates me anyway. You know that. Besides, I told you I have friends up this weekend." Nate's fingers brushed her bikini top as he set a white pebble between her breasts.

Nate started digging around in the sand again. "Busy. House projects. I've been repainting the bedrooms."

"Yes, of course I know I could hire someone. I wanted to do it myself." Sky held the cell away from her ear and made a face.

"Mother, it isn't bizarre. It's what people do." Sky poked Nate's chest and mouthed, "What are you doing?"

"Yes, I'm seeing people. Winky and Prescott stayed with me the other weekend. And I went to a big party with them, your sort of thing. The Hutchinsons were there." Sky pushed Nate as he tried to balance a clamshell on her nipple.

Grinning now, Nate persisted trying to place his shell. "No, I didn't talk to them. I saw Francisco that weekend too."

"I know you like Francisco. And that his father is the ambassador. I've told you already: he's just a friend." Sky gave up and let Nate put the shell where he wanted.

"Winky and Prescott might buy a house up here."

"Yes. I'm sure it'll be much nicer than my house." Sky rolled her eyes.

Nate returned to his project with two more shells. He teased the other side, flicking the edge against the thin fabric. "Nate, stop that!"

"Who's Nate? Who is that?" Lucretia demanded.

"I've got to go. Have a safe trip. Give my love to Daddy." Sky hung up the call.

"What were you doing?"

"Trying to distract you," he said, adding the final shell on her bikini bottom to complete his tableau.

"Well, it worked." She looked at her decorated torso. "This is the first time in ages I've talked to my mother and not gotten in a fight. Nice design you made on me."

Nate grinned. "Yep."

Sky pointed to the pair of paddlers. "Look, there's Eva and Trip." The shells and pebbles fell as she sat up to wave. "Let's see if they want to go for a swim."

🐐 🐐 🐐

"I'm going to throw in a line before it gets dark. Dusk is always fishy," Sky announced, pulling her rod out of the sand.

Sky cast effortlessly, her long rod making a graceful arc as she hurled her lure beyond the breakers. There were fish. Sky pulled in a schoolie striper, which she released by gently holding the fish in the outwash until it revived and darted off.

"I think this one's a blue," she called to Nate. "A big one." Her rod danced as she reeled in the thrashing fish.

"You need a hand with that?"

"Nope. I've got it," she called back. Avoiding the razor-sharp teeth, Sky dehooked the fish with one deft shake of her needle nose pliers, administered a solid smack to the head, and knifed it through the gills to let it bleed out. Eva, a vegetarian, watched in horror.

"Geez, Sky, couldn't you have let that one go too? I didn't know you were such a fish killer!" Trip was delighted. He was tired of eating nothing but tofu and vegetables. And he found Sky's skill and fearless fish slaying rather sexy, as did Nate. And, of course, Sky was still in her bikini with just a plaid flannel shirt for warmth.

"I wonder if fishing mags do anything like the *Sports Illustrated* swimsuit edition. Sky, you wear that bikini and you could star in the Hot Girls with Big Rods edition," Trip joked, knowing he was going to pay for that remark.

"Trip, that's so sexist. You pig!" Eva yelled, whacking him with a s'mores stick.

"I know, Year of the Pig, remember, I can't help myself. Hey guys, can we have fish for dinner tonight?"

"Yup. I'll plank it over the fire," Nate called back. He turned to Sky. "You want me to fillet that?"

"Nope. My fish," Sky insisted. She pulled out the fillet knife and scaled the blue. Quickly and cleanly, she sliced through the side of the fish, starting at the gills, cutting down to the backbone, and finishing with the ribcage to avoid the smaller bones. No ribs, no gut wall. Nate was impressed.

Nan crept up, belly to the ground, eye on the skeleton. "Nice job," Nate said, giving Sky a kiss as he brushed fish scales from her cheeks. Seeing her opening, Nan slunk to within biting distance of the tail. "Nan, no!" Nate scolded.

He filled the bucket with sea water, placed the fillets and shakes inside, and carried it back up the fire. After they'd soaked, Nate set the shingles on two pieces of wood at the edge of the fire and pushed a pile of coals underneath to singe the planks. When they started to smolder, he flipped them over and set the brined fillets on top to cook, skin side down.

Eva pulled her rubbery hotdog off the end of her stick and took a bite. "That smells awesome." She reluctantly took another bite of the vegetarian hotdog, which tasted as bad as it looked. Trip could see her thinking. The aroma of the cedar smoke with a hint of fresh fish cooking was intoxicating.

"I'm going to try the fish." Trip stared at Eva in amazement, and Eva shot him a look. "Well, most scientists believe that fish don't feel pain like humans or other animals. Their neural structures are different, and they don't react to painful stimuli. I think that smell triggered some sort of primal thing in my brain. I *really* want that fish."

Sky sucked her cheeks into her mouth and moved her lips into a fish face. "If you won't regret me in the morning…" Eva burst out laughing.

The fish tasted as good as it smelled, and even Nan turned her nose up at the vegetarian hotdogs. Sky drooled over the clams, smoky and hot from the fire, awesome with a spritz of lemon. And the s'mores were as they all remembered. Sky was meticulous about toasting her marshmallow. She would slowly turn it over the coals to maximize the chances of getting an even golden crust over a gooey center, the confection almost falling off the stick at the end in the glorious perfection that is an expertly toasted marshmallow. Eva was a burn-and-eat-and-repeat person. Nate would try for golden but get distracted—usually by watching Sky, and his marshmallow would catch fire. Trip reverted to his kid days. He simply mashed and pulled his marshmallow into a stringy glob before sandwiching it between the graham cracker and chocolate.

"You're missing the best part," Eva said.

"Nope," said Trip. "This is how I like them, and this is how I eat them. Sushi s'mores."

The friends sipped Trip's fine scotch and stared into the bright shape-shifting flames of the fire, listening to Eva quietly strumming Jorma Kaukonen's "Water Song" as the flames leaped and crackled. The night had gone dark and chilly, and the four friends moved closer together. A sense of peace and belonging settled over Sky as she sat in her beach chair next to Nate, watching the sparks rise in the air.

Eva put down the guitar and crawled over on hands and knees to where Sky sat. "This has been such an amazing weekend," Eva said, planting a kiss on Sky's forehead. "I love you, you know."

Trip leaned over in his chair, tipping sideways in the sand, and kissed Sky's smiling cheek. "Double over here. Love you, sweetheart."

Then it was Nate's turn. He didn't think. "Me too. I love you, Sky."

TWENTY-FIVE

After fresh goat milk café au lait (not bad, Trip had to admit) the four headed over to Nate's to pick wild blueberries for breakfast. It had been a bumper year for berries. Even late in the season, the bushes remained full of fruit.

The air was soft and calm. Walking through the misty fields, picking berries from one bush, then moving to take a handful from an even more heavily laden bush—a Zen-like experience. Trip and Sky were amazed at the variety of the diminutive berries. Some were large and a chalky blue; some were tiny and shiny and almost black; and others, a bit larger, were a true blueberry blue. They'd grown up with supermarket blueberries: giant, sweet, flabby, and almost flavorless. These were a revelation.

"Hey guys, stop eating them all. We won't have enough for the recipe," Nate mock-scolded the trio.

Back home, he began to assemble his world-famous muffins. OK, maybe Island-famous.

"How'd you learn to make these?" Eva asked. She'd heard about Nate's muffins from Sky and had insisted that he bake them a batch.

"I wanted to win a prize at the ag fair, to beat my cousins," he replied. "I came in second, but I kept trying, tinkering with my recipe. The next year, I got a blue ribbon." He pulled out the big pale-green milk-glass bowl and quickly measured and mixed the batter, working from memory.

"What's your secret?" Sky asked.

"Triple berries, a bit of cinnamon, don't overmix."

Soon the warm smell of fresh muffins filled the cottage, masking the mustiness of the old place that no amount of cleaning could eliminate. Nate joked with Eva and Trip in the kitchen as if he'd known them forever.

Sky tried to imagine Winky and Prescott here in Nate's house, with its mismatched chairs and stained wood walls. Sky's old life, and most of the people in it, had overlapped like circles in a Venn diagram: prep school, camp, college, work, friendships, dating. That line—with Winky and Prescott, her career, and her family—was a road familiar and, until now, one she thought she'd been happy to follow. But now there was a new, parallel line, with Nate and Elly and Eva and Trip. Right now, it felt much more real, and the other felt, well, not false but somehow less true to herself, like an expensive outfit that fits and looks great but doesn't quite feel right compared with an old pair of jeans and broken-in boots.

Trip must have gone through the same thing after meeting Eva. Surely no one, himself included, would've predicted that Milton Blair Hamlin Page III would become a tofu-eating environmental filmmaker living in a ramshackle farmhouse in Vermont. His great-grandfather Frick must be turning over in his grave. Sky took another sip of coffee as Nate glopped batter into his beaten-up muffin tin. Perhaps she was deluding herself, like that time she'd gone to Krabi in Thailand and wanted to live forever in a bungalow on the beach with a sailboat and a snorkel. Or the time she'd decided that she could live in that old miner's cabin in Aspen, with a pair of skis for winter and hiking boots for summer. Each time, however, her old life had called to her. It always did.

Then her mind drifted to the beach fire. He couldn't have meant it, not that way. They'd agreed this would be a summer romp, nothing serious: lovers, but not in love?

Nate had noticed Sky's distracted look and leaned over to pop a blueberry in her mouth. "You OK?" he asked, raising one eyebrow. "You look a million miles away." Sky bit the berry and smiled to show him the blue flecks on her teeth.

"Yup, I'm back—right where I want to be."

Zeke, as usual, had sensed the baking of blueberry muffins all the way from the tent, showing up at the door just as they were coming out of the oven. Eva and Trip were fascinated by his lifestyle choice. "And how many months a year can you live there?" Trip asked.

"Depends. It's less the temp inside—I've got my sleeping bag—than the temp of the, uh, outdoor facilities," replied Zeke. "I can always head over to Nate's but whizzing out in the cold wind and rain and sleet sort of loses its appeal after a while." He turned to Nate and took another muffin off the plate. "Damn, these are good. Hey, man, I had that weird goat dream again last night."

Eva had picked up Nate's guitar and was strumming "Sweet Baby James," but her eyes lasered in on Zeke at the mention of a goat dream. "What happens in your dream?" Eva asked.

"Well, I'm on this farm. It's a dream, so it isn't like a real farm, but I know it's supposed to be a farm because there are all these goats around. A bunch of goats have climbed onto these big boulders like they have at Waskosim's Rock."

Eva stopped him. "That's good: lots of goats on a farm are supposed to represent future wealth and prosperity and, goats on rocks symbolize good luck."

"Then it starts to get really weird. This one big white goat jumps off the rock and comes up to me and tells me—well, it bleats, but I know what it is saying—that I have to ride it."

"Male goat or female goat?" asks Eva.

"Girl goat. So, I get on this nanny goat and I'm riding around…"

"Oh, that's easy, that's a new sexual encounter."

"So I am riding this big old fat white goat, and a black billy goat trots up and knocks me off, then starts with that head-butting thing, but somehow I'm kind of a goat, so I'm using my head to butt him back."

"Oh, that isn't so good. The butting billy goat is obviously your foe, and he's trying to get your business or your money."

"Well, hell, I don't have any money, so I guess that isn't a problem," continued Zeke. "And he's welcome to my job. Anyway. So then the white goat gets even bigger and fatter, sort of like in that Miyazaki film where the spirits get all crazy big? The white girl goat gets like twelve feet high and turns on the billy goat and butts him to kingdom come. Then that giant nanny goat walks up to me and at this point, I'm like eye level with her udders and bleats at me to suck on her. Told you this was a weird dream. But that part totally freaks me out so I wake up."

Eva thought a minute. "I don't think I've ever read anything about how to interpret that," she started. "But it kind of seems obvious. I'd say that, one, you're heading toward a new phase of wealth and prosperity. And, two, you are going to start a sexual relationship with a powerful woman with strong maternal instincts who will take out your enemies for you. Anyone like that in the picture?"

Nate choked trying to suppress his laughter. Zeke stared at Eva with a look of dismay. "You can't mean Batty."

An image of six-foot Batty, arms akimbo, flashed in Nate's mind. Yep, he could see her kicking that billy goat. And udders were not, unfortunately, an inaccurate description of her significant chest.

"It's fate, Zeke," said Nate. "Sorry man, but you can't escape fate."

With Zeke's dream as inspiration, they headed over for a hike at Waskosim's Rock. Zeke tagged along with the foursome, still trying to convince Eva that there must be another interpretation of his dream. "A goat can just be a goat, right? Maybe this means I'm supposed to go into business with Nate or something?" he asked, almost pleading.

Eva shook her head. "Goats can be goats, but not when they are interacting with humans in a dream. And the fact that this is a recurring dream means that you know, on some level, the truth of what it's trying to tell you."

"How about you, Nate. What do you dream about?" Eva asked.

"Yeah, I have a goat dream, too, but I think my goats are just goats. They escape. I chase, but can't catch them." Nate didn't tell Eva that in the dream there is only one goat that escapes, a beautiful one that he loves, letting him get tantalizingly close, then slipping away from him, over and over.

"And you, Sky?" asked Eva. Sky shook her head. She didn't want to talk about her recurring Gil dream/nightmare. Besides, she hadn't had that dream since she'd met Nate. "Sometimes I'll get bits and pieces, but I don't really remember my dreams." Eva looked disappointed. She loved to interpret dreams but was soon distracted as she caught sight of the huge boulder that gave the Land Bank property its name.

"Waskosim means 'new rock' in Wampanoag," explained Zeke. He had a surprising store of obscure Island history filed away in his otherwise flaky brain. "I think it was 1669 when there was a treaty between the Wampanoags and the English— the Mayhews. They drew this imaginary line—the Middle Line—between this rock and Menemsha Pond. Everything on the right was Wampanoag, and the English took everything on the left."

"Real history right here. That's cool. I wonder if they each thought they got a good deal, or if the Wampanoag felt ripped off?" Trip considered. "I'm heading to the top. Anyone want to join me?" Trip and Eva started up using handholds in the crack that split the giant twenty-five-foot-high boulder.

"I wonder why this one is called new rock? It must've been dumped by glaciers at the same time as the other erratics," Nate said.

"Maybe aliens dropped it later," suggested Zeke. "You know, like to mark a landing zone or something?"

"It does look like it dropped out of the sky. Geez, this really is a huge rock," Sky said as she, Nate, and Zeke walked around the base of the boulder watching Trip and Eva make their way up. Eva sprang up the last pitch to the top. "Hey, Eva, you're looking pretty goat-like up there!" called Sky.

"I'm a goat! And I see goats! All over the place!" Eva called down.

"Oh yeah, the Land Bank keeps a big herd, like a hundred or something, to bring back the pasture on the properties. They must be clearing over here now," said Nate.

"And I think I can see Menemsha pond too. It's beautiful up here. Come on, you guys, it's easy, you can get up," Eva urged.

Nate, Sky, and Zeke scrambled to the top to join Eva and Trip. In the distance to the right, Vineyard Sound was visible as was much of the north and south shores. The Treaty of the Middle Line had divvied up a lot of real estate.

Nan ran around the base of the boulder, emitting anxious little yips. "Chill, little dog, we're fine," Trip said. Then, putting on a Monty Python-esque voice and demeanor, he gestured out over the landscape. "I say, chaps, I think I'll take the left side, from here to there. You don't mind now, say what?" Trip trilled in a silly British accent. "And how about a puff on the peace pipe to close the deal, old chaps," he added, pulling out his pipe, Eva giggling at his side.

"None for me. I'm heading down," said Nate.

"Me too," said Sky.

Nan, relieved to have her people back on the ground, ran off to chase what they hoped was a feral turkey and not a skunk. "What do you think, guys? You ready to come down? It'll be time to leave for the ferry soon."

Got a client meeting. Say goodbye to Eva and Trip for me, Nate texted from his truck. This was a ruse: Nate was on his way to pick up Baby Face and Cooper. Eva had cooked up the plan to meet him and the goats at the ferry terminal in Oak Bluffs. She'd checked the rules, and the Steamship Authority allowed "domesticated animals restrained by a leash." Eva knew goats were nothing if not domesticated: they'd been so for ten thousand years.

Nate checked to make sure that he had an old leash of Nan's, a collar, and a length of rope. After the usual struggle to get the goats into the despised trailer, he was on his way to Oak Bluffs. He wasn't nearly as confident as Eva that this was going to work: a goat restrained was by definition not a goat cooperative.

Stares and laughter followed as Nate half-dragged, half-lured the mama and baby goats up the sidewalk with Nan nipping at their heels.

Sky, Eva, and Trip were exchanging goodbye hugs when they spotted Nate and his four-legged companions. "Shit," Trip said as Eva ran down to Nate. Sky, on the other hand, hadn't yet put two and two together.

"What is Nate doing here with his goats?"

"Eva's goats, you mean," Trip replied.

Eva came running up with baby Cooper in her arms as Nate continued to pull Baby Face along the sidewalk.

"Oh my goodness, are those goats going on the ferry?" asked a white-haired woman attempting to restrain a pair of yapping corgis. "Shush, Elizabeth. Shush, Philip," she scolded.

"I hope so!" replied Eva, eyes alight. She was prepared with a printout of the Steamship Authority's animal policy to show to the ticket taker.

"Well, isn't that something new. Do you need a poop bag, dear?"

"I didn't think of that, thank you! Sky, can you put it in my pocket?" she said. "Oh Cooper, don't be scared of the dogs," she reassured the tiny goat as he bleated his dismay.

Nate handed Trip Baby Face's leash. "Here you go, buddy. Her idea, not mine. Sorry. I take returns, though," Nate joked.

Trip just gave him a look. "You'll love having goats," Sky said. "Really! Goat milk lattes every morning."

"Mommy, I want to pet the baby goat," cried a tow-headed child, yanking on her mother's arm. More and more people turned to check out the commotion, pointing, laughing, and taking pictures.

With a resigned sigh, Trip took the handle of a rollaboard in one hand and the goat leash in the other. "Bye guys, thanks for everything," he said, shooting Nate another dirty look. He then looked at Eva's beaming face and sighed. He loved his wife, and his wife loved goats. Trip turned to Nate and gave him a lopsided grin. "Forgiven, mate." He tugged on the animal. "Let's go, goat."

"Meh," Baby Face said. She planted her feet, bent to pick the leash up in her teeth and chewed.

"Yo, goat, don't eat that," Trip said. "Nate, how do you get this out of her mouth?" Then Baby Face spotted a patch of delicious-looking zinnias. She darted in that direction, yanking the leash from Trip's hand. "Whoa, hold on, where are you going? Boat's that way!" He dropped his bags and began chasing the escapee, who picked up speed as the crowd parted. "Grab that leash, somebody! Runaway goat! Baby Face, stop!"

"Guess I better help," said Nate. "C'mon, Nan."

Eva picked up baby Cooper and ran after Trip and Nate. "Watch the bags, Sky! Trip, don't you lose my new goat!"

Sky was nearly doubled-over with laughter, tears streaming from her eyes and so regretting that she didn't have her camera. It was like a slapstick comedy from 1920s, the goat dodging and veering through legs, Trip waving his arms and yelling, baby-goat-laden Eva shouting instructions, and Nan barking as she tried to herd the animal.

Finally, Nan got Baby Face cornered against a fence. Nate picked up the leash and handed it to Trip. "Hold tight, OK?"

"Yeah, I think I've got it now," Trip said, chagrined.

Eva ran back to Sky, still hugging tiny Cooper. "Omigod, I thought we'd be chasing Baby Face all over Oak Bluffs! She's so fast!"

"And tricky," Sky said. "But you'll figure it out."

Eva kissed Sky's cheek. "This was the best trip ever. Promise you'll invite us back?"

"Anytime," said Sky.

"Call if you need any advice," Nate said.

"Oh yeah. You'll be hearing from us," said Trip.

The entire ferry crowd's attention turned to the young couple as they walked up the ferry ramp with their rollaboards and goats. The ticket taker simply shook his head in disbelief as he waved them through.

As Sky had predicted, Eva had indeed got her goat.

When Nate drove back to the barn to drop off the trailer, he was surprised to see a pair of strange cars, nice ones, a Lexus and a BMW, parked there. Lost tourists? Nate walked to the barn to see what was going on.

"Too nice a view to waste on goats!" brayed a familiar voice. Nate stopped in his tracks.

Then a woman's voice. "And I'm sure you can subdivide. I'll check that there aren't any restrictions, but it's three-acre zoning in Chilmark."

"What do you think, Winkster? Or would you like being in town better?"

"The views are pretty, Prescott, but I don't know. We'd have to build."

"Ah, but that way, we get exactly what we want. My wine cellar. Your spa. We can even buy you a horse."

"I don't like horses. You know that."

"Ponies, then, for the children to ride."

The real estate agent's eyes were bright. Her nose twitched with the promise of an impending deal. "It should be no problem to put in a stable, but there are strict set-back and height restrictions on building a house. I'll get you the information. I must tell you, this is a very special property. Honestly, I was quite surprised when the owners said that they were willing to let me show it. If I were you, I'd make an early offer before they list it."

Nate had heard enough. Monday's family dinner. His aunt and uncle weren't going to borrow money. They were planning to sell. And if not to Winky and Prescott, to someone just like them. The thought kicked Nate in the gut. He'd call his uncle to tell him he already knew that they were putting the property up for sale. That was one dinner he did not want to sit through.

Nate couldn't imagine his uncle not owning the farm. He'd sworn to Nate he'd never sell a foot of land that belonged to the Batchelor family. The barn had been a big part of Nate's life. It's where he'd chased chickens as a toddler and played endless games of hide-and-seek with his cousins. Hours spent as a teenager with a pack of friends and a case of beer. Nate had always thought his own children (a vague, distant prospect, for sure) would play there with their cousins. Uncle John's money troubles must be worse—much, much worse—than he'd suspected. And Nate couldn't help him.

The voices grew inaudible. They must have been walking down to the pond. Nate unhitched the trailer and pulled it around to the side of the barn, still trying to process what he'd heard. Only later, thanks to Zeke, would the unthinkable occur to Nate.

TWENTY-SIX

"No offense, Sky, but I think I prefer Edgartown. The houses are so pretty, and you can walk everywhere," said Winky. "But the property Prescott likes best is somewhere around here, I think," She glanced at her Rolex. "Help me keep an eye on the time. We need to get to the airport at 6:00."

"No rush. It takes only two seconds to check in." Sky took a sip of her wine. "Did you see anything in Edgartown that you liked?"

"There was one place on Cooke Street, not far from the Charlotte Inn. It doesn't have a water view, but it's just beautiful inside, with a new kitchen and a gorgeous rose garden."

"What about the other one, the place Prescott liked?"

"That one's waterfront. Somewhere on the Chilmark side of Tisbury Great Pond. That's this pond, right?"

Sky nodded. "If you bought that, we could boat to each other for cocktails."

"Wouldn't that be fun?" Winky exclaimed. "I'll have to have the agent send me a map. I get lost on all these dirt roads. It's just land, though, but a lot of it. I think Prescott wants to play country squire and build his manor house or something. I can't decide if that's good or bad."

"Probably both."

"Prescott likes it as an investment play. We could subdivide and sell off the back lots. But here I am, rambling on. Tell me, how are things with Nate? I hope you didn't mind our dropping by the other night."

"No, of course not. I still can't believe you and Trip remembered each other from Mrs. Shippen's. I'm not sure Eva and Nate knew what to make of the two of you dancing the foxtrot around my house."

"That was too silly. But it seemed like Nate and Prescott were starting to hit it off."

Sky let that one go. "Nate and I are getting along really well. This is what I wanted, a summer off just to have fun and do what I want. Last year, I think I spent all my vacation days going to other people's weddings."

"At least mine was in Saint Kitts!"

"That was fantastic. But do you remember how summers felt when you were a kid? That's how I feel now."

"You forget you were lucky and got to come up here. I had to go to ballet camp," said Winky. "But have you thought about what you're going to do in the fall?"

Sky screwed up her face. "Not much. I've been taking a lot of photos recently. Video too. In retrospect, I wish I had gone to film school instead of law school." She took a sip of wine. "I really don't want to work for a law firm again. But maybe I can go in-house somewhere, so I can get more control over my life."

"That makes sense," Winky said.

"Unfortunately, it's what everybody wants to do, once they've worked in a firm for a couple of years. But no one hires in August anyway, so I'm not worrying about it now. I'll start looking in the fall, I guess," Sky said.

"You promise you're coming back, right?" Winky checked her watch again and stood up. "I should take off. It was so great to see you. We may be back up to look at a few more places. I'll give you a call and let you know how it's going." She leaned over to give Sky a kiss. "Be sure to give Nate and those goats a big hug from me."

The post-house-guest laundry chores could wait; Sky much preferred to ride along with Nate on his rounds. She had to say something about the other night, about that unexpected "I love you," but what? The old refrain, wrong guy, too soon, ran through her head.

"Do you mind if we swing by my cousin's alpaca farm on our way back?" Nate asked, interrupting her thoughts. "Duncan needs to borrow some of my extra baby goat supplies. His new mother stopped letting the baby nurse."

They turned into the dirt drive that led to a big inland farm with a handsome gray-shingled post-and-beam barn. The parking area was almost full of cars with out-of-state plates. "Everyone thought Dunc was nuts when he bought this place and said he wanted to raise alpacas, but he's doing pretty well," Nate explained. "The farm gets a ton of visitors. Kids love this place, especially petting the alpacas. He put a gift shop in the barn with hand-knit sweaters and stuff, and he's made a website with an alpaca-cam for the real alpaca groupies."

They stepped out of the truck, and Sky wandered over to the fence while Nate pulled the box of supplies out of the back.

"Oh, look, Nate. The alpacas are so cute!" Sky exclaimed. Nate walked over to join her. "See that fluffy white one? He looks just like a toy I used to have when I was a kid. My father brought it for me from Peru. It had real alpaca wool—so soft—and a tiny halter made out of yarn." Nate smiled as he thought of a nice surprise for Sky.

"Let's go see if Dunc's around." Duncan was blond and shorter than Nate, but Sky could see the family resemblance. Like his sister Jessie, Duncan not so subtly checked her out.

"So how long are you up here for?" he asked.

"I don't know," Sky honestly answered. "It's been so beautiful this summer. I haven't wanted to think about leaving."

While they chatted, Nate had slipped into the gift shop. He came out a few minutes later with a small paper bag. "For you," he said shyly, handing her the bag. Inside, like a pouf of white wool, was a small toy alpaca with a tiny red halter.

"Oh, Nate! It's just like the one I used to have."

Duncan looked uncomfortable as Sky kissed Nate. "Uh, you guys want to see the new baby?"

Sky rode home in a state of baby alpaca bliss. "I thought baby goats were cute, but that little baby alpaca was the most adorable thing I've ever seen," she sighed.

"You're good with the babies," Nate remarked. Sky did seem to have a way about her that the animals liked. The tiny ball of white fluff had tottered right up to her and settled into her lap to feed from the strange bottle.

"Did you feel how soft Fuzzybutt was?" The farm had let the visiting kids suggest and vote on names for the babies. Fuzzybutt had won this time, narrowly beating out Princess Rainbow Cookie and Pikachu.

After the chilly receptions in the coffee-shoe shop and at the barn, Sky was relieved that Duncan had seemed to like her, extending an invitation to drop by anytime to help feed baby Fuzzybutt or just hang out with the alpacas.

She pulled out her little toy. "Nate, thank you again. It's funny how this," Sky stuck her nose into the wool, "brings back so many memories. My father used to travel all the time for work. I think, now, it was, in part, to get away from my mother. But he'd always bring something back for me. When I'd start missing him, I'd sit on the floor and set up all the little toys and trinkets around me, and it would make me feel better."

"I'm glad you like it," Nate said.

Sky sat stroking the little toy alpaca on her lap, then took a deep breath. "You're a sweet guy, Nate. But you shouldn't. Um, we can't." Her words failed as she floundered to avoid hurting him. "What you said to me, at the beach fire…."

"It's OK," Nate interrupted, not wanting to hear her say it. "That just came out. You know, copying Eva and Trip. Not like in a serious way. We're good." Sky wasn't sure she believed him, but she was relieved nonetheless. She settled back against the seat and ran her fingertips over the leather-hard callouses on his fingers. And after a while, she reached over to tickle his neck with her alpaca. He caught a wanton—nay, a goatish—glint in her gray-blue eyes. He read the look, returned his own, and they headed home.

TWENTY-SEVEN

Nate had tried to keep the date of the cut opening quiet to avoid drawing a big summer crowd, but Chris had let it slip in the riparian owners' meeting. The weather wasn't likely to be a deterrent: the day was forecast sunny and warm. Nate hustled Sky out of bed at daybreak, employing Nan's help as a face-licking alarm clock.

"Why do you have to get there so early?" Sky yawned, rubbing her eyes.

"I'm a Sewer," Nate replied. "I'm in charge."

"A what?"

"A Sewer. It's an elected position. The oldest one in the State, all the way back to the 1600s. One of the Sewers has always been a Batchelor."

"So I can tell my friends that my boyfriend is a Sewer. That might impress them even more than a goatscaper." She tried to pull Nate back to bed. "Hmm, how about you check my pipes."

Nate gave her a look and tugged her to her feet instead. "Ha ha. C'mon, sleepyhead, time to get up. Sewers have one job. We decide when and where to open the pond. We've got to get to the beach before the backhoe."

The pond was like glass in the early morning calm as they walked down to the boat. "See the mirror image of that tree there? And the pink streaks of the clouds?" Sky whispered to

Nate, reluctant to break the silence. "It's almost perfect like the reflection could be real, and the real the reflection."

Nate nodded, hoping that Sky sensed the pond's spirit. Tisbury Great Pond was, for most people, just a pretty setting for a waterfront vacation home. It was different for Nate. He'd rarely lived more than a hundred yards from its shores, had spent endless hours on the pond, and caught at least one of every creature in it. He'd studied the science behind the pond's fragile ecology and tracked nitrogen levels, temperature, and salinity. But more than that, Nate had an almost animistic belief in the spirit of the pond. He understood the pond as an ancient living organism.

"You should see it here in the fall," Nate said, again leaving unasked the question of how long she might stay. "There's only me and old Sarah and Sloan who year-round on the pond and…" Nate paused, struggling to describe the pond in the off-season. "It's so empty and quiet. The water, the air, the colors, the light. It's all different. Like the pond tolerates the summer people, but in the fall, it gets to be itself again."

"I'd like to be here then," Sky said, meaning it. They continued to walk down the path through a shady tunnel of gnarled white oaks.

"This will sound crazy, but when I'm here on the pond by myself, time seems to collapse. Like I can see the pond through the eyes of my father, my grandfather, back to the first Nathaniel Batchelor."

"Not crazy," she said, squeezing his hand. "Special."

Nate paused. "My parents used to joke that I had pond water flowing in my veins instead of blood, I spent so much time here as a kid. You know how much I missed the Island when I went off to college? There was this one dream I'd have over and over: I was a striper that had gotten caught in the pond after the cut closed. I'd swim up the cove and look through the surface of the water at my old house. Sometimes I'd see my parents working in the yard, my mother hanging laundry on the line. But I was a fish and couldn't go home."

"Nate, if you were a striper, you'd be a keeper for sure," Sky said, gently teasing. Nate squeezed her waist.

The path opened back up to meadow as they neared the small wooden dock. Sky stepped into the boat with Nan close behind, paws scrabbling for purchase on the cold metal.

"How long will we stay?" Sky asked.

"Probably five, maybe six hours. We want everybody off the beach before we leave," Nate replied.

The sound of the engine broke the quiet, and the small boat began to plane as it picked up speed, skimming the pond's surface like a tern. "I can't think of anywhere I'd rather be, Sky thought," idly rubbing Nan's ears and gazing at gorgeous, sensitive, sexy Nate—*her* gorgeous, sensitive, sexy Nate—as he sat relaxed, his hand on the throttle, the boat's wake spreading out in smooth widening vees across the pond.

🐐 🐐 🐐

A thin scrim of fog shrouded the beach. They could barely see the giant backhoe trundling down the beach from Black Point through the mist. Chris, the other Sewer, had yet to arrive, so Nate and Sky started to set the stakes for the safety perimeter.

"Let's put another stake there," Nate said, pointing.

"How do you decide when to open the pond?" Sky asked, rocking the stake down into the sand.

"Mostly by the height of the pond. So it depends on how much rain there's been. But we open it for the spring herring run and like it closed for the oyster set in August. What's best is opening on a full moon at high tide, so we get a good flush." Nate explained how the hydraulics of the pond opening could look deceptively safe to the casual beachgoer, especially away from the cut itself. "But in reality, it's closer to a dam break: think of the beach as the dam and the pond as the reservoir. The pond can drop a few feet in less than twenty-four hours until it gets tidal. It's really dangerous that first day." Nate handed a fresh roll of safety tape to Sky, and she tied the end to the next stake. "The cut also drains Black Point Pond through Crab Creek, about eight, nine hundred acres in total."

"That's a lot of water," Sky said.

"I always worry about the kids," Nate said, with a flicker of concern as he remembered his own terrifying ride in the rip.

He dug in another stake. "The opening looks a lot like a water park ride. Wait until you see the outflow make standing waves." Sky was excited by the chance to see the whole process from start to finish. "The main thing is just to keep people behind the tape and out of the pond anywhere near the cut. Here, take one of the whistles. That usually gets people's attention," he said pulling a silver lifeguard's whistle out of his pocket. Sky put it around her neck and tested it with a soft, sharp trill.

"I haven't had one of these since the most boring summer job of my lifeguarding at Point O'Woods."

"You were a lifeguard?" Nate asked.

"Yup, CPR-certified and everything."

"Well, I hope we won't need your training today."

A few early beach walkers joined Nate and Sky to watch the backhoe, like an overgrown Tonka toy, dig a narrow trench from the pond to the ocean. The early flows through the two-foot-wide trough were unimpressive, like water draining through a hole in a bucket. To kill time, Nate chatted with the Chilmark cop on her ATV. Chris would cover the Long Point side where a second cop, a friendly, burly Wampanoag, was stationed on his vehicle.

"Oh, hey, there's Batty," Nate said. "She must have launched over at Sepiessa." A kayak cut across the pond, powered by a figure with short blond hair and broad shoulders. The paddler beached the kayak, and lifting it over her head, walked over to Nate and Sky. Weirdly, she reminded Sky of the incredible wall-sized portrait of a Nubian woman warrior in her old boss's apartment, only with a kayaking vest and without spears and, obviously, the blue-black skin. Same biceps, though, and direct fierce gaze that softened on seeing Nate.

"Hi, Nate," Batty paused, eyes hardening again to fix Sky with a judging blue look.

"This is Sky. She's going to be filming the opening. Sky, this is Batty, an old friend." Batty extended a hand that was almost as large and strong as Nate's.

"I heard you bought Pennywise. Congratulations." She turned back to Nate. Sky realized they were nearly the same height; she really was an Amazon, and not one Sky would want as a foe. "Zeke here helping today?"

"Naw, he's on the schedule today, so he's off mowing somewhere." Disappointment crossed Batty's face.

"What side do you want me on? Nice day like this, we're probably going to get a crowd. But I can stay for only a few hours. I've got to lead a kayaking trip over on Sengekontacket later."

"Hey, I'll take any help. Why don't you stay here? If we need to launch in the ocean, it'll be from the beach on this side." Batty hoisted her kayak again and carried it across the soft sand toward the surf.

The first groups of beachgoers came across the pond. Nate directed them to pull up their boats down toward Quansoo. "But I've got heavy coolers," one guy in Ray-Bans and a pink Vineyard Vines polo complained from his Boston Whaler with its huge forty-horsepower motor.

"Sorry. Not today," Nate said with a tone that shut down any argument. More and more people arrived and wandered up to the safety-taped perimeter; Nate patiently explained over and over again why the pond needed to be opened and the history of the cut. Sky learned it had been dug with hitched oxen, and even sometimes by hand with a shovel, in Nate's parents' time, and more about the dangerous conditions it brought.

Sky brought her camera out from time to time to film the progress. Over the morning hours, the cut had slowly broadened to an eight-foot-wide flow, establishing a channel from the pond to the waves at the ocean's edge. Crabs and fish were flailing about in the water on their emancipating trip to the sea. It looked no more dangerous than the small river that ran through her grandparents' country estate, and she wondered what all the fuss was about.

Then the outflow reached some sort of hydrological tipping point as it picked up speed and volume, appearing to double every few minutes. No longer a lazy river, the water began to swell and roil as the channel deepened and widened, creating sand cliffs that fell into the cut as it expanded, growing higher with each collapse—first three feet, then six, then twelve—unstable and impossible to climb. Standing waves, so large that they rolled back to break on themselves, formed in the canyon. A terrible natural force, the waters flowing through the cut were as treacherous and uncontrollable as a river in high flood.

Sky and Nate moved the perimeter back ten feet, then twenty feet as the placid pond waters transformed into a raging current. Sky filmed from different angles, trying to capture the power of the torrent of water pushing out into the ocean in a massive riptide and turning as it caught the ocean currents running parallel to shore. The foam, pushed by the breeze, floated a mile out to sea.

She turned to film across the broad two-mile long pond. The volume of water yet to exit through the channel was staggering. "This is amazing," Sky said, bringing her camera down.

"I thought you'd like to see it," Nate replied with a shy grin. "We're hoping this opening will last a long time. The longer it's open, the better. We've got to flush all the summer nitrogen buildup out and set up a good exchange with the ocean. So far, so good."

"Are you ready for a sandwich?" Sky asked. She put her camera back in a Ziplock bag and slid it into its case.

"Sure. I'll take the turkey." Sky was on her way to the cooler when her eye was caught by a heavyset man standing on a paddleboard far out in the pond. He was heading their way.

She ran back. "There's some guy out on a paddleboard!"

"Shit. He must have launched from one of the houses." Nate picked up the megaphone and headed to the edge of the pond. "Paddle over to the boats," he instructed, gesturing with his arm towards Quansoo. Oblivious, the guy continued his wobbly but steady progress towards the cut.

Sky blew her lifeguard whistle at full blast. "Nate, I think he's wearing earbuds. I don't think he can hear you."

"Damn. Next time, I'm bringing flares." Nate and Sky started waving their arms, and Sky again blew the lifeguard whistle at a piercing pitch. Batty heard the whistle and ran over.

"Nate, should I get my kayak and paddle out to him?" she asked.

"Sure," Nate said in an even voice, as he calculated the possible scenarios. Others on the beach shouted and waved as well, and by the time Batty sprinted back with her kayak, the paddleboarder realized all the commotion was about him. He changed his path but it was too late; the current had caught him and was dragging him toward the cut.

"I'm going to get the rescue float," Sky said. Her heart pounded with anxiety.

"And the extra rope—quickly," Nate was calm as he walked along the edge of the pond, but he saw fear in the man's eyes as he fought the current. "Keep paddling to shore," Nate said through the megaphone. "You're doing fine. Just keep coming toward me. You've got it." The terrified paddleboarder got within six feet of the shore when he panicked and jumped off the board, but the mass of his body dragged him even faster towards the powerful flow at the neck of the opening.

The cop had joined Nate on her ATV and Sky ran up with the rope and orange float. At the same time, another guy started to wade into the cut to reach toward the panicked victim, who was still holding onto his board with one arm and frantically attempting to paddle to shore with the other. "You! Get out of the water. Now!" Nate ordered the would-be rescuer, but it was too late; the second man lost his footing in the unstable bottom. Both were going through. "We're throwing you a life ring. Let go of the board." Nate jogged farther down the beach, and judging the distance and current, threw the rescue float with a prayer to the pond gods.

"Nate, should I tie the end of the rope to the ATV?" Sky asked, trying to steady her voice as she imagined Nate being pulled into the cut.

"No. We need to keep control over the tension if they get ahold of the float. Bring the second rope. And the megaphone." They lost sight of the victims frantically reaching for the float as they and the float were swept around the corner into the canyon of the cut. The seconds passed like hours as Nate, Sky, and Batty ran toward the top of the cliff with the ATV behind them, Nate playing out the rope as they ran.

"They've got it," they heard an excited voice shout.

"Move back! Get out of the way," Nate yelled at the beachgoers who had breached the safety tape barrier to peer over the edge at the two men desperately clutching the float as the current tossed them like leaves in a rushing stream. Nate continued to run along the edge of the cut to where it met the ocean. He dropped the end of the remaining coil, still playing out the rope with the barest degree of tension.

"Batty, tie the second rope. Quickly," Nate said, his voice now tense. Batty secured the end of Nate's rope to the extra length. The men floated further out to sea, any screams inaudible over the roar of the water. "OK. Once they get to where the current swings around, we're going to angle them back to shore."

"Do you want my kayak?" Batty asked. "I think I can get out to them."

"No. Too dangerous," Nate said, playing out a few more yards. "We won't do that unless I run out of rope." The coil of remaining rope was getting shorter and shorter.

"Can't we pull them in now?" Sky asked, her voice pitched high with anxiety.

"Soon. Move down the beach. We need the current to help us bring them towards us." The victims, still caught in the center of the rip, began to move—not away—but in a westerly direction parallel to the beach. Nate followed, still playing out rope as he walked down the beach.

"OK. We can start angling them out of the main current and then pull them in. It's like landing a fish, Sky, we got to keep the tension just right. Batty, you're anchor. Sky, when it's time to pull put your arms around my waist and brace me."

"Do you need me to help pulling?" asked the cop.

"No. It's easier with two. Get on the megaphone and tell them to hang on tight. The rope is going to yank when we start to bring them in."

Nate stopped walking, and Batty and Sky got into position. The cop picked up the megaphone and ordered the victims to hold onto the float, telling them that they were coming in. Nate slowed the release of the rope, increasing the tension. Gradually, then, he began to haul the rope in, keeping a careful eye on the rip still buffeting the men. "Nice and easy. We don't want them to lose their grip if they hit a wave."

Slowly, the force of the waters abated as the victims were eased out of the strongest part of the rip's flow. At that point, Nate and Batty were able to haul them quickly to shore. Sky heard the crowd clapping and cheering behind her. The cop and Batty took over, checking the men for injuries and shock.

"Idiots," Nate muttered, turning his back on the scene and walking back toward the cut. A few people tried to congratulate him on his rescue, but Nate was not in the mood to talk to strangers. Sky caught up and took his hand, feeling it tremble. They walked in silence back to the opening.

"Nate, you probably saved their lives," she said.

"Maybe," he said, staring at the torrent of water moving through the cut. We were lucky. They were lucky." He looked back to scan the pond for any more boats coming in. "A man died here in the cut a few years ago. Same thing, no one saw him go in. He'd walked out into the pond where the water was shallow but the hydraulics make the bottom like quicksand. He lost his footing." Nate paused, feeling the adrenaline drain from his body and being replaced by faint nausea. "My dad was a Sewer. I was still in high school. I saw the guy go through." Pain showed in his eyes. He looked back at the flow. A standing wave rose up and broke back on itself. "I thought it was going to happen again with those two idiots," he said with a flash of fear. "Well. Back on duty. We should probably move the perimeter again."

Sky yanked on a stake. Gil would have run around in a panic, but Nate was different. He stayed calm, totally in control and did exactly what was needed to save the two men, knowing what could happen if he failed. Sky felt a rush of admiration and affection, maybe more. A hero, that's what he was.

They were rocking the last stake back into position when the rescued paddleboarder walked over. "Thanks," he said shaking Nate's hand. "But, shit, couldn't you have pulled us in faster? You kept us dangling on the end of that rope for what seemed like forever." Nate stared flatly at the man.

"No."

"Well, can you send a boat out to get my paddleboard? You told me to let go of it and now it's out in the ocean somewhere. It cost two thousand bucks."

"No." The man's face twisted and he looked pissed. Nate turned his back and walked away. "Fuck him and his rich man's toy," he muttered to Sky as he headed back to the cut.

TWENTY-EIGHT

Sky couldn't stop thinking about paddleboard man's cluelessness. "Nate, what was he thinking? Did he have no idea you'd just saved his life? Did he really think you'd go out to get his stupid paddleboard?"

Nate's flash of anger had long passed. "Probably. Can you hand me the mallet?" She handed it to him. Nate drove a stake for the goats' new pen. Sky had seen plenty of muscles flex in the gym, but there was something different about watching them accomplish something useful. So practical and so very sexy.

"Can I try that? I feel like pounding something."

"Yeah, sure. Here, you can set this one. I'll hold it for you."

"Stupid, stupid man," she said with each wallop of the mallet.

"Ah, Sky, it's not worth staying mad. Not that you're insensitive or anything, but you don't get it."

"Tell me what you mean," Sky said as she kept whumping on the stake. "It's not going in. I think I hit a rock."

"Here, let me try," he said. No way could Sky understand what it's like to have one summer client be the difference between paying the bills through the winter or not. "Different worlds, Sky. The economy here, not the whole thing, but a lot of it, depends on keeping rich assholes happy on their vacations. So they're on vacation, and hey, they've just paid a zillion dollars for their house and beach key. So they feel entitled to act like jerks. Especially to the locals." He handed her the mallet. "Here. It's going in now."

Sky resumed pounding with a determined look on her face. "Like that guy I told you about who wanted me to cut twenty-five percent off my bill because I'd brought over six goats instead of eight. He claimed he was only paying for goat hours, whatever the hell that is. He seemed to really enjoy getting all pissed off, yelling at me when I refused to discount the bill. Some don't yell, but I can tell that they think they're better than I am because they've got money. If you work with your hands, it means you weren't smart enough to do anything else." Nate paused as he eyeballed the height. "Sorry, but that's your friend Prescott. OK. That's good enough. You want to do the next one too?"

"Sure." Sky thought back. Had she ever acted that way? She didn't think so, but Nate was right about Prescott. Nate pulled another stake from the pile.

"How do you deal with it? It's so obnoxious."

"You can get angry and stay angry and turn cranky and bitter—I know people like that—or you learn to let it go." Nate held the next stake for Sky. "You know, thinking that it's their problem, not mine. But that's easier said than done," he added with a grim smile.

"You know, I had a weird thing happen last week," she said, trying to keep her strokes clean and even. "I ran out of painters' tape so I went to Alley's to get more. I was all covered in paint and in my crappy clothes, and this woman in a Hermès scarf cut right in front of me to get rung up first like I was totally not there. She probably thought I was a local."

"Probably," Nate said. Sky didn't seem like a summer person, not anymore. They used the Island as a set for their annual play, Our Vacation at the Vineyard. That wasn't her. Sky belonged here. "I like that you're invisible under paint. That means I get to scrub you clean to find you again."

Sky glanced at her gorgeous boyfriend and sighed at the delicious memory of the loofah and the outdoor shower. "Promise?"

"Anytime."

As she pounded, Sky's mind returned to the rescue. She had had no idea how dangerous opening the cut could be. Fear clenched her gut as it occurred to her that Nate could have died if he'd gone out after the paddleboard. "Well, I'm still mad at that guy you rescued. And a little scared. Promise me you won't ever go into the cut after anybody or anything," Sky said firmly, fixing Nate in the eye.

"Don't worry, Sky. I don't take risks like that." He reached over and gently stroked her arm. "Nice muscles. But don't stay angry. As Zeke puts it, dicks don't stop being dicks when they go on vacation. I still get mad sometimes. But not now—not about that."

🐐 🐐 🐐

Sky was reading a book under the deck umbrella when her phone rang. "I'm so excited. We've decided. We're putting an offer in!" Winky said.

"You're kidding. Wow. Where?"

"The land that Prescott liked on Tisbury Great Pond. We'll be neighbors!"

Sky forced excitement into her voice. She'd almost forgotten about Winky and Prescott's real estate idea. "That's great. But I thought that you liked Edgartown better?"

"Well, I did, but Prescott convinced me that this was a much better investment. The only thing there is an old barn, so we'll have to build. We met with an architect. You know, the guy who designed Nicole and Howard's in Southampton? I think it'll be fun to build just what we want."

"Really fun," Sky said. She'd been to the Southampton house for a party. It was as un-Vineyard-like as she could imagine. Town building restrictions would keep a new house low, but couldn't do much about big, or anything about ugly. Prescott would build to impress.

"I've always wanted to live in a new house, where I've picked everything out myself. Well, me and my decorator. No more fusty old family antiques!" Sky thought of the ghastly chartreuse and raspberry vase and shuddered.

"Sky, I think we are really lucky to have found it. It isn't even listed yet," Winky said.

"Then how…?"

"Prescott had his assistant look up property owners on this pond and Chilmark pond, then cross-check the tax records for delinquencies. He came up with a couple of names he gave to Elisabeth, the real estate agent, and she made 'discreet inquiries.' Wasn't that clever?"

"Very," Sky said. And, yet, despicable.

Winky heard the note of disapproval. "It's not like we are making the owners sell. We're just giving them the option, information about what their property is worth to someone. But the agent said the owners are seriously considering our offer."

Suddenly, Sky had an awful premonition. "You mentioned a barn?"

"Oh, we'd knock it down. It's right on the house site."

"But what does it look like?"

"Nothing like the nice one the Cupertons had their party in if that's why you're asking. It's really old and the roof looks like it's about to fall in. And smelly, with cows inside. They were cute, though, black with white tummies. Oh, and there was a pen of goats. That reminds me, how's Nate doing?"

Sky's heart pounded. It was like a slot machine, in reverse. The fates had conspired, of all the properties on the Island, everything that was for sale, to come up three unlucky cherries on the old barn. If Nate found out—when Nate found out— he'd think she was behind it. And never forgive her. Yet, this was Winky. Dear, wonderful, Winky whom she'd do anything for.

"He's fine. Listen, I've got to go. Let me know when you hear something!" Sky said with forced brightness.

"Fingers crossed!"

"Fingers crossed," repeated Sky. But for what?

"Sky, you got anything for the dump?" Nate called out from the cab of his truck. Sky stood with her shovel, glaring at the patch of dirt by the side of her house that was foiling her attempts to plant several gallon pots of black-eyed Susans.

"Yes. And can you help me with those holes?" she asked, making another stab at the ground. "The dirt here won't dig." Sky pouted as about a cup and a half of earth came up with the blade. Nate walked over to inspect the shallow scrapes in the soil.

"It's mostly sand and rocks here. You've got to dig straight down, stop when you hit a rock. Did you get compost to mix with the dirt?"

"No. Do I need that?" Sky asked.

Nate stood directly over the shovel, then using his full weight rocked the blade into the ground and lifted out a sizable chunk of ground. He moved the shovel over and leveraging the first hole, dug up another shovel-full. "I can stop on my way back and pick up a couple of bags for you if you want."

"Can I go with you? I want to pick up an old shirt at the Dumptique to wear when I paint, so I don't get it all over my clothes." Sky retied her blond ponytail. "And we've got the fair later. Remember we promised Elly and John we'd look for them."

"Yup," said Nate.

Sky wrapped her arms around Nate's midsection and rested her face against his sweat-dampened back, breathing in the slightly acrid scent. She'd decided not to tell Nate that Winky and Prescott had made an offer on Nate's uncle's barn. If they got it, she'd tell him. His aunt and uncle hadn't listed the property, so that probably meant they weren't serious about selling it. The more she thought about it, the more she was convinced she was right. "Thanks, Nate. I was about ready to throw in the towel. The shovel, whatever."

"Glad I come in handy for more than just the one thing," he teased, bending from the waist to lift her off her feet.

Nate lowered Sky down. "Go get your trash together. I'll be done here in a minute."

Nate's cell rang. "Nate Batchelor." A funny expression crossed his face. "Hi. Yeah, long time." Sky caught a woman's voice.

"Great, sure. I'll be there early, so I can do that. Looking forward to seeing you too." Nate was smiling. He put his cell back in his pocket.

"Who was that?"

"Marianne. Ex-girlfriend. We're both in that wedding over Labor Day weekend."

"Do you see her often?" was all Sky could manage.

"Naw. It's been ages."

Sky sulked as she inspected the blisters on her hands during the ride to the dump. Of course, Nate has ex-girlfriends. Probably lots of them. "Nate, it's totally pathetic that I got blisters after twenty minutes with a shovel."

"I've got no problem with soft hands. We'll put some Band-Aids on you when we get back. You want me to drop you at the Dumptique while I do the trash? I'll meet you back there."

Sky wandered into the shack and said hi to the white-haired lady sorting through a box of housewares in the back. She walked over to the men's rack and found a well-worn blue oxford with ink spots that would work for a painting coverup. Leafing through the rest of the rack, she pulled out a black polo shirt with the logo of a Kenyan game lodge, still sporting its sales tag, and a newish pair of khakis that looked Nate's size. She folded them in a pile, then wandered through the jumble of housewares and toys to a bookcase of used books. Sky smiled as she added two paperbacks to her pile.

"Nate, what do you think about these?" she asked, holding up the polo shirt and pants.

"Um, they're ok. But I don't think I need them."

"What if we go out to a nice dinner? Look, the shirt is new."

Nate made a face. Great, something to wear when they 'dine' with Winky and Prescott. "I'm not a 'nice dinner' kind of guy, Sky."

"And see what else I found," she said, holding up an almost-new copy of *Love in the Time of Cholera.* "I read it ages ago. It's great. And this one," she added with a saucy smile, showing Nate the cover of a lurid pink paperback featuring half-naked lovers in a passionate embrace. "My Grams's favorite author. She had a secret weakness for trashy romance novels. Elly and I would steal them and read the sex scenes."

Nate took the book, opened it to a random page and started reading out loud. "'William felt an overwhelming desire to take Victoria in his arms. Her hair shone gold in the light of the single candle, and her soft, ripe curves barely contained by the stays of her emerald dress made it nearly impossible to resist the urge to ease the lust in his loins. But he saw disdain in her eye as she surveyed his unkempt hair and ragged clothes…'"

He looked up. "Are you kidding me, Sky? You really want this?"

With a mischievous look, Sky tugged on the loose neck of her shirt baring her shoulder and half of her lace bra. Imitating the lovers on the book's cover, she pressed herself against Nate's chest and threw back her head, then moaned with desperate intensity, "Yes, Nate, yes!"

A chuckle came from the back of the shed. Sky's face reddened as she quickly pulled her shirt back up.

"Oh, hey, Aunt Betsy. I didn't know you were working today," Nate called.

The woman walked up and gave Nate a big hug. "You must be the new girlfriend we've heard about. I take it you found what you were looking for?" she asked with a cheeky smile.

"A polo shirt and pants for Nate, if they fit," Sky replied. "A painting shirt for me. And a couple of books."

"Let's see what you picked, dear," said Aunt Betsy. "Oh, that's an oldy but a goody," she added, reading the back cover of *Passion's Flaming Flower.*

"I don't read romance novels. Not usually," Sky said, still flustered.

"Ah, but they have their uses. Especially during our long winters." Betsy winked at Nate. "Or so your Uncle John says. Have you tried on your clothes? I hate it when people take things that don't fit. Go," she said, shooing Nate behind the sheet that hung in the corner.

Aunt Betsy turned back to Sky. "I hear you have a lovely house."

"Thanks. I've been doing some work on it, painting bedrooms and stuff. Nate's helping me plant a garden today."

Betsy then got to her real question. "Will you be staying up past Labor Day?"

"Um, yes, I think so. I'm still figuring it out," Sky replied. To her relief, Aunt Betsy's attention turned to Nate.

"Those fit well," Aunt Betsy said.

"I hate trying on clothes," he grumbled.

"You look great," Sky added. "All you need is a haircut and some nice loafers, and I could take you anywhere."

Nate made a face and shoved his hands in his pockets. "The pants are stiff. And the pockets are too small."

Aunt Betsy walked around Nate with a critical eye, then tugged at his waistband. "That button looks loose. Here, try a belt." Nate fussed as she threaded a woven belt through the belt loops. "Nate, grow up," his aunt scolded. "There."

"Thanks. We'll keep the outfit, right Nate?"

TWENTY-NINE

Sky leafed through *Passion's Flaming Flower* to find an even steamier passage. *This sounds like us, almost,* she thought with a smile to herself: two worlds collide when the handsome virile hero meets the initially reluctant (OK, maybe not so reluctant) buxom heiress and, overcome by passion, they break the rules of class and station and succumb to overwhelming desire. *Yup, that pretty much sums us up.*

She glanced at Nate leaning back against the seat with one hand on the wheel and, with a naughty thought, ran her hand along the inside of his thigh. Her touch jolted him like a bolt of electricity, and he almost ran off the side of the dirt road. Nate corrected the steering and adjusted his shorts. "What was that for?" he asked. "Not that I mind, but a little warning next time."

"Just checking," she replied with a grin. And like the best romance novels, Sky didn't want this happy story to end. But weren't the lovers always divided by fate before they could find each other again and live happily ever after? Or maybe it wouldn't end that way. It could be even worse: she and Gil had seemed like a happy love story, too.

Sky returned to her book and smiled. "Hey Nate, here's an even better one." Her voice dropped to a husky, sultry register. "'An involuntary groan escaped her lips as she felt his mouth slip downward, tracing the dewy length of her throat as his rough hand bared the round creamy orbs of her breasts to the cool night's breeze. She gasped as his moist searing tongue gently traced the sensitive peak before the entire risen pinnacle was devoured within the heat of his mouth, and she willingly succumbed to her fate—their fate—as passion's flower burst into flames….'"

Their own passion inflamed by the passage (and in Nate's case, by the lingering traces of Sky's hand on his inner thigh) induced them to shop quickly, picking up two forty-pound bags of compost and six deep-purple-blue lavender plants. Playtime, with searing tongues and creamy orbs, awaited them at home.

Sated after a time, they turned to the planting project. Nate taught Sky to make a half-and-half mix of rich compost and poor sandy soil, loosen the pot-bound roots, and spread them so they could take hold in the dirt. It felt good to put something in the ground. Something that, if properly tended, would grow and flourish, becoming lovelier every year. Sky felt like one of the plants, setting root in a new home, tended and watered by a man who knew about those things.

"Make a little dip in the soil, like this, so when you water it, it doesn't all run off. Don't worry about overwatering in the beginning, but then you should taper off so the roots will start to go deep." Sky nodded, half-listening to Nate explain and imagining her scraggly plants, now half-flopped over with the stress of being transplanted and pelted by the hose, transformed into a lush garden.

She looked at the dirt under her nails and blurted out, "Nate, I feel I belong here, really belong here, on this island."

"Of course you belong here. I realized that a long time ago. You thought you didn't?" He looked up from the watering to examine Sky in his fishing hat, lightly dusted from top to bottom with compost.

"You're a dirty girl. Shower and I'll do some paperwork. Then we'll head to the fair?"

"Umm hmm," she replied with a broad wink, "I am a dirty girl," catching Nate's eye as she pulled off her tee. "Care to join me?"

🐐 🐐 🐐

"Nate, man, I've got to talk to you," Zeke said, banging the screen door behind him.

"What?" Nate said, putting down his calculator. He hated sending out dunning letters. Why were his wealthiest clients always the slowest to pay?

Zeke rocked back and forth on his feet. "Shit. You know how you told me your uncle put the barn up for sale?"

"I'm trying not to think about it," said Nate.

"I told Laurel and she tried to look the listing up in her office's system. It's not there, man."

"What do you mean? I saw a real estate agent there with Sky's friends. And I talked to my uncle," Nate said. He ran his fingers through his hair. "Do you think he changed his mind?" Nate asked with a glimmer of hope.

"Nope. It was never there. But there's an offer on it."

"I don't get it."

"Laurel figured it out. They're doing it under the table—negotiating a private sale."

"Why would my uncle do that?"

"I don't know, man. He should talk to Laurel, though. I think he needs some advice."

"Yeah. I'll tell him. I don't want him getting ripped off." If Uncle John was going to sell, he needed to be smart about it.

"There's something else." Zeke looked unhappy and was rocking again.

"What."

"Laurel said she's only seen private sales where the people know each other. And I'm pretty sure Sky's fancy friends don't know Uncle John or Aunt Betsy."

"Yeah. So?" Nate asked.

"I warned you about her. It was Sky, man."

🐐 🐐 🐐

The bright lights outlined the Ferris wheel against the darkening sky. It was all so familiar: the clackety rides, the calliope music of the carousel, the carnies barking out their entreaties—C'mon, everyone's a winner—the crowds, the bright colors, the bells clanging, and the smell of fried and sweet and salty wafting by.

Nate was still reeling. He felt like he was on a fun house ride—the one that spins before the floor drops out. Sky was behind his family losing their land. And the last thing he wanted to hear was that the deal was a "win-win" for everyone.

"C'mon, Nate, let's see if Pearl and Lizzie won," Sky said. "I'm so excited."

"All right. I'm coming," said Nate.

Sky pulled him through the animal barn past cages of chickens and ducks and stalls of wooly sheep, miniature horses, and pigs with their litters of snorfling pink piglets. At the end were the seven entrants in Department 103—Goats. "Our goats are the cutest. Why didn't we get first?" Sky asked, surveying the competition. She stuck out her lower lip prettily and fingered the white third-place ribbon.

It all made sense. She'd been clear what the deal was: no-strings sex, as much as he liked. Next summer, she'd have moved on from hooking up with a goatscaper. Of course, she'd want her "dear friends" to have a house on the pond too.

"Nate? Yoo-hoo?" Sky tugged on his arm. "How come we only got third?"

He turned to look at her with a pang of love tinged with nausea, a horrible mix. No question: his options sucked. "Yeah. They judge mostly on health and grooming but also on breeding and form. These guys aren't purebred anything. All we did was run Nan's dog brush over them. Third's not bad," Nate said. "I forgot you were so competitive. You're used to getting what you want."

"Yeah, I am." Sky smiled and squeezed his biceps. "Still, next year I'm using my shampoo and conditioner on them. They may not be purebred, but we're going to have the shiniest goats at the fair."

No way he or his goats would be with Sky at next year's fair. But Nate's heart, refusing to listen, leaped anyway. He knew that he still loved her and couldn't stop loving her just like that. No matter what she'd done.

Sky took out her camera and posed Pearl and Lizzie with their ribbon. "Nate, get in the picture too. Here, put on the ribbon even though it should be a blue for you!"

"I don't think so," Nate said.

"Nate, how come you're so grouchy? I thought you wanted to come to the fair."

"I'm just tired." No use accusing her. What was done was done. Soon, it would be the end of summer, end of the old barn, end of their relationship. Then fall would sink into the long, dark winter.

"Oh, OK. Do you want a soda or something? First I want to see the baby pigs and go to the fiber tent. Didn't you say Duncan was bringing Fuzzybutt?" Sky asked.

After a quick hello to her favorite alpaca, Sky dragged Nate to the spinning teacups. "C'mon, Nate, let's go on this one," she said. "That's our deal. You'll ride with me on whatever I want, so long as it doesn't go upside down."

Spinning in a teacup certainly didn't help, and Nate begged off a second ride. "You can go by yourself," he said. "Do what you want. I'll be fine." Anger began to overtake the sharp shock of betrayal. How could she have done that?

"Oh, you're no fun," Sky said frowning. "Let's get something to eat then."

Nate took a deep breath. "The library's booth has pie if you want that. Jessie's there tonight," Nate said, trying to remember what normal sounded like. He could blame Sky all he wanted, but he should've listened to Zeke and Jessie and Batty and everyone else who warned him about her. Nate's anger turned on himself. Idiot. Fool.

They made their way down to end of the food stands lining a row of picnic benches. Jessie, in an "Eat–Sleep–Read" tee, was putting slices of pie on paper plates. "Hi, Nate!" she called. "And Sky. Nice to see you again." Jessie's smile stayed in place, but her eyes cooled as they did a quick girl-assessment of Sky, warming again as she looked back at Nate. "And you, cuz. What have you been up to?"

"Usual. Goatscaping, I crewed on Jak's boat one day." Jessie shifted ice-blue eyes back to Sky. Nate was oblivious to the unspoken communication going on between the women:

you'd better not be playing games with my cousin, rich girl, or I'll take you down.

"You guys want a slice? The cooks made a special fair pie this year. Pecan-chocolate chip with an oatmeal crust. Tons of calories," she added, glancing again at Sky's figure and judging her one of those annoying I-never-eat-sweets types. "Even better with whipped cream." Sky read the challenge.

"Thanks. Big slice, lots of whipped cream, two forks. Right, Nate?"

🐐 🐐 🐐

"I don't think I can go on any more rides after that pie. How about a game? I haven't played since I was a kid," Sky said.

"They're rip-offs. Waste of money. No one wins," Nate said, still chewing over the bitter gum of Sky's duplicity.

"You want to bet?"

Sky paid for a shooting game, and Nate went first, missing his first three shots and hitting the last two.

"Go again? Win the lady a prize?" the carny asked, eyeing Sky.

"My turn," she replied. Nate had seen that look on Sky's face before: the target was toast. "Can I have a practice shot?"

"Sure. Line the center of the target with that little bump right there. That's your sight," the carny explained, leaning in and breathing mint on Sky. The first shot hit the second ring, and Nate could see Sky calculating the degree of inaccuracy. She shouldered the gun, narrowed her eyes, and fired. The next four hit the bullseye, and the fifth barely missed.

"Nice shooting, lady. Take your pick from the top row," the carny said, impressed. After some deliberation Sky chose a five-foot-tall inflatable alien and handed it to Nate.

"Here's your prize, handsome."

"So I take it you shoot, too?" That was it. He felt like he'd been shot by her, flattened by a blast of pellets fired at close range.

"Skeet, mostly. I don't like the killing part of shooting real birds, though I love being in a blind with a thermos of coffee to watch the sunrise," Sky chattered. "My godparents had a big farm out on the Eastern Shore. And fresh goose breast on the grill, yum."

She turned her attention to the neon-green alien, and Nate could see her thinking. Staying with Sky meant accepting what she had done. It was like when he was eight and his cat killed his pet dwarf bunny and brought it to him as a gift, purring and rubbing herself against his leg. Like the cat, Sky was acting true to her nature. He'd just been blind to what that was.

"I'm going to call him Ian," Sky said at last.

"Ian?" said Nate.

"Yup. I-A-N. Interstellar Alien, uh…" She paused. "Nerd. Or Nate. Your choice." Sky wrapped her arms around Nate's waist and rose on her tiptoes to plant a kiss. Love rose and swelled, unbidden. Like a wave washing over a sandcastle, he felt the pain subside and smooth. He wanted her, loved her. No matter what. Shit.

"Let's look around. Maybe I can talk you into another ride," Sky said. She snuggled under Nate's arm, and they strolled the midway with Ian-the-Alien, watching the parents empty their wallets as their kids ran around from game to ride to game to ride in a frenzy of sugar-accelerated excitement. He felt ridiculous carrying the alien, but Sky insisted. She'd won it for him, after all.

"Hey! We haven't been on the Ferris wheel yet!" She dragged Nate over to the old-fashioned wheel. "I wonder if you can still see the pond from the top."

"Probably," Nate said.

"How about a ride, then we'll get a burger?"

"OK." Nate pulled down the safety bar as Sky wiggled close and rested her head on his shoulder. He'd have to find a way to deal. Any other option meant losing her before he had to, and the hooks were set too deep.

🐐 🐐 🐐

The West Tisbury volunteer fireman's booth had the best food (and the longest lines) at the fair. "Looks like we're in George's line. He's a second cousin once removed or something.

Anyway, he's the fire chief. Don't be surprised if he tries to flirt with you. He fancies himself a ladies' man."

When they got to the front of the line, an aging-but-still-handsome man with thick white hair leaned over and extended a hand. "Ah. This must be the lovely Sky. I've heard tell of your charms." Sky reached out to shake a burger-greasy paw and found her hand trapped in his grip. "So tell me what you see in this crumb bum of a relative of mine? You can do better than a goatherd, my dear."

"Hey, burgermeister, hit on her later. You've got a line here," called a loud voice in a New York accent. To Sky's relief, George finally released her hand.

"Hold your horses, guy. This isn't New York City, you know," George yelled back. "So, what'll it be, kids?"

"Two burgers, please. The works," said Nate.

"You got it. Hot sauce too?"

"Yup," said Sky, "Give me everything."

"Two burgs, the works, put them on fire!" George hollered at the cooks.

They found seats at one of the picnic benches and dug into the burgers. "These are really good," said Sky, wiping ketchup off her chin.

"Got room for two more?" Jak asked as he and Duncan walked up with plates of Jessie's pie.

Nate moved Ian off the table. "Sure. Sit down. Good pie this year, huh?"

"Excellent. Hey, I've got a couple open slots between Labor Day and the Derby if you guys want to go out. I promised you some fishing, Sky," said Jak.

"Absolutely," Sky said with an excited look.

"I'll get back to you with a date. Maybe we can even leave this loser behind. He can't fish worth a damn," he teased. Sky giggled. Both Jak and Dunc were on her side. That she knew. "And nice alien, Nate."

Nate rolled his eyes. "Sky won him for me."

"How's Fuzzybutt doing, Dunc?" Sky asked.

"Great. That little guy is my best alpaca ever for the fair—not fazed by anything. I think it was your bottle-feeding, Sky."

Dunc polished off his pie. "I should get back to the tent. Catch up with you guys later."

The lights of the midway grew brighter as the sun set behind the trees. Friends and neighbors came up to chat with Nate, meet Sky, and hash over local issues. Architects had confirmed that the First Congregational Church steeple was doomed to collapse if money wasn't found. Inexplicably, a ferry had stopped dead in the water that afternoon and had to be towed back to Vineyard Haven. There were rumors that the candidate to replace the West Tisbury police chief didn't want the job after all. And the past night's moped accident—a minor one this time, fortunately—had the anti-moped forces hopping.

A bit bored by Island politics, Sky wandered off to find some cotton candy. Disgusting. But what was a fair without cotton candy? The exhibits in the Ag hall were too much to take in at a glance, but she did pause to admire the graceful carving of the heron that had won first prize and the fair's special achievement award. She'd come back and look around with Nate later.

Sky returned with her fluffy pink treat to find Nate talking with Elly and Zeke, who sat hugging Ian-the-Alien. Nate read Zeke's look and shrugged as Sky plopped herself onto Nate's lap, biting off wisps of sugar. Suddenly, a gust of wind swirled around, picking up trash and blowing Sky's hair into the dark-pink sticky fluff. When she pulled her hair out, big pink tufts came attached. "I'll take care of that," Nate said and popped a candied blond lock into his mouth.

As he sucked on Sky's hair, an almost overwhelming rush of joy hit her like a stupid smack in the head. I love him. Omigod, I love him. The utter rightness of those words, I love Nate, lodged in her core. Sky hadn't noticed the shield over her heart had loosened and fallen away. This wasn't supposed to happen. I love him.

She sat, stunned. The Ferris wheel still turned, and people walked by eating corn dogs and ice cream cones. Nate, done working on Sky's hair, was asking Elly what she knew about the new principal at the high school. Nate shifted her on his lap. "You doing OK there?" Nate asked.

"Fine," she said automatically. She looked into his eyes. No doubt in her mind. None. Sky looked out at the crowds, heart as light and taught as a helium balloon. I. Love. Nate.

Then, Sky spotted a familiar elegantly dressed couple coming their way. The Cupertons, the couple who threw that over-the-top party in Chilmark that Winky and Prescott had taken her to.

"Nate, it's the Cupertons. We have to go. Now," Sky said jumping up from Nate's lap and grabbing his hand. She wanted—needed—to flee. He looked around.

"Who?" he asked.

"I'll explain later. Can we go?" she added, tugging on his hand. "Sorry to run off," she added to Elly and Zeke. Sky yanked again on Nate and got him up, then practically ran, pulling him along, until they reached a big tree behind the fireman's booth.

"What's going on? Are you OK? Why are we hiding?" he looked hard at Sky. Nate had no idea what was going on with her. Then it hit him. Back came the hurt and the anger. Of course. "You were embarrassed to introduce me to those people, weren't you?" he asked.

Sky was appalled that that was what he'd thought. "No. Not that, Nate! You don't embarrass me. I…" She stopped. She was about to say "I love you" but something stopped her. Mind spinning, Sky leaned against Nate. He wrapped his arms around her and felt her shiver.

"Hey. It's OK." Nate believed her. He was probably an idiot, but he believed her. The anger drained away. "No worries. Had enough of the fair?"

Sky was quiet in the truck, rattled by her instinctive flight from the Cupertons and even more by her realization that she loved Nate. So stupid not to have seen it. She'd fallen in love with Nate the Goat Guy.

"Are you all right? What was going on back there?" Nate asked. Sky pulled herself back to focus on Nate's question.

"I saw some people from…" she'd almost said, "my real life," but she corrected herself. "From my old life. It's not like they're ax murderers or anything. They're perfectly nice, but I just really didn't want to talk to them. I'm not sure why it freaked me out so much." She snuggled in closer. "I know. I'm not making any sense. I'll have to apologize to Elly and Zeke. They must think I'm nuts."

Nate patted her knee then rested his hand on her leg, gently brushing a rough thumb along the inside of her thigh. She'd be gone soon. He should just enjoy the time they had left. "You want to come to my place? I can set a fire and we can work on that jigsaw puzzle."

"Uh huh," she sighed. "That sounds perfect."

THIRTY

Sky's mind was made up. It was the text from Winky that did it. Prescott had put in a low-ball offer on the old barn, expecting the owners to ask for more. Now, things were moving, and Winky and Prescott were expecting a counteroffer. And soon. Which meant they could be signing a sales contract within days. Sky was now certain where she belonged. And whom she belonged with. And what she had to do.

"And you said this is your barn, dear? I didn't quite hear you," said the white-haired receptionist at the Martha's Vineyard Preservation Trust. Sky had seen a flyer for the organization's annual fundraiser on the bulletin board at Alley's and knew that they worked to preserve old Vineyard buildings, like the Grange and Alley's General Store. Why wouldn't they want to save a barn, too?

"I'm asking for some friends," Sky said in a loud voice.

"They've applied for a raze permit?"

"No. They want to save it, not raze it," she explained. "But they might sell it to someone who would try to tear it down. Can the new owners do that?"

"How old did you say the barn was again, dear?"

"Late eighteenth century, we think," Sky shouted.

"Oh my, that is old. We do have a strong interest in keeping our historic buildings standing. Where did you say it

is?" Sky gave her the information. "Let me speak to the
director. We'd have to get permission from the landowners, of
course, to do a preliminary study."

"But if it is deemed historic then the Preservation Trust
could pay to restore it, right?" Sky asked.

The lady chuckled. "Wish we could," she said in a kind
voice. "We can offer our expertise, but there is very little
money for anything other than maintaining our current
properties. Just the other day, we got an estimate for repairing
the plumbing at the Grange. Oh my, the cost!"

Sky's face fell. "I'm sorry, dear. Once in a while, we find an
angel donor." She reached out to pat Sky's hand. "A couple of
years ago, there was a wealthy couple who restored their
neighbor's barn. They liked seeing it in their pretty view."

"Thank you," said Sky. "I really appreciate all the
information."

The woman had given her a new idea. A great idea. Sky
drove straight back to West Tisbury and turned at the sign for
Solitude Farm. She knocked on the door of the nicest
farmhouse she'd ever seen.

"Hi. My name is Schuyler Harrington. I live nearby. Are
you the owner?"

The large woman in overalls and a toolbelt laughed. "You
think I look like Lady Nelson?"

"Oh." Sky had heard that a British lord had a summer place
on the pond but had no idea where. "Is either the lord or lady
at home?" she asked, feeling like a character in a Jane Austen
novel.

"No, I think they're in France. Or London. Actually, I have
no idea. I'm the caretaker. Can I help you?"

"Do you have a phone number? Or their emails? It's urgent
that I get in touch with them."

"I'm not allowed to give those out. Sorry." She started to
shut the door.

"It's a legal matter," Sky said, improvising.

"Legal matter?" She woman shifted her weight. "Maybe I
can give you the name of their lawyers in Boston. I think that
would be OK. You're not trying to serve process on them or
something?"

Sky smiled. "Nothing like that. I promise."

The woman still looked doubtful. "Wait here. I'll text their personal assistant and ask. I have to go get my phone."

Sky turned around on the porch. Across the cove, the old barn sat squarely in their view. The last thing the lord and lady would want would be a Hamptons-style monstrosity sitting right there in front of them. Even worse: Prescott might subdivide the farmland into house lots. Sky felt a surge of optimism. This could work.

With hope—and love—giving her energy, Sky tackled the last two painting projects in a single day. Her house would be perfect by Labor Day when her houseguests arrived. She repainted the violently violet bathroom with a soft bachelor's button blue to match the flowers blooming in her field and transformed the school bus yellow one with oyster white paint that had a pearlescent glaze like the inside of a shell. The guest room beds were made up with creamy Frette sheets and pale-flax down duvets, and the newly painted bathrooms were appointed with fluffy white towels and the handmade goat milk soaps from Flat Point Farm. Sky had taken the plunge and bought Kris's painting. The huge beachscape in its driftwood frame looked fantastic in the main guest room.

Franny—a sturdy woman with a booming voice, giant heart, and the energy of a dynamo who came with the house—came by Thursday morning to help Sky do the big clean. Sky had learned that all she had to do was call, and the next thing she knew, every grain of sand had been vacuumed up from between the floor boards, and the house was spotless.

"Skyla, looks like you got yourself a guy," bellowed Franny from the bathroom in her heavy New-Jersey-moved-to-New-England accent. She had spotted Nate's razor and a pile of dirty men's clothing in the hamper. Sponge in hand, a grinning Franny poked her head into the bedroom where Sky was making up her bed with fresh sheets. "You can keep your secrets to yourself, honey, but I am glad to see you all glowy.

Just hope he treats you right." Franny's thirty-seven years had
been full of not-so-good guys. She had moved to the Island a
couple of years earlier to escape an abusive ex and had stayed.
"If he turns out to be a bad one, you just let me know. I'll take
care of him." Sky laughed. In another life, Franny would make
an awesome hit man.

Next, Sky did the big-weekend shopping at Morning Glory
Farm. Along with half the Island, it seemed. The farm stand
was a madhouse. She picked up some of the fabulous (and
fabulously expensive) Goldbud Farms peaches, figs to serve
with cheese and honey, heirloom tomatoes, lettuce, and basil
(green and purple—it was too hard to choose!). She'd already
picked up cheese at the Grey Barn and Farm, honey at the
roadside "our honey" stand, and yogurt and decadently
delicious lassis at Mermaid Farm. A stop at Cronig's Market in
the morning would take care of the rest. Sky added a big bunch
of sunflowers to her basket and joined the checkout line.

She felt a bit overwhelmed with the idea of hosting eight
people for a long weekend and wondered how much she'd
miss Nate. They hadn't spent a night apart in weeks, but
having him out of town did make things easier, at least for this
crowd. That thought brought a guilty twinge.

Sky used the time painting and cleaning and running
errands to plan the special evening when she'd tell Nate she
loved him. It felt good inside, her secret, like when you know
you've found the perfect gift for someone and it sits waiting in
its box. Still, she had to resist the temptation over and over to
blurt it out. She also had the little voice telling her that falling
in love with Nate was a terrible idea. No, it isn't, she told the
voice. We'll figure it out together.

It was a silly romantic idea, but she wanted there to be
candles and a wonderful wine poured into nice wine glasses at
a table set with flowers and white linen napkins. She'd make it
a surprise: she'd tell him she'd picked up a pizza or something,
but she'd answer the door wearing a sexy dress and there
would be a delicious dinner ready to serve.

But the fates had conspired against her. Nate had a Pond
meeting Tuesday night, they were going to Elly and John's
Wednesday, and Nate had to work late Thursday, checking his

jobs before he left the next day. No matter, Sky told herself. Her secret could stay secret a few more days.

Nate threw his dad's old canvas duffle onto the passenger seat. He hoped that the borrowed suit wouldn't come out all wrinkled for Geoff's wedding. The suit and shirt belonged to his fishing buddy, Jim—probably last worn at Jim's own wedding five years earlier. The suit was almost an inch too short in the sleeves and legs, but fit well enough across the shoulders and waist. And the shirt was OK if he left the top button undone and tugged the sleeves down.

Sky had insisted on buying him a new tie after seeing the broad maroon-and-gold-striped number that he'd borrowed from Jim. Too wide, too narrow, too short, too long: Nate didn't see what difference it made so long as he didn't have to wear one of those ridiculous bow ties that reminded him of Pee-wee Herman. His new tie was nice, he admitted, blue with a tiny overall pattern of fish. "Blue fish. And you catch bluefish. And it's sky blue. That's me. This one," Sky had insisted after looking at what seemed like a hundred ties at the Vineyard Vines store. She wouldn't let him see the price, but he was sure it was a waste of money for something he'd never wear again.

Nate's first attempt to knot the thing was pathetic: the front ended up four inches too short, and the narrow end dangled to his belt buckle. Giggling, Sky had adeptly retied it, showing him the prep school trick of slipping it over his head without undoing the knot.

First stop: drop Nan off at Zeke's tent. Leaving Zeke in charge was maybe not the best idea, but Nate didn't really have another choice. He had reset the enclosures on his five jobs, leaving the biggest job, the three pens over in Chappy, for last. The goats would have plenty of fresh brush to eat, reducing the risk of a breakout. Or so he hoped. Mindful of the tree-climbing goat video, Nate had paid attention to where he'd set the fencing and pounded in extra stakes for security. Nan would make the rounds with Zeke to check that the goats were OK. Or at least that was the plan.

Zeke was dead asleep in his blue sleeping bag, snoring like a moose. "Sorry, girl," he apologized to Nan. "You have to stay here." Nan dutifully lay down on the green bathroom mat that served as Zeke's rug. Nate dropped a bag of dog chow onto a table along with his instructions for care and feeding.

"You stay. I'll be back in a couple of days," Nate said, giving Nan a rawhide bone to keep her busy.

"Too early, man," Zeke mumbled as he rolled over. Nan kept her eyes on Nate as she licked her bone, uneasy with this turn of events.

He hadn't been off-island since the spring, too busy with work. Nate pulled into a spot in the ferry line; he was on an early freight boat with most of the Island's garbage. Not the best way to start the day, but a clear blue sky and stiff breeze made the ride pleasant anyway. The garage mechanic had pronounced the beater roadworthy, so long as he didn't go over maybe forty-five miles per hour. That meant that Nate had a back-roads drive of at least four hours to get to Amherst. He'd have time to think.

The beater made the trip without complaint. Nate checked into his hotel and texted Geoff, who was hugely grateful to hand off a long list of errands for Nate to run before the wedding. He spent the day dropping off welcome bags—locally brewed beer, hangover kit, Sky could have his scented candle—at various hotels and inns, picking up someone's turquoise-dyed pumps at the bridal store, and buying a beribboned cake knife at a frou-frou gift shop. Last stop was the tux-rental place to pick up his monkey suit for the wedding ceremony. He hadn't dodged the bow tie after all, but the genteel Italian proprietor sized him up and thoughtfully included a pretied version along with the floppy length of black satin.

Nate showered back at the hotel and reluctantly dressed for the rehearsal in Jim's suit. He slipped on his tie and looked at the pattern of fish on blue. Sky had been so pleased with her choice. Nate grabbed the stack of wedding programs from the printer and headed to the chapel.

"I am so glad you came, Nate. It's great to see you!" called Marianne wearing a snug red wrap dress and teetering heels. She was a bit softer and curvier than in college, but she still had the same bright eyes and dark curls, now with a strand or two of grey. She rose on her tiptoes to kiss Nate on the lips. Nate had almost forgotten the positive force of Marianne's personality. She was both bubbly girl-next-door and indisputably sexy.

"You too, Mari." Nate couldn't resist tugging on one of the dark ringlets that had escaped her bun. "Hey, you look terrific. Are Tad and your little boy here too?"

Marianne's smile dimmed. "I guess you haven't heard. Tad and I divorced last year." Nate hadn't known Tad well in college but hadn't much liked him. Still, he wouldn't wish divorce on anyone.

"I'm sorry, Mari. What happened?" Nate blurted out without thinking. "Probably none of my business."

"No, it's OK. I don't mind telling you. Infidelity. That old story." They sat down in one of the pews. "Tad was working on his doctorate. Comparative religion of all things. Teddy had colic, and Tad decided he needed to pursue field research into the rise of Buddhist retreats on the West Coast. Right." Mari made a wry face. She went on to explain that what Tad found instead of a thesis topic was a lithe yoga instructor named Lindsey, and he also discovered that he didn't much want to be a father.

"That's tough, Mars," said Nate, unsure what to say. "Where are you now?"

"Back home with my parents in Fall River. I know." She shook her head. "But Teddy's the sweetest thing, and my mom is nuts for him, too." Marianne pulled out her phone to show Nate a photo of a chubby-cheeked toddler. "I work in the financial aid office at Brown. I help the kids with scholarships and stuff. And I can telecommute a couple of days a week, so I get to spend time with Teddy. It's not what I thought I'd be doing, but it's OK. Enough about me though." She turned up the voltage on her smile. Nate felt a tingle when she reached for his hand. "Are you still living on the Vineyard? What have you been up to?"

"I have a goatscaping business. The goats clear brush by eating it," he said.

"That's interesting," Mari said. "I didn't know they could do that."

"Marianne!! There you are. You have to help, the florist can't get the roses we picked, and they have to use something else," said one of the other bridesmaids, running up to Marianne. "Meggie's in tears."

"Sorry, Nate. Floral crisis. Catch up later?" Marianne asked, giving his hand a squeeze.

The rehearsal went fine, but the evening afterward with a bunch of people who knew each other really well—and Nate not at all—made for one of the longest nights Nate could remember. He vaguely recognized a few faces but could retrieve no names to match, and he wasn't sure people recognized him without his long hair and scraggly college beard.

It also didn't help Nate's comfort level that he and the groom's father were the only men dressed in suits. At least Geoff's dad's suit fit. Nate felt increasingly like a country bumpkin as creases set in at his elbows and knees, shortening his sleeves and pants even more. Marianne had complimented his blue tie, at least, standing so close that her dark curls tickled his chin as she made a tiny adjustment to the knot. Nate tried a couple of times to pick up his conversation with Mari, but she kept getting pulled away by one group or another, promising "to be back in a minute" over her shoulder.

Despite the dorky suit, Nate was sure he wasn't misreading the looks from a couple of the other bridesmaids, and he had one incredibly awkward encounter outside the restrooms with a tipsy, homely, and apparently horny girl from his freshman dorm he couldn't remember at all.

Back in his hotel room at last, Nate shed the suit with relief and checked his phone. A text from Sky—just a single red heart. He replied with three and fell asleep.

🐐 🐐 🐐

It had been a crazy day of arrivals, and Sky was happy and excited to have succeeded in getting the old gang together again. Some hadn't seen each other since Cole and Inez's wedding, and she wasn't sure if the old connections would still be there. But she needn't have worried. They were all still the same beneath the fancy degrees and successful careers, instantly relaxing in each other's company and falling back into the old affectionate patterns of teasing and nicknames. Alexandra—back to being Lexie and being needled with the rightfully despised "Sexy Lexie"—and Russ had arrived first on a morning ferry to beat the Labor Day traffic. Sky hadn't needed to worry about food: they came off the boat sharing the weight of a big soft-sided cooler. "I figured you still didn't cook, and Russ and I have gotten totally addicted to cooking videos, so we've been making stuff all week! We've brought cinnamon-pecan monkey bread and Cajun shrimp jambalaya and stuff to make Vietnamese banh-mi meatball sandwiches..."

"Don't forget the peanut-butter-stuffed skillet cookies. Those were so good we ate the first batch and had to make 'em again," Russ added. Nor had she needed to worry about her stock of wine: Colin and Keke flew in from New York a couple of hours later and had arranged for a mixed case of Bordeaux to be ready for pickup at MV Wine & Spirits. Hadley and Max had been on the same plane and had checked an extra bag filled with fabulous goodies, including a big box of La Maison du Chocolate pralines, Koeze colossal cashews, elegant pastel Payard macarons, and a bubble-wrapped magnum of Veuve Clicquot champagne. Cole and Inez arrived last on a late afternoon flight. Their house gift had arrived a few days earlier: a set of ten martini glasses and a silver-plated shaker. They needed only to stop to pick up a bottle of Hendrick's gin and jars of olives and pickled onions for their famous filthy dirty martinis.

Her friends loved the house and were amused by the almost completed goatscaping view-enhancement program Sky had undertaken. "We thought Prescott was joking when he told us about your goats and your goatherd," said Hadley. "So, what's next? Chickens and pigs?" she asked.

Dinner had been a raucous affair, starting off with Sky's cheese plate and a bowl of the massive cashews and, of course, a round (or two) of filthy dirtys. Someone—maybe Cole?— had made a college-era playlist on Spotify which had them dancing and singing along to some truly terrible songs, and they were all appalled to find they still remembered all the words. Lexie and Russ insisted on being in charge of food. They served their spicy pasta with a simple salad of the Morning Glory Farm lettuces and tomatoes with an avocado-lime dressing. Hadley popped open the now-chilled champagne to serve with the hedonistic offering of chocolates and the to-die-for peanut butter skillet cookies.

After dinner, Cole and Inez swept in to do the dishes, and Sky pulled out the rest of Trip's blue bottle of single malt for a nightcap on the deck.

The Milky Way was spread across the night sky in a broad arc, an almost-supernatural cloud dotted with bright pinpoints of light. "I didn't know there was anyplace left on the East Coast where you could see, really see, the Milky Way," Colin said. "This is way cool."

"It's magical here. And you seem so happy and relaxed. I don't see how you could ever leave," Hadley whispered to Sky. After a round of warm hugs and good-night wishes, they woke Max, softly snoring in his chair, a half-drunk glass of scotch balanced precariously on his chest, and headed off to their beds.

Trite, but true, there's nothing like old friends.

"Bleah, I really shouldn't have had that scotch. Not after Cole's martinis and the red wine. I thought I'd had enough water, but my mouth feels like a kitty litter box," Hadley said tipping the bottle up as she and Sky sat nursing the baby goats and their hangovers. "Hey, what's that?" A familiar black and white shape came streaking across the field.

"What are you doing here?" Sky exclaimed. Nan lay down outside the pen wagging her tail and panting. "You're supposed to be with Zeke."

"Who's the doggy?" Hadley asked.

"This is Nan, she's…" Sky had almost said "my boyfriend's dog," but she caught herself. "She's a neighbor's dog. I may need to take her home."

"She's cute."

"Supersmart too, and a real sweetie."

Sky wedged the bottle with Clyde still attached between her knees and got out her phone. "Hi Zeke, this is Sky. Nan's here. Do you want me to run her back?"

"Can you keep her? I'm already out on Nate's rounds," Zeke replied.

"Sure. I can drop her off later."

Back at the house, Nan greeted Sky's friends with friendly tail wags and allowed herself to be petted before returning to Sky's side. Sky pulled off a piece of the nearly-demolished monkey bread and munched on the warm cinnamon-sticky sweetness under Nan's adoring eyes. "You're probably hungry too," she said, pulling the dog bowls out of the cabinet. Nan thumped her tail approvingly as Sky filled them with food and water. "Is everyone up now?" Sky asked.

"Almost. Russ is still asleep, that lazybones. What's the plan for today?" Lexie asked.

"I thought we might rent bikes in Oak Bluffs. Anyone who wants some exercise can do the ride on the bike path along Beach Road to Edgartown. It's really nice. Runs along the water almost the whole way," Sky said.

"Biking for me," said Cole.

"Me too," added Inez.

"Anyone else can come to Edgartown with me and look around. The riders and the shoppers can meet for lunch," Sky suggested. "There's a bike trail here from Edgartown so we can keep the bikes for the weekend. I'll borrow a friend's pickup truck to return them to Oak Bluffs on Tuesday."

"To the beach in the afternoon?" asked Cole.

"And I'd love to get down to Menemsha at some point. I've been dreaming about getting littlenecks at Larsen's," said Lexie. Sky's college gang still remembered their favorite Vineyard spots.

"And I want ice cream from the Galley," Colin added.

"I was thinking we'd grill some fish tonight, so we could send people down to Menemsha after the beach to pick up dinner stuff," Sky replied.

"OK. We've got a plan. Time to motivate, people!" Colin announced.

Sky felt like a local, greeting Rob at the Tank and recommending (to Rob's delight) his clam chowder as the best on the Island. Now back at the house, those who weren't riding bikes were getting everything ready for the beach, filling the bags with towels and the coolers with drinks and hunting for hats and spray-on sunscreen. Sky was changing into her swimsuit when she heard the crunch of gravel and slam of a car door.

Nan ran to the door, barking wildly. "Nan, stop that, that's not like you," Sky scolded as she walked to the door. Nan obeyed, but the fur of her ruff stayed raised like a wolf's. Sky was immediately and literally swept off her feet by Francisco's embrace.

"What are you doing here?" Sky sputtered, her voice muffled by his chest. Francisco released Sky briefly, then firmly held her shoulders and planted a soft kiss on her mouth. Irritation rose in Sky like a patch of poison ivy.

"I have been dreaming about you, my cielo, my heaven, my Sky. I was so close. Nantucket. When I heard that my friend Robert was sailing his boat over, I knew that I had to see you."

Sky backed out of his reach. "Oh," said Sky. Now, what was she supposed to do?

Nan began to growl. "Could you ask the beast to let me in?" he asked. "And the sailing made me thirsty. I'd love a glass of ice water. Pellegrino or Perrier, please."

"Nan, to bed," Sky ordered. Nan took up a position on the living room rug where she could keep an eye on the intruder, the fur on her neck still announcing her instinctive dislike of the man wearing the white yachting cap. Francisco dropped his tan Ghurka duffle bag by the door and strode past the kitchen into Sky's living room in full yachting attire—navy blazer, faded Nantucket-red pants, Sperry boat shoes, and a white polo shirt—and sat in the middle of her sofa.

Putting his feet up on the coffee table, he spread his arms across the back of the sofa and smiled. "Come sit next to me, and we can catch up," he said, patting the spot next to him.

Still stunned by the appearance of her uninvited and unwelcome guest, Sky poured Pellegrino into a tall glass with ice, handed it to him, and returned to stand by the counter gritting her teeth. She should say something—what?—and tell him to go away. Nice to see you but please leave now?

"So what is our plan? Shall I change for the beach?" His gaze glided up her bare legs to the sliver of her pink bikini bottom visible at the bottom of her gauze top and up to linger on her chest and go no further.

The front door swung open to admit the first of the sweaty bikers. "Yo, Francisco man, I didn't know you were going to be here," said Cole, giving Sky a broad wink.

"Neither did I," replied Sky under her breath. A mental groan that she hadn't quashed that rumor that she and Francisco were an item.

Next in were Inez and Russ. "Hey, Francisco, good to see you. Just in time for the beach. You coming with us?" Unfortunately for Sky, her friends liked Francisco. He was sociable and fun. And, to be fair, he was good company when he was not in seduction mode. Easy on the eyes as well: darkly handsome, gorgeous hair, and a perfectly sculpted torso—the result of hours spent with a personal trainer.

"I'm just about to change into my swimsuit," Francisco replied, picking up his duffle and heading to Sky's room. All three faces turned to her with eyebrows raised. As the door shut behind him, she realized too late she'd missed her chance. Oh well, what's a couple more hours of Francisco?

🐐 🐐 🐐

"The waves look totally rideable. Come on, let's go," Sky coaxed. Her friends looked like a bunch of lazy sea lions flopping in the sun. Only they had much better physiques.

"We don't have any boogie boards," said Lexie, rolling over. "Russ, put more sunscreen on my back?"

"You don't need boards. We can bodysurf," said Sky.

"I'll just get water up my nose," said Colin.

"I don't want to ride, but I'll go in," said Hadley. "I'm hot."

"Indeed you are," said Cole. Hadley kicked him.

"C'mon you guys. I'll show you. You just wait until the wave is about to break, then kind of jump up and on top of it, with your hands like this," Sky demonstrated as the group walked down the beach, putting her arms out and hands together like she was diving into a pool. "You won't always catch the wave, but when you do, it's like you're the surfboard."

"We bodysurf in Argentina. Schuyler, have you been to Mar del Plata? My family has a house there. You would love it," said Francisco, as they waded into the surf.

"Nope," Sky said as she chased a swell. She was a good bodysurfer, picking her waves carefully and almost always riding all the way onto the beach if she didn't pull up first to avoid getting sandpapered. The waves were breaking clean, helped by a northerly breeze, and most of Sky's friends were able to catch rides. Hadley tired of bodysurfing first and climbed up onto Max's shoulders, leaving him to get smacked by the waves.

"Hey, it's nice up here, Keke. Get up on Colin!" Hadley called. Keke complied, climbing onto Colin's shoulders. Francisco smiled and moved to lift Sky by her waist.

"Sorry, Francisco. No. I'm going to catch that wave." A few quick strokes, and Sky was speeding away.

Sky pulled up in the shallows. That was close. She started to head back out, then stopped as a huge swell rose up in the far line of breakers. Unable to duck, the wave broke over her double-decker friends, knocking them like a line of dominos into the surf.

"I think I've had enough," Colin announced, snorting ocean as he waded to shore. The others followed.

"How about a dip in the pond before we dry off?" Sky suggested. "There's a special on fish exfoliations." Sky was met with dubious looks. "C'mon, I'll show you."

Everyone headed over to the shallow warm water at the edge of the pond and, at Sky's instruction, sat down with just their heads and shoulders sticking out of the water. "Now try to stay still." Before long, dozens of tiny fish were nibbling off flakes of skin. "You know, you can go to fancy spas in the city for fish pedicures and pay a lot of money, but here you can get a full body treatment for free."

"Hmmm," said Hadley, watching the minnows through the clear water. "Interesting. I sort of feel like a fish buffet. I think my flakey feet are the main course."

"OK, Sky. This is weird," Cole added, putting his hands behind him, then leaning back and closing his eyes. "But it's not unpleasant. I wonder whether we're nutritious."

Francisco, less keen to be part of the food cycle, squirmed uncomfortably. "Uh, Sky? I'm going to get out now. The fish are trying to get into my trunks."

🐐 🐐 🐐

Back from the beach, Lexie and Colin collected a few of the others for the drive to Menemsha. "Swordfish steaks, three dozen littlenecks, and some smoked bluefish from Larsen's. And you want us to pick up corn at the farm stand on our way back?" Colin asked. "You sure you don't want those littlenecks on the half-shell?"

"Yup. I'll do it," said Sky. And she could. "What's everybody else up to?"

"Francisco's on a run, and I think the rest of us are going to the Granary Gallery. Maybe stop by a couple of others," said Hadley. "You want to join us, Sky?"

"No. I'll stay here and do some stuff. I still need to take a shower."

For the first time all weekend, the house was quiet. Though she'd managed to stay mostly out of the reach of Francisco's hands, if not his eyes, it still felt good to soap the lingering virtual grease of his gaze off her body. She took her time, scrubbing every inch of her body with the lavender bar and washing her hair twice to get out all the sand.

Sky started to dress then changed her mind. She'd have a cup of tea in her robe in bed and catch up on emails while everyone was out, maybe even sneak in a catnap. But there, standing at the bar was bare-chested and wet-haired Francisco, wearing what must have been one of her hand towels, so small, its ends barely met at his waist.

"You're back from your run," Sky said. She sucked in her breath as irritation popped her shower bliss. It was time to stop being so freaking nice. She wouldn't have picked this scene, but it would have to do.

"Yes, it was fabulous. All that fresh air and nature," Francisco said, puffing out his chest. "I ran into Colin on my way back, he said everyone was out. You were in the shower." He touched his phone. The plaintive guitar chords of a bolero filled the room. Francisco picked up the silver shaker, shook it with a flourish, and poured. He held out a martini glass with a perfect spiral of lemon peel suspended in clear liquid. "Hendrick's, dry, with a twist," he said swiveling his hips. "Just what you like. And then…." He swung his eyes toward the open bedroom door behind Sky.

This was ridiculous. It had to end. She marched into the room and planted her hands on the countertop to face him. "Francisco, keep your towel on," she snapped. "I'm not playing games. I like you as a friend, but I really, truly, absolutely am not interested in you that way."

"The more you say 'no,' the more passionate the 'yes' when it comes." Holding his martini in his hand and her eyes with his, Francisco stepped back and snaked his body to the beat of the music. "And it always comes." Francisco knew that he was good looking. Like a bird of paradise, he puffed and preened and waggled to impress his would-be mate.

"Ugh," Sky puffed in exasperation. She smiled and shook her head. His brio was thicker than marsh muck. "No. No doesn't mean 'maybe later,' Francisco. It doesn't mean 'I'm thinking about it.' It just means no."

He reached for her hand. "But that night, Sky, you know we were good together. Fantastic. But it was just too soon after Gil."

"It was a mistake."

"But you admit we had a connection? I could tell you enjoyed it as much as I did, mi cielo. And I know what you told Winky when she visited."

Again, Sky kicked herself for letting Winky put the Sky-and-the-goatscaper gossip to rest by hinting Sky was interested in Francisco. "It isn't what you think. I don't want to explain. Just believe me: I like you, but I don't want to date you." Francisco just raised his eyebrows. Sky seethed. Nothing she said was going to make a dent. She looked at the kitchen clock. "Don't you need to be getting back to Edgartown? I can take you now."

"Robert's yacht? He was only stopping for lunch. I told him I would be staying the night and would catch the fast ferry back in a day—or two." Sky's heart sank. The last ferry to Nantucket left in less than 30 minutes. There was no way he could make it. "If I miss the boat, no problem. If not your bed this time, your sofa?"

The wedding went off without a hitch. The tiny ring bearer looked terrified but didn't drop the rings. The Old Chapel was lit only by candles. The bride's gown and pale flowers glowed in the dim light, and the short ceremony was just as lovely and romantic as the bride had hoped. The reception started as a dignified affair but soon turned raucous as the wine flowed and a reliving-our-college-days party vibe took over.

"Why Nate, I haven't seen you in a hound's age." An impeccably barbered man in gold-rimmed glasses dropped into the chair next to Nate and clapped him soundly on the shoulder. "To Geoff," he said, raising his glass in a toast. "He's looking as happy as a dead pig in the sunshine." Nate drank, then searched his memory, trying to figure out who this could be and what he meant about the dead pig.

"Greg?" If he hadn't heard that voice with its soft Georgia vowels, he'd never have known his freshman suitemate, the wildest of the bunch. He'd been nicknamed Chong for his looks and bad habits.

"Wasn't sure you were going to figure out who I was." He grinned. "Turns out I had a fine legal mind under all that hair. I'm back in Atlanta: excellent wife, two little girls, joined my father-in-law's firm," Greg said anticipating the next set of questions. "C'mon, let's get refills and head outside for a doobie, for old time's sake."

Greg had always been a bad influence, and tonight was no different. By the time the reception was winding down, Nate was sitting glazed and dazed, watching the final few wedding guests dance with drunken abandon as Marianne led them in a conga line. Greg, guided back to his room by his wife, was long gone. Nate's tux jacket was off, and he'd lost the bow tie. He thought that he'd been dancing at some point too, but wasn't sure. Not that it mattered. He was drunk and very tired, and he was way too stoned. The pale-yellow table top looked like a very fine place for just a little nap.

🐐 🐐 🐐

When Nate woke up, his head was throbbing and his bladder uncomfortably full. Light streamed through a crack in the brown and maroon striped curtains, piercing his eyelids, and intensifying the sharp pain behind his eyeballs. He lay in bed, flat on his back, unwilling to move. Nate wasn't quite ready to open his eyes yet. He lay there, hoping that he'd remembered to pack Advil. Oh, never mind, the hangover kit. Realizing he was awake, his bladder forced him to action and he swung his legs over the side of the bed.

Marianne sensed the shift in Nate's weight and propped herself up on one elbow. Nate felt the movement and turned with an expression that mixed bewilderment and alarm. "Oh, don't look like that," she said, one side of her generous mouth turned up in a wry smile.

"Uh, hi," he replied, "I'll be right back." Nate relieved his discomfort and swallowed two Advil tablets and a glass of water. He paused in the doorway of the bathroom in his boxers. Nope. She really was in his bed. He had no recollection of how Marianne—or, for that matter, he himself—had made it to his room. She had propped up the pillows on his side of the bed and, with an inviting look, patted his side of the mattress. Nate lay down, sick with his hangover and at what he might have done.

"No, we didn't," she replied to his unspoken question with a laugh. "But we can if you want to? For old time's sake?" Marianne's hand moved lightly across his chest, then started to slip under the sheet. Nate held her wrist, stopping her before the hand could move into dangerous territory. Unfortunately, his self-control did not extend to his entire body.

Marianne looked longingly at the part of Nate that did want her before rolling back to stare at the ceiling. "Sorry. It was worth a try. How are you feeling?"

"Pretty crappy. Thanks for getting me back."

"Yeah, it took a couple of us to get you in bed. You were zonked out." She turned onto her side. "I always wondered what would have happened to us if you hadn't left school. A lot of the time, I think I really screwed up. I could have tried to make it work long distance." She looked at him wistfully. "I really was in love with you, you know. And my marriage turned out to be a disaster. Obviously. But, of course, then I wouldn't have had Teddy." She patted Nate's shoulder. "Still, it's nice to wake up with a man in bed next to me. That hasn't happened in a while." A shadow passed over her face. "It's lonely being a single parent. Guys aren't exactly lining up to date a woman with a little kid."

"No, Mari, it's not that. And you're still beautiful and sexy and…. It's just that I'm seeing someone." For how much longer, he didn't know. Maybe he should think about what would happen after Sky left.

It was as if Marianne had read his mind. "Fall River isn't far, so if it doesn't work out with her you'll let me know? No excuses. I'm going to put my number in your phone."

Marianne paused to look at Nate and sighed. "Or we could just see each other as friends. Maybe Teddy and I can come over on the ferry sometime? He'd love it—and your goats."

"He's what, two now?"

"Two and a half, and all over the place," she said with a fond smile. Marianne reached across Nate to take his phone from the bedside table. "You've got a bunch of messages here. Zeke's still around?" She tapped in her number, put the phone on Nate's bare chest, and stood up to go. "I'd better get ready for the brunch. Don't worry, I won't ruin your reputation. See you there?"

"Yeah. And thanks again."

Bleary-eyed and nauseous, Nate looked at his cell: three voicemails and four texts. The last one, at 7:22 a.m., was from Zeke: *Going back to Chappy call me.* Heart sinking, he looked at the texts, all from Zeke: 5:57 p.m., *goats loose in Mytoi shit call me*" 7:22 p.m., *got 3.* At 7:41 p.m., *too dark to look call me.* Nate's queasiness set into a painful lump in the pit of his stomach. If the goats had eaten the Japanese gardens at Mytoi, there was no limit to what it would cost to repair the damage.

He listened to the voicemails. The first was from Sky, hoping he was having a good time, that she missed him, and that he should give her a call to tell her how the wedding went. The second was from an unknown caller. "Mr. Batchelor, please call me as soon as possible. This is Julie Clark from Mytoi, and it's about your goats. My cell is…." The last message was left by an almost incoherent Zeke: "Hey man, it's pretty bad. I tried. We all tried. We couldn't catch those damn devil goats, and I went back for Nan, and the ferry line was, shit man, when I got back they were all over Mytoi, and one is still out there somewhere. I'm sorry, dude."

Marianne emerged from the bathroom and saw Nate's stricken face. "What's wrong?"

"I think I just lost my business."

THIRTY-ONE

Still feeling like crap on toast, Nate found Zeke sitting up against an unchewed Japanese maple. A blanket-covered lump lay nearby. Zeke looked thoroughly dejected, his eyes red and puffy.

"He's dead, Nate. Nan found him here this morning." Zeke rubbed his face, trying to hide the fact that he was about to start crying again. He didn't particularly like goats, but dead or injured animals, even a squashed bunny in the road, could bring tears to his eyes. "I think that's Dillinger, but I'm not sure." Nate lifted the blanket to look at the lifeless black goat. "Yup, that's him. I wonder what he ate." Nate looked around and spotted the distinctive flower stalks of the foxglove plant now gone to seed. "It's OK, Zeke. It looks like he ate foxglove—you know, digitalis, the heart medicine. He would have just had a heart attack and died instantly. Probably didn't even know what was happening."

A group of people clustered around one of the bigger Dr. Seuss bushes on the far side of the garden. Even from afar, Nate could tell it looked like it was a victim of a botanical Texas Chainsaw Massacre. Zeke explained as they walked over. "I don't know what happened, man. I came on Friday morning, and all the pens were fine. Then I came back yesterday afternoon, and the far pen, you know, the one down by the swamp, was completely flattened and the goats were gone." Zeke rubbed his eyes again and went on with his story.

"So I start looking around. I don't have Nan because she's decided to go over to Sky's. She doesn't much like my tent. I've got the rope, but there's no sign of goats. Then the owners see me marching around and come to tell me that they've gotten a call from Mytoi, and the goats are there eating all the plants, and they've given them your number."

"Yeah, they left a message, but I didn't see it," Nate explained, kicking himself again for having forgotten to turn his ringer back on after the ceremony.

"So I hop back in the Jeep and head over there. There's all these people running around yelling at the goats. You know how they wait until you are just about to grab them and then dance off and look at you with those yellow devil eyes? So everything's all chewed up, and they've caught one that they've tied to a bumper with a garden hose. I think the people who work here are in shock. I figured I wasn't going to have any more luck catching them, so I tell them I'll be right back with the sheepdog—goatdog—whatever you call her."

Nate paused to inspect the damage to a low-growing threadleaf maple. "You were probably right to get Nan," he reassured Zeke.

"So I get stuck in the ferry line again. I tried to tell the ferry lady it was an emergency, but she was like 'wandering goats are not an emergency.' We finally get over, Nan gets them herded up in no time flat. You know how she gets down low and stares at them. It's like she's got doggie superpowers or something. They just freeze. We catch three more, and now it's dark, and we look and look but no number five. I give up and try to get the other goats back. You ever tried to walk four goats on a rope down a long dirt road in the dark? It's hard, man. And the pen was still busted, so I had to add them to the other goats, who were not happy." Zeke shook his head, still looking traumatized. "And then old Dillinger has to up and die..." Nate patted Zeke on the shoulder.

"Thanks, Zeke. I mean it. You did the best anyone could do. I'm just really sorry you had to go through this."

Zeke's expression shifted from sadness to concern as he decided whether to unload one more piece of bad news on his best and oldest friend. "And I hate to say anything, but I guess you should know. That guy, the rich Latin-lover dude I saw all over Sky the other week in Edgartown? Looks like he's staying with her this weekend." Nate's expression froze as Zeke continued. "When I went to get Nan, it was just the two of them in her house." Zeke stopped there to save his friend the details. The sick lump in Nate's belly constricted to a ball of pure pain. He winced. "Shit. When it rains it pours," Zeke said. "I'm sorry. I warned you, man."

They crossed the arched wooden bridge over the pond over to the Mytoi staff. A small white-haired woman stood stroking the devastated remains of a leafy puff with her hand, tears streaming down her cheeks.

Nate sighed. "Let's see how bad it is."

Weeks would pass before Nate would know what it would take to restore Mytoi, or what it would cost. The staff would arrange for a team of master gardeners to come from Boston to do an assessment. Despondent, Nate spent the rest of the long weekend contemplating the awful turn of events. One day. Two disasters. Just like that, his life was as tattered as that tiny threadleaf maple.

His brain toggled back and forth between two images, one real, one imagined, like a slide show with only two slides: the first, the ravaged Mytoi garden, and the second, Sky and her Latin lover. Nate had dragged a few more details out of an unhappy, reluctant Zeke: that Sky had been in her robe, music was playing, both were drinking martinis, and that after saying something that made Sky smile and shake her head, the guy did one of those sexy salsa hip moves for her in his little towel. Nate could only come up with one explanation for what Zeke had seen.

It all fit. Prescott and Winky, Francisco: this was Sky's life. These were her friends. And her other lover. The thought of Sky with another man was a jagged knife. Even when he could push that image away, he couldn't stop thinking about her. He'd look over in his truck and expect to see her there, the wind through the open window whipping her light hair, a half-smile on her face as the fields rolled by. How could she have lied? About the old barn, about this guy. She had seemed so honest, so loving.

Or maybe she didn't see it as a lie. She'd never promised to be faithful or said a word about the sale of the barn. She could be one of those people who think a lie by omission isn't a real lie. He remembered that brief—but unmistakable—look of relief on her face when she'd learned that he'd be away that weekend.

Pure cluelessness on his part. He had missed what he hadn't wanted to see. He'd let their lovemaking blind him to who she was. He should have known. The clues were all there. Maybe a different guy could deal with an open relationship, but he couldn't. Like Zeke said, just do it clean and fast, and try to move on. Nate had no interest in bringing up this Latin lothario and hearing her try to explain. Or the barn. What he knew already was enough. Too much.

A half-truth would be best, he decided. He'd tell Sky that he'd reconnected with Marianne at the wedding and felt honor bound to break it off with her. Who knew? Maybe someday, he would look up Marianne and pick up where they'd left off.

No need to let Sky know he was back early, let her enjoy the rest of her weekend with her friends and her lover. With that thought, the knife twisted again, deeper this time. Nate simply couldn't understand how—why—she could have done this. And his mind slid to rest in a dark, devastated place.

THIRTY-TWO

Hosting that big gang had been hugely fun, but after three days of nonstop socializing and partying, Sky was relieved to make the last trip to the ferry. Getting rid of Francisco had been easy. She'd checked the ferry schedule and announced to him that he was leaving, and that was that. Sky had shut down her friends' questions with a simple "he left." They could think what they wanted.

Her thoughts drifted over the highlights of the weekend. As she'd hoped, her shucking skills had impressed the gang. "How did you learn to open clams?" Hadley had asked, dabbing a bivalve with cocktail sauce.

"A friend taught me," Sky had replied as she twisted off the top shell and loosened the clam with her knife. "The trick is to put them in the freezer for a few minutes first." She'd figured out the rest on her own—the Zen of imagining the knife sliding between the shells before giving it a gentle push.

Sky would be doing sheets and towels for days, but a quiet week with the washer and dryer and—best of all, Nate—would be wonderful. She felt a bit guilty that she hadn't thought about him all that much. Mostly, she'd missed him in her too-big and too-empty bed. With the guests gone, her mind was free to return without distraction to thinking about her Nate and their pending reunion. Like a giddy schoolgirl, she played out scenarios worthy of a Harlequin romance: the two of them running into each other's arms, kissing passionately, and uncontrollably ripping off their clothes before succumbing to thrusty-lusty lovemaking on the kitchen counter. Or maybe the sofa. No way would they make it all the way to the bedroom.

But Sky's real plan was different. She took a deep breath and, just to be sure, emptied her mind and asked herself again, Could this be just a rebound, an infatuation rooted in sexual desire? Was she sure that this was love? The answer, bypassing her brain, came straight from her heart. No hesitation. No doubt: I love him. Relieved, she felt happiness wash over her body. Tonight, she'd tell him.

Nate was going to catch the 5:30 ferry, so she had a few hours to get ready. They'd start with a few littlenecks, then have the leftover lobster salad with avocado and blueberry pie. Sky brought down the dahlias from the guest rooms as a centerpiece, set the table with linens, and arranged the leftover cheeses on an oval wooden platter with cashews and figs. She decided on her soft cotton halter dress, hair up in a loose bun (Nate loved tugging the strands that fell out down her neck), and an aquamarine pendant to rest low in her cleavage. Dusk was falling, the candles were lit, and Sky was turning on Nate's favorite playlist when she heard the truck pull into the drive. Smiling, she opened the door.

Nan jumped out first and ran to Sky, tail wagging with joy. "Good girl, so you went back and stayed with Zeke like you were supposed to," Sky said as she patted Nan's head. Nate was slow getting out of the truck, and she could see from a distance that something was wrong. Very wrong.

"Nate, what is it?" she said stepping carefully on the gravel drive in her bare feet. "Are you OK? What happened?" Nate's whole body wore his dejection, and his face was grim. "Come in. I'll get you something, and then you have to tell me what's wrong." Nate dragged himself out of the truck and, with hundred-pound feet, walked toward the thing he didn't want to do but had to.

He slumped onto a stool at the kitchen counter, his head in his hands. Sky poured him a glass of wine and walked over to touch him gently on the shoulder. She couldn't imagine what had happened. "Nate. Tell me," she pleaded. Nate lifted his eyes. Sky had never looked so lovely or desirable. No wonder she had lovers. He needed to just say what he needed to say and follow Zeke's advice: "Just make it clean and fast, man. Get it over with, and get out of there."

"Sky, I saw my ex-girlfriend at the wedding, and, well, there was still a spark. I'm not the kind of guy who can see two women at the same time so…" Sky couldn't believe what she was hearing.

"What do you mean?" Sky asked in a tiny, tight voice. Was this really happening?

Nate continued, looking down at his hands. "So, what I'm saying is that we need to break up." He stood and bit his lip. "I'm sorry. I don't want to hurt you, but this is how it is. I'm sorry." Sky sat stunned. Nate turned to his dog. "C'mon Nan, let's go."

THIRTY-THREE

A northeaster was coming in, and Nate needed to get all the goats off their jobs and into his uncle's barn or risk another escape during the three-day storm. The goats had sensed the drop in the air pressure and had become uneasy and skittish. Nate drove from one end of the Island to the other collecting goats. It was exhausting work, even with Nan's help, but it helped keep his mind off Sky. At least a little. At the Homets', he collected four unhappy, bleating goats. He thought he had them secured in the trailer when he went to rope number five, but the unhappy creatures were jumping around so much, they worked the latch loose, leaped out, and scattered. Chasing them down took more than an hour. Nate was miserable and tired and bruised. He had been butted—hard—by sweet Bugs and kicked by both Butch Cassidy and Wyatt. Yet the physical pain was nothing compared with the hurt he'd inflicted on himself in breaking up with Sky.

Not wanting to face Sky, he had left her goats for last. Nate couldn't get rid of the vision of her standing in her kitchen in her pretty blue dress, stunned, her eyes wide with disbelief at what he had said. It had felt deeply, fundamentally wrong. He kept running down all the reasons why it was the right thing, the necessary thing. The cheating, of course. But she was also behind the sale of the barn, which was unforgivable, her knowing how much it meant to him and his family. And all the rest—her money, education, snobby rich friends, city life, all of it. No way he wasn't some sort of summer fling, a way of amusing herself for a few weeks. The summer was over. And she was, after all, a summer person; it was just a matter of time before she left him to pick up her real life again. He had maybe moved up the inevitable by what, a week or two? The outcome was going to be the same either way. But Nate couldn't shake the persistent feeling that he had made a terrible mistake.

The wind had picked up when he arrived dirty and bone-tired at Sky's, and the first fat raindrops were beginning to pelt him from the dark sky. The weather was fast turning ugly; he'd better get this done quickly and check that the rest of the beasts weren't knocking down the walls of the barn. Nate parked the goat trailer in Sky's field and walked across to the enclosure, his brain telling him that he wanted her to stay inside and his heart yearning to see her and undo what he had done.

Sky sat on the sofa where she had just spent the previous two hours in an almost catatonic state as the reality of the breakup finally sunk in. Turning sideways, she pulled up the throw and stared out the window. Nate was striding across the field, rope in hand, faithful Nan at his heels, as the rain pushed across the pond from the north in narrow, intense bands.

The night after Nate had left was a blur. She must have put the food away and cleared the table, but she had no recollection of doing so. Still in a daze, she had picked up the notes she had jotted the afternoon before—yoga, laundry, kayaks, check windows, deck furniture, supermarket (milk, TP, dish soap)—and began to follow it unthinkingly.

No Elly at yoga: the school year had started and she was back teaching. More out of habit than hunger, Sky stopped to pick up a scone and coffee and drove back to the house. She checked her list and moved from task to task like an automaton, stripping the beds, starting the washer, and moving on to batten down the house for the storm. It was the strangest thing: the feeling of being detached from reality, like being in a dream or under some mind control drug.

Sky had been getting texts and emails throughout the day from her houseguests effusively thanking her again for the weekend. She'd replied, over and over again, *So much fun! Be sure to pencil in next year!* Her mother had left a message: "Call me, Schuyler, dear, I want to talk to you." That, she had ignored.

Then the storm began in earnest. Great sheets of rain lashed the man and dog in the field. His work shirt now plastered to his chest like a dark blue stain, Nate struggled with the goats huddled, catatonic in a corner of the pen. Sky wanted to be with him, to help him, to love him, but he didn't want her. With that thought, the tears began.

Nate listened to the banshee wind howl and roar around the tiny cottage as the rain battered the roof and windows. The sky was dark, and he turned on the kitchen light. He started the coffee and looked over at Zeke still snoring on the sofa. Zeke had already settled into Nate's house for the storm by the time Nate got back from putting Sky's goats in the barn. "Yeah, I put the tent and table in your shed. Sorry I brought over all my crap. You don't mind if I do some laundry while I'm here, do you?" Piles of Zeke's clothes, bedding, and cardboard boxes of who knew what were strewn around Nate's small living room.

Nate turned on the weather radio to get the latest marine forecast for the Cape and Islands, not caring if he woke Zeke. The automated Scandinavian voice he'd nicknamed Sven was intoning: gale warnings, sustained winds up to forty knots with gusts up to sixty-five, sea heights eight to ten feet, small craft immediately to seek protected anchorage. The small cottage had weathered hundreds of such storms and would do fine in this one, give or take a few shingles, but he'd better fill the oil lamps and get out the flashlights. It was only a matter of time before they lost power. He thought of Sky weathering the storm by herself, another painful pang. She probably hadn't been through a true northeaster before. Nate had almost stopped by the house to make sure she was prepared, but, in the end, he couldn't. Just couldn't.

The sky had turned an ominous purple, and the pond roiled dark and angry. His buddy provided a welcome distraction. They'd talked Red Sox for a while as Zeke sorted through his clothes. Then, the conversation had moved to the new girlfriend. Maybe it was Eva's prediction coming true, maybe not, but Zeke and Batty had become an item.

"I don't know if you want to be hearing about another guy's love life right now, man, but Batty, she's voracious." Afraid he'd put his foot in it, Zeke looked at Nate with concern. "How did it go with Sky yesterday. You guys broke up, right?"

Nate's expression grew even more grim. "Not fun, but it's over. I don't feel like talking about it." A powerful gust bashed the north side of the cottage, and he heard a few shingles work loose. "But tell me about you and Batty. She's been after you for years. What happened?"

"Ah, fate, kismet. You know her Labor Day party? She pulled out this limoncello stuff she'd made. Like lemonade liquor. Damn. It's good. I think I killed a bottle. Party went late, so I was crashing on her sofa." Zeke made a pile of socks and started sorting through them. "Middle of the night, I'm looking for the bathroom and go into her room instead. She's asleep, naked in this blue moonlight. With no clothes on, she's beautiful, man." Nate didn't particularly want to envision Batty's high school champion discus-throwing body nude, but Zeke kept on. "Then it's like I'm the tide and she's got this pair of big full moons pulling me to the bed…"

"Good for you, Zeke. Batty's a fine woman," Nate interrupted.

But Zeke wasn't done yet. "Maybe she put some love potion in the lemon liquor stuff, I don't know. But like I said, she's one voracious female. You ever noticed the muscles on the inside of her legs?"

"Uh, not really."

"Man, with Batty, it's like she's the nutcracker and I'm the nut. I'm getting crushed!" A faint smile came across Nate's face as he pictured skinny Zeke trapped in a pair of massively muscled thighs. "This storm, I am so glad to hang with you for a few days and recharge. That woman's drained me dry."

"Happy for the company, Zeke," Nate said, meaning it.

"Oh, and you know how she cooks," Zeke continued on, smitten. "Her Italian grandmother taught her how to make pasta like a dozen different ways. It's carb city over there. And her sourdough bread, whoa, it is so good I have to get her to bake you a loaf. She's got this little glob of dough that lives in the fridge, and she has to feed it flour and water. She calls it SpongeBob…" Zeke rattled on as Nate listened with half an ear and finished his coffee. He got up to find his yellow oilskin.

"Good on you. Really. I've got to get over to the barn to check on the beasts."

The goats were not happy. Nate had gotten soaked just walking from the truck to the barn. He didn't really have enough room in the empty pens and stalls for them all, so he'd put them where he could, trying to keep compatible goats together. At the end of the barn in the old pig enclosure, two gangs were ramming each other in a goat version of street fighting. Nothing he could do about that. He hoped they'd figure out who was top goat before any of them got hurt. The goats loudly bleated their complaints as Nate replenished their hay and water. He stopped where Sky's goats stood uncomfortably close together, glaring at him with their yellow and tan eyes. Billy voiced a particularly long and articulate meh to protest being stuck in a horse stall and butted the door. Hard to believe it had been only a month since he'd taken them to Sky's place. He remembered that day, watching her laugh as she ran after the escapees in her boots and cutoffs, Nan at her heels. Nate felt sick. She'll be gone soon, he thought, and things will have to get better.

A long, horrible night.

The outdoor shower door crashed against the house, waking Sky with a start to a familiar, sick feeling. The door bashed against the house again, hard. She sat up and looked at the clock: 6:42. Shit.

Standing brought a wave of nausea, paired with the acid bite of bile in her throat. *Omigod, I hope I'm not getting sick too.* Sky went to the bathroom for a Pepto and a glass of water and then looked for twine and her raincoat. If she didn't secure the banging door, it would either tear off its hinges or drive her crazy.

Outside, the storm, pleased to find a new victim, whipped the hood from her head and beat Sky's face and hair with cold, stinging needles. The door hung loose with a busted latch, swinging on its hinges. A gust of wind bashed it open again, and this time something cracked. Sky struggled to thread the twine through the gaps in the boards to tie the door shut. If nothing else, she'd keep her house from blowing away.

Chilled and wet on top of being tired, sick, and heartbroken, Sky unzipped her slicker and let it drop to the floor. Unable to stop thinking about Nate, she stood there, dripped, and sobbed. Sniveling and shivering, Sky finally changed out of her wet pajamas and put on a pair of sweatpants. She shouldn't, but she let herself, for a moment, pretend that it hadn't happened. Pretended that she was waiting for Nate to come in from the storm soaked and muddy. Sky would take off his wet clothes, and they'd make love with the wind howling and rain pounding against the windowpanes. Then they'd lie curled together, warm and dry and sated, and sleep.

Sky started some toast and tea to settle her stomach. For the first time, she felt abjectly, miserably alone in this house that she loved. Maybe she'd feel better if she talked to somebody. She could call Eva and Trip. Or maybe Elly. There wasn't anyone else she could talk to about Nate. Winky would be kind, but she wouldn't understand. And she'd have to say— out loud, what Nate had told her. No. *I'm not ready.* Not ready for sympathy and hearing all the reasons she and Nate didn't belong together or that she'd get over him and soon realize this was all for the best—for them both.

Her cell beeped with a text from Winky. ESP, huh. Sky clicked on the message. *Bad news, Sky. There's another offer. How could that happen? And the historic preservation society has been looking at the barn. Awful if we couldn't tear it down! Will let you know—fingers crossed. Love to Nate, W.*

"I guess that's good news, sort of," she said to the empty house. Lord and Lady Nelson must have offered to buy the whole thing, not just repair the barn. But they'd want to save the barn, right? The glimmer of hope was dashed by another thought: it was just as likely they'd take it down as an ugly eyesore.

Sky's stomach rumbled a complaint over her despair. She had just sat down on the sofa with toast and jelly when the house went dark. "Oh, great," she groaned. She lit a candle and put it on the table next to the sofa (more for its company than its light) and dug around in the kitchen drawer for a flashlight.

Hours passed in the near dark. She began to feel unhinged, sitting with the rain lashing at the window, the wind howling. Before this summer, Sky had never taken a break from the pressure of thinking about the future. She'd been so totally focused on planning the perfect life that was expected—demanded—of her: the Ivy League education, ideal career, perfect wedding. Until that life fell apart. And she nearly had, too. She'd put the pieces back together, but like a new mosaic, the pattern wasn't the same. She couldn't go back to the way she'd been before. And the blissful option—not thinking about the future, just doing what she loved on the Island she loved, and loving Nate—was gone.

She had to think about what she'd do next. Stay here? That was obviously a terrible idea under the circumstances. Go back to the city and put some version of her old life back together? That probably makes the most sense: it's what everyone expected. But the thought of all the people and the buildings and noise and grit, let alone apartment hunting and finding a new job, just added depression to the basket. Maybe she could try a new city. San Francisco, perhaps. She could couch surf with friends and study for the California bar until a job turned up. Or go to stay with Eva and Trip. They'd been pestering her for ages about visiting Vermont. It would be lovely there in the fall, and they'd understand about Nate. Or even travel for a while. She could go to see all the places her father had told her about when she was a child: Asia, South America, even Africa. I could afford that on the income from Grams's trust if I hang out with the backpacking crowd.

Sky felt paralyzed. Closing her eyes, she took some deep breaths to clear her mind. Then she asked herself, "What do I want to do next? Where do I want to be?" Anguished, she knew. Here, on Martha's Vineyard, in Nate's arms.

THIRTY-FOUR

The northeaster, like a stumble-drunk uncle, appeared to have no interest in relinquishing its grip. The gale-force winds bowed the Blacksmith Cottage's walls like a sail, opening gaps in the flashing. Nate set up a saucepan to catch the rain and sat in his chair staring out the window, a book in his lap, listening to the incessant drip-drip-drip of water hitting the metal pan. Other than that, and the howling wind outside, the cottage was quiet. Nate was alone with his thoughts. Batty had braved the storm around midday to pick up a rested Zeke for another bout with the nutcracker, kindly leaving a still-warm loaf of sourdough bread for Nate's lunch.

Nate looked over at the big brown paper bag in the corner that held the gift he had intended for Sky's birthday. He got up and stretched. Then he walked over to pull out the sailor's box that Joan had painted. On a whim, Nate had stopped at Joan's gallery one day. Joan had suggested a barter if he really wanted the box. She and Dick had some land they were putting up for sale up on the moraine, and they were pretty sure there would be a distant water view with the right clearing. Nate had agreed to bring his goats over once his other fall jobs were finished, and the box was his.

He examined the delicate painting of the catboat cutting through the waters of the pond. It was exquisite. The artist had perfectly captured the angle of the hull and sail to the wind and the lines of wake trailing the small boat. The small trunk, called a seaman's ditty box, was the sort sailors had used to hold personal items—letters, tobacco, mementos, shaving supplies, and the like—while they were at sea. The lozenge-shaped piece of wood on the top bore the original owner's initials, N.A.B. Not quite his initials, Nate's much-loathed middle name was Tristram, after one of his forebears, a whaling captain on the *Charles W. Morgan*. He opened the box to look at the lucky stone he'd put inside for her and sighed. He couldn't take the box back: you don't go back on a barter. He wondered if he should give it to Sky anyway, but would she want anything from him?

A wave of sadness washed over Nate. Sky had loved the box, and he wanted her to have it, and it didn't belong here in his dump of a mildewed shack. He'd write a note and drop it off after the storm, and she could do what she wanted. Nate tore out a piece of notebook paper and tried to think what to say. After several failed attempts, he simply wrote, "Sky, this was meant for you. Nate."

By the third day of the storm, Sky was feeling crazy, lonely, and still not well. The days she'd been trapped in the house—the dark gale pounding at the windows and roof and nothing to keep her company but thoughts of Nate and her suddenly rudderless life—had taken their toll.

As Shy climbed out of her rumpled bed, a wave of nausea rose in her throat. Running to the bathroom, the remains of the previous night's scrounged dinner made an unexpected exit. She looked in the bathroom mirror as she brushed her teeth and rinsed her sour mouth: greasy hair, bleary red eyes, skin like the green witch Elphaba's, wrinkled pajamas. What a prize. The last time she had looked in the mirror, it was to admire the effect of her outfit-to-seduce getup. Like her spirits, the pretty blue dress now lay crushed in the corner.

Sky had gotten the idea that this was some sort of karmic backlash, that the jealous and fickle gods were punishing her for her happiness. She could feel the dark edges of depression lurking and needed to get out even if it was just to talk to the grumpy storekeeper at Alley's.

But where could she go? Places in Vineyard Haven might be open, she could try there if the driving wasn't too bad. And get something to eat too. Everything in the refrigerator had grown warm and had been tossed into the trash. Another almond butter and jelly sandwich held no appeal. Over to Elly's? Elly would offer sympathy and good sense along with a strong cup of tea: an appealing combination. Sky had just turned on her cell to look up Elly's number when it rang. Shit. Lucretia. Unwillingly, she hit answer.

"You've been a terrible child, Schuyler, not returning your mother's calls," Sky's mother scolded in her elegant voice, "I have been trying to reach you for days and days."

"We've got a big storm up here, and the power's been out, so I've been keeping my cellphone off to save the battery," Sky explained.

"Well, you should have called me anyway."

"How was the Galapagos?"

"Too many animals. Tedious people on the ship. Your father loved it."

"I'm sorry you didn't have a better time," Sky said, remembering with pain that the last time she'd talked to her mother, Nate had distracted her with pebbles and shells.

"That wasn't why I was calling. The doctors were able to reschedule my little operation to Monday afternoon, and while it is nothing to worry about, your father went off gallivanting around chingchung province or something, so I had hoped you might be back."

"What little operation?" Sky asked. Her mother always downplayed her ailments, so the fact that she was hearing about this worried Sky.

"As I said, dear, it's nothing to worry about. Just one of those things we older people need to have done." Sky knew she wasn't going to get any information out of Lucretia if she didn't want to give it. "But I need someone to go with me."

"Yes, of course. I'll come. I'll look into flights and let you know when I can get in," Sky said, relieved to have some sort of plan, a decision made for her.

"Oh, and dear, you might want to think about giving Francisco a tad more encouragement. He seemed not quite in high spirits after his last visit with you. I've counseled him to be patient while you were getting over that whole Gil fiasco, but it may be time to reel him in, else some other woman will move in and take your catch." That, at least, was good news.

"We can talk about Francisco, if we must, when I get home," Sky said.

Nate spent the day checking on and repairing the storm damage to the enclosures on his jobs. The air was clear and blue and fresh. He listened to the WMVY local news report as he drove up-Island: a forty-two-foot sailboat had come loose from its mooring in Menemsha, bashing into a bunch of fishing boats, and the ferries were back on a normal schedule. Nate wondered how Sky had done by herself in the storm. He'd debated whether to bring the painted box with him or to wait a few more days before risking seeing her. Nate put the brown bag on the floor of the passenger side of the truck. Better to get it over with. He continued on his loop next to the North Shore, then back around to Edgartown and Chappy. It was afternoon by the time he was back in West Tisbury.

An unfamiliar car sat in front of Sky's house, and there was no sign of her Jeep. Nate had told himself that it would be best not to see her. "Nan, stay here. I'm only going to be a minute." Nan sat on the bench seat, wagging her tail and looking at Sky's house.

A woman of indeterminate age answered the door with a mop in her hand. "You looking for Sky? You just missed her. Cab took her to the airport. I'm here doing the closing up." The carpets were rolled and furniture covered by sheets for the winter. Nate's heart sank. She'd left.

Franny cocked her head to look more closely at Nate. "You Sky's fella? I don't like getting into other people's personal business, but she wasn't looking so good. Like she's been sick or something. All pale and weak and kinda green around the gills, you know. Worried me. You might want to give her a call and make sure she's all right."

"Thanks, uh, yeah," said Nate. "Would you put this inside somewhere for her? There's a note."

"Sure, but she told me to close up the house tight like she isn't coming back until next summer," Franny said. "She even unhooked the battery from the car in the garage. You'd better send it to her if it's something she needs."

"No. It's nothing she needs," Nate said. "It can wait."

Sky lugged her rollaboard and duffle bag up the front steps, pausing for a moment on the portico before ringing the bell. The door was answered almost immediately, and Sky happily found herself in Georgie's strong round arms. "It's been too long. You never come home anymore!" Georgie said in her faint island accent. "Let's get these bags in and get you something to eat and we can catch up." Sky felt better just being in the presence of her old nanny. She was a fabulous cook, wicked funny and smart, and she loved Sky to bits.

The last time Sky had been home, the elegant hall, living rooms, and dining areas had been decorated with large, dark antique Persian carpets, mahogany furniture, and overstuffed tapestry sofas. Now, modern carpets in shades of gray and azure blue looked like abstract art paintings on the floor, and sleek contemporary gray and chrome sofas flanked the fireplace. The white dining room table with its spindly metal legs looked like it belonged in the Jetsons' Skypad apartment, and her favorite Queen Anne grandfather clock had been replaced with a stainless-steel timepiece.

"Yes. Your mother has been redecorating again. Absolutely nothing wrong with that old furniture, but she went and changed it all up. Don't worry. She left your room alone this time, and she wasn't allowed to touch your father's library. Or my kitchen," Georgie said. Georgie had fiercely resisted Lucretia's efforts to redo Sky's room into a more spacious office for herself.

Sky took her usual place at the kitchen island. Queen Catty, Lucretia's nasty Himalayan, hissed as Sky walked in.

"Yeah, I missed you too," Sky said.

"Shoo, you old cat," said Georgie. She pulled a large pan out of the warming oven. "Here. I've made your favorite macaroni pie." Sky's mouth watered as Georgie scooped out a generous portion of creamy cheesy pasta with a toasted brown crust. She pulled two farmers' market carrots out of the refrigerator and peeled them without taking off the green tops—bunny carrots, she had always called them—and poured Sky a glass of milk. "Eat up, now. You look starved, little bug."

"It is so good to see you," Sky sighed. "Mother called me to say she needed me here for her surgery tomorrow. Do you know anything about it?" Sky asked.

"You know your mother. She won't tell me. She's out again at some opera performance or something tonight, so whatever it is, it's not slowing that one down." Georgie looked Sky up and down and turned down the corners of her mouth. "You don't look like you've been taking care of yourself. I would've thought you'd be back all tanned and rested after a summer at the beach, but…"

"But I'm looking awful. I know," Sky interrupted. Georgie's familiar broad face and warm brown eyes smiled at her. She would make everything better.

🐐 🐐 🐐

Georgie handed Sky a napkin to wipe her eyes. "Sounds like a bad broken heart to me. Not fair that this next one turned out to be another cheater, but there are good men out there. Don't you worry, you'll find one," Georgie said.

"But I thought I had this time." Sky looked impossibly sad.

"Here. Have another cookie. Listen. You bring the next fellow to me early on, and I'll check him out for you before you get in too deep." Georgie hadn't trusted Gil, and after Sky had broken the engagement, she had told Sky how she knew. "He wouldn't meet my eyes," Georgie had said. "And when I did catch his eye once, he could tell that I could see he was a no-good man. He was handsome and charming and all. I'll give you that, but I saw a hole where his heart should be."

Georgie patted Sky's arm and gave her a smile. Sky took a bite of the still-warm oatmeal cookie and a sip of milk. Despite her tears, she was feeling immensely better.

The two women had turned to discussing Georgie's grandbabies when they heard Sky's mother open the front door. "Not a word to my mother, remember," Sky cautioned. Not that she needed to.

"Schuyler, where are you, dear?" Sky's shoulders tensed at the sound of her mother's voice.

"In the kitchen with Georgie," Sky called. She rose to join her mother in a stiff hug. Lucretia looked around the kitchen and the remains of her daughter's dinner.

"Why Georgie, I didn't know I had you working late tonight."

"I'm on my own time, Mrs. Harrington. Just heading home now. I'll see you tomorrow morning." Sky's mother gave her daughter a hard, appraising look.

"You look just terrible, dear. Your eyes are all red. And I do hope that you've brought some better-looking clothes with you." Lucretia was, as always, impeccably turned out—from the top of her blond coiffured head to the tip of her Louboutin pumps. She wore a sleeveless pale-gray silk sheath dress with a matching wrap that showed off her toned arms and flattered her pencil-thin figure. Sky did feel like a schlub in her yoga pants and baggy striped top. Her Birkenstock sandals were kicked under the counter, and she'd pulled her almost-clean hair back into a black elastic band on her way to the airport.

"Yes, Mother. Remember I left most of my clothes here when I moved out of the apartment."

"And we do need to get you over to Jean-Pierre for your hair immediately. I'll leave him a message tomorrow on our way to the hospital."

Sky gave her mother a tight smile. "Well, you look wonderful as always. But do you want to tell me what is going on tomorrow?"

"We need to arrive by 9:00 for my prep, and you can drive me home a few hours afterward. They'll do the procedure at the new outpatient surgery center. It should take us about half an hour to drive there and park. That's all you need to know for tonight. Don't forget to set your alarm. I'll see you tomorrow, 8:30 sharp. Don't forget." With that, Lucretia turned and left.

She's just the same: my mother, the ice queen.

Sky looked through her closet for an outfit that was unlikely to trigger maternal criticism and was comfortable enough for a long day sitting around a waiting room. She pulled out a pair of crisply pressed khakis, a fine white button-down shirt, navy and white D-ring belt, a navy cardigan (in case the waiting room was chilly), and the pair of striped espadrille flats she'd bought in Barcelona. Pure prep. She'd risk Lucretia throwing barbs about the outfit making her look like she'd put on a few pounds and had she thought about trying one of those new diets, dear?

Sky had showered the night before but took care to blow out her hair (and yes, she was due for a haircut; her mother was right about that) into sleek waves. She needed a real mani-pedi, but a careful trimming and filing of her nails and a coat of pale pink polish would do for now. Her tan had faded from being inside for days during the storm, so she used a touch of bronzer to make her look healthier than she felt and applied makeup with a light skillful hand. Unaccustomed to spending so much time getting ready, she hurried downstairs to find her mother waiting in the living room.

"This is dreadful. They told me I can't have even a drink of water this morning," Lucretia complained. "What took you so long? It's time to go. We can take my car."

"Good morning, Mother. I'm ready. Let me just get my purse." Sky ran back upstairs and grabbed her bag. She hadn't thought to shift her phone and wallet into something more suitable, and her mother looked with dismay at the handmade hippy leather-and-tapestry hobo she and Elly had so much fun selecting at the Chilmark Flea Market. Lucretia's lips tightened and Sky braced herself for the-quality-of-one's-bag lecture, if not now, then later.

"So we've gotten that Gil business out of the way, and now that you've had your little summer playtime, what are you going to do? Have you told Francisco that you're back?" Lucretia quizzed Sky.

"No, Mother. I keep telling you that I have zero interest in Francisco."

Lucretia looked hard at her daughter. "You're not thinking of getting back together with Gil, are you?" Gil had known just the right tricks to charm and flatter and deftly appeal to Lucretia's vanity without appearing to do so. She had welcomed him as a future son-in-law until she found out he wasn't one of the Newport Smiths. By then it had been too late. Furious as she was, Lucretia reconciled herself to the fact that Gil had excellent prospects—good looks, education, charm, a promising career, friends in the right circles—and if she hadn't realized he wasn't one of those Smiths, well, neither would anyone else. Still, she felt that she'd been sold a bill of goods and, but for the mortifying gossip, she had been delighted to unwind Schuyler's wedding.

"No, Mother, I am not going to get back together with Gil," Sky said with a sigh.

"I do take some blame for that, you know." Sky's ears perked up. Her mother never took the blame for anything. Everything was always someone else's fault. "I should have known to hire someone to look into his background the first time you brought him home. We could have avoided all that unpleasantness." Sky smiled at the thought of her mother reading the dossier compiled on Nathanial Batchelor, college drop-out goatscaper. Then her smiled faded. Nate was gone.

"What were you smiling about?" her mother asked in an acid tone. "I'm about to have surgery."

🐐 🐐 🐐

The sign on the glass door at the surgical center—Aesthetic Center for Plastic and Laser Surgery—told Sky all. Her mother's "little surgery" really was a little surgery, a little nip and tuck for a vain, aging woman. Lucretia walked to the front counter, cutting in front of two women who were standing in line.

Sky had long ago ceased being mortified by her mother's refusal to wait in line, but she still hated when it happened. She headed to the far corner of the room to skim an issue of *Town & Country* while her mother checked in. A few signatures on a form, and Lucretia was being escorted through the big double doors.

Sky, regretting she hadn't brought a good book, got up. "Is there anywhere to get a cup of coffee?" she asked the nurse at the desk. The woman's face looked just a bit too smooth for her neck, and Sky wondered whether the center offered an employee discount.

"Sure, down the hall to the main entrance and left past the elevators."

The busy coffee bar made a decent cappuccino. It was helping to be away from everything that reminded Sky of Nate. And dealing with Lucretia was nothing if not a distraction. Suddenly, the coffee demanded an exit and Sky rushed to the ladies' room.

When Sky emerged from the stall, she saw the nurse from the clinic washing her hands at the sink. She looked over at Sky with concern. "Are you all right? I couldn't help overhearing." Sky went to the other sink to rinse her mouth.

"Just stress, I think."

"Oh, I assume that was your mother I just checked in? I see the resemblance." Sky nodded. "She'll do just fine, as you know, she's often here to see Dr. Mahmud. Today's procedure won't set her back but for a few days of puffiness," she said in a reassuring voice. "But what about you? Perhaps you're the one who should be seeing a doctor? I can check you for a fever back in the clinic."

"No, I'll be fine. This has been going on for a few days, and the coffee probably just set me off. Thank you though," Sky said.

The nurse thought for a minute. "It could be stress, as you say, but it isn't normal to have nausea and vomiting for more than twenty-four hours unless it is food poisoning or a virus. Or if you're pregnant."

"No. Definitely not any of those," Sky said forcing a wan smile.

"Then there are a couple more things—serious things— that you should get ruled out. And if it is just stress, medication can help. You have some time to kill, your mother won't be ready to come home until early afternoon. If I were you, I'd go down the street to the walk-in clinic and ask to see Dr. Wing. I used to work with her. She's a very good internist."

"Yes, thank you," said Sky feeling another wave of nausea. "I think maybe I should do that."

THIRTY-FIVE

"Hi, Nate, it's Marianne. Is this a bad time to call?"

"No. Not at all. I'm just at the post office. Hey, how are you?" Surprised, but pleased, to hear Marianne's voice, Nate put down the mail he was sorting through.

"I'm good. Listen, I've been thinking about you since the wedding and hoping things were OK. I couldn't imagine what had happened, but you seemed really upset," Marianne said.

"Well, not exactly OK. But I'm hanging in there," Nate said.

"Anyway, tell me if this is totally awkward. Tad's back East for a conference and wanted to take Teddy up to see his parents for a few days. Which is a good thing for Teddy. So if I'm kid free anyway, I thought I'd take a day off from work and come over to the Vineyard. Maybe have lunch with you and your girlfriend? And meet the goats?" Nate didn't reply right away. "But no problem if you're busy. I also wanted to go up to see a friend in Back Bay," she added quickly.

"No, no. It would be great to see you, really, anytime. But Sky's off-island this week. It'll just be me," Nate said, not ready to go into the breakup yet.

Nate headed over to his uncle's. Uncle John had left a message that there was news about the barn, and he wanted to talk to Nate about it in person. He pulled up to the tidy cape and knocked before letting himself in.

"I'm in the kitchen," Uncle John replied. "You want a lemonade? I was just fixing myself some." Nate sat down at the kitchen table, and his uncle set down two glasses of his favorite raspberry lemonade.

After a couple of minutes of small talk about the storm, whose house had gotten a tree limb through the roof, and which boats had loosed their moorings, Uncle John dropped his bombshell. "Nate, we've accepted an offer. We're going to sell." That sentence, delivered as matter of factly as if they had been discussing whether the sow would have her piglets before the fair, floored Nate. "Hear me out. You know we let that real estate lady show the property to that couple from New York. I needed to know what the land is worth. We got an offer."

"I'd heard," Nate said.

His uncle took another sip of lemonade before continuing. "You know that English lord who owns Solitude Farm across the cove?"

"I did some goatscaping there last summer. That's the place the first family used to rent."

"Well, as you know, their house is smack dab in my view and my barn is smack dab in his. Somehow, he'd heard that we might sell it to someone who would build a big ugly vacation McMansion right in his 'bucolic viewscape,' according to his agent. Like what happened down at the old Ewald place. He matched the other offer. He's promised to fix up the barn and put it into conservation."

"I see." Nate wasn't sure how he felt. Foremost, he felt relief that it wasn't being sold to Winky and Prescott. Sky would be upset, but hell, Winky and Prescott would just buy some other place. Nate studied the familiar lean, furrowed face of his uncle, seeing sorrow at losing the land mixed with pragmatic certainty he was doing the right thing.

"We weren't going to get an offer like that again. So the money, well, it means we can keep this place up, get that new tractor, put some cash in the bank, and help your cousins out if they need it. And you too, Nate. Have you heard back from the folks at Mytoi?" Nate shook his head. "The conservation easement means that it will forever look like it did when your great-great-grandfather—there might be a few more greats in there, I can't keep it straight—built that old barn. The lord'll keep some horses in there for his daughters to ride, and conservation rules mean he has to keep the barn up and can't change it. But, well, we've got to clear out all the animals, and that means your goats have to go too, Nate." Nate still hadn't said anything. It was the longest speech he'd ever heard his uncle make. "So your Aunt Betsy and I, we've decided it was the right thing. There's a bunch of legal stuff to be done, but the lawyers say we can sign the deed over after Columbus Day." He looked at Nate with concern. "I hope you aren't too upset, Nate."

Nate tried to put a reassuring expression on his face. His uncle was looking glum. "You're doing the right thing."

"It makes good sense. It just does," his uncle said. "And it means that old barn'll keep standing for a long, long time. That's part of our family's history, and we don't have the money to keep it up. It's not just the roof, Nate. The whole structure is going to fall down if we don't do something."

Nate smiled as best he could. "It's OK, Uncle John."

🐐 🐐 🐐

"Schuyler Harrington?" Sky heard her name called by the receptionist. "This way, please." Sky was directed to one of the examination rooms where the nurse took her temperature and checked her weight and blood pressure. A young doctor came a few minutes later and introduced herself as Dr. Wing.

"So, what brings you in today? I heard that Leslie over at Dr. Mahmud's sent you over." The doctor had kind gray eyes and a reassuring voice. Sky relaxed and described her symptoms.

"Well, let's rule out the obvious first as you don't appear otherwise to be sick. What was the date of your last period?"

"Oh, that's not possible," Sky laughed. "I had a bunch of ovarian cysts removed when I was a teen. I'm infertile."

Dr. Wing raised one eyebrow. "Well, I'll just ask the nurse to pop the stick in your sample while I do the physical exam."

A few minutes later, the nurse knocked on the door and handed the doctor a white plastic stick. The doctor slipped it out of its cover and showed Sky what she never thought she'd ever see: a bright pink plus sign. "No, that's a mistake. She must have tested the wrong sample." Dr. Wing raised that eyebrow again.

"We can bring the sample in here if you want and do a second test, right in front of you, but I think I know how it's going to come out," Dr. Wing said. Sky sat in shock and stared at the doctor and then at the plastic stick.

"How is this possible?"

"That's a question for your ob-gyn."

Sky walked back to the plastic surgery clinic in a daze. She was pregnant with Nate's baby. An impossible thought. Sky remembered the day she'd learned that the cyst surgery had left her infertile. She was seventeen, and at the time it didn't seem that big a deal. It took care of the whole birth control thing. And besides, pregnancy looked like a hugely uncomfortable bother. But as her friends had started marrying and having their own families, she'd felt twinges from time to time. Still, never ever had she expected to see that pink plus sign.

Nate was hauling old tools out of the loft when he heard his cousin Jessie call to him. "Nate, it's me. Are you up there?" Nate clambered down the ladder and Jessie wrapped his dusty, sweaty body in a bear hug. "I've been worried about you. You didn't call me back," Jess said, looking up at him. "I heard about Mytoi and that you'd broken up with Sky, and Dad said he'd told you about signing the contract. Are you OK?"

"Not really," Nate replied giving a brotherly kiss to the top of her blond head.

"Do you want to talk about it? It might help." They sat down on hay bales and looked out the barn door at the pond. The sun lit motes of dust floating in the dimness of the old barn, and Nate breathed in the familiar scent of hay and animals.

"I'm sorry, Nate," Jessie said simply at the end of his story and lay her small hand with its short, practical nails over Nate's grubby one. "You know what those people are like. Remember Gus-the-shithead? I thought he was different too." Jessie had seen Nate bummed and broken hearted before. But never like this.

"Yeah. But at least we aren't selling this place to Sky's snobby friends. They'd have torn all this down and built some huge vacation house."

"What?"

"The other offer. It was from Winky and Prescott, Sky's best friends." Nate stared at his hands. "She went behind my back and told them about this place, and our money problems."

"That little bitch."

"I guess," Nate said.

Jessie thought for a while, then patted Nate's hand. "You should get away from here. Come back to Peru with me. Sell the goats, give them away, whatever. Zeke can stay in your place and take care of Nan. It's so beautiful, Nate. Machu Picchu will blow your mind, and you can live for next to nothing. The expat scene in Cusco is really fun too." Jessie had been trying for years to get her brothers and Nate off Gilligan's Island, as she called it, to see something of the world. "You can stay with me for long as you like—maybe even make money teaching English."

"Thanks, Jess. I'll think about it. I promise."

🐐 🐐 🐐

Nate finished up with the barn chores and headed down to the beach to clear his head. Whitecaps on the pond tossed the boat, and he throttled down the motor to avoid getting drenched. September was his favorite month, the summer palette of greens shifting to autumn golds and browns and the beach back to empty and wild.

The ocean was rough from the remnants of the storm, and a strong chilly northeast wind set long streams of misty-white mare's tails flying from the tops of the waves. Other than a kitesurfer in the distance, the blustery September beach was entirely Nate's. His heart wrenched when he remembered beautiful, loving Sky casting into the surf and joking that she'd thrown out her lure and reeled him in, the biggest fish she'd ever caught. Yeah. He'd been hooked but good. He had gotten himself back into the sea, but he felt like that schoolie striper he'd once seen badly unhooked and thrown into the cut, half swimming, half belly up.

The kitesurfer raced closer, virtually flying across the ocean, lifting into the air as if the board had a gravity release button. Nate felt earthbound, leaden. As expected, the storm had closed the opening early. The unbroken line of beach gave no indication that where he stood had been, just a week earlier, a broad current of water carrying happy vacationers from pond to sea.

It was the nature of things to change. He had no option but to accept what was lost to him: the barn, his business, and Sky. His uncle and aunt would sell. That was set but for the final papers. They would get a fair price, and the old Batchelor barn would be preserved. Never would a rich man's ego-driven McMansion take its place.

The sale had introduced the practical problem of the goats. Nate had a few fall contracts to finish up, and they would keep about half the herd busy. He might be able to sell a few of the goats as livestock, but the rest would have to go for meat. That thought, and the knowledge that he'd make the most money by doing the butchering himself, made him sick. The baby goats, the kids with their tender meat, would fetch the highest prices. No, he was no butcher. The goats were irritating, uncooperative, destructive, even capable, he suspected, of affirmative malice, but they'd earned Nate's grudging respect. And affection.

He still didn't know what it would cost to repair Mytoi. Restoration, he knew, was impossible. He'd have the money from the sale of the goats and could borrow from his uncle if he needed to, but he'd have to find a job. Maybe it was finally time to try working as a car jockey for the Steamship Authority. He hated the idea of being trapped in the belly of the ferry for eight hours a day, forty hours a week, fifty weeks a year, but it was steady work with good pay and benefits. With a sinking feeling, he determined to call his buddy Bruce to ask if there might be any job openings.

Nate's cell buzzed and he looked at the message from Zeke. *Batty's doing carbonara. Cheese heaven. Come over?* Yeah, he needed to get out of his head, and friends and cheese couldn't hurt.

THIRTY-SIX

Nate hadn't seen Zeke since Batty had dragged him out into the teeth of the storm, but Zeke's clothes and a couple of boxes of his junk had disappeared from Nate's living room. "Yeah, thanks. It's been a pretty crappy week. Smells great, Batty. I really appreciate the dinner invite," Nate said, accepting a cold can of 'Gansett from Batty. "How've you been doing there, Zeke? I haven't seen you around." Zeke put his hands behind his neck and stretched, giving his friend a satisfied grin.

"I've just been settling in. Batty's convinced me my tent'll be too cold soon." Zeke said. Nate sipped his beer and filled Zeke in about his uncle's plans to sell the farm, the lack of news from Mytoi, and Marianne's upcoming visit. "That's good, at least. I remember Marianne. She's solid. Best way to mend a broken heart is a roll in the hay. Right, Bat?" Zeke asked.

"That and food," Batty called from the kitchen where she was grating a small mountain of Parmesan. "Especially chocolate. So chocolate balls for dessert. Hey, Zeke. I think it's cold enough for the first fire of the season. Can you get that going?"

For all her tough outdoorsy style, Batty had decidedly feminine taste in decor. The sofa was overloaded with throw pillows. Photos and doodads—including Batty's collection of chubby porcelain birds—covered the tabletops, and her old gray cat, Ji, slept curled in her egg-shaped rose-colored plush cat bed by the hearth. Everything was floral, soft, curved, or all three at the same time. A little froufrou for Nate, but with a fire blazing, it felt homey and relaxing. Zeke had once again found a warm comfortable nest where he could spend the winter. Which meant that he wouldn't be spending it on Nate's sofa.

Nate wandered over to see whether Batty needed any help in the kitchen. "Here. You can slice the tomatoes for the caprese," she said, taking a break from her grating to hand him a razor-sharp chef's knife and well-used cutting board. A bowl of ripe late-summer heirloom tomatoes sat waiting on the kitchen island. "And you can slice the mozzarella, too. I just made it this morning. Let me know what you think," she said. "It's totally different from the kind you buy; my Nonna taught me. Her carbonara recipe too, of course."

"You make your own cheese?" Nate asked, impressed.

"It's dead simple. You just need good milk, rennet, some citric acid, and a thermometer. I make ricotta too: that's even easier. I have my Nonna's recipe for Parm but that needs a cave to cure in for at least six months, so I've never tried it."

Nate sliced off the end of the irregular ball of cheese. It was, as Batty had claimed, a whole different experience—richer and softer, with a clean taste of milk.

"This is great, really," Nate said. Batty was pleased with the compliment.

"I'm happy to teach you how to make it sometime. Hey, do you ever milk your goats? My Nonna used to use milk from her goats to make cheese, but I've never tried that." Nate remembered the time he'd taught Sky to milk. She'd been so surprised by the powerful jet of liquid that she tipped backward off the step. He wondered when he'd be able to think of her without feeling like he'd been sucker-punched.

"I'm just crackers about cheese," Zeke said in his best Wallace and Gromit voice, sneaking a piece of mozzarella from the cutting board. "Hmm, not quite a Wensleydale, but a fine cheese for all that."

🐐 🐐 🐐

"Georgie, where is that Pellegrino? And don't forget my straw. And fresh ice packs." Georgie gave Sky a well-known look as she headed downstairs. Sky sighed as she sat down in the steel-blue Arne Jacobsen Egg chair. Queen Catty glared at her from the end of her mother's chaise.

"What else can I do for you, Mother?"

"You can check my email for me. Mimi is quite useless as a chairwoman—as I should have known. All money and no taste…" Sky tuned out her mother's voice as she walked over to pick up the laptop from the glass and steel desk. "Your password?" Sky asked.

"Duchess1. Capital dee. One advantage of the bandages was that her mother couldn't see Sky rolling her eyes. Lucretia no longer chaired the Opera Ball, but as the committee's chair emeritus, she exerted a veto right over all decisions.

"All right. I'm in. Here's one from Mimi about the lighting. Do you want me to read that?"

"Yes, do. Twinkle lights. Can you believe? She wanted to use twinkle lights. The place would look like a freshman girl's dorm room.…"

Sky was able to escape to the kitchen, finally, when her mother fell asleep after taking her pain pill. Sky's mind was still struggling to process that little pink plus sign.

"I see something is up, baby girl," Georgie said, giving her a quizzical look. Sky had almost forgotten her old nanny's ability to read her mind and hearing the words "baby girl" gave her an unexpected jolt. She wasn't ready to say anything yet, not even to Georgie, at least not until she'd seen Dr. Dixon on Wednesday.

"I'm sorry, Georgie. I'm just not ready to talk about it yet."

"You tell me when you're ready. No problem. You hungry for dinner? I did chicken coconut curry for my man yesterday and brought us some. That one upstairs can't eat. And I can make some rice. Or do you want that good macaroni pie again?" Thank god it wasn't goat curry. That was Georgie's favorite, and Sky had pretended her whole life to like the chewy, gamy bits of meat floating in muddy brown sauce.

Now, the idea of eating goat meat was absolutely repulsive, as if she weren't nauseous enough already. But Georgie's rich not-too-spicy chicken curry was a different story.

"Curry would be wonderful," Sky said.

Georgie's broad smile broke across her face. "And special for you, I made that key lime pie with the nutmeg crust you love. I bet you don't find that on that little island of yours."

🐐 🐐 🐐

Marianne was easy to spot in her bright red fleece as she walked down the gangplank. Nate had arrived in Vineyard Haven early, intending to stop by the Steamship Authority office to fill out an employment application, but he'd found he just couldn't bring himself to do that, at least not yet. Marianne waved when she caught sight of Nate's lanky frame, Nan sitting at his side, and a grin spread across her face, rosy-cheeked from the brisk breeze.

"Nate, I didn't know you were going to meet me at the ferry," Marianne exclaimed as she gave Nate a big hug. He rested his chin briefly on her curly dark hair and felt her generously proportioned chest yield against his. "And you still have Nan! She was just a pup when I saw her last," Marianne said, rubbing the pleased dog's soft ears.

"Do you mind an early lunch?" Nate asked. "We can walk over to the Black Dog and get something to eat and then head out." Marianne slipped her arm through Nate's and told him about her trip up from Fall River as they walked along the harbor. They stopped to look at the two gorgeous tall ships anchored among the few remaining summer pleasure craft.

"I'd love to go out on one of those someday. Look at the size of that mast," Marianne exclaimed, squeezing his arm. Nate was comfortable with Marianne. It was as if the years apart hadn't mattered a bit. Maybe Zeke was right about what he needed. They continued along to the restaurant and were seated at a table overlooking the harbor.

"Tell me what happened. I was so worried about you, the way you dashed back here from the wedding," Marianne said as she put aside her menu. Nate went into the story of Zeke's call and the Mytoi disaster and was relieved to find that the story was less painful in the retelling. Marianne's brown eyes welled up as she listened to the tale of poor Zeke and the dead goat.

"I'm sorry I'm dumping all this on you. Zeke knows most of it, but I haven't really told anyone the whole story. But I haven't asked you a single thing about your life."

Marianne looked perplexed. "Nate, can't you talk to your girlfriend about all this?" He'd forgotten about the lie of omission he'd told Marianne, that Sky was "off-island this week."

"Well, yeah. I didn't tell you everything. Sky and I broke up, and she's gone." Marianne reached over to squeeze Nate's hand.

"I am so sorry. You really are in a big pile of poo…. Oh, right. You're a grownup. I guess I can say shit in front of you," Marianne said with a hint of a smile. "Maybe we should order you a beer? I'm a good listener, and I think it might help to talk about it—that is, if you want."

Nate found it easier to start at the beginning: their unexpected connection, falling into bed after the "tick check" (which made Marianne laugh), Sky's friends—both the snobs and the awesome couple from Vermont, and, finally, finding out about Sky's other lover. Marianne listened quietly, taking bites of her spinach salad.

"She's not who I thought she was, Mari."

"When you told her about what Zeke had seen, what did she say? Did she think you'd be OK with her seeing both you and that other guy?" Marianne asked.

"I didn't say anything about that. I told her I was breaking up with her because I'd run into you at the wedding. And that I couldn't see two women at the same time."

Marianne stared at Nate. "But that wasn't true. Was it? The part about breaking up with her over me," Marianne said sighing. "Oh Nate, I wish it were true. But look at what you've done. You still love her. That's so clear. If you could see how your eyes lit up when you talked about her—the good parts, that is," Marianne said. She pursed her lips. "But Nate, you didn't give her a chance to explain. I know. I can't imagine how she could, but maybe Zeke thought he saw something that didn't happen. Maybe she had a friend there who looked like her, and that's who Zeke saw. You don't know. And you lied to her about why you broke up. That's not right."

A glimmer of hope, mixed with shame at Marianne's judgment, crossed Nate's face. She continued, "I've been through that. Omigod. The lies Tad told me as our marriage was falling apart. I'm not saying it wasn't what Zeke said he saw, but you need to talk to her. You owe that to her—and to yourself," Marianne said. She took the last sip of her iced tea. "But enough lonely-hearts advice from me. It's a beautiful day. Let's get the check and go find some goats."

Sky wandered into her father's study, uncertain as to whether—or how—to break the news. She was grateful that Lucretia had been given the all-clear from her doctor and had flown out to finish recovering at Sedona Ranch, almost passing Sky's father at the airport. Lucretia had been so caught up playing the poor recovering patient that she hadn't noticed her daughter's distracted state. Sky had half-convinced herself that the clinic doctor had made a mistake. She wasn't a specialist, and perhaps there was a problem with the test. But the kindly young bow-tied gynecologist had confirmed Sky's pregnancy. "Not quite a medical miracle," he'd said. "But the closest I'm likely to see." He'd explained her options, of course, but Sky had made up her mind. Georgie would be delighted by the news. Babies were nothing but all goodness in her eyes, but her mother would be horrified and appalled—more so when she learned who the father was. But Sky had no idea how her father would react.

Sky loved Courtland's study, with its dark wood-paneled walls, large old-fashioned desk, and cordovan leather hobnail armchairs. Like her father, she found it a comforting retreat from her mother's domination over the rest of the house. Her father's tall figure was bent as he inspected an object with a magnifying glass under a green-shaded banker's lamp.

"Hi, Daddy. What's that you're looking at?" Sky asked. He held out a gourd and jade cricket box, barely six inches long.

"I brought this back with me. My dealer in Taipei believes it was owned by Emperor PuYi, but he and I have no way of proving the provenance. Regardless, it is beautiful." Sky studied the carved jade top with its intricately detailed dragon and pearl design. It was a lovely piece. "I think it finer than the one in the Met's collection," he mused.

"The carving is wonderful. The dragon almost looks alive. Did you have a good trip?" Sky asked, handing him the box.

"Very pleasant, except for the flights of course. The meetings went fairly quickly, so I had time to meet with my dealers. It is getting rather hard to locate good pieces, but they keep an eye out for me," he said, resting his new treasure back in its box. "Here, sit down and we can catch up. Would you care for a small whiskey?" Sky demurred and took a seat in one of the comfortably worn leather armchairs by the fireplace as her father poured himself a measure of scotch from the crystal decanter. "I'm so glad you were able to come home and help Georgie with your mother," he said, sitting in the other chair. Sky rolled her eyes. "Yes. I quite know what you mean. How was your summer? Are you feeling rested and recovered from all that business with Gil?"

"I'm better, Daddy. I really needed a break to pull myself together, and, well, the Vineyard was a good place for me to be." Sky paused, gathering up her courage. "I don't know how to say this. I can't believe I am saying it." Sky paused again. Her father regarded her through his old-fashioned gold-wire-rimmed glasses. "The doctors said it couldn't happen, but it did."

"Schuyler, my dear, what is 'it'?"

"The it…. The it is that I'm pregnant." Courtland leaned back in his chair and sipped his scotch. Nervously, Sky waited for him to say something.

"Well, this is rather unexpected. Do you want to keep the baby?" he asked in a neutral tone. Sky nodded. "And the father? Is it that Francisco fellow that your mother keeps talking about?" Sky shook her head.

"He's a local guy I was dating. He and I. Um, we're not together anymore. I'm going to be doing this on my own." Courtland took a few moments to process the information as his logical lawyer's mind assembled the facts and worked through the potential outcomes.

"Well, it's not like the Victorian era when we'd have to ship you off with a spinster aunt on an extended tour of Europe." Sky's father smiled and reached over to pat her hand. "I admit this is a bit of a shock, but I do hope you have an easy time of it. Your mother was quite ill. And she hated getting fat." This, Sky knew: it was the reason she was an only child. "Georgie would be delighted to have a baby to fuss over. She is absolutely bored to tears with no one but your mother and me to take care of. I hope you'll stay here?"

"I don't know what I'm going to do, Daddy. I just found out. I have a lot to think about. But what about Mother?"

"I will deal with your mother. You needn't worry about that," he said. Sky's lovely, eccentric, unflappable father was the one person Lucretia could not overrun or manipulate, and Sky breathed a deep sigh of relief. Her father patted her hand again.

"And the father? Does he know?" Sky shook her head. "You do need to tell him, you realize, my dear. I assume you wouldn't ask him for child support, but he has rights as the biological father," Courtland explained. "But most important: is this happy news?" Sky smiled. She'd been so worried about how to tell her father that she hadn't asked herself that basic question.

"Very happy news, Daddy. I think I can do this."

THIRTY-SEVEN

The weather was perfect for flying: blue sky with just a few wispy cirrus clouds high in the atmosphere. Ordinarily, the flight into the Vineyard was her favorite part of the trip up—especially when she got to sit in the copilot's seat of one of Cape Air's little planes. This time, though, Sky found herself distracted and anxious as she watched the Island grow larger. Over the steady loud hum of the plane's propellers, Sky considered and reconsidered how she would break the news to Nate.

She hadn't told him she was coming. She'd been continually spinning out scenarios, trying to decide what she'd say and to guess how he'd react. Upset? Indifferent? Unhappy? Angry? In none of these imagined scenarios would this come as welcome news. In the worst, he'd ask her to terminate the pregnancy.

The plane bumped down onto the tarmac. Sky climbed down the wobbly aluminum stairs and walked into the small terminal. She had planned to head first to her house, and then she'd call Nate to find out when they could meet. At this thought, a jolt of stress doubled her nausea, and she ran to the airport ladies' room to throw up. Wiping her mouth with a brown paper towel, she glanced at the mirror and saw a pale, anxious face looking back. *I can do this*, she mouthed to the mirror. *I have to do this.*

The trees and fields were showing the first burnished hints of autumn. On impulse, Sky drove past her turn down South

Road towards Nate's, passing the general store and white steepled church before bumping down the dirt road to his house. Either he'll be home or he won't, but if he is, best to get it over with.

Nan was sleeping in a patch of sunshine outside Nate's door. She stood up at the approach of the strange car, getting ready to go into watchdog mode, but her wariness turned into paroxysms of doggy joy when she saw Sky.

"Oh, Nan, you sweet girl," Sky said as she rubbed her head. Nan's feathered tail went round and round with happiness. "You've missed me. Me too, girl." She could hear music playing from inside the house, which usually meant that Nate was cooking. "Courage, Nan, give me courage," she muttered as she knocked on the door.

"Come in. Door's open," she heard Nate call over Pearl Jam's "Better Man." Sky's heart pounded, and she hoped she wouldn't throw up again. Nate had his back to the door. He was stirring a huge lobster pot of something on the stove and dripping white baseball-shaped globs were hanging from poles suspended over the dining table. A smell like hot milk filled the house.

"Nate, what are you doing?" Sky exclaimed. Nate turned, and the color drained from his face.

"Sky???" Omigod. It had been a mistake to surprise him.

"I'll come back when you're not busy. I… I have something I need to talk to you about," she sputtered.

"No, it's fine," he said. "Let me just turn off the flame. I didn't know you were back." He'd been thinking about Marianne's advice, but he hadn't screwed up his courage to call Sky. Now would have to be the time.

"I just flew in for the weekend. I'm really sorry, I should have called first," she said.

They stared at each other feeling a ghastly cocktail of emotions rise and mix. "We can sit out on the deck," Nate said at last. "Do you want a drink?"

"Water, please," Sky replied. Sky sat down in the old Adirondack chair. The sunlight flashed off the ripples in the pond as the resident pair of swans paddled down the cove toward the marsh, followed by their nearly full-grown cygnet.

Nate came out with two glasses and sat in the other chair. "I'm trying to make goat cheese," he said after a time. He could barely look at her. It hurt too much. "Zeke's girlfriend has been teaching me," he added.

"Oh," Sky said. The awkward silence continued. "That sounds interesting." Nate's handsome face in profile looked thinner and more drawn than Sky remembered. She knew from the airport bathroom mirror that she looked even worse.

"Nate, the something I need to tell you..." Sky couldn't get the words out.

He looked at her. He couldn't figure out why she would have come back. "What?"

"It's not anything I thought would ever happen."

Nate stared at the water. It was easier than looking at her. "OK," he said. Whatever it was, he wanted her to say it, and go. No, not go. Stay.

"But I kept throwing up, so I went to the doctor," Sky said.

She didn't look good. Nate remembered with dread his father's last days, battling cancer. "What's wrong? What do you have?" Please don't let it be cancer.

"I'm not sick, Nate. I'm pregnant. You're the father." Dumbfounded, relieved, Nate stared at Sky. She waited for him to say something.

"Pregnant? Are you sure?" he asked stupidly.

"Yes. Of course, I'm sure."

He turned back to look at the pond. "Oh," Nate said, realizing the inadequacy of his reply. He wracked his brain for what to say next. Sky sat looking miserable. "I guess the doctors made a mistake—about your infertility, I mean."

"Almost a medical miracle, they said."

A long, uncomfortable pause as Nate's head spun. "Will you keep it?"

"Yes, I've decided to have the baby. I'm not here to ask you for anything, but you need to know you're the father."

Or not. The pain of Sky's betrayal stabbed Nate once again. "Um, are you sure?" Nate asked. Sky nodded, tight-lipped. "Not that other guy?"

"What other guy?" Sky stared at Nate. "Why would you say that?" Nate floundered for an answer.

"Uh, Zeke saw you with him."

"With who?"

"You know. That rich guy. Francis or something."

Sky shook her head. "Francisco—that lunch, remember? We talked about it. Nate, I didn't sleep with Francisco," she replied. What was Nate thinking, did he think she'd lied to him?

"There was another time. At your house, Labor Day weekend. Zeke saw him—and you—again."

Sky's temper flashed. Effing Zeke. "What did he tell you? Yes, Francisco showed up—uninvited—and I got rid of him as soon as I could. Did Zeke tell you I was sleeping with him?

"Yeah. I mean, sort of."

"And you didn't think to ask me about it? Why?" Here furious eyes drilled blue ire into Nate. "You didn't trust me?"

"I don't know, Sky. Zeke told me....He told me what he saw, there were towels and martinis and music and you had wet hair, and it was that same rich guy, the one you were with in Edgartown who was after you."

"And?"

"Shit, Sky. I was really messed up. I'd come back early because the goats had gotten into Mytoi and everything was totally fucked."

"You took what Zeke—*Zeke*—thought he saw and made up your mind that I was cheating on you." Angry red circles dotted Sky's cheeks. "I can't believe this."

Nate stared at his feet. "It hurt too much to ask you why you were with him. There was only one explanation. I didn't want to hear you say it. I couldn't bear it." His face had lost all color, and his eyes looked up at her with pain. "I'm sorry."

Nate looked so miserable. His shoulders slumped as he put his head in his hands. Pity tempered Sky's fury. She let out a sigh. "Oh, Nate. That was the real reason you broke up with me. Wasn't it. That ex-girlfriend? The spark? That wasn't true."

Nate's face gave Sky her answer. "And the other thing," Nate said, head still in his hands. He couldn't look at her. "I still can't believe you did that to me, to my family. That hurt, Sky."

"What are you talking about?"

"Shit. I shouldn't have said anything. What's done is done."

Sky reached over and gripped his arm. He raised his eyes. "No. Tell me," she said.

Nate bit his lip, struggling to speak. "The old barn."

"What about the old barn?"

"I can't believe you are making me say this. You told Winky and Prescott about my family's money problems and that they should put in an offer. Prime waterfront, right?" He pulled his arm away. "That land has been in my family for more than 350 years."

"Goddammit, Nate! I didn't tell them anything."

Nate looked at her. "What?"

"Prescott found the property by searching the records for tax delinquencies. He was looking for a 'good deal.'" Sky gave a dead laugh. "I tried to stop it. I told Lord and Lady Nelson— well, their lawyers—that there was an offer on the property, and that I knew the people and they'd build a big Hamptons-style house where the barn was, right in their view. But they could stop the sale, maybe, if they offered to restore the barn as a historic structure." She leaned forward in her chair and stared at Nate. "It never occurred to me, not once, that they would put in an offer themselves."

Nate was stunned. "Why did you do that?"

"Because I love the Island, and I loved the barn because you did. And I loved you." Sky stood up. "I'm going now, Nate."

Nate was still sitting outside on the deck when Zeke came banging through the house. "Whoa, you got cheese world going on there in the kitchen. How's it taste? Batty teach you right?" Nate could hear him rooting through the refrigerator and opening cabinets. "Hey, where are you, Nate?" Zeke called.

"On the deck," Nate said in a flat voice. Zeke came through the screen door with a bowl and spoon and flopped onto the chair Sky had vacated earlier.

"You really think you might be able to sell that cheese? Looks like lots of work for a couple of globs," he said, slurping a big spoonful of cereal from the chipped blue bowl. Zeke looked over at his oldest friend. "Oh no, man, what is it now?" he asked.

"Sky came over," Nate said, his face distraught. He told Zeke what she'd said, about the baby, about the barn. Zeke choked on his cereal, nearly snorting milk from his nose. He wiped his face with his hand and stared at Nate in disbelief.

"No way. Whoa. This is messing with my head." Zeke stared out at the pond for a few minutes, cereal forgotten. He turned back to Nate. "How's she know it's yours?" Zeke said finally. "It could be, you know, that other guy's."

"Zeke, I screwed up. There was no other guy. I really, royally screwed up."

"You're sure."

"I'm sure," said Nate, putting his head in his hands.

"Man, I was totally wrong about her," Zeke said, shaking his head. "Fuck." Zeke looked out at the water. "I can't believe it. I was so sure she was in it for her. That she was just using you, buddy."

"I should have trusted her."

Zeke put his face in his hands and rubbed his eyes. "I just feel so bad."

"Hey. Shit happens," Nate said.

"But a baby."

"Yeah."

Zeke sat rubbing his face, thinking. "Oh man. It's not about you anymore. Or Sky. It's about the baby, dude," Zeke said, sounding un-Zeke-like in his seriousness. "You still love her, don't you?" Zeke looked into his best friend's eyes. Nate nodded. "If there's any chance that you can give that little goober two parents that love each other and love him…" Zeke grabbed Nate's arm, spilling cereal onto the deck. "You've got to go find her. Tell her that, tell her that I am so fucking sorry.

I'm so sorry." Zeke's eyes filled with tears. "You go find Sky, man. You've got to try to fix this."

Nan leaped across Nate and out the open door of the truck emitting quiet little yelps of happy anticipation. Nate sat a few moments longer, trying to pull himself and his thoughts together. I have no idea what to say to her. Zeke might be a screwup, but this time he's right; I have got to fix this.

Nate slowly walked to the front of the house and looked through the side window into the living room. Sky was asleep on the sofa, a sheet pulled up to her chin. Her blond hair was mussed, her face pale and childlike in sleep. Nate's gift—the painted box—sat on the coffee table next to a pile of wadded tissues. Nan, now impatient with Nate's delay, gave a sharp bark. Sky opened her eyes. She pulled off the sheet and walked to the door.

"Nate," she said. Nate stood silent and sad. He struggled to speak.

"Sky," he choked out finally, "Please forgive me, Sky."

Red-rimmed eyes looked at Nate. "I don't know. I just don't know."

She leaned her back against the closed door. She'd change her flight. It was time to go.

Zeke sat waiting in Nate's kitchen eating an anxiety meal of pie and ice cream. "How'd it go?" he asked, face tight with worry.

Nate shook his head. "I tried. She didn't want to talk to me."

"You told her you were sorry?"

"Yeah." Nate stared at his feet. Of course, she didn't forgive him. Why should she? Crestfallen, Zeke shoveled pie into his mouth. Nate dropped to a chair and looked at the cheese-making mess in his kitchen, then out the window at the pond. Sky's baby would be the first in the family not to be born on the Island. His baby, a Batchelor, being pushed by a nanny down city sidewalks.

"Shit," said Zeke.

"I better clean this up," said Nate.

"Maybe she just needs time. It's like…like you're both shell-shocked. She drops a baby bomb on you then finds out you've been thinking she's a …."

"I know," Nate interrupted.

"I'm just saying that it's a lot to process, dude. Don't give up, buddy."

THIRTY-EIGHT

It would have been too easy to fall into Nate's arms and say, "I forgive you." That was for simple misunderstandings. This was serious. He had rendered a fundamental judgment against her. Deemed her disloyal. Dishonest. Capable of betrayal. Guilty of cheating. Nate didn't trust her. She'd done her duty: she'd told him about the pregnancy. Still, that impulse to touch him, kiss him, make love to him until he couldn't see straight.

Shit.

After a delayed connection in Boston, Sky was relieved to arrive in Burlington. "I hope you don't mind me showing up like this," Sky said as she dropped her overnight bag in the back of Eva and Trip's pickup.

"It's the best surprise ever," Eva said. "We've only invited you a thousand times. But we figured you'd be spending September…" Trip gave Eva a warning look. "But Vermont is better. Peeper season's almost here. It's amazing. You have to stay for that," Eva said. "And I can't wait to show you the farm. You're not going to believe how big Cooper is! And Trip and I made the most awesome pen with ramps up to the hayloft in the barn. The goats spend all day going up and down the ramps." Sky felt a twinge at the mention of goats. "It's really funny. Nate would love it." Eva slapped a hand across her mouth.

"We're really glad you're here," Trip said. "And like I said, stay as long as you like."

"Thanks," Sky said. She blinked away threatened tears. The mask slid. She was a hot mess. "Tell me more about how Baby Face and Cooper are doing."

"They're goats. They eat, they poop, they wake me up going 'meh-meh'," said Trip.

"Oh, you love them now too. I catch you petting Cooper all the time. My gosh, did we tell you about the ride back?" Going back to the city and facing her mother would have been a bad idea, staying on the Island and seeing Nate everywhere even worse. Trip had promised her space and quiet—as quiet as it could be living with Eva—and no questions. "Trip wanted to put them in the truck bed but we'd have had to stay on the back roads because you can't do seventy on the highway with goats in the back! Plus, it would have taken forever to get home, so we put Cooper on my lap and Baby Face in the back seat. We tried a seat belt, but that didn't work, so I had to hold her the whole way because she kept trying to eat Trip's man bun…."

Had Nate really expected she'd forgive him, just like that? She still couldn't believe it. "Then when we finally got here…. Oh, wait. I didn't tell you about what happened at the gas station. That was funny too…." No, she couldn't forgive Nate. Not yet.

They pulled up in front of a ramshackle white farmhouse with a big wrap-around porch and a hot pink door. "Here we are. Home sweet home," said Trip. "It's not fancy, but it's ours."

Sky fell in love with the farm immediately. To the west, the gentle shoulders of the Green Mountains rose up behind the house. To the east, a sliver of Lake Champlain splashed silver in the distance. Black and white spotted cows grazed in a field in front of a big red hip-roofed barn, like a Vermont postcard come to life.

"Wow," Sky said. "You weren't kidding when you said you had great views. Are those your cows?"

"No, we lease the land to our neighbors. That's their barn. Two goats are enough animals for me," said Trip.

"And Boo. Oh look, there he is, come to say hello." Eva picked up a chubby black cat. "He's really friendly; just doesn't like to be picked up, do you, Boo-boo?" she asked as the cat wriggled out of her grip.

Sky kneeled to stroke his back. "Aw, he's sweet. I love cats. Will he sleep with me?"

"Probably. But he'll walk all over your head in the morning. Let's go in. You can pick your bedroom. Lake or mountain view?" Trip asked.

"And then we'll go see the goats," said Eva.

The short gold September days passed quickly. Sky managed with the help of saltines and pretzels and long morning walks to keep her morning sickness a secret and explained her abstinence as a desire to "get healthy" after a long, wine-filled summer. Like the sun fading a photograph, the passage of time muted the bright, sharp colors of her hurt. She hadn't forgiven Nate, but she wasn't angry anymore.

She was best when she could focus on the bright spots in the day. A perfect autumn leaf and the scent of wood smoke in the air. The warmth of wool socks worn to bed on a cool night. Waking to a breakfast tray of waffles and maple syrup and a crisp, sliced fall apple. The soothing background chatter of Trip and Eva, the best unlikely couple she could imagine. The future wasn't any clearer, but she felt readier to face it.

Sky picked up a book to read in her favorite spot, the daybed on the glassed-in sun porch. Boo, the cat, jumped up, kneaded her chest, lay down, and purred. Sky had just opened the novel when her phone rang.

"Hi, Winky," she said. Winky had found nothing surprising in Nate and Sky's post-Labor Day breakup but was miffed that Sky hadn't called when she was in town.

"Are you still in Vermont? When are you coming home?" Winky asked. "I haven't seen you in such a long time. It was Rob and Debbie's engagement party last weekend. Even Mitch and Arlene showed up. You're missing everything."

"I know. But I want to see the fall colors, it's so pretty here. I'll be back soon, I promise."

"Listen. I have a great idea. Prescott's firm is looking for an in-house lawyer. You'd be perfect."

"I don't know anything about his business. Don't they want someone with experience?"

"Oh, that doesn't matter. They have law firms on retainer to do the real work. You'd just coordinate, look things over— the easy stuff. You'd figure it out in no time."

Sky's heart sank. The one thing she had ruled out was going back to being a lawyer. "And the salary is super." Winky quoted a figure that took Sky's breath away. "You could get a really nice apartment, maybe even near our place, and you and Prescott could ride to work together. And it would be totally flexible. You could even telecommute summers from the Vineyard if you wanted."

"Wow," Sky said with a sinking heart. "I'll think about it."

"You'll need to move fast. The headhunter has already found a few candidates, and they want to start interviewing soon. It's perfect, Sky. Prescott thinks so too. Can I tell him you'll send him your résumé?"

It didn't feel perfect at all. It felt like the first time Lucretia had forced her to "dress" and attend the annual Children's Hospital gala. The designer gown had made her feel—and look—as if she'd been wrapped in a giant ace bandage. And worse were the nude stiletto pumps that pinched her toes and rubbed her heels but tilted her pelvis and buttocks to just the right angle. She'd been gorgeous. And miserable.

"I don't know, Winky. I've been thinking I might do something other than law."

"At least come for an interview. You can always say no."

She tried to read again but couldn't concentrate. Winky's call had left her paralyzed. Sky lay the book on her chest and closed her eyes.

"Sky, Trip and I need you," Eva called. "We can't agree— again—on what footage to use. Come on," she said, pulling Sky up from the daybed and dislodging the cat. "Then we can make lunch. Tomato sandwiches?"

"OK, sure," said Sky.

Trip sat in front of a laptop and three computer monitors. "Trip, I got Sky. Play what I want to use." Other than weeding the truck garden, Sky's biggest contribution to the household was to act as tie breaker.

"See? Trip's up the tree," Eva said. "You can see the claw marks and how big they are compared with his hand!" Eva and Trip were down to the final edits on their documentary short on the now-extinct Vermont catamount. "And he looks so cute."

"But the audio's no good. This is better," Trip said clicking on the keyboard. He hit play on a close-up-but-Trip-free video of the scratches.

"Um, could you redo the audio in the first one. Voice-over or something?" Sky suggested.

Eva crossed her arms. "That's what I've been telling him."

"Oh, all right. It's going to be a pain, though," Trip said.

Eva smiled in triumph. "Sky, do you want to go with me this afternoon to Waitsfield? My friend Meg called. She needs help with a new shipment of antiques for her store."

"You should go, Sky. It's a nice drive. I'll sit here and figure out the audio," Trip said. "Eva, don't come home with anything crazy this time. Sky, I'm delegating my veto right to you."

"OK," said Sky. No surprise that there would be any risk of that, given the eclectic assortment of items already scattered around the farmhouse. The real carousel horse mounted on a pole in the living room. The someday-to-become-a-lamp butter churn. A row of vintage irons displayed like fine china in the dining room hutch. And Sky's favorite—the huge salvage art picture of the mountains made out of bits of old license plates.

Eva bit her lip as they headed out the driveway. She was under strict instructions from Trip not to ask Sky any questions about Nate, but she couldn't understand why anyone would keep something so obviously major like a breakup bottled up inside. But Eva had agreed, so she talked about trees instead.

"You know why leaves turn colors in the fall, right?" she asked as they drove past a thicket of firethorn.

"The trees stop making chlorophyll or something," Sky had replied. "I didn't pay much attention in bio."

"Right, and the yellow colors are there the whole time, just covered up by the green. But the red colors come from a different process. The trees actually put energy into making the anthocyanins. That's the red."

"Oh really," said Sky, trying to fake interest in the topic. The drive was pretty, but it was going to be long if she couldn't get Eva off trees. Maybe she should send in her résumé. Maybe it wouldn't be so bad to be an in-house lawyer.

"You'd think they'd want to rest up for the winter, but maples trees are killers—chemical warfare! The red leaves fall off and poison whatever is underneath them. No competition from other trees next spring!"

"Wow," said Sky. As Winky had said, she'd have control over her time. She'd even be able to telecommute.

"And sugar maples have sap that's four times as sweet as most other trees. In Scandinavia, they make birch syrup, but it takes way more sap. There's also something special in how the sap flows up maples that makes them easier to tap." Eva looked over at Sky gazing out the window. "I'm boring you."

"No, not at all. Do you guys make your own syrup?" The salary would let her live somewhere nice, maybe with a view. A good nanny would be expensive: she couldn't just impose on Georgie.

"We try, but Trip gets cranky carrying buckets. You know it takes like forty gallons of sap to make a gallon of syrup? Oh, but it is so good though. Our neighbors have a gravity feed system with tubes for the sap. It's supercool how that works." Sky made a decision. She'd fix up her résumé and apply. She probably wouldn't even get the job, but it would get her moving forward, toward the future.

Lost and Found Antiques sat in an old barn at the edge of town. A miscellany of housewares and furniture, organized by style—country in one corner, Victorian in another, midcentury modern in a third—filled the dusty, cavernous space.

"Meg?" Eva called.

"In here," came a voice from the back.

Eva introduced Sky to the dark-eyed proprietress sitting in the middle of a tangle of furniture and boxes. "Thanks for coming. I hit the jackpot at an estate sale over in Shelburne. I took one look around and bought the whole thing."

"How do you know how much to ask?" said Sky, peering into a box. "If I'm not sure, I check out comps on eBay. No science to it. Ask a little less if its ugly, a little more if I like it or it has something to do with Vermont. Grab a box."

They settled down to work. Sky sat at an old-fashioned school desk and opened up a carton of antique kitchen tools. "What's this?" she asked, holding up a silver star-shaped disk on a wooden handle.

"Pie crimper," said Meg. "Just mark $5 on each of those and feel free to keep anything you want."

Eva and Meg gossiped as they sorted and priced. A cougar, the human kind, had taken up with Meg's baby brother, and the neighbors were trying to keep an old couple from being evicted from their condo.

The pile of unsorted boxes dwindled. "You've done enough, guys," said Meg. "Why don't you take a look around?"

Sky stood up and stretched. "Sure."

She was nearly overwhelmed by the volume of treasures—or junk—depending on how one looks at it. Sky picked up a pair of antique spool candlesticks that would be perfect for the Vineyard. Sadness formed a lump in Sky's throat as she remembered the romantic dinner that she had planned for Nate. She took a deep breath and slowly exhaled: look forward, not back. Then, her eye caught a wooden bassinette hidden behind a table. She wandered over and gave it a little push to rock the cradle. It was a lovely piece, airy and light.

"I don't usually stock baby items," Meg said, carrying in a box of woodworking tools. "Safety issues—the slats are too far apart, that sort of thing. But I fell in love with this. Victorian, probably from India originally. The caning was in bad shape so I had a friend replace it, and I added wheels so it can be moved from room to room." Sky ran her hand over the smooth, intricately woven sides. She could see it on the deck, swinging in the breeze. "The pattern is called lace caning. Pretty, isn't it?"

"How much are you asking?"

Eva walked up with two taxidermized bullfrogs nailed to a board, a vintage Town Talk Bread advertising thermometer, and a perplexed look. "Why do you want to buy a cradle?"

Sky didn't feel like lying. The news had to come out, one way or the other. "I'm having a baby. In May."

Eva gasped and stood gaping at Sky.

"Congratulations," said an uncomfortable Meg.

"Nate's baby?" Eva choked out. Sky nodded. "Does he know?"

"Uh, I'll be in the back," said Meg, beating a retreat. "I was asking $950, but I'll give it to you for $550," she added over her shoulder.

"Oh Eva, I've been trying to figure out how to tell you and Trip. It's a long story."

🐐 🐐 🐐

"I can't believe Nate thought all those awful things about you," Eva said. Her mind was racing. She'd been so sure that Nate and Sky were meant for each other—cosmic soul mates.

"Me neither." Sky felt much better. As the saying goes, a sorrow shared is a sorrow halved. "But I need to figure out what to do next. You remember Winky and Prescott? They were the ones who dropped by after dinner one night when you guys were visiting me."

Eva wrinkled her nose. "Yeah." Hard to forget Miss dancing school and the yodeling boozer.

"His firm is looking for an in-house lawyer. I think I'm going to apply."

"You don't want to work for Prescott, do you? And live in the city again?" Eva said, failing to disguise her horror.

"I don't know, Eva. I mean, where else would I go? I can't stay here forever. I have to be realistic about my options. It makes sense at least to interview."

"But you said you didn't like being a lawyer. Don't you want to do something you like, something that makes you happy?" Eva asked, getting out of the truck.

"I'm thinking in-house wouldn't be so bad. It's not like a law firm. And it would pay well. Really well."

"Hey, guys. How was your afternoon?" Trip called from the porch. "I think I've finally got the audio right. I suck at lip-synching. Did you get anything?"

"Well, I'm not convinced," Eva said to Sky. "Hi, Trip, I got these," Eva said, pulling the frogs from a paper shopping bag to show him.

"What the heck is that?" Trip asked, blinking at the oddest decorative item he'd ever seen.

Eva patted an olive-green head. "Bullfrogs. Playing dominos. For the mantle."

Trip made a face. "Veto power, Sky?"

Sky shrugged. "I thought they were kind of cute."

"And a neat old thermometer for the barn to make sure the goats don't get too cold this winter."

"OK. I guess we can use that," Trip said.

"Sky bought a cradle for her baby," Eva said with a sidelong look at Sky. "And some candlesticks and a pie crimper."

"A what??" Trip exclaimed.

"Pie crimper," Eva said with an impish look. "You know, to seal the edges of the crust."

"Trip," Sky said. "I've got something to tell you."

After unloading the truck, Sky sat Trip down on the porch to watch the sunset and talk. Eva stayed inside and chopped vegetables for dinner. "So Nate turned out to be, well, not exactly a jerk, but you can see why it could never work out. Right?" She sighed. "It's hard, but I'll get over him. And I'm happy about the baby. I should probably be more scared, but I think it'll be OK."

"I'm glad of that."

"And I've got a job prospect. Back in the city. Eva doesn't approve."

Trip sipped his scotch. "I don't know, Sky. I keep putting myself in Nate's shoes. I mean, Zeke's his best friend. Why wouldn't he believe him? And if I ever found out Eva was cheating on me, I hate to say it, but I'm not sure I could face hearing her make excuses."

Sky had expected sympathy and outrage. Not this. "I see."

"He should've talked to you. Sure. But you know him better than I do. Does it really surprise you that he didn't?"

Sky stared at the clouds over the horizon. "No. I guess it doesn't."

"You didn't say anything when you figured out that Winky and Prescott had put in an offer on the barn. Right? What if you had?"

Sky hadn't considered that possibility.

"Oh."

🐐 🐐 🐐

Trip's call had come as a surprise, igniting a speck of hope, no bigger than a match. "Hey, I am probably sticking my big long nose where it doesn't belong, but Sky is here and I think you should come up. Eva thinks so too," he'd said. "You guys have more you need to talk about."

The exhausting ten-hour drive on back roads ended in front of a warmly lit farmhouse. Eva wrapped Nate in a giant hug and launched into a long story about her goats and the neighbor's cows. Casting glances at Nate, Sky sat petting an ecstatic Nan as Trip warmed up a plate of leftovers. She bit her lip. It was hard seeing him here—in her refuge. Doors to carefully controlled emotions flew open. She wished that Nate hadn't come, wished that he hadn't let Trip and Eva convince her to see him again. Sky wanted to move on, not look back.

"Goodnight, guys," Trip said after Nate finished eating. "We're going to bed." Eva followed him up the stairs with a hopeful glance over her shoulder.

"Let us know if you need anything."

"Sure. Thanks for the dinner," said Nate.

Sky took a deep breath. "Let's sit in the living room," she said.

"OK."

They sat on opposite ends of the lumpy Victorian sofa. Eva's taxidermized treasure adorned the mantle. Nan circled the hearth rug twice and lay down in front of the blazing fire, eyes on Sky to make sure she didn't disappear.

"Are those stuffed frogs?" Nate asked.

"Eva's," said Sky. "She found them the other day in an antique store. They're playing dominos."

"Oh," said Nate. He had no idea what to say. "Uh, the bluefish derby has started."

"I still want to enter that someday," said Sky.

"Yeah."

Nan rolled over onto her side and closed her eyes. "How'd Nan do in the truck coming up here?"

"She was good."

"Pretty drive?"

"Very. Just long." Nate took a slug of beer. "Trip called me. Asked me to come."

"I know," Sky said with a sideways glance at her ex.

"How have you been doing?"

"So-so. Eva and Trip have been taking good care of me. You?"

"Not great. Zeke and Batty keep trying to cheer me up. Zeke feels awful about…" Nate struggled for words. "You know, about the stuff he said. About you."

"Tell him I understand. He was just trying to protect his best friend from the evil rich girl."

Nate turned sad eyes to look at her. "Don't say that, Sky."

Sky stared at the flames. "Eva thinks we have a cosmic connection. You know, fate. That's why we got together like we did."

"I thought it was because you asked for a tick check."

The corner of Sky's mouth turned up. "I'd forgotten that." She relaxed back into the sofa.

"I haven't," Nate said. Couldn't, even if he wanted to. Sky was so close, so lovely. Not angry anymore. The tiny flame shone a bit brighter.

"Eva thinks certain people come into your life for a reason. To teach you something about yourself. I think maybe that's right," Sky said.

"I sure learned something. That I'm an idiot."

"Nate, you're not an idiot."

"It's true." He rested his hand on the cushion between them. "I put you in the box with all the other rich summer people."

"…who come to the Island and take what they want," Sky finished Nate's sentence. "Because that's what we do. We buy properties, drive up the prices, push out all the local people." She sighed. "Why shouldn't you assume that about me—and my friends?"

"Because I was wrong."

"You weren't wrong about Winky and Prescott."

"I guess," said Nate. She was so near, it hurt.

"I stuck my head in the sand. I could have told you, warned you, that they wanted to buy the barn. But I didn't. And I didn't tell you when Francisco showed up again."

"No, it's my fault. I was an effing idiot for listening to Zeke. For not talking to you."

Sky's heart thumped. "Why didn't you?"

Nate struggled to explain. "I tried to stop myself . . . I tried not to get serious. That's what you said you wanted, no strings." Flames crackled in the hearth. "Remember that night with Eva and Trip and the beach fire? I said I loved you. It wasn't a joke. It was true. Even when I thought you'd gone behind my back, I still loved you. But if I knew for sure, then I'd have to walk away."

"No," she whispered.

"But it all fit. You have no idea, Sky, how bad it was." Nate told her everything. From passing out at the wedding and waking to find Marianne in his bed, to the Mytoi disaster and his despair when he thought he'd lost everything he cared about—the goats, the land, and her. "Then Marianne came back to visit. She straightened me out. I was trying to get my nerve up to call when you showed up." Nate's heart wrenched loose. "I love you, Sky," he choked out. His shoulders shook. "I can't help it. I love you."

Sky reached out for Nate's hand, then released it. "I love you too, but—"

Nate moved to kiss her. "It's not enough. I don't think I can be with you," she said, pushing him away. The words pained her, but they had to be said.

"Why not?" He refused to let the ember go out.

"You said it yourself. We come from two different worlds. I'm the rich summer person with the snobby friends. Your friends are snobs too—*reverse* snobs. You deserve some nice Island girl, a normal life. I need to go back to my real life, in the city." Like Winky said, it was time she came home.

"No. It's not just about you and me. There's a baby. Our baby." Nate's voice cracked. "You are true and loyal and the most beautiful woman I've ever seen. I want you and our child in my life. We love each other. We have to try."

Sky closed her eyes, heart thumping. This time, she thought of her childhood: her fond but absent father, her coldly critical mother. The best nanny in the world couldn't replace a loving, present father. Emotions tore loose from their lines, setting Sky, like a boat, wallowing in the sea.

She choked back tears. "I need to think, Nate. I'm going to bed."

🐐 🐐 🐐

Sadness pulled at Eva's normally bright face. "I was sure it would work, that they just needed to see each other again," she said, whisking pancake batter. Both she and Trip had heard Sky go upstairs, alone, then Nate, later, to the other guest room.

"Well, we tried," said Trip. "Oh hi, Nate. How did you sleep?"

Hollow-eyed, Nate poured coffee into a mug. "Not great. I mean, the bed was fine." The night had been torture. Sky so close. "I'll be getting an early start back, I guess."

"Can't you stick around just a little and rest up from your drive? We'll show you Vermont," said Eva.

"Thanks, but I should go."

"Let's stay," said Sky, walking into the kitchen. "Your goats will be fine for one more day. We can drive back to the Vineyard tomorrow." Sky's face was alight as she beamed at the stunned trio.

Nate stood dumbfounded, his mouth agape, disbelieving his ears. Sky laughed and planted a kiss on Nate's open mouth. "Yup. Ooo, pancakes. These guys make their own maple syrup. Wait until you try it. You can taste the terroir," she teased. "Then I want to show you something upstairs after breakfast, Nate."

Eva clapped her hands. "But what happened? You guys slept in separate bedrooms."

"None of our business, Eva," Trip said.

"Sure it is," Eva replied.

Nate blinked at Sky. "You – I – we…?"

"I was really upset and stayed awake for a long time thinking about what you said. What I wanted, what would be best, for me, for the baby, for you. It was like I had all the pieces but couldn't make them fit. Everything kept spinning around." Sky took Nate's hand. "But when I woke up, I knew."

"I can't believe this," Eva said.

Sky looked over at her. "You know how you said dreams give advice, insights that you can't see when you're awake?"

"Scientifically proven," Eva said, bouncing on her toes.

Sky squeezed Nate's hand. "I dreamt I was sitting at a school desk—you know, like that one at the antique store." Eva was rapt. "Eva was at the blackboard writing math equations: Sky loves Nate plus Nate loves Sky equals question mark. Then Sky plus baby plus Nate. Then Sky plus baby minus Nate. I stare at the equations. I should know the answers. But I'm drawing a blank."

"Then what?" asked Eva.

"Trip is there. He raises his hand and answers: two, true love; three, a family; and zero. You say, correct, and give him a sticker." Sky wrapped her arms around Nate. "I don't know what I was thinking. I don't know if or how it'll work, but I want to be with you."

Eva gave a whoop and hugged Trip so hard he nearly tipped over. "I knew it!"

Hurried breakfast over, Eva and Trip listened with great satisfaction to the headboard knocking against the wall upstairs. "Told you, Trip," Eva said with a smug grin as she handed him a plate to dry. "Cosmic soul mates."

🐐 🐐 🐐

Eddies of emotion: disbelief, joy, wonder. And love. Sky fit into Nate's arms, the missing piece of the puzzle. They lay quietly, Sky resting her head on Nate's bare chest. A cool Vermont breeze fluttered the curtains, and Sky pulled the covers up. "You're sure we can make this work?" she asked, biting her lip.

"I'm sure we can try. Try like crazy. I love you, Sky."

"I love you more," she said, adding a kiss. "But you have to promise to tell me everything. Always. And I will too."

"I promise," vowed Nate. "No more listening to other people. Especially Zeke."

"Especially Zeke."

Sky opened up about her misgivings, about how Nate would fit into her world and her fear that she would not fit into his.

"It's not going to be easy, Sky. I wish it were different, but you've got to make choices. You either go to Chilmark cocktail parties, or you work at them. And there are some people who aren't going to accept you, no matter what you do, simply because you're not from the Island."

"Never?" she said.

"Not most people. Look at how much Elly loves you. But there'll be some. That's just how it is."

"I see," she said.

"What about your friends and family, how're they going to feel? I mean, look at me," he'd said, spreading out his rough calloused hands. "I keep goats for a living."

"I don't know, Nate. The same, I guess. Eva and Trip—well, we know what they think about us being together." She smiled and stroked his cheek. "But others…." Sky paused, thinking about her circle of friends. "No."

"Not much we can do, I guess," Nate said. "But that's OK with me if it's OK with you?"

"It's OK with me."

She let her fingertips slowly trace a line down Nate's breastbone and listened to his heart beat faster, then picked up his hand and gently bit down on his thumb.

Nate smiled. "Testing? I'm real. And I'm not going anywhere." He drew a circle with his fingertips in her palm. "Remember when you did that, at the Galley?"

"That was pretty shameless. Then, I think, I grabbed your thigh."

"You did," he said. Nate placed his hand on her leg, sending an electric shock into her core. "Right here."

"I missed you, Nate. So much."

"I've missed you more. I've missed this," he started, kissing her forehead. "And this," he whispered as he slowly, gently, set out to explore all he had thought lost.

"Oh," Sky sighed.

THIRTY-NINE

The side of the bed sank under a man's weight. Sky opened her eyes as Nate leaned over to plant a soft kiss on her forehead. "Hi, sleepyhead," he said. "It's a beautiful day. I can't believe the pond geese didn't wake you up. They were really noisy this morning."

Sky sat up and stretched, then flopped back on the pillows gazing at Nate's familiar, scruffy, beloved face. "I can't believe that I'm back."

"Me neither," Nate replied, and leaned over to brush back a tangled blond lock from her face. Lovely Sky, a Botticelli in an Up-Island Automotive tee shirt. "Sit tight, I've got something for you."

Sky watched Nan stretch into an elaborate downward-facing dog pose before padding over to rest her furry snout next to Sky's pillow. She blew morning breath in her nose (Nan's favorite. Go figure, dogs) and stared at the water glittering in the morning sun. Nate returned with a custard cup filled with something white drizzled with golden honey.

"Thanks, Nate," Sky said, sitting up in bed to accept the cup. "I've been queasy a lot. I should eat in the morning." She dipped the spoon in. "Yum, is this yogurt?"

"Nope. Ricotta. Try it and tell me what you think. The milk's from my goats, but I've added something," Nate said.

Sky took a bite. There was a faint almost-floral aroma under the fresh creaminess of the ever-so-slightly tangy ricotta, sweet with honey. "Nate, you made this? It's—wow, I'm not sure what to say. It's really good. Is there more?"

"Plenty. I got up early to finish this batch. You were my inspiration, how you always smell a bit like lavender? I threw some in the pot from the plant outside as an experiment. It works, though, don't you think?"

"So what smells better now, me or the ricotta?" she teased, lifting an eyebrow.

"Hmm, not sure... I'd better check." He leaned in and pig-snuffled her neck. Sky tried to pull him back down into the bed. "Tempting, but it's time to milk some goats if I'm going to try burrata today. Be back in a bit," Nate added, giving her one last ticklish snorfle in her armpit and making her giggle.

Sky got up to get some fresh coffee and climbed back into the still-warm bed, alone with her thoughts and a happy Nan.

"Oh, you're not supposed to do that, you sweet naughty dog," Sky said, as Nan jumped on the bed and rested her head in Sky's lap, tail thumping on the blankets.

Sky's cell rang, interrupting her thoughts. Home. That would be Georgie or her father. Lucretia would be away for another week.

"Schuyler, this is your father."

"Yes, Daddy. Hi. I know."

"Your mother's back early. I just told her your news, and she's not taking it well. I wanted to ask you not to take her calls. Delete any messages, too. I don't think you need—or want—to hear what she's saying. She'll be rational in a bit, I expect, but we'll have to be patient."

"Oh. Is it that bad?" Sky asked with a sinking heart.

"I'm afraid so. She's convinced you're making a huge mistake."

"I'm not," Sky said.

Courtland sighed. "You've been gone a while. Have you talked to the fellow yet? What did he say?" Sky wasn't ready to tell her father about her plans. She didn't even know what they were. Not really.

"He took it fine. We're talking. He's a good guy. I think it'll be OK."

"I'm relieved to hear that, dear. You can tell me about it at home. When are you getting back?"

"I'm going to stay on a bit longer, Daddy. I'll let you know. But thanks for the warning."

Nate clumped in with two buckets of warm milk. "Come on, lazy girl, get up," Nate called. "You can help." Sky put the call out of her mind as she wrapped herself in one of Nate's flannel shirts.

"OK. What do you want me to do?" she asked as she took a seat at the counter.

"Here. You can read Batty's recipe and run the timer," Nate said. "This is a lot harder than making the ricotta." The first burrata leaked out its creamy center—delicious and really messy—but Nate got the hang of the shaping and sealing by the second.

"It's probably a ridiculous idea," Nate said, "and I'd need to find money for the equipment. My aunt and uncle might be able to help me out, and I'll have to get another job to pay the bills at first, but…" Sky had waited for him to finish. "I like making things, I always have. I'd like to see if I could make a go at this. At the cheesemaking business, that is," he said finally.

"It's not ridiculous. I mean, look at Grey Barn and what they charge, and they can't keep their cheeses in stock. You have to try. It's a good idea, Nate." Sky thought. "How about your friends in the restaurant and catering businesses? We could invite them over for a cheese tasting, and maybe you could start selling to them?" Sky was getting excited about the prospects. "And then, in the summer season, you could get a stand at the farmers' market. You'd sell a lot there. And a farm stand too. Maybe with an honor system, like Mermaid Farm. People are always looking for a reason to see what's at the end of a dirt road. Maybe you'll need more goats!" Sky's enthusiasm was infectious. Nate laughed and shook his head.

"I think you're getting ahead of yourself. So far, I've made a half dozen ricottas and one-and-a-half burratas. You'll have me stocking gourmet stores up and down the East Coast next."

"Well, maybe not the first year, but you never know."

Finished with cheesemaking for the day, Nate put the creamy white balls into the refrigerator. The failed burrata drizzled with olive oil and sprinkled with sea salt on toast made a fabulous quick lunch.

"I have to go over to Chappy today," Nate said. "Want to come?" The weather was clear and cool, and Sky could think of nothing she'd rather do than spend it with Nate driving from one end of the Island to the other.

"You bet," Sky said.

Nate couldn't bear to look at Mytoi again, but Sky wanted to see the damage herself. He dropped her off and went to move a client's goat pen while she wandered around. The staff had evened out some of the damage, but it still looked like a crazed barber had taken massive scissors to the garden.

Back in the truck, she tried to convince Nate that it wasn't so terrible. "It's like a bad haircut. It'll grow out OK."

Nate wasn't convinced. "I don't know, Sky. I don't even want to think about it." She reached for his hand. "They haven't sent the bill yet. I'm still waiting."

They drove right onto the ferry—no line this time of year—and, when they landed, headed to Chilmark. Sky turned the radio to WMVY and opened her window to breathe in the fresh air. The road up-Island was almost empty, no more New York and Connecticut plates to be seen. The familiar but still breathtakingly beautiful vistas of field and pond and sea worked their magic on Sky, sending her back into the state she called Island bliss. She gazed at the view with a relaxed, half-smile on her face.

"Happy?" Nate asked.

"Hmmm, yes, very. Can we stop at Squibby and check out the ocean?"

"Sure, the turn's right ahead." Nate headed down the road to Squibnocket Beach and pulled into the empty parking lot. Sky slid across the seat to nestle under Nate's arm and slipped a narrow hand through the buttons of his shirt to warm her fingers on his skin.

"Chilly hand," he said, pulling her closer. They sat in comfortable silence, watching the waves break against the rocks and the narrow beach. Nate leaned over and gave Sky a smile and a kiss. "Ready to go? One more stop. Remember Joan, who painted your box? I want to check out some land I'm going to goatscape for her. Then we could head down to Menemsha for fried clams and the sunset."

"That sounds wonderful," Sky replied, sighing. "And I never thanked you for the box. It's perfect. Really beautiful. But we should return it, Nate, it's much too expensive."

Nate shook his head. "Not a problem. That's how Island barter works. I goatscape, she paints, we both get what we want, but can't afford. It's yours, love."

The Bite hadn't yet closed for the season and the chatty server was happy for the midweek business. They ordered fried clams and oysters and—over Sky's misgivings—fried mac 'n' cheese. "You've got to try it. Totally unhealthy and unfortunately delicious," Nate said.

The greasy takeout smelled wonderful. Nan, drooling slightly, stared at the bags on Sky's lap as they drove to park in the almost-deserted beach lot. Nate pulled out a couple of towels and his canvas fishing jacket for Sky to wear against the chill as Nan ran ahead to the beach in search of birds to herd.

"I still can't believe this is real. Nate, I'd been so miserable. And now." Nate muffled the end of her sentence with a kiss.

"Me too." They walked hand-in-hand to the end of the beach by the breakwater, where they could lean against one of the big granite boulders to watch the sunset. The breeze had dropped, and the waters across the sound were glassy and calm. Nate spread the towels and opened up the bags of food. Sky was grateful that she suffered from morning sickness only in the mornings. The warm crunchy clams with their soft melting bellies had never tasted better, and the oysters were even more delicious.

Sky savored another. "Nate, the oysters—and the clams—umm, yum," Sky said, wiping grease from her mouth. "And this," she said, holding up a crunchy nugget, "is a close second to Georgie's macaroni pie. You'll have to meet her someday. She's such a great lady. More of a mother to me than my own mother—by a long shot. And the best cook in the world."

Nate reached for more fried mac 'n' cheese. "It's clear tonight. We might get a green flash. Have you ever seen it?"

"Nope," Sky replied. "I didn't think that was a real thing."

"It's real. Just rare. Has to do with the atmospheric refraction of the light or something." Nan, who had been distracted from chasing birds by the food, lay waiting for crunchy bits to be thrown her way. "I read a lot of Jules Verne when I was a kid," Nate said. "You know, *Around the World in Eighty Days* and *Twenty Thousand Leagues Under the Sea*. But there was this one book called *The Green Ray*. I kept waiting for it to get exciting or science-fiction-y but the characters just ran around Scotland looking for the green flash." Nate took another clam, dipped it in tartar sauce, and popped it into his mouth. "Anyway, the girl in the book won't get married—she had these two guys after her—until she's seen it. They all believed that if you've seen the green flash, you can't be deceived in love, that it gives you this power to see into others' hearts, and your own."

"Nice if that were true," Sky said. "Oh, Nate, look at the colors now—how the blue gets lighter then turns almost pink then yellow then orange…" Sky's beautiful, happy face glowed in the light of the setting sun.

Nate reached into the top pocket of Sky's coat. "What are you looking for?"

"Just seeing what I have in here," he said, pulling out one of the little fishing bits he used to attach his lure. Nate started bending and unbending the wire. "Now pay attention. Just after the top rim of the sun drops down we may see the flash."

A few minutes later, the sun slid out of sight, and a small flattened green disk floated for a brief second above the horizon. "That was it!" Sky said. "I saw the green flash!"

"Me too." Nate leaned over and kissed Sky, a long, lingering kiss, as he screwed up his courage. "I'm probably a fool to ask," he said showing her the now ring-shaped object. "But, I love you. I'm pretty sure I can make you happy. And be a good father. Sky, will you marry me?" Sky sat stunned looking at the wire ring held in Nate's calloused fingers.

"Nate, I... I... I don't know," she sputtered. Nate's face fell. "I mean, I need to think about it. I didn't expect—I hadn't thought... not yet. I'm sorry." Nate didn't respond, just looked out over the darkening sea.

"Well, I guess that was the sunset. I'll drive you back now," Nate said, getting up from the sand. "It'll be dark soon." He was about to leave the piece of wire on top of the boulder when Sky stopped him.

"Can I hold on to that?" Sky asked. Her voice had an almost pleading note. "I'm sorry. I don't want to hurt you. I have to think."

🐐 🐐 🐐

The wood stove had burned through its fuel during the night, and the air inside the house was frosty. "What are you looking for?" Nate asked, carrying in an armload of split firewood. Sky, in his old terry robe, too-big wool socks, and an earflap hat, was poking around for something in one of the kitchen drawers.

"Do you have string anywhere?" The bent wire snap-swivel engagement ring sat on the kitchen counter.

"Try the lower drawer. You look ridiculously adorable," he said, patting the plaid hat down over her eyes. Sky shoved the hat up and stuck out her lower lip. Even if she didn't marry him, he was still amazingly, incredibly lucky to have her in his life at all.

"It's cold." She tugged open the next drawer. "I want to keep this with me. You know, while I think." She picked up the ring. "I thought I'd put it around my neck on a string."

"Hold on, I might have something better." Nate went into the bedroom and rooted around in the back of his sock drawer, finally finding a small, dark-blue velvet box. "I didn't have this with me yesterday, but here," he said opening the box. Inside was a fine gold chain and a small silk pouch, which he unzipped to pull out a sapphire ring. "My mother's engagement ring. It's nicer than the fishing wire. That is, if you want it. It's too big though."

"Oh, Nate, it's lovely," Sky said, looking closely at the old-fashioned platinum and gold filigree ring—a small oval cobalt-blue sapphire, flanked by two tiny diamonds. Sky slipped both rings onto the chain and then hooked the clasp around her neck. "There," she said. Nate's eyes dropped to look at the rings nestled in Sky's cleavage, and he slid his hand inside the top of her robe. Sky giggled and tipped her head, dislodging the hat, and gave him a kiss.

"You know what today is?" she asked. His hand had slid lower to tug at the knot on her robe, and she swatted it away.

"Uh, Monday?"

"It's my birthday." Sky found herself lifted in the air.

"Happy birthday! I lost track of the date." Nate swung her around in a circle. "When I was little, my mom had me make a birthday list," he said, putting her down. "Not toys, but stuff I liked to do. Then we'd spend all day working our way down the list."

"You got some paper?" Sky asked, eyes bright. Nate handed her a steno pad and pencil. "Beach. That goes at the top. Do you think I'm allowed to eat raw clams?"

"Nope." Nate laughed as he looked over her shoulder at the list. "OK, OK. We've only got one day. What's first?"

"Quansoo. Can we go by boat?"

"Your wish is my command, birthday girl." Nate kissed the top of Sky's head. "And if you want to look for oysters, I'll make you my famous Oysters Batchelor."

"Where'd the cut go?" Sky asked, climbing out of the boat.

"It closed in the northeaster. That always happens in a big storm." The line of the empty beach stretched unbroken. Like the two of them, back together and whole, as if they'd never been apart. "You can kind of see where it was. Right there." Nate pointed to a dip in the dunes. "How far do you want to walk, birthday girl?"

Waves swelled and crashed on the beach as Nan raced off into the distance after seabirds. "Not too far. It's chilly. But beautiful." The earflap hat slipped as Sky bent to pick up a shell. "Nate, I'm a bit terrified of the whole baby thing," she said, shoving the hat back on her head.

"You'll be fine. You're great with baby goats and alpacas."

"Not the same. And my mother's hardly a good role model."

"Don't worry. You just keep 'em clean and dry and fed and loved." Nate wrapped his arms around Sky. "And I'm here. You're not doing this by yourself, except for the one thing," he teased, dropping his eyes. "Mmm. Fun and functional." Sky swatted his chest. "And there's Nan. She'll herd and clean up the Cheerios. But seriously, I've been thinking a lot about babies."

"You like them, right?"

"Yup." Nate reached for Sky's hand as they continued their walk. "I remember holding Caroline's kid when he was like a month or two old. He had these chubby legs and fuzzy hair that stood straight up. His head smelled so good." Sky couldn't see herself with a baby, but she could see Nate. "And a funny gummy smile. Caroline said it was gas, but I think he liked me." A warm lightness filled Sky. Their child deserved—was lucky—to have Nate as a father. Of that, she was sure. "Ready to go find some oysters?"

"Sure." It would be OK. Together, they'd figure out the parenting thing.

When they reached Crab Creek, Nate crouched and said "Hop on, birthday girl. I'll carry you across."

Sky climbed on Nate's back. "Giddyap!" she said. "Tell me about oysters. All I know is I love to eat them." She adjusted her arms around Nate's neck and whispered into his ear. "And I love you."

A wave of pure happiness. "I love you too, Sky."

"I'm serious. I want to know about oysters."

"OK. Stop me when you get bored." Nate, said as he waded into the water. "Oysters are filter feeders. And they're hermaphrodites," he explained. "They spawn in the summer. Not sure how they decide whether to be a boy or a girl, but I've read they switch back and forth. Are you sure you're interested in this?"

"Yup," Sky said, climbing down from his back on the other side. "Do you know why oysters are an aphrodisiac and not clams? I always thought raw clams seemed more like, uh…" Nate snorted. He knew exactly what she meant, although that particular thought hadn't occurred to him before. "You know, especially littlenecks?" she added, wide-eyed.

"Uh, yeah, I see that. Hmm, thanks. I think." Nate shook his head. "OK. Oysters. Scientists think the aphrodisiac thing may be true. They found these rare amino acids that increased levels of sex hormones in rats."

"We'll have to eat more," Sky said.

"If you say so. There's the spot up ahead." Nate put the bucket down. "This is a lot easier than clamming," he said, wading out to pick an oyster up off the bottom. "Or getting scallops. Those little buggers swim away from you. The only hard part is telling an oyster from a rock." Nate reached into the shallow water. "This one's big enough. And see the tiny baby oysters stuck there? That's spat."

Sky wandered around peering into the clear water. "Found one! Ahh! Wet!" Sky yelled as her boot filled with water. She picked up her prize then marched, sloshing, back to the beach. Ridding herself of quarter-wet jeans and soggy socks, she stuck her feet in her boots and strode, bare-legged and undies-bottomed, back into the chilly water.

"Laugh if you will, Nathaniel Batchelor, but I refuse to be defeated by an oyster!"

🐐 🐐 🐐

Sky sat wrapped in the blankets from Nate's bed as he built a fire in the woodstove. The house was cold, but she felt snug and warm and utterly content with her birthday day. After oystering, they had headed into Edgartown where Rob's secret-ingredient clam chowder was on the fall menu at the Tank, and Sky's favorite boutique was having an end-of-season sale. She chose a thick, ultrasoft, white hooded fleece that reminded her of Fuzzybutt, the baby alpaca. And then she added a side trip to the alpaca farm to her list.

After a stop at Morning Glory Farm for a yummy monkey bar and the ingredients for Oysters Batchelor, they went to Nate's for a lovely afternoon nap-and-tumble before the trip to Menemsha. Nate stayed true to his word that her wish was his command, starting with the gentlest of massages and ending as she and Nate, like the lovers in Grams's romance novels, succumbed utterly and completely to true love's passion.

"It was really sweet of Zeke and Batty to make that birthday dinner," Sky said.

"Zeke still feels bad."

"Well, he shouldn't."

"But mostly, Batty loves an excuse to cook."

"That Nonna cake was to die for." Sky sighed with pleasure, thinking of the whipped-cream-frosted cake layered with cherries and sweet mascarpone cream. "They sort of look like Mutt and Jeff, but I think they're really good together."

Zeke had pulled her aside before dinner to apologize again. Then he told her that Nate was the best and most honest and loyal friend in the world, and she could get a richer guy, but she'd never find a better man. Green flash or no, Sky knew that was true.

Nate closed the door to the woodstove and joined Sky on the sofa. "It'll warm up in here soon."

Snuggling next to Nate, Sky took off the chain and tried on the sapphire ring. Then she picked up the handmade one. "Do you have any pliers?" she asked.

"Sure, I think there're some in the junk drawer. Why?"

"Well, there's this little piece of wire sticking up. I think it might catch on things," she said. "And I want to make the ring a tiny bit smaller, so it won't slip off."

"You don't mean…" Nate started.

"Yes, Nate. I mean yes."

🐐 🐐 🐐

Sky's cell chirped a brief reggae tune. "Hi, Georgie. What's up?" she asked, putting a bookmark into her novel.

"I figured I'd better call and warn you. That mother of yours has made up her mind, and there is no stopping her. It's been hell an powda house around here, I tell you," Georgie said.

Sky's happy bubble popped. "Oh no. What's going on?"

"We're on our way. We land at 2:00, I think. I've got to go." The line went dead. Sky flopped back on the sofa and stared at the ceiling.

Nate looked up from his pile of bills. "What was that?" he asked.

"Trouble," Sky said. "My mother's coming. Today."

Back at her cottage, Sky went into a frenzy of cleaning, yanking dust covers off the furniture, unrolling the carpets with a flurry of mothballs. She was just finishing up the vacuuming when the crunch of tires in the drive announced her mother's arrival. Sky, flushed with sweat and anxiety, opened the door to a coldly furious Lucretia.

"I am livid, just livid, that the only way I can talk to you is to travel all the way to this godforsaken island." Lucretia marched in and fixed her eyes on her daughter. Georgie followed her in with an apologetic what-can-you-do expression on her face.

"Hello, Mother. I'm surprised to see you. And, hi, Georgie," she said, grateful to stop for a moment in Georgie's comforting arms. "Did Daddy come too?"

"He had to get on a call this morning, but he's taking the next flight up," Lucretia answered through tight lips. "Not that we need him."

"Well, uh, welcome to my house, Mother. May I show you and Georgie around?"

"No, I don't want a tour of your little…" Sky's mother ran her eyes around the room with a sniff. "Your little playhouse. Your father made me promise to wait until he arrived, but that's ridiculous. We have to talk now about fixing this dreadful situation you've managed to get yourself into." The tone in her mother's voice triggered a hot swell of unpleasant emotions. Sky took a deep breath, and slowly releasing it as she'd practiced in yoga, did her best to stay calm.

"Let me make us some tea. I don't have much else. I haven't stocked up since I've been back," Sky said in a level voice.

"Let Georgie do that. Then she can go look for her mouse holes to plug up or whatever it was she said she needed to come along to do. Sit down, Schuyler," Lucretia ordered in a tight, peremptory voice. "I understand from your father that you are pregnant and that you insist on keeping the baby. You have no idea what a ridiculous idea that is, but I have managed to figure a way out of your predicament." She wore a cold, determined look. "I've spoken to Francisco. He is willing to marry you..."

"What?" Sky shrieked, appalled.

"Yes. He'll marry you to keep that child from being born a bastard. I've made the arrangements in Saint Lucia. After a waiting period of only twenty-four hours, you can marry. Privately. Francisco has a friend with a yacht you can use for your honeymoon or stay on at Anse Chastanet. I don't care. You and he can work that out."

"Omigod," Sky said, sitting down. "You're not serious."

"Oh, yes. I am very serious," said Lucretia. "Francisco was, of course, quite surprised. You are a very lucky young woman."

Sky sat stunned. She turned toward the kitchen to look at Georgie, who simply pursed her lips and shook her head. Lucretia continued. "Very lucky. He's willing to give this child his name. You don't meet men anymore with that sense of honor. Your child will grow up a de Santos."

"You told him…" Sky sputtered.

"I find it hard to believe, but Francisco is willing to let the biological father see the child if that man insists on parental rights. But it's far better if you have full custody, and our lawyers can ensure that we get that outcome." Unnoticed, Georgie set teacups onto the table. "I've told Francisco that you will call him to accept his offer after we've spoken. The sooner we can wrap up this mess you've made, the better."

Sky's head was spinning. The staggering magnitude of her mother's interference was breathtaking. That she would go so far to manipulate Sky's life. And Francisco's, the poor dupe. Sky felt the heat rise in her chest, her neck. "This time, Mother," she said, between clenched teeth, "you have gone too, too, far."

A knock. Sky turned to see Georgie open the door to admit an uncomfortable-looking Nate. Georgie looked him over from head to toe, fixing him in the eye with a firm stare. After a brief moment, her expression turned from calculating to friendly as a broad smile split her face. Nate, relieved, smiled back.

"Hi. You must be Georgie. Sky's told me a lot about you," he said.

"Georgie, tell whomever it is to come back later," Lucretia ordered, looking toward the door.

A rush of affection rose in Sky at the sight of Nate's anxious, freshly shaven face. His hair was still damp with comb marks and he wore the almost-new black polo shirt and khakis from the Dumptique.

Lucretia knew. She turned her back to Nate. "As I said, Georgie, tell whomever it is that Schuyler is not available."

"Mother," said Sky.

"Why don't you and I take a walk," Georgie whispered to Nate. "These two have more talking to do."

"Sure," Nate said.

Georgie pulled the door closed behind her. She put her hand on Nate's arm and they started down the path toward the pond. "Um, have you visited the Vineyard before?" Nate asked.

"No, but I like islands. Makes people behave, be civil when there's nowhere to escape."

"I guess."

"Oh, it's true."

"This is where my goats cleared this summer," Nate said, pointing out the goat-munched area.

"My great uncle in Jamaica used to keep a herd of goats," Georgie began. "One thing he liked to say was 'lickle bit a ram goat have beard, and big bull no got none.'" She stopped and turned to look hard at Nate again.

"I'm not sure I understand."

"Hold on, I'm not done." They continued down the path. "I got lucky in life with my man. And I want my Sky to find the same. I told her that I was going to look her next man in the eye, and I would know—I can always tell—whether he is a good man or a bad man."

"I promise, I'll…" Nate began, but Georgie cut him off.

"Let me finish. That old proverb about the goat. That means that little people can have fine qualities that big people do not. Do not let these big people with all their money and fancy things make you feel like you're not good enough. I know Sky's heart as well as I know my own. I saw how she looks at you. And I saw that bit of metal she's got on her ring finger—though you might want to think about something a bit nicer," Georgie teased, squeezing his arm. "But put on your shining armor, man. There's a dragon in there."

The battle was over. A pair of alabaster-cold faces turned to watch Nate and Georgie come through the door. Sky stood up and walked over to stand stiffly next to Nate. "Mother, this is Nathaniel Batchelor, my fiancé," she said.

"I know very well who he is. The goatherd," Lucretia said, the words dripping with contempt. Lucretia rose to her full height, imposing in an impeccable cream-colored pantsuit and pearls. Making Nate invisible in the horrible way she had of not seeing people who were "beneath" her in social standing, Lucretia looked right through him, searching for Georgie. "Georgie, get your bag. I have nothing more to say here. Take me back to the inn."

The door slammed shut, and Nate wrapped his arms around a still, unyielding Sky. Her face was drained of blood and her eyes flashed cold-blue fury and pain.

"Sky, are you OK?" he asked softly. She shuddered.

"It was horrible, Nate," Sky murmured into his chest. "The things she said to me—and I said to her." She pulled out from his embrace. Her face was still a rigid mask. "I need to be by myself for a while. I'll call you later," she said.

"Are you sure?" Sky cut him off.

"I'll be OK. Please go."

FORTY

Sky looked blankly out the window as her mind ran through the encounter with her mother. Nothing was more important to Lucretia than keeping the image of her perfect life with the perfect house and the perfect husband and the perfect daughter. And she had no qualms about manipulating others to serve her purposes. But Sky couldn't forgive her mother for the venomous things she'd said. And, at the end, the unbelievable threat.

Sky couldn't shake her anger. "Open, goddamit," she said to an uncooperative package of rice crackers. She put down the crackers and started rummaging through drawers. "Where are the stupid scissors?" she muttered.

A car door slammed shut, distracting Sky from her search. She opened the front door to find the slightly stooped figure of her father standing in the drive.

"Oh, hello there, dear. I wasn't sure if this was the right place. Georgie gave me directions, but the dirt roads around here all look the same. But I made it," Courtland said, walking up and giving her a hug. "I am so sorry. Your mother promised me she would wait to talk to you until I'd arrived. I didn't know," he added. "Georgie said you and your mother ended up having quite the row, a real battle royal."

"It was awful, Daddy," Sky said. "I've never seen her so angry—or been so angry with her. But come in. Can I get you a drink?" Sky asked.

"Just water, dear. Your mother is resting back at the inn. I didn't know she was cooking all that up with poor Francisco. I am genuinely sorry."

"I'm sorry she did that too," Sky said through compressed lips.

"She wants what's best for you. She just can't see that her choices may not be right for other people. And I'm afraid she's even worse when it comes to you." Courtland squeezed Sky's hand. "You don't realize how much she loves you."

"You always say that."

"Trust me, Schuyler. Your mother is truly worried—convinced—that you are throwing away your life, your education, everything you've worked so hard for. I've never seen her so upset."

"What about me?" Sky said.

Courtland patted her arm. "Of course, you're upset too. But put yourself in her shoes. She can't imagine you being happy on an island with a man who is, well…" her father paused. "He is not someone with whom you have much in common. Please try to forgive her, dear. She may come around in time."

"I don't know if I can, Daddy. She's threatened to disown me if I marry Nate—I would no longer be her daughter, and our child would not be her grandchild. I think she means it." Saying this, a wave of sick, cold anger washed over Sky.

Sky's father looked at her with concern. "You're terribly hurt. I understand. Let's sit down. I do want to talk to you."

"Are you going to try to convince me that I should not marry Nate too?" Sky asked.

Courtland patted the sofa cushion next to him. "Come here, dear Schuyler." He waited until she was seated to go on. "I'm not going to try to convince you of anything. I know you well enough to know that won't work. But please think about your decision. Are you really, truly sure that this is the man you want to marry? And that this is the life you want to live? I need hardly point out that it's quite different from what you're used to. This is a charming cottage, and the Vineyard is lovely, of course, but to live here all year round…"

Sky cut him off. "I'm as sure as I've ever been in my life, Daddy."

"Well, perhaps it sets my mind at ease that Georgie agrees with you. She says that Nate is a good man and that he will make you happy."

"He does," Sky said.

"It may take some getting used to, dear heart, but I will try. Now, would you like to show me around your house?"

After the tour, Sky and her father sat on the deck. The late-afternoon sun lit the fields bright gold, and the cocktail-hour geese made their daily splashdown into the cove.

"I haven't thought about this in years, but I want to tell you a story. You wouldn't happen to have any scotch?" Sky went into the house and poured her father a small measure of single malt with a splash of water.

"Here, Daddy," she said, handing him the tumbler.

"Perfect. Thank you, dear." He paused to gather his thoughts. "Back when I was in college—before I met your mother—I was absolutely and madly in love with a girl named Eliza. She was a local New Haven girl who waitressed in the coffeehouse by the campus. Nights, she played the guitar and sang. Eliza had such a beautiful voice." Courtland took a sip of his drink, and his eyes took on a faraway look. "She was so lovely, so kind and gentle. Clever, too. I was young and naive and thought everyone could see how perfect Eliza was. But when I brought her home, my family—quite expectedly, in retrospect—absolutely rejected her. Sent her back on the next train without even telling me and forbade me ever to see her again."

"That's awful. What happened?"

"The family arranged for me to study at Cambridge the next year, and when I got back to Yale, she was gone." He stopped and took another sip. "Then, my parents introduced me to Lucretia. She had looks and brains. And a fortune. At this point, my father was on the verge of bankruptcy. Your great-grandfather Van Devers bailed him out, and no one ever knew. And I married Lucretia."

"Oh, Daddy, I didn't know," Sky said, saddened by the wistful expression on her father's face.

"It hasn't been the worst marriage in the world. Your mother loves me, in her way. But I've lived my whole life wondering where Eliza went, whether I had made a mistake, what would have happened if I had defied my family and followed my heart. No way of knowing, of course." He turned and looked affectionately at Sky. "I've lived my life with regret. But you are strong and brave. Not like me. If you choose to follow your heart, I will support you. Fully."

"Thank you," Sky said, filled with love for her gentle, courtly father.

Sky pulled up to Elly's modest shingled saltbox with the apple trees and big deer-fenced garden. "Hey, Sky! I've been meaning to call you. The beginning of the school year has been supercrazy with the new principal," Elly said.

"No, no. I'm the one who's been out of touch. Do you have a minute or are you busy?" Sky asked.

"I'm free. Unless you call folding laundry busy. Would you like something to drink?"

"Just some water, thanks. And maybe an apple if you don't mind. I'm feeling a bit queasy," Sky said, taking an apple from a big pottery bowl and sitting down at the table in Elly's bright, warm kitchen.

"I've just come from having coffee with my father. And my horrible mother was here too. I've got so much to tell you." Worried about her friend's reaction, Sky cut to the quick. "Nate and I are engaged. And I'm pregnant."

Elly's eyes went wide, and she jumped from her chair to hug Sky. "That's wonderful news. I can't believe it. I knew you seemed really happy with Nate but…" Sky cut her off.

"But I was a summer person. I know."

"And your parents?" Elly asked.

Sky took a deep breath. "It's a long story." An understatement, for sure.

Elly started giggling halfway through Sky's story. "Omigod, Sky. I know she's your mother and I shouldn't laugh, but it's like a telenovela."

"Oh, Elly, you're right," Sky said, cracking a smile. "And poor Nate," Sky said. "Mother was so awful to him. And then my father asked about the wedding plans. I just don't think I can go through all that again."

"Lots of couples don't get married—even after having kids," Elly said. "You don't have to."

"That's not what I mean. I want to marry Nate. I mean like the whole guest list and ceremony and reception and flowers and cake and bridesmaids and… it was so stressful and six months out of my life."

"Wait. Is that a snap swivel?" Elly asked, finally noticing Sky's ring.

Sky laughed. "Nate made this, but we're replacing it, don't worry! He's got his mother's beautiful sapphire that we'll get sized."

Elly smiled at her old summer friend, then put her chin in her hand. "Don't worry about the wedding. This time it's up to you and Nate—not your mother. Do you know John Alley?"

Sky shook her head. "I don't think so."

"He's an old family friend and a justice of the peace. He'd be happy to marry you in a rowboat if that's what you want. But…" Elly cocked her head. "I think a wedding is no more than an excuse for a big party with people who love you and Nate and wish you well. Throw in some food and drink and maybe some music, and you're done." In a flash, Sky saw the old barn, swept clean, with oil lamps hanging from the beams, buckets of chrysanthemums in milking pails, and a fiddle band playing in the corner. A sawhorse table with a white tablecloth and platters of lobster rolls. And a big three-tiered cake topped with flowers.

"We could use Nate's uncle's barn…" Elly clapped her hands with excitement.

"Hold on. I'll get a pad of paper and start writing things down," Elly said. The list and assignments went quickly. "Nate can ask his uncle about the barn and his friend Mairi is in the Flying Elbows fiddle band."

"I'll check to see whether the church is free," said Sky.

"Don't forget to mention Nate's name. His uncle is a deacon. My friend Felicia's a caterer. She can make anything. But lots of people do their reception as a potluck if they don't want to spend much money. Nate can probably borrow the mums from Island Gardens..." Elly went on. They were gathering steam.

"Do you think it would work to use the watering troughs as the ice buckets?" Sky asked. "I can't believe this. I'm so excited. I wonder if Batty would be willing to make the cake?" Sky added.

"She'll insist."

"Invites? Email will do. We can design something cute— something with a goat on it," Sky said. "What about bridesmaids? I had nine before... ugh. But I don't want to hurt anyone's feelings."

"If it were me, I'd just be as happy never having to buy another bridesmaid dress," said Elly. "You can skip that too if you want."

Sky recalled the stupidly expensive Pepto-pink horror her mother had selected for her wedding party. No bridesmaids equaled relieved and grateful friends. "You're right. But would you be my matron of honor?"

Elly leaned over to hug Sky again. "Honored. If get to wear what I want," she teased.

"Absolutely. Anything." Then Sky groaned. "Oh no. But I need a wedding dress. Not again." She could still see her unworn gown hanging in the closet, swooping acres of gorgeous, abandoned white silk.

"Hold on," said Elly. She ran upstairs and came down a few minutes later with a dry-cleaning storage bag. "No obligation, but I think this'll fit you. My great-grandmother made it for her own wedding." Elly unzipped the bag and pulled out an ivory gown with a simple scoop neck and cap sleeves, covered in a hand-crocheted pattern of flowers and leaves.

Sky gasped. "It's so beautiful. But, really. I couldn't."

"Try it on. I insist. Let's see how it looks." Sky went into the bathroom to change. She slipped on the light silk slip underdress and then the heavy lace dress itself. Elly was right, it fit her perfectly.

This time it was Elly's turn to gasp.

"Please say yes, Sky. My grandmother wore it, and my mother, then me. Granny said that the dress was made with love and that it brings the luck of the Irish to anyone who marries in it."

"Oh, Elly. I don't know how to thank you," Sky said, eyes welling with gratitude.

"Seeing you and Nate happy together will be thanks enough," Elly said. "This all takes care of old, and borrowed, and your ring is blue. Just buy yourself some new shoes, and you'll be set!"

🐐 🐐 🐐

The night wind whistled through the dark trees. Inside, where it was warm, Nan sleep-barked muffled little yelps as she lay curled on her rug. Sky put down her novel. Never, in a million years, would she have thought that she'd be lying in bed with such a man—impossibly happy, wearing a fishing-tackle engagement ring, and thinking about their future.

Sky rolled over and stuck her nose into Nate's side, remembering the first time she'd inhaled his clean Nate-smell, scented with just the tiniest hint of goat. Her Nate. The Island—what had been Sky's escape, her vacation place—now felt like home. The city, when she'd been back, had felt all wrong. The glass and concrete buildings pressed down on Sky, and the sounds—trucks rattling and clanging over potholes, cars and taxis honking, ambulance sirens blaring—had set her nerves on edge.

"Ready to turn out the light?" asked Nate, putting down his book.

"In a minute. I was just thinking about New York."

"Do you miss it? Here we are, like an old married couple, reading in bed. Pretty dull stuff, city girl," Nate said.

"I don't miss it at all. That's what's weird. I really feel like I'm meant to be here."

He kissed the top of her head. "I hope so."

"I know so." Sky traced the line of his farmer's tan and kissed his shoulder.

"But what about your career?"

"You know what I used to do? I read boring two-hundred-page documents that pushed money from one company to another. I'm not going to miss that at all." Sky rolled over onto her back. "I've got some ideas for my own business. I'm good at photography, especially portraits. People always want that perfect vacation photo of the kids and the dog to put on their Christmas card and to give as gifts to the grandparents. And I'm going to do a Vineyard goat calendar."

"You think that would sell?" Nate grinned at his happy fiancée. "Be right back. I think I forgot to plug in my laptop. You want a glass of water or anything?"

Nate glanced at the computer screen as he connected the power cord. His heart stopped when he read the subject of the top email: *Mytoi—Important Message.*

"I think they've sent the estimate for the Mytoi damage," Nate said in a constricted voice.

"Let's read it together. I'm sure it's not so bad," Sky said as convincingly as she could. She slid on her robe and joined him in the kitchen. Nate's anxiety was palpable. *Dear Nate,* the message read, *I am forwarding the attached letter to you. Please read first and call me asap. Sincerely, Julie Clark.* He clicked the icon for the attachment labeled with Japanese characters.

Ms. Julie Clark, Head Gardener, Mytoi Gardens
Chappaquiddick Island, MA

Dear Ms. Clark,

I had thought at the end of my long career that there would be no more challenges, no more excitement. I was wrong. I have reviewed the photographs you sent of the damage inflicted by goats on the Japanese gardens at Mytoi, and I am excited.

In my work, I follow the concept, the philosophy, as it were, of wabi-sabi. It is based on the view that beauty comes from transience, from imperfection. The perfect, the unchanging, can please the eye, but it can never be truly beautiful. In Japan, we do not seek symmetry and perfection as the ideal of beauty; we say that nothing lasts, nothing is finished, nothing is perfect. This is sometimes referred to as "flawed beauty." Perhaps you are familiar with the small, imperfect bowls used in our tea ceremony as exemplars of this concept.

I recognized my good fortune to have been given the gift to see what goats—with wonderfully natural energy—have unlocked within your gardens. You may not realize it yet, but you have been blessed with the opportunity to create something in Mytoi that reaches for true beauty.

I offer my services. If you are willing to cover my travel and lodging expenses, it will be my honor to oversee the restoration—no, the rebirth—of Mytoi.

Sincerely yours,
Harumi Nagashima

"Omigod, Sky. Everything's going to be OK."

The days sped by, and Sky and Elly's plans fell into place more easily than Sky could have imagined possible. The church and minister were available after the Sunday morning service on Columbus Day weekend, and offers poured in from friends and family to help: cousin Jessie, slowly warming, would make the bridal bouquet with flowers from her cutting garden; Jak promised to catch and cook a few stripers; Zeke volunteered to put on his shucker's hat and open oysters; and Suzanne from Island Gardens would bring over gallons and gallons of fall asters and mums. Sky ordered a big tray of Chinese dumplings and miniature egg rolls from Elly's caterer friend, Felicia, and lobster rolls from the Menemsha Fish Market. Rob insisted on supplying a keg of Katie's summer IPA and a vat of clam chowder, and Sarah and Claire, a selection of vegan cookies from Coffee and Clog. The Flying Elbows were available, and Katya offered to play guitar and sing at the after-party. Batty would, of course, make the wedding cake and a giant tray of lasagna; she also had the idea of "registering" the couple at a goat supply website for cheesemaking supplies and a milking machine. And Nate would debut a selection of Naughty Goat cheese.

The sapphire ring was resized for Sky's narrow finger within the week, and she was delighted that the 1930s-inspired ivory lace and leather shoes she'd loved (rejected before by her mother as "too clunky") with the ankle straps and retro heel were still available in her size and were on sale online.

Sky finally met Nate's uncle whom she liked immensely. He seemed to like her too. "A right and proper sendoff for the good old barn," Uncle John announced, leaning over to place a gentle peck on Sky's cheek. "And thank you for trying to save it."

Sky's friends—except for Eva and Trip—were shocked and baffled by the news that Sky was pregnant and getting married in less than two weeks. To a Vineyard goatscaper-cum-cheesemaker. More than a few made it clear that they thought she was off her rocker, and Sky knew she'd be suffering through *Green Acres* jokes (and worse) forever.

When the day came, Billy and the Kid wore wreaths of periwinkle blue fall asters—not pink roses—around their goat-necks, minded by dear, perplexed Nan, festooned with her own garland of flowers. The long warm rays of Indian summer painted the white steepled church bright gold, and the leaves on the old maple tree in the churchyard glowed crimson and orange. Glorious sprays of asters and white-petaled Japanese anemones tied with streamers of ivory satin ribbon hung from the church doors, and the faint strains of Mairi's violin playing "The Skye Boat Song" floated into the churchyard.

Sky paused at the door in the wedding dress of love and old lace, Grams's double strand of pearls clasped around her neck, her fair hair woven with ribbon and anemones. Her father looked down at her with a kind expression. "I'm sorry to surprise you, but we've got an unexpected guest, my dear. She needed to be here."

"Mother?"

"She's trying, Sky. It's going to take her a while."

A moment of silence, then Sky heard the violin begin the first notes of "Ode to Joy." She gripped the satin tying Jessie's cascading bouquet and laid her other hand on the arm of her gentle father. Courtland nodded. "Ready?" he asked.

Heart pounding, Sky took a deep breath and smiled at her father. "Ready."

They paused in the doorway of the church. In the last row, Lucretia sat, her face nearly hidden beneath a broad-brimmed hat. She turned and, with a rueful smile, nodded at her daughter.

Filled with joy, Sky barely noticed the glad faces that turned to watch them walk down the aisle. There was Nate, waiting for her, movie-star handsome in a navy blazer and the sky-blue tie she'd chosen for him. She kissed her father and with a radiant face stepped forward to stand by Nate, taking his hand in hers.

"Love releases in each of us the capacity to be happy," the minister began.

And so it was to be.

As I tumble and spin through fields
My star-cross'd lover, never yields
His pursuit, my fair hoof in marriage
And whisk away in jolting carriage

But we must run, and not be seen
For my mother-goat, she's not so keen
And my father-goat, he must disparage
This bouncy, flouncy, trouncy, marriage.

DBM

RECIPES FROM GOATS
IN THE TIME OF LOVE

INDEX

TOFU—AND MEAT

SIDES, BREAD, AND CHEESE

DESSERTS

COCKTAILS

NATE'S TELL BLUEBERRY MUFFINS
(12 muffins)

1½ cups flour
½ cup sugar
1 tablespoon baking powder
½ teaspoon salt
¼ teaspoon cinnamon
6 tablespoons unsalted butter (cold, cut into ½ inch pieces)
1 egg
½ cup milk or buttermilk
1½ teaspoon vanilla
2½ cups fresh (or frozen – keep frozen else the batter will be blue!) wild blueberries
Demerara or brown sugar to sprinkle on top

Preheat oven to 350 degrees. Line a muffin pan with cupcake liners (or lightly grease).

In a large bowl, whisk together the flour, sugar, baking powder, salt, and cinnamon. Cut in the butter with two knives (or a fork) until the mixture resembles coarse crumbs.

In a small bowl, whisk the egg, milk, and vanilla together until combined. Pour the egg-milk mixture over the flour mixture and stir until about three-quarters of the dry ingredients are moistened. Add the blueberries and mix just until the dry ingredients are moistened, and the berries are distributed.

Fill the muffin pans, pressing down lightly if needed (batter will be thick and lumpy). Sprinkle the tops with demerara or brown sugar.

Bake for 15-20 minutes until brown and slightly firm to the touch (or until a toothpick comes out clean, except for berry juice). Note: muffins made with frozen berries may take slightly longer. Serve warm.

BOLLA'S BLUE RIBBON UP-ISLAND BREAKFAST BREAD
(One 9-inch loaf)

3 tablespoons unsalted butter
2 medium onions, chopped
¾ pound bacon (12 slices for recipe – plus 2 for eating!)
2 cups flour
1 tablespoon baking powder
1 tablespoon seasoned salt, such as Jane's Krazy Mixed-Up Salt
1 cup milk
¼ cup extra-virgin olive oil
1 egg
½ pound shredded Gruyere cheese (about 2 cups)
(Optional – extra eggs and freshly snipped chives)

Preheat oven to 350 degrees. Grease a 9 x 5-inch loaf pan.

In a large skillet, cook the onions with the butter over low heat, stirring occasionally, until brown and caramelized (about 30 minutes). Let cool on paper towels. In another large skillet, cook the bacon over medium heat until crisp. Let cool on paper towels, then crumble by hand.

In a large bowl, whisk together the flour, baking powder, and salt. In a small bowl, whisk together the milk, oil, and the egg. Slowly pour the milk mixture into the flour mixture, stirring just until combined. Gently fold in the cheese, onions, and bacon just until combined.

Scrape the batter into the loaf pan. Bake until golden brown and a toothpick inserted into the center comes out clean, about 45 minutes. Let stand for 15 minutes to cool slightly. Remove from pan and let cool completely. If desired, serve slices topped with fried eggs and snipped chives.

(adapted by Bolla from Christina Tosi's Bacon and Cheese Quick Bread (Oprah.com))

COFFEE AND CLOG VEGAN CARROT MUFFINS
(16 muffins)

2¼ cups flour
1 cup sugar
1 tablespoon cinnamon
2 teaspoons baking soda
½ teaspoon salt
2 cups shredded carrots (packed down)
1 apple, shredded
1 cup crushed pineapple
Equivalent of 3 eggs (vegan egg substitute)
¾ cup canola oil
2 teaspoons vanilla

Preheat oven to 350 degrees. Line muffin tins with cupcake liners (or lightly grease).

In a large bowl, whisk together the flour, sugar, cinnamon, baking soda, and salt. In a small bowl, whisk together the egg substitute, oil, and vanilla. Add the egg-oil mixture, carrots, apple, and pineapple to the flour mixture. Stir well to combine.

Fill the muffin cups to the brim. Bake for 30-35 minutes or until firm to the touch.

CINNAMON-PECAN MONKEY BREAD
(12-15 servings)

½ cup unsalted butter
½ cup chopped pecans
1 cup brown sugar
2 tablespoon water
½ cup sugar
1 teaspoon cinnamon
2 cans (16 ounces each) jumbo buttermilk biscuits

Preheat oven to 375 degrees. Grease a 9 or 10-inch Bundt or tube pan. Sprinkle the bottom of the pan with 2 tablespoons of pecans.

In a saucepan, heat the butter, brown sugar, and water, stirring over medium heat until it comes to a boil. Set aside.

Separate the biscuits and shape each roughly into 3 balls. In a medium bowl, mix the sugar and cinnamon. Add the balls and toss to coat with the sugar-cinnamon mixture.

Put half of the balls into the bottom of the pan. Drizzle with half the sugar syrup and sprinkle with half of the remaining pecans. Repeat with the remaining balls, syrup, and pecans.

Bake for 30-35 minutes. Invert immediately onto a plate.

YUM, WAFFLES
(makes about 5 double waffles)

1¾ cups flour
1 teaspoon baking powder
1 teaspoon baking soda
½ teaspoon salt
2 cups buttermilk (or substitute scant 2 cups milk + 2 tablespoons white vinegar, set aside to curdle)
5 tablespoons canola oil
2 eggs

In a large bowl, whisk together the flour, baking powder, baking soda, and salt. Add the buttermilk, oil, and eggs, and beat until smooth. Cook in a preheated, greased waffle iron as directed.

(Adapted from "The New Good Housekeeping Cookbook" (Hearst Books, 1986))

ROB'S (SECRET INGREDIENT) QUAHOG CHOWDER
(Serves 10-12)

1 quart of shucked quahogs (clams), including their liquor
¼ pound bacon
2 medium onions, chopped
3 large red potatoes, cut into ½-inch dice (about 3-4 cups)
2½ cups whole milk
½ cup heavy cream
2 tablespoons butter
2 teaspoons salt
½ teaspoon freshly ground black pepper
1 pint sour cream (at room temperature)
Oyster crackers for serving

Defrost the clams if frozen and coarsely chop, saving the clam liquor. Strain out any sand in the liquor by pouring through cheesecloth or a coffee filter.

Cook the bacon until crisp in a big heavy pot or Dutch oven. Saving the bacon fat in the pot, cool the bacon on paper towels and crumble into small pieces.

Add 1 tablespoon butter and the onions to the bacon fat. Cook slowly over low heat until the onions are tender and transparent (about 20 minutes). Add the diced potatoes, clam liquor, and sufficient water to rise about 1 inch above the potatoes.

Simmer uncovered until the potatoes are tender (about 15-20 minutes). Add the chopped clams and bacon and simmer for 5 minutes. In a separate saucepan, heat the milk (do not let boil). Add the hot milk, heavy cream, 1 tablespoon butter, salt and pepper to the pot. Taste and add more salt if desired.

Take the chowder off the heat, cover, and allow it to "ripen" on the counter for an hour.

Reheat, uncovered on low heat, until the mixture begins to steam (do not let the chowder boil or it will curdle). In a bowl, combine the sour cream with 2 cups of liquid from the chowder and whisk until smooth.

Add the sour cream mixture to the chowder pot and stir. Reheat briefly (if needed) and remove from the heat. Serve with oyster crackers.

(Adapted from "The Martha's Vineyard Cookbook, A Diverse Sampler from a Bountiful Island" (Harper & Row, 1971))

AUNT BETSY'S BLUEFISH
(Serves 4)

1¼-1½ pounds fresh bluefish (two small or one larger filet)
3 tablespoons butter
3 ounces bread crumbs
2 tablespoons chopped parsley
2 tablespoons lemon juice
1 cup white wine
Salt and pepper
Lemon wedges for serving

Preheat oven to 325 degrees. Line a 9x13-inch pan with foil and grease with butter.

Place the fish skin-side down in the pan and cover with the bread crumbs. Sprinkle with the parsley, lemon juice and a pinch each of salt and pepper. Dot the top evenly with butter.

Bake for 25 minutes. Take the pan out and pour the wine over the fish. Switch the oven to broil (high), and set a rack about 8-inches below the flame. Return the pan to the oven and broil the fish for 10 minutes. Serve with lemon wedges.

SEA-AND-CEDAR PLANKED BLUEFISH
(serves 4-8)

2 bluefish filets (allow ¼ to ½ pound per person)
2 cedar grilling planks (or untreated cedar shingles)
2 quarts of salt water (or 2 quarts of tap water + ½ cup sea salt, stirred to dissolve)

In a large deep pan, soak the cedar planks (or shingles) for at least one hour. Add the filets to brine for 15 minutes.

Build a fire in the grill (or on the beach). When hot, char one side of the planks, then place the bluefish (skin side down) on the charred side. Return the plank to the grill (fish-side up). Cook until the fish is opaque and flakes with a fork.

FIRE-GRILLED CLAMS
(Serves 2)

12 littleneck or cherrystone clams
Lemon wedges

Make a fire in the fireplace or firepit and let it burn down until there is a good bed of coals (or set a hot fire in a grill).

Cut 36 inches of aluminum foil and double it over. Make an open-top pouch by folding over 5 inches from each end, then tightly rolling the open ends to make an open 8 x 8 pouch.

Rinse the clams and place inside the pouch in a single layer. Push the coals from under the logs and nestle the pouch in the coals (or set the pouch on the grill). When most of the clams have opened (5-15 minutes – start checking after 5 minutes), use tongs to carefully pull the pouch from the fire.

Discard any unopened clams. Serve with lemon wedges.

SKY *CAN* COOK LOBSTERS
(Serves 4)

4 live lobsters, 1½ pound each
3 tablespoons salt
½ cup (1 stick) melted butter
Lemon wedges

Fill a large stockpot (4-5 gallons) two-thirds full of water and add the salt. Bring to a full boil over high heat.

One at a time and head first, add the lobsters to the boiling water.

Cover with a lid and return to a boil. Reduce heat to medium and cook for approximately 15 minutes, until the lobsters are bright red.

Use tongs to remove the cooked lobsters. Split the underside of each lobster with a sharp knife and drain. Serve with melted butter and lemon.

OYSTERS BATCHELOR
(Serves 8 as a first course)

2 shallots, finely chopped
¼ teaspoon red pepper flakes
4 cups loosely packed fresh spinach
1 cup chopped parsley
1 cup (2 sticks) butter
½ cup bread crumbs
24 whole oysters, opened with top (flat) shells removed
Salt and pepper

Preheat oven to 450 degrees. Loosely crunch up aluminum foil and place in the bottom of a 9 x13 pan to make a bed to balance the oysters (or use rock salt).

In a medium skillet, sauté the shallots and red pepper flakes in 3 tablespoons of butter over medium-low heat until the shallots are tender and beginning to brown. Add the spinach and cook just until wilted. Drain any excess liquid from the pan.

In a food processor, combine the spinach-shallots mixture, parsley, remaining butter, and breadcrumbs. Pulse briefly to coarsely chop.

Set the oysters in the pan, balancing the shell on the foil. Top each oyster with 1 tablespoon of the spinach mixture. Sprinkle with salt and pepper. Bake 5-6 minutes.

GRAMS'S LINGUINI WITH CLAM SAUCE
(Serves 2)

6 ounces dry linguini
2 cloves garlic, minced
3 tablespoons extra-virgin olive oil
¼ teaspoon red pepper flakes
¼ cup dry white wine
18 littleneck clams (in their shells)
2 tablespoons chopped parsley (optional)
Salt and pepper

Cook the pasta according to directions until barely al dente, saving out a cup of the cooking water before draining.

While the pasta is boiling, sauté the garlic and red pepper in the olive oil in a large skillet over low heat just until the garlic begins to turn golden. Add the wine and clams, and increase the heat to high.

Cover the pan and cook until the clams start to open (5-7 minutes). Take the clams out as they open to avoid overcooking them. Discard any unopened clams.

Add the cooked pasta to the pan with ¼ cup of the reserved cooking water. Cook over high heat, stirring constantly until pasta is al dente and has absorbed some of the clam sauce (add more cooking water if the pasta starts to get dry). Take off the heat.

Add salt (if needed) and pepper to taste. Add the clams and parsley to the pan, toss to combine, and drizzle with a bit more olive oil. Serve immediately.

BATTY'S CHEESE-THERAPY CARBONARA
(serves 4)

½ pound diced pancetta (or bacon)
2 tablespoons extra-virgin olive oil
½ cup white wine
16 ounces dry spaghetti
3 eggs
1 cup grated fresh parmesan, plus extra for serving
1 teaspoon fresh minced garlic
¼ teaspoon freshly ground pepper

Bring a pot of water to a boil for the pasta. Place a big ovenproof bowl (pottery or ceramic) in a very low oven to warm.

In a medium skillet, cook the pancetta (or bacon) in the olive oil until crisp. Remove the pancetta, saving about 2-3 tablespoons of the oil in the pan. Add the wine and bring to a boil. Cook until reduced by half. Return the pancetta to the pan and set aside.

Cook the pasta according to package directions and drain, reserving a ½ cup of the cooking water. Take the warm bowl out of the oven, add the pancetta mixture, reserved cooking water, eggs, cheese, garlic, and pepper and whisk well. Add the hot pasta and stir well to coat. Salt to taste. Serve with additional grated parmesan.

GEORGIE'S MACARONI PIE
(serves 4 as a main course, 8 as a side)

2 cups grated sharp cheddar cheese
4 slices American cheese or Velveeta
4 tablespoons butter
2 tablespoons flour
2 cups milk
2 cups dry macaroni
½ cup breadcrumbs
Nutmeg, salt, and pepper

Preheat oven to 350 degrees. Grease a 2-quart casserole dish. Cook the macaroni according to package directions just until tender, drain.

While the macaroni is cooking, put 2 tablespoons of butter and the flour in a large saucepan. Cook over low heat, stirring constantly, until it just starts to brown. Add the milk and stir until smooth and thickened. Add the cheeses and stir until smooth. Add the cooked macaroni and combine thoroughly. Add a tiny shake of nutmeg, then salt and pepper to taste.

Place in the casserole dish, top with the bread crumbs, and dot with 2 tablespoons of butter. Bake at 350 degrees for 30 minutes. Serve hot or cold.

BATTY'S STRACOTTO (ITALIAN POT ROAST) FOR GETTING A MAN
(serves 6-8)

3-4 pound rump roast
3 tablespoons olive oil
5 cloves garlic, peeled and smashed
2 onions, chopped
3 carrots, chopped
28 ounce can Italian plum tomatoes
1 cup red wine
3 bay leaves
Preheat oven to 350 degrees.

In a Dutch oven, sauté the meat in 1 tablespoon of olive oil over medium-high heat until well browned on all sides. Remove the meat from the pot. Add the onion, carrots and the rest of the olive oil to the pot. Sauté over medium heat until the vegetables are lightly browned. Return the meat to the pan and add the garlic, wine, tomatoes (including the juice), bay leaves, and some salt and pepper. Add enough water to cover the meat and bring to a boil. Remove from heat.

Bake covered at 350 degrees for about 3-4 hours, until the meat falls apart with a fork.

EVA AND TRIP'S THREE-PEPPER TOFU HOTPOT
(serves 6)

1 bunch scallions, thinly sliced (keep white and green separate)
1 cup flour
Vegetable oil
28 ounces firm tofu, patted dry and cut into 1½-inch cubes
1 to 2 tablespoons Sichuan peppercorns
5 tablespoons of butter, cut into chunks
2 teaspoons toasted sesame oil
2 shallots, thinly sliced

2 jalapeno peppers, seeded and thinly sliced
6 cloves garlic, peeled and smashed
1 inch peeled fresh ginger root, cut into matchsticks
2 tablespoons soy sauce
1 to 2 tablespoons sugar
2 tablespoons coarsely ground black pepper
Cooked Japanese rice (for serving)

Heat about 3 tablespoons of vegetable oil in a large skillet. Pour the flour onto a rimmed plate and coat the tofu cubes a few at a time. Add one-third of the tofu cubes to the oil and sauté over medium-high heat until golden, about 8 minutes, turning as needed. Drain on paper towels. Brown next batch of tofu cubes, adding oil as needed, repeat.

Wipe out the pan with paper towels. Add 2 tablespoons of vegetable oil and the Sichuan peppercorns and sauté over low heat until the peppercorns turn brown. Scoop out the peppercorns with a slotted spoon and drain on paper towels (leave the oil in the skillet). Crush the peppercorns by putting them in doubled ziploc bags and banging them with the handle of a big knife.

Add the butter and sesame oil to the peppercorn-spiced oil in the skillet. Add the shallots, jalapenos, garlic, and ginger. Sauté for a few minutes over medium-low heat, then add the white parts of the scallions and continue cooking until the vegetables are soft, about 8 minutes. Stir in the soy sauce, sugar (to taste) and the black pepper. Add the tofu and green parts of the scallions to the sauce and toss to coat evenly.

Serve over rice with a pinch (or more!) of crushed Sichuan peppercorns on top.

(Adapted from "Feast: Generous Vegetarian Meals for Any Eater and Every Appetite" (Chronicle Books, 2013))

GEORGIE'S COCONUT CHICKEN CURRY
(serves 8)

3-4 lbs. boneless skinless chicken thighs, cut into 2-inch pieces
2 tablespoon curry powder (preferably Jamaican)
3 tablespoons canola oil
3 cloves garlic, minced
2 medium onion, chopped
1-inch fresh ginger, minced (about 1 tablespoon)
1 cup coconut milk
Optional: 1 hot pepper (Scotch bonnet or habanero), split lengthwise (or 1 jalapeno, minced)

Sprinkle the chicken with 1 tablespoon of the curry powder and set aside.

Heat the oil in a deep skillet. Sauté the garlic, onion, and ginger over low heat for about 10 minutes or until lightly brown. Add 1 tablespoon of curry powder and sauté another few minutes. Add the chicken, hot pepper (if desired), and 1 cup of water.

Simmer covered for 15 minutes, then uncovered until the chicken is done and the gravy is thick (about 30 minutes total), turning the chicken from time to time. Take out the whole hot pepper (if used) and add the coconut milk. Salt and pepper to taste. Simmer another 10 minutes. Serve with rice.

SUPER-CORN CORNBREAD
(serves 6-8)

1 cup cornmeal
1 cup flour
¼ cup sugar
1 tablespoon baking powder
1 teaspoon baking soda
1 teaspoon salt

2 eggs
1 cup buttermilk
1 tablespoon honey
¼ cup vegetable oil
1 cup frozen corn, chopped in a food processor
2 tablespoons butter

Preheat oven to 425 degrees with a dry 9-10-inch cast iron skillet inside the oven.

In a large bowl, whisk the dry ingredients (except for the frozen corn) together. In a small bowl, whisk the eggs, buttermilk, honey, and oil together until smooth. Add the egg mixture and the frozen corn bits to the dry ingredients. Combine with a few swift strokes – don't overmix.

Take the hot skillet out of the oven, add the butter and turn to coat the bottom and sides. Pour in the batter. Bake for 20-25 minutes, or until firm and lightly browned.

COLE'S FAMOUS COLESLAW
(Serves 8-10)

One small head of green cabbage
2-3 large carrots, peeled
1 Granny Smith apple, peeled and cored
¾ cup mayonnaise
3 tablespoons cider vinegar
1 tablespoon maple syrup
½ teaspoon salt
¼ teaspoon pepper

In a large bowl, whisk the mayonnaise, vinegar, syrup, salt, and pepper together until smooth. Shred or finely chop the cabbage, carrots, and apple. Add to the bowl and mix well.

Taste for seasoning, adding more salt, pepper and/or syrup if desired.

Serve immediately. (If prepared in advance, shred and add the apple immediately before serving to avoid the slaw turning brown.)

SPONGEBOB SOURDOUGH BREAD
(One loaf)

3 cups "lively" sourdough starter
5 cups bread flour, preferably King Arthur
1½ cups warm water
2½ teaspoons salt.

In a large bowl, mix the ingredients together (dough will be sticky). Cover with plastic wrap and let rise until doubled, about 4 hours.

Line another large bowl with a square of parchment paper. Sprinkle some flour around the edge of the dough bowl and push the dough down into a rough ball. Tip the ball out into the center of the paper-lined bowl. Cover and let rise until doubled, about 2-4 hours.

30 minutes before baking, place a large Dutch oven (or other heavy covered pot – an 11 x 8-inch oval is ideal) in the oven and preheat to 450 degrees. Transfer the dough into the hot Dutch oven by picking up the four corners of the parchment (enlist a helper, if possible), and carefully setting the dough, still in the paper sling, into the pot. Trim the excess paper and cover. Bake for 30 minutes; remove the lid and bake for another 20-30 minutes.

(Adapted from No-Knead Bread recipe, New York Times (November 8, 2006))

HOMEMADE MOZZARELLA
(1 ball)

1 gallon of whole milk (not ultra-pasteurized)
1 teaspoon citric acid
¼ rennet tablet
1 teaspoon kosher salt

Crush the rennet tablet in ¼ cup cool water to dissolve. Set aside. In a large pot, add the citric acid to 1 cup water and stir, then add the milk. Heat the milk to 90 degrees over medium-high heat, stirring occasionally. Remove the pot from the heat. Add the dissolved rennet and stir for 30 seconds. Cover the pot. Wait 5 minutes, then check if the mixture has set. It should look like soft tofu or custard. If the curd (solid) is too soft or the whey (liquid) is milky, let sit a few more minutes.

Using a large sharp knife held upright, cut down through the curds to the bottom of the pot to make a 1-inch checkerboard pattern. Put the pot back on the stove and heat to 105 degrees, slowly and gently stirring curds (try not to break curds). Take off the heat and gently stir a few more minutes.

Scoop the curds out with a slotted spoon into a colander, gently pressing out excess whey. Put the pressed curds in a bowl and microwave for 1 minute. Drain off the whey and quickly work the cheese with a spoon (or your hands) until it is cool enough to touch. Microwave for 30 seconds and repeat working/folding to drain off the whey. Repeat microwave-and-folding a third and final time. (The microwave should bring the cheese up to 135 degrees.)

Quickly knead the cheese until smooth and shiny, stretchy and taffy-like, returning to the microwave to heat if it gets too cool to stretch. Add the salt near the finish. Form into a ball.

(Adapted from New England Cheesemaking Supply Company)

NATE'S LAVENDER RICOTTA WITH HONEY
(makes about 2 cups)

2 quarts whole milk
1 cup heavy cream
½ teaspoon salt
3 tablespoons lavender flowers
3 tablespoons lemon juice
Cheesecloth
Honey

Cut a 6-inch square of cheesecloth, set the lavender in the center and tie into a bag. Cut another piece of cheesecloth to line a strainer and place it over a large bowl.

Slowly bring the milk, cream, salt and lavender bag to a rolling boil in a 6-quart heavy pot over medium heat, stirring occasionally. Remove the lavender and add the lemon juice. Reduce heat to low and simmer, stirring constantly, until the mixture curdles, about 2 minutes.

Pour the mixture into the cheesecloth-lined strainer and let it drain 1 hour, then refrigerate. Serve with a drizzle of honey.

(Adapted from Fresh Homemade Ricotta recipe on Epicurious.com)

FABULOUS FAIR PIE
(one pie, 8-10 servings)

Crust:
    1 cup quick cooking rolled oats (not instant)
    ¼ cup brown sugar
    ¼ teaspoon salt
    5 tablespoons butter, melted
    ¾ cup pecans (or walnuts), finely chopped

Filling:
1 cup good-quality bittersweet chocolate chips
2 eggs
½ cup flour
1 stick salted butter, melted and cooled
1 cup pecans (or walnuts), coarsely chopped
Whipped cream for serving

Preheat oven to 350 degrees. Watching carefully, toast the oatmeal on a cookie sheet in the oven for 10 minutes to brown. In a small mixing bowl, combine the crust ingredients. Press into a 9-inch pie plate and bake for 15 minutes or until lightly brown.

While the crust is baking, whisk together the eggs, sugar, and flour in a mixing bowl. Gradually mix in the butter. Add the nuts and vanilla extract and stir.

After the crust has cooled, place the chocolate chips in an even layer on the bottom of the pie crust. Carefully pour the filling in a circular motion over the chips. Bake for 1 hour, until the filling is set. Serve with whipped cream.

(Adapted from the Oatmeal Nut Pie Crust recipe from MI Mitten (Food.com) and Not Derby Pie recipe from Phyllis Richman (washingtonpost.com))

PB-STUFFED CHOCOLATE CHUNK SKILLET COOKIE
(12 servings)

2 cups flour
1 teaspoon baking soda
½ teaspoon salt
¾ cup butter, softened
¼ cup sugar
1 cup brown sugar

1 teaspoon vanilla extract
1 egg
8 ounces (2 bars) high-quality bittersweet chocolate
¾ cup peanut butter

Preheat oven to 350 degrees. Greased an oven-proof skillet (10-inch cast iron is ideal).

In a large bowl, beat the butter, sugar, and brown sugar with a mixer until creamy. Add the vanilla and egg and beat until combined. In another bowl, whisk the flour, baking soda, and salt together. Add the flour mixture to the butter-egg mixture and mix well. Break or cut the chocolate into small chunks. Add to the bowl and stir.

Spread/press half the cookie dough into the skillet. Spread the peanut butter over the dough and cover evenly with the other half of the cookie dough. Bake for 35-40 minutes or until the edges are golden brown and cookie looks done.

Let cool down in the pan. While still warm, cut into wedges and serve.

(Adapted from the Peanut Butter-Stuffed Skillet Cookie Is a Dessert You Need, Tasty video recipe on BuzzFeed.com)

LITTLE BUG'S FAVORITE OATMEAL COOKIES
(4 dozen)

1 cup (2 sticks) of butter, softened
1 cup brown sugar
¾ cup sugar
2 eggs
2 tablespoons milk
1 tablespoon vanilla
1¾ cup flour

1 teaspoon baking soda
½ teaspoon salt
3 cups old fashioned rolled oats (or 2½ cup quick oats, not instant)

Preheat oven to 375 degrees. In a large bowl, beat together the sugars and butter with a mixer until creamy. Add the eggs, milk, and vanilla; beat well. In another bowl, whisk the flour, soda, and salt together. Add the flour mixture to the butter-egg mixture and mix well. Stir in the oats and mix well.

Drop by rounded tablespoons onto an ungreased cookie sheet and bake 9-10 minutes for a chewy cookie or 12-13 for a crisp cookie.

Cool 1 minute on cookie sheet then move to a rack to finish cooling.

(Adapted from Quaker Chewy Choc-Oat-Chip Cookies recipe)

CHOCOLATE BALLS THAT CURE
(about 25 balls)

8 ounces (2 bars) high-quality bittersweet chocolate
½ cup heavy cream
½ teaspoon vanilla
Unsweetened cocoa powder

Break the chocolate into pieces. In a small microwave-safe bowl, microwave the chocolate and heavy cream for 20 seconds. Stir until the chocolate is melted and smooth. (If lumps remain after stirring, microwave for a few more seconds and stir again.) Add the vanilla and a pinch of salt and stir. Set aside to cool.

When thick enough to shape (about 1 hour), scoop the chocolate into small balls onto a wax (or parchment) paper-covered cookie sheet. Chill in the refrigerator until firm, then roll each ball in cocoa powder to coat.

ISLAND KEY LIME PIE WITH NUTMEG CRUST
(one pie, 8-10 servings)

½ cup key lime juice
1 cup sweetened condensed milk
4 eggs, separated
¼ cup sugar
1½ cup gingersnap crumbs (pound cookies to crumbs in a plastic bag or use a food processor)
½ teaspoon grated nutmeg
6 tablespoons butter, melted

Preheat oven to 350 degrees. Mix the crumbs, nutmeg, and butter together in a bowl, then press evenly into a 9-inch pie pan. Bake for 8-10 minutes.

With a mixer and bowl, beat egg whites until soft peaks form, about 5 minutes. Add the sugar gradually, beating at high speed until stiff peaks form, another 2-3 minutes.

In a separate bowl, beat the egg yolks until pale, then add the lime juice and condensed milk. Pour into the crust and top with the egg whites. Bake 20 minutes on a low rack in the oven.

Cool for 1 hour at room temperature before placing in the refrigerator to chill for at least 3 hours.

(Adapted from a recipe from my neighbor Craig)

NONNA'S ITALIAN RUM BIRTHDAY (AND WEDDING!) CAKE
(serves 10-12)

Cake:
> ¾ cup sugar
> 4 eggs at room temperature
> Zest of 1 lemon
> ½ cup flour
> ½ cup cornstarch

Mascarpone Filling:
> 1 cup mascarpone
> 1 cup heavy cream
> ¼ cup sugar
> ½ teaspoon vanilla extract

Almond filling:
> 1¼ cup blanched almonds, slightly toasted in a dry skillet
> ½ cup water
> ¼ cup sugar

Whipped cream:
> 2 cups heavy cream
> 3 tablespoons sugar

To assemble:
> 8 ounces Amarena (or fresh) cherries, halved
> ½ cup rum (substitute cherry or orange juice)
> ½ cup syrup from the Amarena cherries (substitute cherry or orange juice)
> Cherries or toasted almonds to decorate

For the cake:
Preheat oven to 350 degrees. Butter and flour a 9-inch springform pan.

With a mixer and bowl, beat the sugar, eggs, and lemon zest at high speed until very fluffy and pale yellow, about 15 minutes.

Sift the flour and cornstarch 3 times, then sift a little at a time over the egg mixture, folding gently so as not to deflate the batter. (It is ok if a few tiny flour lumps remain.) Pour into the prepared pan.

Bake for 40 minutes, or until a toothpick inserted in the center comes out clean (do not open the oven for the first 30 minutes of baking). Turn off the oven, prop the oven door open and leave the cake inside for another 10 minutes. Remove from oven and wait 10 minutes before running a knife around the edge of the pan to loosen the cake. Cool the cake on a wire rack.

For the fillings:
Mascarpone filling:
With a mixer and bowl, beat the mascarpone, heavy cream, sugar, and vanilla until fluffy. Refrigerate.

Almond paste filling:
Place the toasted almonds in a food processor and process for about 2 minutes until very fine. Bring the water and sugar to a simmer in a saucepan over medium heat. Add the almonds and stir until the liquid is absorbed. Set aside to cool

Whipped cream:
Immediately before assembling the cake, beat the heavy cream and sugar in a bowl until stiff peaks form.

To assemble the cake:
Slice the cake in half. Mix the rum and cherry syrup together. Drizzle (or brush) the bottom half of the cake with half of the rum-cherry liquid. Crumble the almond paste over the cake. Place an even layer of cherries over the almond paste. Spread

the mascarpone filling over the cherries. Add the top half of the cake. Drizzle (or brush) the rest of the rum-cherry liquid on top. Frost with the whipped cream and decorate with cherries and almonds. Keep refrigerated until serving.

(Inspired by the Wedding Cake recipe from "Cooking with Nonna" (Race Point Publishing, 2017)

SHEEP DIP COCKTAIL
(one serving)

2 ounces Hendrick's gin
½ ounce St. Germaine elderflower liqueur
¾ ounce fresh lemon juice
¼ ounce maraschino liqueur
¼ ounce creme de violette
3-4 large basil leaves, plus a small leaf for garnish
Dash Peychaud's bitters

Muddle (crush) the basil leaves in the bottom of a half-pint mason jar or rocks glass. Measure the gin, liqueurs, lemon juice, and bitters into the jar and stir well. Add ice and basil leaf garnish.

FILTHY DIRTY MARTINI
(one serving)

3 ounces Hendrick's gin
½ ounce dry white vermouth
½ ounce olive brine
Drop or two of onion brine
1-2 olives and 2 pickled onions as garnish

Measure the gin, vermouth and brines in a cocktail shaker with ice and shake vigorously for 45 seconds. Pour into a chilled martini glass. Garnish with olives and onions.

NOTES

ACKNOWLEDGEMENTS

Thank you to my husband, Chris, for his constant support, encouragement, and edits, and to my readers with particular thanks to Adrienne for patiently going through multiple drafts and early-reader Lauri for her insights. Huge thanks to Dina, Mary, and Eliza for their encouragement (and edits), Jodi, Betsy, Susan, Nancy, Dina, Arlene, Debbie, and Felicia for their thoughts and suggestions (and more edits), to Sherri and Claire for their enthusiasm and technical assistance, and to Bolla for her recipe. Thank you, dear friends Tory, Caroline and Meg, my fall frolic, work, book club and yoga friends, and finally my kids and family for their love and support. The kind words from unexpected corners (Hadden, Mitch, and Greg, men enough to read a book in a pink proof cover) gave me a boost. And a special shout-out to Brenda Copeland for guiding me along the path of becoming a writer. Her insights and edits were invaluable.

And thanks especially to the Island and those naughty goats for inspiration.

ABOUT THE AUTHOR

Thanks to the power of telecommuting, the author splits her time between Washington, D.C., and West Tisbury, Massachusetts. She has a husband, three children, and a dog— no goats. *Goats in the Tine of Love* is not only her first novel but also her first attempt at writing anything other than legal memos. This was more fun.

www.telizabethbell.com